Mid-Century

Mid-Century

Charles Angoff

South Brunswick and New York: A. S. Barnes and Company
London: Thomas Yoseloff Ltd

© 1974 by Charles Angoff

A. S. Barnes and Co., Inc.
Cranbury, New Jersey 08512

Thomas Yoseloff Ltd
108 New Bond Street
London W1Y OQX, England

Library of Congress Cataloging in Publication Data

Angoff, Charles, 1902–
    Mid-century.

    I. Title.
PZ3.A592Mi   [PS3501.N569575]   813'.5'2   72-9853
ISBN 0-498-01339-1

PRINTED IN THE UNITED STATES OF AMERICA

Mid-Century

one

David was in the kitchen, drinking a favorite concoction that he
had only recently heard about: extra-dry beer mixed with a tea-
spoon of lime juice. He had heard a man talking to a companion
on a bus: "There we were, my wife and I, in a pub, not far from
Buckingham Palace, one of those side streets, a narrow street,
but clean, real clean, and the English pubs are not like our
saloons, they're real nice; women, real, refined women go into
them, and sit and have a beer and some cheese or sausages, anything you want; many people have their lunch in them. But we
went into this one in the late afternoon; not many people there,
and we sat down, and I ordered a beer for me and a little port
for my wife. They call the beer bitters in England. And a man
who was sitting next to us told me to put some lime juice in the
beer and he told the barmaid to bring me some—they have girls
and women tending bar in England—so she put it into my beer,
and it tasted real good." David tried it that very night, and it
tasted fine. David was not much of a beer drinker, but the lime
juice did make the beer more drinkable.

David felt at ease and he wasn't quite sure what had filled him with this pleasant feeling. He turned the beer glass around and around, and all sorts of thoughts ambled through his mind. . . . He would like to visit England, but, no, that would come after he had visited Israel; perhaps he could go to both countries on the same trip . . . would he ever make this trip? . . . how would he feel at the tomb of King David? he had heard people tell how they had climbed Mount Zion, "and there was the tomb of King David." And they said little more . . . but, then, what can one say? David was a little fearful about what he would feel at the tomb of the man who had written some of the Psalms . . . King David . . . *Dovid ha-Melech* . . . the phrase was so sweet on the tongue. So, indeed, was the word Jerusalem, *Yerusholayim* . . . Jerusalem, Jerusalem. . . . William Blake came to David's mind, Blake who had written so much about Jerusalem, about the whole inner meaning and mysticism of Israel. Blake knew what angels were and what God had said to them, and what God had whispered to men and women . . . and David wondered what Blake whispered to his wife Catherine in bed and in the evening, and what feelings went through him as he approached her, and as she approached him. Did he tell her what was going through his mind? Did he tell her everything in the deep silences of their embraces, and did she understand? . . . David was sure she did understand: women understand everything that is born in the act of love, even in the evening kiss, even in the mystical afternoon's secret look. And there was Keats and there was Coleridge, the brother of Blake . . . Coleridge was an intellectual Blake. And there was John Dryden and Andrew Marvell and John Donne . . . yes, John Donne; strange that he should think of Donne now, for Donne had so much in common with King David. Both were in love with women and with God and with life and with the past and the hereafter and with the silences of emotion and the urgencies of dreams. Both were above and within all things worldly, and they sensed the otherworldly in this-worldliness . . . a woman's breast was a miniature sky of the night and the aroma that came from far-off planets, and from time itself, and from infinity itself. . . .

Now a soft loveliness came to David's ear. His daughter Anne was playing "Für Elise" on the piano, slowly, gently, the melody winding and winding around his heart and around the ceiling and up and down the walls, gently, tenderly . . . and now she was playing something else that was lovely. David wasn't sure what it was—probably Mozart, or Schubert; no, Mozart—and now she was playing her own version of the oboe solo in the second movement of Brahms' violin concerto . . . Anne was deeply attached to that theme . . . her version was good, but it was an oboe theme, not something for the piano; it was a wind theme, not a string theme. Anne repeated it slowly, caressing every note.

David walked into the living room quietly and watched his daughter as she played . . . here was a lovely creature trying to have communication with forever by way of the piano, by way of song and quiet. She turned to face her father, smiled, and went back to her playing. David looked at her neck and at her shoulders and at the back of her head . . . there was something in common between the music and her neck and her head and her shoulders. . . .

"I love that oboe theme, Daddy," Anne said. "Sometimes I wish I went to the High School of Music and Art, not to Bronx Science. There is a course in music in Bronx, but it's not very good, I hear."

"You can still play by yourself, the way you're doing," said David.

"Yes, I guess so, but there's so much I don't know. Next year when I go to college I may take a course in theory." She smiled. "That is, if a college accepts me."

"I have no doubt about that."

"Why do they make it so difficult to go to college?"

"They shouldn't, if someone has the capabilities. But you don't have to worry."

"But I do worry."

"Next year this time, you'll forget about your worries now." As soon as David said this he realized what a foolish remark it was. "I was thinking, Anne, how wonderful it would be if next summer we went to Israel and England and maybe Rome, too, and Paris."

"Oh, Daddy, that would just be grand, especially Israel. I sometimes think to myself, Daddy—I mean, I wonder what was it like when Israel was a nation, way back, when all those kings

9

and prophets were there. It all seems so almost unbelievable that Israel is a nation again."

"I hope we can go next year—I mean, next summer, if I can get the time."

"I could study Hebrew more. I can speak it a little already. But I'll study more. Daddy, early this week, in social science class, we were talking about Presidents, and some said that President Truman was a bigger man than President Eisenhower, and that's what I think, too, not just because President Truman was the first to recognize Israel, but in general. He is a good man, like Lincoln was, and I said it in class. I don't mean President Eisenhower is a bad man—but you know something, Daddy?"

"What, Anne?" David was always deeply drawn to his daughter when she became serious about political or broad social issues. A stark honesty and bewilderment, mixed with the softness of young womanhood, spread across her face . . . she seemed like an island of paradise in a wide world of ugly reality.

"I didn't say it in class, but I can't love a man who is a general. Being a general is killing. I often think to myself, at night, how can anybody decide to be a general, go to military school, how can anybody do that?"

" I can't imagine it, either."

Anne began to smile, and she put her face in her hands. This action always reminded David of Anne when she was hardly a year old . . . she would become shy when a strange person, especially a strange man, came to the house, and would look and look at the person, then hide her face in her hands, and then dig her face in her mother's shoulder.

"What are you thinking of?"

"I'd like to marry a man like President Truman, or like Dr. Herzl. And you know something else, Daddy?"

"Tell me."

"I sometimes imagine President Truman with a black beard, and then he looks just like Dr. Herzl. But something else, Daddy. You know I like Adlai Stevenson, I like him very much, but I never think of him with a beard. Why is that?"

David was amused. "I don't know either. Stevenson can't have a beard; you know what I mean."

"You know, Daddy, when I was playing 'Für Elise' I was

10

thinking that it was a Jewish tune, sort of—don't you think so, sort of sad? I know Beethoven wasn't Jewish; still when I was thinking about this I remembered what Rabbi Cohen once asked us in class, when I was studying for my *bas Mitzvah.* He once asked us in class what holiday we liked the best, or what we thought was the most important, you know."

"What did you say, Anne?"

"I didn't know. I mean I wasn't sure. Danny Goodman said he thought that Rosh Hashonoh was the most important, the new year. And Evelyn Schrifft said she thought Passover was the most important, that was when the Jews stopped being slaves, you know. And somebody else, I forget who—I think it was Phyllis Weintraub, said she liked Succoth best; it wasn't the most important, but she liked the whole idea of building a *succeh* in the open, and covering it with fruit and flowers, you know; she said it was so pretty."

"And what did you say, Anne?"

"Well, I thought and thought, and when it came my turn I said *Simchas Torah,* because it was a holiday dedicated to the Torah, the Bible, and that's the most important part of Judaism. Besides, there is dancing right in the synagogue; but the whole idea is wonderful. Rabbi Cohen said that the Jews are the only people who have a holiday dedicated entirely to a book, the Torah. You know, the Jews are the People of the Book. That's a wonderful thing to be called. Sometimes, Daddy, I think I'd like to be a teacher when I grow up. Books. I still can't make up my mind if I want to specialize in French or in English, or maybe history. I like them all, so it's hard to decide. I really like French, I like to speak it and to read it. But my English teacher, Mr. Levine, he says he thinks I should major in English in college, because he likes my poems and my stories. So I don't know. But sometimes, daddy, I get all mixed up, about everything."

"How do you mean, Anne?" She seemed especially lovely when she became philosophical, David thought.

"Well, at night, before I go to sleep, I think of many things. Especially when I look out the window and there are many stars and the moon is bright, a full moon, and the sky is light blue, near the moon and near the stars. Daddy, the blue of the night,

11

in the sky, is so much finer and more wonderful than the blue of the day, and I wonder about that. It almost looks as if the angels—or maybe it's God—like the night sky more than the day sky. Can that be?"

"Well . . ." David was startled by the question. Anne was right, the blue of the night was lighter and softer than the blue of the day.

"And I think," continued Anne, "was the world always like this? Wars and troubles everywhere, Russia and Korea and China, and then I think all these troubles are really nothing. I mean there's more wonderful things in the world than troubles. Sometimes I think one thing, sometimes I think the opposite. Are you that way, too?"

"Yes, there's nothing absolutely definite to be said about the world," said David, who was troubled by the pomposity of his remarks. "There's good and there's bad, but I suppose in the main the good is more plentiful than the bad, when you add it all up. After all, we have no more religious wars, you know . . . the Thirty Years War and the Hundred Years War."

"We studied that. What you say is true, in a way."

"And in a way it isn't," said David. "The Jews are still not liked by a great many people in the world. That's true of both Christians and Arabs. Look what's happening in Israel. The world isn't doing very much to help the Jews, even though the United Nations created Israel."

"I know."

"But maybe it will be easier now to fight this anti-Semitism—I don't mean win the fight, I doubt we'll ever win it, really, as long as the Christians don't repudiate the New Testament, which is filled with anti-Semitism; and it is unlikely that the Christians will do that for hundreds, maybe thousands of years. But now that the Jews have a nation, it will be possible to fight back openly, and not remain silent as much as we used to. A government can denounce anti-Semitism openly, an individual can't always do that, so it will be a little easier. And it will be easier to be a Jew, I mean for those who used to hide their Jewishness, or made little of it." David suddenly realized that he was talking to his sixteen-year-old daughter the way he would talk to a much older person, and he liked that. She probably didn't get

12

all the implications and nuances of what he was saying, but she did follow his general line of thinking, he was sure of that.

Anne turned toward the piano again, and with one hand was playing, lazily, the opening theme in Schubert's "Der Erlkönig." "Isn't it marvelous, Daddy?" She began to play the same theme with both hands . . . she stopped now and then, put her head in her hands, resting them on the edge of the piano, and looking off into the spaces of her wandering mind.

David looked at her and looked at her, and a tightness came to his chest with love of her . . . and also a sadness at what she would meet in life, as she went to college and got married, and. beyond. He was sure that she would always be proud of her Jewishness, but he also knew that she would meet rebuffs because of it and would suffer from the encounter as she combated it. All Jews go through life wounded from such encounters, bitter at first, then accepting it as in the order of nature, but never entirely free of a pervading sense of resentment at the Christian world that has so persisted in its anti-Semitism.

Lately David had read an article in a magazine by a well-known Jewish sociologist claiming that it could well happen that, in the not too distant future—perhaps in twenty-five or thirty years— the Jews will win a friend from a source at the time held very inimical to the Jewish state, namely, the Arabs. The argument of the sociologist went like this:

The Arabs have a history of friendship with the Jews . . . the two cultures worked together, complemented each other in Spain for centuries . . . indeed, some of Maimonides' major works were first written in Arabic. He was held in high respect by Arab philosophers. There is a basic area of agreement in the religious field, for Islam, like Judaism, is a monotheistic religion. This is not true of Christianity, which is really polytheistic: the concept of the Trinity, no matter how interpreted, implies a polytheistic belief in the equality or near-equality of the Father, the Son, and the Holy Ghost. Only Islam and Judaism insist that God is One. The Jewish state, in time, will have to become more and more Middle-Eastern, and hence closer and closer to its Arab neighbors in general outlook, and less and less Western, though the Western outlook will be stronger (perhaps always) with the Jewish state than with the Arabs. As the greater Middle-Easternization, so to speak, becomes more dominant in Israel, and the "fanatics" among the Arab "hate Israel" politicians pass out, the Arab statesmen will see more and more that economic and political rapport with Israel makes great sense; there will arise a deeper bond between the two peoples. After all, the Mohammedans have suffered almost as much at the hands of the Christians as the Jews. One need only recall the Crusades. . . .

This was an enticing speculation, thought David, and he hoped that Anne would live long enough to enjoy the benefits of this rapprochement—David definitely would not—and when that rapprochement took place, perhaps then Israeli culture will bloom and once more achieve a grandeur at least approaching the grandeur of the days of the prophets.

Meanwhile, there will be trouble and war and death and despair, and David wished he could do something to make Anne's life in this sort of world easier. Perhaps there was nothing specific he could do . . . all that any Jew could do for his children is to strengthen their character, to teach them to persevere and to fill them with a conviction that continuing to be a Jew was worth the struggle. David hoped that Anne would never feel that Jewishness was her way of life only because there was no other for her: the world would insist, as it had for two thousand years, that those born as Jews always remained Jews, no matter when they were converted or assimilated or just "passed." Dr. Shmarya Levin, the great Zionist, long ago pointed out that the Christian world is schizophrenic about its attitude to the Jews: it wants them to abandon Judaism, but it takes every effort to make sure that those who have left it do not act "as if they really were full-fledged Christians." Jews must be "kept in their place": that was one of the guiding thoughts of the Christian world, not merely of "vulgar, commonplace" Christians, but also of many intellectuals and artists and writers.

Lately David had done some teaching in a writers' conference and also on a part-time basis at several colleges and universities in the New York area and also in Detroit and Kansas City and Chicago and Trenton. He liked the life of teaching very much and thought seriously of going into it on a full-time basis. It would be a pleasant way to end his working career;

14

it afforded time for writing more . . . this was very important to him now that he had two collections of short stories published, and also two novels . . . all three had been well received. He was eager to do more and more writing. Almost every day he found he had more ideas for stories and poems. But there were also problems associated with the academic life. Those in it were not as dedicated to the life of the mind as he had imagined. There were many mediocrities and even incompetents and also psychopaths, who were uncomfortable in the presence of those among them who had achieved publication or been elected to office in professional organizations. He also learned that the Ph.D. degree was often a badge of mediocrity, that the Ed.D. was even more so—that, in short, the love of learning for its own sake was almost as rare in the academic world as outside it. David learned that the academic world was rife with anti-Semitism, often unspoken and subdued, but present nevertheless. The anti-Semitism worked hand in hand with the politics of the academic world in complicated and revolting ways. David recalled having read what President Woodrow Wilson had said, during the time he was President of Princeton University: "Academic politics makes big-city politics look like child's play."

What hatred there was in the world! There was enough, even in a small group, someone has said, to blow up a whole city. But how can this hatred be stifled? An old, old question, said David to himself, staring into the distance, but still with us. David recalled overhearing a university dean say to a colleague: "I've been going through the names on our liberal arts faculty, and I've come across several Goldsteins and Weiners and names like that, and I wonder whether our faculty isn't top-heavy with Jews. Naturally, it's hard to say this in public. There would be an outcry of discrimination and God knows what else, but there should be a balance on the faculty, with no one group predominating. It will be hard to cut down on the Jewish membership of the faculty. Many of them have tenure, but I wonder whether we shouldn't be a bit more careful when considering putting more Jews on tenure, and seeing that we don't hire too many more." This dean was friendly to David. Indeed, it was he who had hired David in the first place and had promised him a full-time job, "as soon as there is an opening. We need alive

15

people like you, people who have done things in the outside world. Our students need you." David was sure that the dean knew he was Jewish.

There were even more subtle forms of anti-Semitism on the faculty. One member, a woman of some distinction in her field, had said after reading some of David's short stories and his first novel, "I like them, I do, but, I hope you won't mind what I'm about to say—I mean only to be honest—I couldn't get rid of the feeling that the stories and the novel were parochial. Maybe that's not the right word, but you know what I mean." David was startled by this comment, especially that it came from one who had impressed him as being free of any anti-Jewish bias. In fact, David was so disturbed that he refrained from being his usual cautious self in such a situation, and said, "Have you heard of Selma Lagerlöf?"

"Of course. A Swedish novelist. She won the Nobel Prize."

"She writes about Sweden, Swedish people, of whom there are about six or seven million."

"I suppose so."

"But you wouldn't call her parochial, would you?" asked David.

"No. Of course not."

"Well, there are about six million Jews in the United States. I write about them. Why call me parochial?"

"But that's different," she said.

"Why?"

"Oh, now, you're taking this personally. I'm so sorry."

David had nothing else to say to her. She sensed it, saying, "David, I hope you don't hold what I said against me. Maybe I shouldn't have said what I said, but you have to believe me . . ."

"Don't worry," said David. She walked off. David hadn't thought about this incident for years. He wondered why it came back to him now. . . .

Anne now was playing some themes from Beethoven's Sixth Symphony, that joyous hymn to nature. David wanted to tell her how much he enjoyed her playing of these themes. He needed their soft comfort so much now, and he was glad that he didn't have to tell her any of the worries that were running through his mind. Someday he would, perhaps, but not now. And as he thought this way, his mind went back to days and nights of sheer

16

delight he had spent at a writers' conference in the West. The university was situated in a woodsy area, far from a large city, though not too far when the urge to go to a motion picture or to visit a city library came to him. There were many trees and hills and two streams running through the campus and there was the university chapel, with the hourly and half-hourly chimes. When David first heard these chimes he was almost unbearably thrilled . . . the soft, round, deep notes seemed to be coming from the uttermost reaches of eternity, bringing comfort and messages of kinship with time and space.

One evening, after a class in the writing of the short story, David walked by himself along a path in a nearby woods. The beginnings of sunset were bathing the trees and resting on the grass. The only sounds he heard were the occasional rustling of leaves, and of a squirrel rushing across the path and then up a tree. A wonderful sense of peace enveloped David. If he could only spend more time in these surroundings, not with his class, not with his colleagues on the faculty, but walking by himself in these woods, and how delightful it would be to spend the night here alone. Then other thoughts came to him, more sobering. All this was fine, but could he tolerate an extended period of this sort of living? he wondered. The first day and the first night he was at this college campus he was thrilled with its quiet; the second night he was, too, but the third day and night he wasn't so sure. He was restless. The very things in New York that he was glad he was away from he now felt were drawing him back. Noise and dirt and confusion and traffic and cement had their own magical powers. But now, as he looked about him, he was glad that he was among these trees at this time of day. He walked on and on.

He heard someone behind him. He could tell, from the light step, that it was a woman. He became a bit concerned. He had never been here before, and it was getting darker every minute. Now the woman was directly behind him, and now she was by his side.

"I'm afraid I was following you, Mr. Polonsky," she said. "Not that I meant to, but as I walked I saw you, you have a sort of rolling walk, so I thought I'd catch up with you. I hope you don't mind."

17

"No, of course not." David recognized her. She usually sat in the front row of his class, her legs crossed. She was about forty, beginning to get plump, and apparently of Irish descent. David, who came from Boston, a predominantly Irish Catholic city, prided himself upon being able to tell on sight if a person was Irish.

"Isn't this a lovely place?" she said.

"It is, very much so."

"I don't suppose you know, but this road leads right out to a big highway. You can't see it from here, but in ten minutes or so you will see it. I walk through here to meet my husband, who is waiting for me with his car."

"Oh, that's good."

"I wanted to tell you, Mr. Polonsky. I've been reading your short stories and your first novel, and I wanted to tell you how much I enjoyed them."

"Thank you."

"But I've wondered about something. Did you know my grandmother, Elaine Hughes?"

"Why, no. Why do you ask?"

"Well, you write about her, to a *t*. Your Alte Bobbe is just the way Grandmother Elaine was, said pretty much the same things, thought pretty much the same way. She lived in a suburb of Chicago, and died well along in years, maybe ninety or more, like Alte Bobbe. They would have liked each other, they're so much alike. The only difference is that your Alte Bobbe was Jewish and my grandmother was Irish Catholic. One went to synagogue and the other went to church. It's really amazing how you got Grandmother Elaine down on paper. I could hardly believe it. I thought I'd tell you."

"I'm pleased to hear this," said David . . . and now he knew that he had written truly about Alte Bobbe, that she was universal . . . and hearing what he had just heard made the whole day so much pleasanter. And as he walked back to his room in the dormitory he looked at the rising moon with greater appreciation and the trees seemed to have more meaning and the future seemed more hopeful.

Another student of his was a young nun. She couldn't have been more than twenty-two or twenty-three. She had a round face, the color of an apricot; there wes eagerness in her eyes and on her lips; she took copious notes. The stories and sketches she submitted were lovingly sculptured, and the color imagery in them was outstanding. Generally he discussed manuscripts with students in the cafeteria or on a bench by a nearby lake. He thought it would be nice if he took the nun to a small restaurant that was on the edge of the campus. He asked her.

She smiled, and said, "I would have to ask the Mother Superior."

"I'm perfectly safe," David said stupidly.

Again she smiled. "Regulations."

The Mother Superior gave the nun permission to have lunch with David.

He said, "There's something I would like to ask you."

"Please do."

"In your manuscripts, the stories and the poems, you show such a deep appreciation of color, the many shadings of color— I've been wondering, I hope you don't mind my asking—how you, who like color so much, how you manage to get along, to adjust to your somber habit."

She smiled, emitting a soft laugh. "Why do you ask? Didn't you know that the combination of black and white is one of the most beautiful there is?"

David was won over completely, so to speak. She really didn't answer his question, and then, again, she did. But she was very likely at peace with herself, and she did not seem to mind his rather personal question. But the rest of that day and for several days afterward, intermittently, he thought about the nun, what made her give up the "worldly" life, and he couldn't help thinking how her celibacy was depriving some man of a good wife and children of a good mother. He couldn't help thinking about the sheer cruelty of her state: Why should a woman deny herself the delights that God had clearly given her and to all women? The Jews were right, thought David: Celibacy was a form of discourtesy to the Almighty. To refuse to accept a gift was impolite—to refuse to accept the gift of God was gross impoliteness . . . still, who can say? Marriage was possible for everybody, but apparently not all were suited for it. Not all gifts were equally acceptable to all. David wanted

19

to ask the nun other questions: Was she happy? Did she have any regrets? Does she have any "normal' desires for sex relations and for children, for family life? What have older nuns revealed to her? . . .

Anne said something about the possibility of her going into teaching . . . she had said it several times lately—teaching and writing. That would truly be pleasant. And how much even more pleasant it would be if Anne married a teacher. How strange, thought David, that he should now be so attracted to teaching. He had gone through a strange evolution in this respect. While still in high school he hardly knew what he wanted to do with his life. He thought of becoming a writer, and he thought of becoming a physician, but his chief interest, as well as he could now recall, and assuming he had a chief interest, was in becoming a sociologist, or, more accurately, a social worker. He remembered vaguely having gone to the Boston State House in search of information about openings for investigators of working conditions or arbitrators of labor disputes. David didn't recall whether he got any of this information, but if he did he certainly didn't remain interested in the subject for long.

In college he was in a state of bewilderment most of the time. He had thought of becoming a doctor, a psychiatrist, a mathematics teacher, a philosophy teacher, and he took several courses in the school of Education because he thought it would be "easy" to earn a living as a high school teacher. But the two courses he took in the School of Education—one was the teaching of algebra in secondary school, the other, civics in junior high schools—appeared so silly to him that he gave up all desire for teaching. Then he went into journalism, and had remained there for about three decades. During that time he had been asked several times to deliver some lectures at institutions of higher learning. He always accepted with some hesitation. He didn't quite know why. But slowly he became attracted to teaching. In the little lecturing he had done he had discovered that there was excitement in speaking before young minds and getting their responses, and there was also a feeling of influencing future generations . . . and the profession somehow seemed "cleaner" than did journalism. It really was an honorable and useful occupation. He had learned some of the unpleasant aspects of

20

teachers as a group. There were mediocrities and "graspers" among them—but in the main they seemed to be decent. It would be something of a wrench to leave journalism completely, but he was getting tired of all the wrangling and all the cheapness and, perhaps more than anything else, of his feeling of having failed to make a mark in the profession. He had a good reputation among magazine people, and among book publishers, too, but he himself was disappointed: he had achieved so much less than he had wanted to. . . .

Suddenly, as if out of the distant past, he heard Anne playing a lovely Schubert dance. There, thought David, was a God-intoxicated man if there ever was one! Anne played the dance again and again, slowly, lovingly, and then she tried to play some variations upon it.

She seemed tired from her effort. She turned to David and said, "How does anyone get such delicious melodies?"

"No one knows the answer to that question. The best questions are those that have no answers. How did Mozart get to write his Adelaide violin concerto when he was about seven, maybe only six? How did Shakespeare write all those plays and poems? How, how, how?"

"But how, Daddy?" She smiled.

A sad thought passed through his mind, and he gasped inwardly as it did so. This lovely daughter of his would soon be older and more "worldly" and more "sophisticated" and all this softness and genuine innocence and youthful bedazzlement would be largely gone.

"When you were very little you asked a question I haven't been able to answer—nobody can answer it."

"What question?"

"You asked—I think you were only three—you asked, 'Where did yesterday go?'"

She put her face in her hands girlishly, "I asked that?"

"Yes. And later—you must have been eight or nine, it was one summer in Atlantic Beach—you asked me, as if I knew the answer, 'Why doesn't God tell us more?'"

"I was a question-asker," Anne said, and he sensed that she was pleased with her childhood self; and he was glad that she was pleased.

David thought back to the weeks he had spent at writers'

conferences. Generally they lasted two weeks, some lasted one week, and some lasted three weeks. Most lasted two weeks, and David got to think that two weeks was just about right, not too long and not too short. The conferences were good and useful but there were conferees who were more eager for companionship than to get pointers on how to improve their manuscripts. On the whole, however, they had value, and David was glad that he was associated with them. In addition, he met many people who fascinated him—wastrels of the literary world, drunkards because they sensed they had failed to be superb poets or short-story writers or novelists. It occurred to David how much more interesting failures were than successes . . . and he had met many women who were unhappy. Unhappy women always interested David . . . at times he thought that women represented God's failure with the human race, far more so than his failure with men. David was entranced with the thought of women, always had been . . . he was deeply attracted to them, all of them, in fact, with their secondary position in life, and yet with their rightful conviction that they were closer to divinity than was man. David loved them and he was appalled by all of them . . . women did things that men would hesitate to do; and yet, David thought, always, nearly always, they had their eye on the real and genuine values, and what drove them to moral horrors was their disappointment with the ways of God. Women were more demanding than God, and perhaps that was the thing about women that attracted David most: they dared to argue with God on moral issues. There was the wife of Job, who admonished her husband, her bed partner, "Curse God, and die." It was this strength of women—they did not hesitate to question ultimate authority. Women were polite to each other, but they did not hesitate to be impolite to "higher authority," and that had pleased David.

As always, David thought of the Jewish attitude to the eternal values, to God, to the infinite. What had appealed to him down the years was that Jews had almost no questions that couldn't be asked. Jews were the supreme atheists, who yet believed in God. Jews accepted no earthly authority, and they accepted hardly any divine authority. In Judaism, questions had to be answered. There was no such thing as accepting anything on faith. Christians, thought David, were half-human beings . . . there were

22

whole areas that they accepted without question: one believed, whether or not one approved. Among Jews there was no such thing as believing without approving.

And there was the matter of humor. Jews looked upon God as One who could accept a joke and laugh at it. Among Christians God was not one who accepted jokes. The Christian God was always solemn. One never told stories in a church; one did not hesitate to tell stories in a synagogue. This lack of Christian humor, in respect to God, David often thought meant that Jews and Christians would really never "get together." And David sometimes wondered how Christians managed to make peace with reality, which was so tragic and often amoral: How can one possibly continue to live without approaching reality with a sense of humor? David thought that the Christian fear of sex also was somehow related to the Christian lack of humor. Sex was glorious and delightful, and it was also humorous. The sex act itself was an act of comedy: it brought engineering into a delightful spiritual experience . . . and it was this very fact that made life so tolerable to Jews, despite all their disappointments and despairs at the hands of Christians. Life was a comedy in the midst of a tragedy . . . a kiss was an act of faith in a world of perfidy . . . love was a temporary cessation of incredulity, and birth was the apotheosis of certainty. The final failure of Jesus was his lack of humor, thought David. One must learn to laugh, or life is intolerable. The Greeks were better Jews than the Christians, and Maimonides would have got along far better with Plato than with Jesus or St. Paul. St. Paul was not a true, genuine, whole Jew; he was a Jew perverted by psychopathic ideas. Jesus himself would have been horrified by St. Paul if he had ever spoken to him at length.

David wondered about the mystery of writing. At bottom, it seemed to him, it was a matter of being utterly honest about one's relations to the world, to men and women, to God. Somehow a whole body of legend has arisen about how people *should* feel about these matters, and few people take the trouble to distinguish between what legend says and what is actually true. The question then arises, how did the body of legend come into being? David had no answer. How could people accept as fact what they knew wasn't so? How did an untruth assume the force of fact and truth? The great writers, he often thought, were those

23

who dared to question the legend and wrote what they actually felt, and so true was that which they put on paper that large elements of the world's population gave them the honor of reading them. Yet those who purveyed the legend continued to crop up, and they enjoyed popularity. Why? Was the truth so bitter that many people preferred, at least temporarily, to give devotion, so to speak, to falsehood?

Writing, thought David, was loneliness seeking for some comfort by expressing itself. But that brought up the question of why God arranged things so. If God is love, why did He create all this loneliness? In the words of his daughter, Anne, "Why didn't God tell us more?" There must be a reason, thought David, and he wished he knew the reason. Perhaps not knowing was a kindness. It made man search more deeply into himself, into life, and that made for art. God does work in mysterious ways His wonders to perform.

These thoughts recalled to David a priest in one of his classes: a young man in his mid-twenties, he always seemed ready to take part in a tennis match. He was so content with himself . . . he sat in class in short pants, short sleeves, a simple sports shirt, and he hardly ever participated in the class discussion, though he smiled now and then. After three or four days, the smile bothered David. There were times when David wanted to ask, "Why are you smiling? Is it about what's taking place in class, or about something else . . . something that has happened in your past life, or something that you have read?" One paper the priest handed in was a page and a half long, and was entitled "A Defense of Immortality." It was little more than a statement of the problem of immortality . . . it really was not even that. It was written so smugly . . . no doubts, no hesitations. David asked him, "Is this all?"

The priest thought a second, smiled, then said, "Yes."

"You mean there is nothing more to say about this problem?"

"Not really."

"But whole volumes, hundreds of them, maybe thousands have been written on this issue, and as lawyers say, to some people at least, the question is moot."

"I know," said the priest simply.

"Are you convinced, yourself?"

"Definitely."

"You think there is absolute proof?"

"It's all logical. It can't be otherwise. It's a matter of reason."

David was staggered by this assurance. "I don't wish to argue with you. You believe as you wish, but don't you think there should be more evidence? After all, Immanuel Kant felt he had to devote more than a page and a half to prove the immortality of the soul. I believe that St. Thomas Aquinas also felt this way, and Spinoza, and, I believe, St. Augustine. The question is one of the unsolved problems of philosophy, I mean to some people."

"I know. But not to me. Frankly, I hardly know what else to say."

"Well," said David helplessly.

"But is it clearly written?" asked the priest.

David didn't know how to answer this question. "Oh, yes, you write clearly."

"That's all I really wanted to know."

Suddenly he heard Anne speaking to him. "What are you thinking about, Daddy?"

"Oh, lots of things, about writing, about immortality . . ."

"Immortality? Of all things . . ."

"I guess I'm in the same state as the whole world is now. *Cul de sac,* it might be called. Maybe even worse. There seems to be only way out of everything, all problems, and that is the recognition that there is no way out. Life goes on and on and on, the same problems over and over again. But I'm sorry I'm talking to you this way, Anne. Your life is beginning. It is not a *cul de sac* for you. You have one great, wonderful advantage over me: you have youth. There is nothing greater than that. But maybe things are really not so bad even for me. There's one great antidote to age: art, music, painting, literature. All these, all the arts, see and express inner holiness, inner joy and beauty in life, and this sense makes everything worthwhile. I suppose a child, a daughter, represents all that these arts say, and much better, more intimately, more enduringly, more wonderfully."

Anne exclaimed, "Oh, Daddy, that's so wonderful, what you said, so very wonderful." She rushed over to him, threw her arms around him and kissed him.

two

The death of his mother, Nechame, and the death of Dryfoos
continued to hover over David's consciousness much of the day
and night, and they also were in his dreams. Sylvia's death was
slowly receding from the center of his mind, though now and
then her soft and lovely face would spring before his mind's
eye, and Helen was now taking the place of Sylvia as the major
object of his affection. Helen didn't replace Sylvia—the two were
different in many respects, but she did supply much of the
warmth and comfort that Sylvia had. There were times, at the
beginning of his relationship with Helen, when he felt almost
unfaithful to the memory of Sylvia, but then he felt that Helen
had left the place of Sylvia in his life almost intact. . . . But the
death of his mother had sunk deep into his being: the terrible,
gnawing sorrow of her whole life, her sheer exhaustion in her
mounting efforts to be a Jewish wife and mother . . . the intricate
schemes she had to make a little money go a long way at the
family table. Seven children and two parents, nine in all, Moshe
often out of work, and even when he did get employment he
generally made $12 a week, seldom more; even in the second and
third decades of this century this was very little. Mother did all

the washing herself, she did a good deal of the baking (nearly all the bread, all the cake), and, of course, all the cooking. Thursday of every week was an especially arduous one for her, as was Friday morning, in preparation for the Sabbath. Often she would stay up till two or three Friday morning, cooking and cleaning, and would be up three hours later making breakfast for Moshe and for the children—and she would also make lunches for those going to school.

So many memories kept coming back to him, and each one filled him with more love and with more sadness. There was the time she and Moshe went to hear David make the *kabolas ponim* (welcome) talk (it lasted about three minutes, but it was listed in the typewritten program of the Hebrew School Ivrioh as "Remarks," by David Polonsky—the word "Remarks" filled David with a sense of importance) for Nahum Sokoloff, the great Zionist leader. David spoke in Hebrew; he had written many of the words of his talk himself, while others and the general tone were supplied by Mr. Hirsch, his Hebrew literature teacher. All David now remembered of his talk was a phrase or two: "You come to us as a beacon of light for all Israel . . . you are a messenger of the glorious past to the glorious future, and a most respected guest of the present" . . . the entire student body sang "Hatikvah," and a wonderful glow spread throughout the assembly hall. David also remembered that at the time he had a sense of something historic having taken place, and he was enormously delighted that he was part of it. As he left the hall with his mother and father, his mother embraced him and kissed him, and said, "I'm so happy, I'm so proud of you. You make everything seem so good," and again she kissed him. His father patted his head and said, "Very good. You were very good, and I am very happy." David still remembered the tenderness in his mother's voice, the deep gratitude, the limitless love that came from her, and he remembered how lovely she looked, her hair done up in a pleasing manner, her ears seemed so young to David—he now wondered why he remembered the ears—and her long dress made her seem so lofty, she looked like some of the women's pictures he had seen in the society pages of the Boston *Post* and the Boston *Herald* . . . and there was her fleur-de-lis watch on her left breast . . . this watch gave her dignity, and made her look so beautiful. What a wonderful, wonderful time that was . . . and suddenly he remembered the slight upturn to her nose, how charming it seemed, imparting a girlishness to her whole face . . . and her cheekbones that protruded just a little bit . . . at this very moment they reminded him of the "horns" on Michelangelo's Moses. What a wonderful, wonderful face Mother had . . . and then he recalled her few days in New York visiting her girlhood friend, Tzipporah: tired, ailing, yet eager to see and hear everything.

His mother had been born to lead, in part, a life of subdued gaiety, but gaiety nevertheless . . . she read about dance recitals and about concerts and about charitable affairs that involved dancing. She liked the theatre, and went whenever she could afford to. She liked the movies and she went now and then (there was the problem of her husband, Moshe, who looked upon dancing and the movies and the theatre as mostly foolishness, but he gave in to her wishes occasionally) . . . she liked singing, and was especially fond of the singing of Alma Gluck and Galli-Curci, which she sometimes heard on other people's phonographs (the Polonskys couldn't afford a phonograph till David was already in college). And there was the time she took David to see Anna Pavlova dance.

Moshe, being a Chassid, found most of his emotional release in religious singing and in watching more active Chassidim dance religious dances. That, to him, was proper entertainment for a mature person. Motion pictures, ordinary dancing, and sports held no interest whatsoever to him. He looked upon them all as childish, and he wasn't at all sure that motion pictures and such sports as baseball and football were not also tainted with atheism. "What requires such tremendous physical effort," he said, "cannot be good in the eyes of God. You say *goyim* enjoy these things?" he asked David. "Well, let *goyim* enjoy them. They are not for our people." David pointed out to him that several distinguished baseball and football players and even boxers were Jews. But this didn't trouble his father. "All I can say about these Jews or so-called Jews that you mention," he said, "is that they were not brought up properly, and I can well imagine how heartbroken their parents must be."

Nechame was a bit more worldly in such matters than was her husband. She wasn't belligerent about it—no good Jewish wife is ever that to her husband—but she secretly enjoyed the movies. On the pretext of watching over her younger children, she sometimes took them to the Olympic Theatre in Bowdoin Square, in Boston, where for five cents one could see two pictures. David still remembered the soft little laughs that came from her as she watched some Fatty Arbuckle pranks, and David also remembered the soft little sighs that came from her as she watched the Gish sisters suffering through *Orphans of the Storm.* Mother also liked "worldly" music, and sometimes, on a Saturday, she would ask her oldest, David, whether he wouldn't walk with her on Tremont Street, especially along a certain block where there were several stores that sold phonograph records and victrolas with the big horns. They all played records constantly, so that if one tarried by the door one could hear Mischa Elman or Kreisler play, or one could hear Caruso and De Gogorza and Schumann-Heink sing. "Such a pleasure," Nechame would say, "such a pleasure!" And David also recalled what a glow would come to her face whenever she heard Elman play "Humoresque," which apparently was a favorite of hers.

One Sunday the great and illustrious Cantor Rosenblatt came to Boston. Mother pleaded with Father to take her to hear him. At first he objected violently. "A cantor belongs in a *shul,* not in a public hall. I will not be part of such atheistical goings-on."

"But he's an Orthodox cantor, who sings in an Orthodox *shul* in New York," said Nechame, "and all the biggest people in New York go to hear him, and the Metropolitan Opera House asked him to become one of their singers—I read it in the *Forward;* but he wouldn't do it, because he wouldn't sing without a *yarmulke."*

"Really?" asked Father in surprise.

"Yes," said Mother, "and he's a real *Shabbes* Jew; wouldn't think of traveling on *Shabbes."*

Father finally consented to take Mother and David to hear Cantor Rosenblatt. Both were deeply moved, as they both looked about the Boston Opera House, where the concert was being given. "Nu, it really is nice," said Father, "that a big place like this can be so crowded with people who want to hear a cantor sing Jewish tunes, and religious tunes, too, many of them, I can see from the program." Later, he said, "That is singing, really singing. In all my born days, I don't think I heard a *chazen* sing like that. May he live to be a hundred and twenty."

three

Dryfoos had been, so to speak, David's favorite uncle with whom he could discuss whatever was on his mind. He had been a free spirit—as free as David on occasion hoped he himself would be, but dared not or simply could not. He had been a spiritual anarchist, a questioner of everything and everybody. He was the ideal older companion for a bewildered young man like David: He admonished, guided, encouraged; he was cynical, he was sentimental, he loved women, he didn't trust them, he was supremely honest, he was strangely devious, and he was always loyal to those he liked. He liked David, he loved him, and David felt enormously comfortable with him, and very grateful. His death deprived David of a mainstay in his life. Happily, Helen Davidson was gradually taking his place in his life. A woman of great resources of affection, she was not as cynical as Dryfoos had been; she was inclined more to pity those she didn't like than to despise them. She was completely honest emotionally. She told David about her relationship with her late husband, Mordecai: "I just couldn't stand him any more getting close to me. I would shiver all over. I knew it the first night, but a young girl is a young girl, and when an older man shows her

30

respect and flatters her, she makes the mistake I made. A Russian writer, I forget his name now, once said by way of a woman character in one of his stories—she had also married an older man she didn't like, 'I liked him for warmth, but not for delight.' That's how I felt about Mordecai. Of course, there was something else that blinded me, his devotion to Palestine, Israel, to the Jews, to the Hebrew language, to the theatre."

Helen knew David's real interests as well as did Dryfoos; she sensed the grounds for his unhappiness on the *World,* where he now worked pretty much in a state of stupor.

"Leave it, darling, leave it, you're too young to be wasting your life, to be dishonest with yourself," she told him time and again. "Youth is a time for being honest, for doing what you want, for love."

"But how will I live?" asked David. "Here I've had two collections of stories and two novels, and I don't think I've made more than a thousand dollars, maybe a little more. I need a job."

"I think you should teach," she said. "I've always thought so. You're excited about literature, about people, and you know everything, and that's all you need to teach."

"Where will I get a job? I've never taught before."

"You'll get a job. Any university will be glad to have you. But you have to let them know you want to teach. Oh, darling, you need a manager so badly. You're bashful. The world has little use for people who are bashful." Suddenly she began to smile, and soon she burst into laughter.

"What are you laughing at, Helen?"

"I can't say," she said hiding her face in her hands, still laughing. She was very appealing as she did this.

"I can't say. Please come here."

He came over and she threw her arms around him and kissed him, and said, "I wish I knew how to get you into some college or a place like that, even a high school—no, you should teach in a bigger place, you know . . . older students. Oh, I wish, I wish . . ." and she kissed him again.

He kissed her in return. "Why did you laugh before?"

"Oh, all right, I'll tell you, but it's funny for me to say it. My grandmother used to say, 'If you're bashful, you can't have children.' That's why I was laughing."

"It is funny; nothing wrong in your telling me."

"Oh, I don't know. After all, I'm a woman. Promise me you'll look for a teaching job. I wish I knew where to look for you. You teach at these conferences in the summer, writers' conferences. They should be able to help you. They'll be very happy to have you, the colleges, I'm sure. Your magazine, the *World,* is terrible. That man Simmons makes me want to hold my stomach; I shake when I think of him. Remember the Christmas party you took me to?—his party. I saw those little fingers of his, his pinched nose, and that terrible smile covering up what's in his mind. I didn't tell you before, but he touched me a few times, and I felt like running. Teaching is clean and your students will like you."

Mordecai had left Helen no money. There was no Hebrew theatre in New York, so Helen could get no job as an actress. Her Russian was fine, but there was no Russian theatre to speak of. There was also the matter of her accent, which kept her from the Broadway and off-Broadway theatre in significant parts. But she was so skillful an actress that now and then she did get a bit part as an Italian mother or Spanish grandmother or Mexican prostitute. She got few such jobs, because there were few such plays. She was forced to seek other means of paying her bills: she translated novels, stories, and articles from Russian into English, for professors and for publishing houses. She earned little for this work, because her English idiom was faulty so that her work had to be gone over by those who knew no Russian but were familiar with English. Then Helen ran a class in acting in her own two-room apartment. Sometimes she had ten students at one time, sometimes she had only four or five. Her fees were flexible: "Oh, I tell them to pay what they can—three dollars an hour, five dollars, two dollars; some pay only one dollar, and one or two pay nothing." This income was whittled down by her "coffee socials." At intermission time she would make coffee for the students and also serve cookies or doughnuts or rolls and jam. Some of the students would, on occasion, bring coffee and doughnuts "to help out," but probably more often Helen supplied the refreshments herself. She made her own clothes, generally from castaways that she would buy at charity bazaars or at HIAS "outlet stores." The Hebrew Immigrant Aid Society has stores in New York, where people leave clothes and whatever else they don't need. These are sold at low rates, and the money is turned over to the Society. She told all this to David, without complaint, without self-pity, merely as facts. There were still other ways she earned money: she would do clerical work at the Farband, a Yiddish workers' organization; she helped out in the theatrical programs of the Amalgamated Clothing Workers and the International Ladies Garment Workers Union.

Once, in a moment of exuberance, she said, "I get along, and I love you. I don't need anything else," and laughing, she held out her arms for David to fill them.

Helen, as the saying goes, knew everybody. She was associated with several groups of Hebrew-speaking men and women, Yiddish-speaking *landsmanschaften,* Russian culture clubs, and Lithuanian culture clubs. She took David to them, and he was delighted. Through her he learned what marvelous cultural activity goes on in New York among these immigrants, and how uninformed about it so many American writers are. Helen participated actively in these groups: she would read parts of plays and novels, stories, poems, she would tell about the latest developments in the various literatures (she read the East European press regularly), and she would help out with the refreshments. She'd roll up her sleeves, put on an apron, firmly place her hands on her hips for a few seconds, as if to make sure they were firm, and get to work in the kitchen. When David saw her do this he almost melted with love of her—love and generosity and unending womanly kindliness seemed to be flowing from her breasts and eyes and mouth and neck and ample hips. She was not a slender woman; she was well-proportioned, and profoundly desirable. She was the proverbial wife, mother, and mistress— open, eager, and joyous.

"I like to see people eat and laugh," she said, as she raised her arms and made a circular motion. "I don't like thin people. What's the trouble with American women, that they like to be thin, with nothing on them, nothing nowhere?" She smiled. "I don't believe they, men, really like such girls and women. There is a saying in Russia, 'A man with a full barn and a fat wife has a good life.' That's true. I don't mean very fat. I mean full, full all over, a woman must be full to be happy herself and

33

her husband likes her that way, too. It's nature. You American men!" And she burst out laughing.

"Don't look at me," said David.

"I don't mean you, you know what I mean."

It was through Helen that David learned about YVOH, the Yiddish cultural organization, and about Camp Boiberick, and about the Workmen's Circle. David had known about the Workmen's Circle in the Boston area, but it was Helen who introduced him to the New York branch.

Helen took David to Camp Boiberick, in the Catskills, one week-end. There, for the first time, he was in the midst of a completely Yiddish-speaking group . . . some also knew Hebrew, but most were dedicated to the survival of Yiddish as a language and as a culture. There were older men and women and some younger ones, there were writers for the Yiddish press, especially the *Forward*. There were "discussions" at night—in the library and in the recreation hall; there were musical concerts, and on Saturday nights there were "gala" affairs, a visiting lecturer, an instrumental recital (a guitarist and a vocalist, in this case), and group folk singing. The preceding evening, Friday night, there was a "special" event: a "secular religious welcoming of the Sabbath," as one of the functionaries put it to David. Because the dominant group was "nonreligiously Jewish," there was barely a hint that Friday night had anything to do with Judaism— it was just another night, but a little different, why or how was not made clear to David. The "services" consisted of a brief talk by one of the officers of the camp about the events of the coming week (especially of the next night), about new additions to the library, and somebody read, in Yiddish, a Sholom Aleichem story, and then somebody else read, in English, an essay on early Jewish-American history, with emphasis on the Yiddish influence among the Jewish customer-peddlers in upstate New York and New Jersey.

David was pleased, yet depressed. He was pleased to be in a group of so many Jews (about a hundred), who got together Friday night. He was pleased to hear so much Yiddish spoken . . . but was this a Jewish Friday night? Is this what is meant by "secularism"? As David looked at the faces of the Jewish

34

women and their men, he was sure that their "principles" would never have suffered if someone had got up and made a blessing over the candles . . . or if the congregation had sung *"L'Cho Dodi"* or *"Adon Olom,"* the traditional songs on Friday night in every synagogue. David also missed the traditional Havdalah service at sundown on Saturday night—a beautiful service involving the blessing of a special Havdalah twisted candle, and the blessing of the *psomim* (spices) . . . the singing of the lovely song *Eliyohu Hanovi* (Elijah the Prophet) . . . all the people making a circle, holding hands, and singing *"A Gute Voch"* (A Happy Week) . . . and the blessing of the wine . . . the wonderful warmth that always came over all on that occasion. The idea itself was very beautiful: the ceremony signified the end of the Sabbath and the beginning of the secular part of the week. Jews make an important distinction between the two periods. For six days a Jew worked for a living, and the seventh day, the Sabbath, he came back home, to God, to holy things. The Sabbath was the important holiday in the year, on a par with Yom Kippur. It distinguished man from the animal, it emphasized week in and week out the fact that man is primarily a spiritual being.

"I like it here," said David to Helen, "but it's cold, and for a coldness to prevail at a gathering of Jews is strange to me. I don't want to complain. I do feel happy here, very happy, but I miss what means a great deal to me, Jewishness."

"I knew you'd say that, darling," said Helen. "A few years ago I would have said you were old-fashioned, narrow-minded, maybe even uncivilized. It's not only the *Yiddishisten* who have made a religion, you might say, out of having no religion. The *Hebraisten,* too. It was all a foolishness, I can see now. And I think others are beginning to say it, too."

"Is that a fact, Helen, what you say, that these secular Jews are, as they say, coming back?"

She smiled, and patted his hand. "Oh, darling, you still have to learn about Jews. Some things about them you know so well, better than anybody I know—the philosophy, the literature, the community leaders, the intellectuals, some of them—but other parts of Jewish life you still have to learn well. You don't mind my saying so, darling?"

35

"No, of course, not. But look what happened or what didn't happen Friday and Saturday."

"I know, David. Jews are stubborn. I believe most of those here would have been pleased if they had had *kiddush* on Friday night, and Havdalah on Saturday night."

"And why not some studying of the Torah and the Talmud and *Pirkay Avot* (Sayings of the Fathers) on Saturday afternoon, just before *mincheh* and *maariv* services?"

"I would like that, too, David, but remember, it's hard for people to admit they have been wrong for a hundred years, it takes time. Nobody is always right. The very Orthodox were for a long time against Zionism, you know, and I think the Reformed were, too. The first were waiting for the Messiah, and the second "—she smiled again—"I don't know what they did, I don't know many Reformed Jews. I used to think they were almost *goyim,* but I was wrong. Many of them, maybe most, are Zionists now. The same with many Orthodox Jews. But, darling, when I'm with you I feel warmly Jewish, so deeply Jewish. But you are right. All those religious ceremonies are really beautiful, they have so many meanings. Ceremony is important in everything. And when you're dealing with God and life, you need a lot of ceremony. Do I make sense?"

"Of course, Helen. Being rational about everything is irrational."

"That's a beautiful way of saying it."

"Lights, candles, blessing of the wine, the menorah, these are Jewish symbols, very dear to Jews, and what's very dear is holy."

"I like that, too, David . . . what's very dear is holy."

"Bialik was an atheist, but he loved Friday night, and he wrote a beautiful poem about it, I believe."

"It's so beautiful, David. In Hebrew it sounds just wonderful."

"When I knew Hebrew well, I used to read it mvself, it was wonderful. He knew the meaning of candles and light and soft music at sunset. He said he was an atheist, but he was religious."

"Everybody is religious, David. You have to be. That's part of being human."

"I wouldn't say it to any of the people here, straight out, but their atheism is childish."

"Of course. What are you thinking of now, David? Your mind seems to be far away."

"My mind is far away, Helen, and yet it is near."

She took his hand, and a stream of comfort coursed through him. He wished he knew how to tell her how much he loved her, how she enriched his life. He didn't know. He only looked at her and kept silent, and sensed how disappointed she was . . . and still he didn't know what to do. Suddenly he took her hand in his and kissed it and put it to his face, and then kissed it again. She looked at him silently, and he saw tears begin to gather in her eyes . . . and this only added comfort to his being. Here was a woman of endless delight, of profound loyalty, of pervasive love. Indeed, so deep was his love of her that he was afraid of it.

"What were you thinking of, darling?" she said, and quickly added, "Before you answer me, tell me you are enjoying it here."

"I am, very much."

"I'm glad, David, very glad. You've looked so tired recently— really, David. I thought you ought to have some relaxation, and that's why I brought you here. The people are the kind you'd like, I thought."

"I like them very much, Helen."

"And it's quiet, and there are trees and grass and the quiet of the evening and the quiet of the morning, and there are places where you can go off by yourself." She put her hand to her mouth. "I guess I haven't let you go off by yourself very much. I've been selfish. I can't help it. Forgive me. I feel so near to you—now, I mean, when I'm with you, it's like being with myself . . . I don't know how to say it. I wish I knew how to tell how I feel better than I can do now. But I will let you be with yourself more in the little time we'll still be here." She clasped her hands to her face. "Oh, I wish I knew what to do and what to say, David. I wish I did. Please forgive me."

"For what, Helen?"

"I don't know. For being so excited, for not letting you alone. I don't know. I think I'm doing something wrong, and I don't want to. But I can't help it. Tell me what you've been thinking about, David."

"It's about a little *shul* in Boston, Helen."

"My father went to a little *shtibbel* in Russia. He loved it, and my mother loved it, and once, when I was a little girl, my mother took me there, upstairs, of course, with the women." She stopped, then she said, "Forgive me, darling. You are talking, and I interrupted you. I don't know, David, why I'm acting this way. Please forgive me."

"Don't worry, Helen. This little *shul* is on Joy Street, in Boston. It's really not on Joy Street; it's in Smith Court, that goes off Joy Street, a little alley. Now, since my mother died, I've been going to several of the places she and my father used to go to."

"I wish I had met your mother, David."

"I do, too, Helen. You would have loved her. But . . . I have so much to say, Helen . . ."

"Please talk all you want, David, say everything, darling, say everything. I love to hear you."

David looked at her. She was perfect now . . . the perfect, loving woman, the ultimate in softness and joy and comfort for him . . . the gift of God, he thought. For a second he didn't want to go on, but to embrace her and kiss her and caress her and love her and tell her how wonderful and desirable and joyful she was. But she interrupted his thoughts and said, "Please go on, my darling. I want to hear you."

This decided what he was going to do . . . he would continue talking, and now he was glad, because what he was about to say was tumbling over and over in his mind.

"I have to tell you about Joy Street, first, Helen. Joy Street in Boston is not just a street, it's a part of my past, of my life, of Boston Jewry, of Boston. Frankly I didn't think about it for years; you know, you get lost in things, here in New York; you go away from your roots, from your past, and then something happens, like my mother's death, and you realize that what really matters you have overlooked, you've been sidetracked. The older I get the more my past means to me, and I've been going to Joy Street a lot recently, I don't think I've told you, I don't know why. We all live secret lives. I meant to tell you, really."

"Of course, darling. I understand."

"I was going to tell you about Joy Street," continued David.

"It's right opposite Chambers Street, where the Hebrew School Yvrioh is, where I went as a young boy, studied Hebrew, I even wrote poems in Hebrew and short stories and essays, everything in Hebrew. I told you this, didn't I, Helen."

"Yes, you did."

"We kids who went to this Hebrew school used to pass by Joy Street, but later went a little way up the street, to see the police station there. It fascinated us and it frightened us. Those two big blue lamps at the bottom of the stairs that led to the station added an eeriness to the whole building, and then a wagon, a police wagon, would stop—they had wagons in those days, paddy wagons they used to call them, not automobiles, like now. Policemen would jump out, and after them there would be the prisoners, derelicts, most of them, I seem to recall, and drunks, and we kids were sorry for them. We saw them line up before the station sergeant, and we were sorry for them. We kids from the Hebrew school often said that not one Jew was among these prisoners, all *goyim*. I guess we said this because they didn't look like Jews, and, of course, we were all taught that a *shikker iz a goy* (drunkards are gentiles), and we were proud of that. Well, we kids for a long time would stop off at this police station, on the way back from Hebrew school. In the summer it was still daylight; in the summer, seven o'clock or even seven-thirty, it is still light, so what we saw at the police station was not so frightening and fascinating. But in the winter, seven and seven-thirty is already night, and that added to the eeriness of it all."

"I wish I knew you then, David," said Helen. "But go on, please."

"Now about the Joy Street *shul* I was telling you about. Its real name is Congregation Anshay Lubavitz, Chassidim, but people referred to it as the Joy Street *shul*, even though it wasn't even on Joy Street. Oh, it must be over a hundred years old. Not very long ago I went to Boston to visit my family, and the three men in the family, I mean the three sons, just rode around the city, but we spent most of the time looking at the places where we had lived, at the Hebrew School Yvrioh I just told you about, at the Catholic Church across the street. My mother and father always spoke about the church, that it was so close to the Hebrew school, and yet there was no pogrom, no trouble at all. 'A really wonderful country,' my father and mother would say. The three of us, as I was saying, just wandered around, even stopped to look at the old Charles Street jail, where one of our mayors, James Michael Curley, was imprisoned for taking an examination for somebody else. He was a real crook, I'm afraid, not because of this examination but for other reasons, he served in jail other times for using the mails to defraud, or something of the sort, but the real reasons the three of us looked at the jail was that on top was a big clock, and we three used to sleep in the attic, and we had no clock of our own, of course. We had no watches—that was riches; so we would look out of the narrow window of the attic where we slept, to see the time. The jail clock was our clock. Then one of us said, 'Let's go to the Joy Street *shul*.' The Smith Court, where it is, is narrow, like all such places in Boston. On one side are some old houses, wooden ones, with flowers in front, nice doors— Boston is known for its fine doors—and I guess some wealthy or artistic people live there. The Bohemians have taken over all that part of Boston. It used to be slums.

"Anyway, the *shul* door was open, the door was weather-beaten—God knows how old it is, and pinned on the door in Yiddish, in some cases, in English in other cases there were scribbled announcements: 'Candle lighting next Friday, 7:37. . . . *Shachris* (morning prayer), every day, 6:30 and 7:15 . . . *Minche* and *Maariv* (late afternoon and evening services) every day, 6:15 . . . The *Chevreh Kadisha* (burial society) will have a meeting next Sunday at 4 in the afternoon . . . Please make another contribution for the care of the cemetery . . . *talaysim* and *sidurim* (prayer shawls and prayer books) can be bought in Green's Bookstore, Leverett Street, also candles and *luochim* (calendars).' Rain had run down these signs, and not all the words were clear, but I liked it better that way.

"We went in, the three of us. A wonderful musty smell greeted us. That *shul* smell is just wonderful, Helen, it's dry, it's strawy, it's timeless, it's indestructible, it's simply good. To the right of the door was an old carton, filled with yarmulkes, and to the left was a rickety table, with old *sidurim* on it, worn and much used, some of the pages sticking out, some of the

40

covers kind of loose. And of course, the benches on both sides, with the red straw cushions, worn and very much used. The *shul* itself is really small. When I used to go there with my father, as a boy, I thought it was huge. Now it looked small. The walls were a sort of faded green, with some streaks of brown here and there. There was, of course, the women's gallery, with a dirty bronze railing all around—well, I don't mean dirty, really, I guess it was just old. Bronze can get old, too, I guess.

"In the middle was the *bimme,* where, as you know, the *chazen* conducts the services, where the Torah is read. The *bimme* is still rather large, I mean, the way I used to remember it. There's a table, or a big desk, up front on the *bimme,* where the Torah is put on Saturday, when there is the usual reading of the Torah. And straight ahead is the *Oren Kodesh* (Holy Ark), where the Torah is kept. There is a velvet curtain, the usual one, with the Hebrew words, *Yehi Or* (Let there be light). And on both sides of the Holy Ark are the two lions of Judah, and directly above are the Ten Commandments, the two tablets, very modest, sort of gray stone. I don't know why I went into all this detail, but I wanted to tell you everything, what we saw, Helen. I guess it's because I love that place so much. I wanted to go to a service, to hear the words of the prayers, to see the faces, the wonderful faces of the old Jews, heads moving right and left, as befits a Jew while praying. I wanted to hear the beautiful hum of Jews in prayer, the waves of prayer going up and down and all around. Oh, I forgot to mention the *Nair Tomid* (Eternal Light) directly in front of the Holy Ark, up above.

"I felt so good while I was in that *shul.* In my mind's eye I saw those faces of the old Jews, in my mind's ear I heard them praying. But I also heard the prayers of all Jews down the ages, I saw these Jews. Here, in this lovely synagogue I saw and heard what has kept the Jews alive all these miserable years, until they got their country, and this same soul in this synagogue will keep the Jews going in all the years of misery to come, for, even with their country back in their hands, the outside world is going to make it difficult for them. The world doesn't like Jews—not just the Arabs, but the Christians, too, they don't like Jews. Oh, there are some exceptions, but you can count them on the fingers of one hand. The strength of the Jews is in synagogues like the Joy Street *shul,* in their faith, in their Torah, in the ceremonies, in their customs, in everything about their religion. And that's why I was so depressed at this camp Friday night and Saturday night. I don't like to see Jews not acting like Jews. Socialism, even Jewish socialism, is no substitute for Judaism, and Jews should have enough sense to know this."

Suddenly David stopped, then he said, "I don't think I really told you what I feel about that little synagogue."

Helen touched his hand, then took it in both her hands, and said, "Oh, darling, you don't know how much, how very much you said. David, you've just given me the whole history of the Jews, all their strength, all their poetry. I am so happy to be with you now."

four

Affairs at the *World* were getting worse steadily. Not one of the schemes that Simmons had concocted by himself or that he had borrowed from others had worked. One of his schemes was to reprint, in very small type, the entire short novel, *One More Spring,* by Robert Nathan. A lawyer friend of Simmons had said to him, "Lester, what people want now is not heavy stuff, politics; they want relaxation, along with some articles, of course, but mostly relaxation. I can feel it in the air. I think you should do something original. Only last week I read for the first time, thanks to my wife, *One More Spring,* it is absolutely beautiful, and comforting; it made me feel good all over." Simmons repeated these remarks several times at the offce. Everybody was against it. Simmons's only reply was, "Maybe it is a crazy idea. But you haven't given me any better ideas, and we are going down hill. Maybe a crazy idea will do the trick."

It didn't. The issue containing *One More Spring* was a horrendous failure, in view of the fact that Simmons printed ten thousand copies more "to take care of the extra sale." The returns on this issue of the *World* were stupendous.

Then Simmons thought of starting a new department, "A Guide to Entertainment and Eateries." Apparently he got this idea from *The New Yorker,* which had notes on movie theatres, Broadway shows, museums, dance recitals. The entire staff claimed that this made no sense, because so much of the circulation of the *World* was outside New York. Besides, they argued, since this sort of department was already in *The New Yorker,* and it was doing a fine job with it, why copy it? To this Simmons said, "There are enough of our readers who don't read *The New Yorker,* who will want this kind of service. Anyway, let's try it." The department involved a great detail of clerical work, checking with theatres, restaurants, and the *World* couldn't afford extra help. The result was a shabby, skimpy department that even Simmons had to admit, in the end, made no sense.

Still another idea of Simmons's was a letter department, "a really big one, let the people know they have their own soap box, so to speak, a kind of Hyde Park in America. We might even call it the *World* Hyde Park. It will be the first idea of its kind in American journalism." Betty Gard pointed out that the *Time-Life* group had experimented with a Letters magazine, pretty much along the lines that Simmons was urging, and it has failed. This didn't stop Simmons. "The idea is still a good one. We can do it our way. Some ideas have to wait for the right time to go over." Betty Gard pointed out that the *Time-Life* Letters magazine had died only a short while ago. "It's still a good idea," he insisted. His wife, Clarice, hardly participated in the discussions, but it was clear that she thought her husband was "way off." David barely said anything. He didn't care. Of course, he had to say something, so, in each case he said, "I have many doubts about this idea." The Letters department was also a failure. Few genuine letters came in, and for some four, five months, fake letters were concocted in the office. This clearly couldn't go on. Again Simmons admitted defeat.

To the relief of everyone, Simmons did not come up with any new ideas for some weeks. The *World* continued to lose circulation, and the advertising was nothing to speak about. The only full-page advertisements now were "contingency" ones, that is, the *World* got a percentage of what came in to the advertisers—and the advertisers were largely "special book offers," some dealing with "Exotic Love Stories of the Orient" and "Peeks into the World's Greatest Romances in all History." There was also a half-page advertisement announcing "a new cure for flat feet, with full, guaranteed exercises." These advertisements ran coupons, and the success of the advertisements was judged by the number of coupons received by the advertiser, and also, of course, by the amount of money that came in with the coupons; some coupon senders only asked for "more information, and perhaps you can send me your book for inspection." These advertisements not only brought in virtually no money to the *World,* they also gave the magazine a shabby reputation in the publishing fraternity and among advertisers of legitimate products.

Then, one morning, Simmons called a special meeting of the editors. He told each of them, "I really got something now. I'm bringing along two people, they'll be at the meeting." Peter said to David, "More phonies." Betty Gard said to David and Peter and Bly, "I don't know, but this frightens me worst of all. This Simmons has an instinct for crazy people and dumb projects. God help us." David only smiled. He laughed to himself, having decided to say, sight unseen, so to speak, "I have too many doubts about this idea."

The two people came, and the entire editorial board waited with bated breath. Simmons was beaming. David could imagine what Peter was saying to himself: "Here are the two Jesuses, full of miracles, but these two guys will have to do a hell of a lot more in the way of miracles than Jesus is alleged to have done."

Simmons took immediate charge of the meeting. He said, "I admit that I have made mistakes, with this and that scheme. Let's not waste time about them, no sense in crying over spilled milk." Suddenly David remembered, vaguely, that he had met both men that Simmons had brought . . . he was sure about one of them: he had been a classmate of David's at Harvard. He had become much stouter and more smug, but he was ninety percent sure that he was a classmate. David also recalled having met the other man, years before, in a dentist's office. David recognized him, or so he thought, by the three huge teeth in his upper set; David had never before, or since, seen such teeth. Simmons continued: "This gentleman [the one with the teeth] is Malcolm Dowd, and this one is Hal Peters. I don't mind telling you, in front of them, that I have found them among the brightest thinkers about the current scene and things in general, anywhere. I've been seeing them at a friend's house. And I might as well tell you right away that I have told them everything about the *World,* and by everything I mean everything. I have kept nothing from them. There's no sense in hiding anything. Besides, we're about as bad, in circulation and in advertising, as any magazine can be, that is, in our class. You know me, I hide nothing from anybody. Now, before Malcolm and Hal start talking I'd like to sort of lay the groundwork. As you know, I'm very much interested in history"—Peter looked at David in controlled amazement, and Betty Gard put her hand to her mouth. She was the most outspoken of the editors, though she had the title only of associate editor; she felt she had to refrain from showing her astonishment—"very much interested in it, as a matter of fact, I have noticed several things lately that have led me to thinking about a lot of things.

"We are living in a very historic period. Important things are happening in the world, very important. You know how I feel about Russia; it's a dictatorship, and it won't last, it can't last. I believe the people there are already disillusioned, and maybe there will be an upheaval there any month, you never can tell about such things. But the tragic thing about it all is not in Russia, but right here in this country. To put it bluntly, the Russian people are seeing the light, but the people here are not seeing the light. That's putting it in a nutshell."

Betty Gard apparently could not control herself any more. "Would you say, Lester, that the United States is going communistic?"

"Not quite, Betty, but—"

She did not let him finish, but contemptuously added, "I read the other day in *Newsweek* or some other magazine that in a recent poll it was revealed that the American people are more conservative now than they have been since Hoover's early days. Maybe you think Franklin Roosevelt was a Communist?"

Lester was getting angry. "I didn't say that. But now that you mention Franklin Roosevelt, he did set this country well on the road to socialism, there's no doubt about that. Had he had his way all initiative in America would have been wiped out."

"That's crazy," said Betty, "plain crazy. FDR was the best friend the American capitalists have ever had. He saved capitalism for the American capitalists. I hope you're not going to try to fill the *World* with that kind of stuff. That would be worse than the astrology and handwriting and chiropractic stuff you put in. We need another kind of magic."

There was a strained silence in the room. Then Betty added, "Now I've said it. I don't know what these two men are going to suggest. I'm willing to listen, but if they say what Lester has just said, I say no. We've been on the wrong track long enough."

Lester turned to her, and in a manner that bespoke pent-up anger, said, "Perhaps you can tell us what the right track is?"

"No, I can't tell you," said Betty. "But I do know what's not the right track, what is wrong for the *World* and will hurt it, and that's important, too. Screwball schemes and printing a lot of things that are not true won't help us either."

Bly, nominally the chief editor, tried to calm the brewing storm. "First let's hear what these two gentlemen have to say. We don't even know what they got on their minds, and Simmons was only sort of giving us the background. We still got to know a situation before we can say anything about it."

"I didn't even have a chance to say what I wanted to say," said Simmons softly, obviously eager not to stir up matters. He smiled a mechanical smile. "I guess I forgot the rest of my speech. Oh, yes, it's about collectivism and the failure of the intellectuals in America and the rest of the world, but, of course, chiefly America. But maybe Malcolm and Hal should talk now."

Malcolm looked at Hal, and started talking. David knew instantly that no good would come out of whatever Malcolm was going to say. He remembered an earlier encounter with Malcolm, a troubled, bitter, largely irrational man. Malcolm said, "I hope Hal and I are not the cause of any domestic turmoil." He smiled.

"Don't take any of this too seriously," said Simmons. "Here we believe in speaking our minds. Remember, I told you this several times, remember?"

"Yes, that is so," said Malcolm. "I think I can say my say briefly, and then you people, who know editing far better than I do—I'm not an editor, I'm only a professor who's taking a look outside the academic ivory tower, so to speak. I'm sure I don't have to say it, but I guess I better should. I have nothing to sell. I don't want a job. I have a job, a good one, and I like it. In a sense, this is only a social call. Mr. Simmons asked us, Hal and me, to come up and share some ideas with you. You can accept them or reject them, whatever you wish. As I said, I'll be brief. America, the United States, is now, in actuality, the intellectual leader of the world. I only mean that the world is looking to us for leadership in how to run the world economically, politically. Europe, of course, is still a great reservoir of culture and learning, of course. But they're all looking in this direction. And they're looking especially to our political leaders, to our philosophers, to our commentators, and I think our political leaders and our philosophers and our commentators are failing the world. More than that, I believe they are also failing the traditions of the United States. So that you'll get my major point insofar as the *World* is concerned, I suggested to Mr. Simmons, it was at a couple of gatherings, that the *World* run a series on the failure of the intellectuals in politics. That's all I had in mind, just a series of articles. I'm not out to save the magazine, though I'm surprised it's having so much trouble. I guess all good publications are having trouble, I've always liked the *World,* I've read it pretty nearly from the beginning; but what was I going to say?—all I had in mind is this series I think people, the kind of quality people who read the *World,* would read. There are corollaries to this idea, if you people are interested; a similar thing could be done about the intellectuals and unions, they are really running them. And, of course, the Communists have a hand in all this. And then there are the colleges and the churches—the Communists and the fellow travelers have infiltrated deeply into all these organizations. This is the whole story in a nutshell."

Betty squirmed, hesitated, then said, "I thought it was going to be something like this. Chasing Communists is crazy."

"But I didn't say we should chase Communists," said Malcolm. "I was only presenting a philosophical thesis, you might say, nothing more. I'm not a chaser of anybody, Communists included."

"I must agree with Betty," said Peter, who had made up his mind to leave the *World* only a short while ago, because he was sure it was going to fold up or be sold to some other magazine. "This kind of crusade will put us in the company of screwballs. Sure there are Communists in all kinds of organizations, but they're a minority, a very small minority."

Lester almost shouted, "What's all this about? You're attacking a man who was courteous enough to come here, and you're attacking him for things he didn't say. What do you think, Clarice?"

His wife, Clarice, looked down at her lap, then at Malcolm and Hal and Betty and David, and then at Bly and Peter, as if trying to make sure all would hear her. She sighed and said, "I'm just listening."

"You're a great help," said Simmons. "Do you see any Communists or anti-Communists in all this?"

"I'm just listening," Clarice repeated.

"What's wrong in listening?" asked Bly.

This question somehow cleared the atmosphere a bit.

"Maybe that's what we ought to do, I mean all of us, just listen," said Peter. "Let's have a seance. Maybe that will help us."

"I don't think it's a joke," said Simmons. "I think there's a lot of sense in what Malcolm has been saying."

For the first time Hal spoke. "I think so, too," he said. "There's a lot of sense in what Malcolm has said, a great deal of it. I agree with him completely. You see, I think I may say so for Malcolm and myself. Both of us were in the radical movement ten, fifteen years ago, he as an educator, I as a writer, novelist, chiefly critic, I suppose. So what we're saying has hard experience behind it. But actually, we're not urging anybody to chase Communists. We're only urging people to be more true to Americanism."

"Oh, my God, there we go again!" blurted Betty. "Now, it's Americanism. We really sound like the Daughters of the American Revolution, or the Knights of Columbus, or, God knows, the Rotarians. This is all so childish."

Simmons exploded, "For Christ's sake, Betty, will you let the man finish? How about some plain, simple courtesy? What kind of place is this? Go on, Hal."

Hal smiled and went on lamely. "I guess I ought to say what Malcolm said. I'm not out to sell anything, and I don't want a

49

job. I got a job, a good one. Lester asked me, and Malcolm, too, to come over to talk to you on the board of the *World*, which I've read and respected for years. I don't mind disagreement. But you people must believe Malcolm and me when we tell you that—well, this lady may not agree"—he looked in the direction of Betty—"the forces of non-American radicalism are very powerful in America now, in the publishing world, which I believe I know well. And, to make my story brief, I think you might have a series of five or six articles, no more, on the influence of the fanatical left in literature, in reviewing, in publishing."

"Yes, I do disagree," said Betty. "The same old nonsense. The next thing you'll be telling us is that General MacArthur or Senator Taft should be in the White House."

"Why not?" asked Malcolm.

"Yes, why not?" asked Hal.

"I think they're both good men, especially Taft," said Simmons.

David sat there appalled. He was going to leave the *World* no matter what, but now he was ashamed that he had ever been associated with Simmons's *World*. David suspected that Communists were, in some way, involved in politics and in publishing and in the whole cultural life of the United States, but to base a whole way of life upon the actions of this minority seemed absurd to him, even sick, and there was the added fact that if the *World* gave space to the Malcolm-Hal type of articles many of the America Firsters and the Gerald Smith fanatics would flock to the *World* as their home, and David was most disturbed about this prospect. Knowing Simmons as he did, he was sure that Simmons had already made up his mind, and that the discussion going on now was only a front of "reasonableness."

Then he recalled that Langston Caxton Patton, a dubious and offensive journalist from Louisiana, had lately been seen walking through the general office to be with Simmons. As David had told Helen on one occasion, "I wouldn't care to be in the same building with Langston Patton." Patton was a shady journalist. He had written many "exposés," and in virtually every instance had been denounced as a demagogue by reputable journalists and had also been sued for libel. One of his exposés was about the "criminal indifference of Southern women" to the mulatto children their husbands have. Another was about the "refusal of Southern Methodists and Baptists, as bodies of religious groups," to help Negroes to get minimum attention in public hospitals. A third was about "the appalling rate of venereal disease among white Protestant ministers' daughters." Patton published these articles in *Collier's,* a magazine of some fair reputation at the time, and the magazine on a half-dozen occasions gave space to correspondents to deny Patton's charges in the most violent terms. The editors said they had submitted the letters to Patton for reply, but that he had refused to do so.

Then there was an occasion when Simmons had told David— David didn't know at the time, nor did he know now, why Simmons told him this—that Patton was "sure mixed up with women. They write to him here, and I open the letters. I just thought I should protect him. I could tell the letters were from women, you can tell their handwriting, and I didn't want Patton's wife to read these letters. She's a simple kind of woman, I don't know what she knows and what she doesn't know, but I thought it's all right for me not to add to her knowledge. Patton sure is sleeping around and I guess he promised marriage to some of them. Some of these women can't even spell correctly; they're illiterate. I wonder how come he tells them his address. I'm going to ask him why he gave the office of the *World* as his address. I did write a recommendation for him when he first began to write for *Collier's* and some other magazine, I forget which, and he's been writing me, but I never gave him permission to use my address for his private matters."

David had no proof whatsoever, but he was sure that Patton was somehow involved in the presence of Malcolm and Hal now in the *World* office. He also suspected that soon or late Patton would be on the staff of the *World.* Suddenly David decided to find out if there was basis for his suspicions. He asked Malcolm, "Do you know someone called Langston Caxton Patton?"

"Yes," said Malcolm. "A good reporter, if a little sensational. He knows a great deal about radicals in American life."

"I know him, too," said Hal. "He stumps me sometimes, I can't say I like his novels. One of them was called *Hilda Tirney,* about a prostitute; rather cheap. It's already sold hundreds of thousands. But he does have an eye for the radicals, as Malcolm says. Why do you ask?"

David decided once and for all to make his stand clear. "I don't like him."

This rejoinder seemed to stun the gathering. David was astonished that it did. What he had said was brief and mild.

"I didn't know that," said Simmons, in a surprised tone. "You never told me before."

"There was no occasion. I don't like him. He's been here recently, hasn't he?"

"Yes, why?" asked Simmons.

"He stopped into my office a couple of times," said David, "maybe four, five times, and we talked about all kinds of things—or, rather, he talked. He likes to do all the talking."

"That part is true," said Hal.

"He stinks," said Betty. "He used to drop in to see me, too, though God knows why. Any sane person would have known the first time that I don't like him."

"I don't like him either," said Bly.

"I wish I knew him to dislike him, too," said Peter, who now didn't care at all what he said or what happened to the magazine.

"But you people really don't know him," said Simmons. "He's a good reporter."

"Good for starting libel suits on magazines that trust him," said Betty.

"I didn't like his smile," said David, feeling a little foolish for this remark. "He looked tricky. His smile is tricky."

"Well, I wouldn't want him to take out my daughter," said Malcolm, "or my son, for that matter, but he is a good reporter. Libel suits or no libel suits, I find him quite accurate."

"To me he stinks," repeated Betty.

"What in hell is all this about?" shouted Simmons. "Patton isn't here. You're all so prejudiced and unfair. How did he get into this?"

"Because he's of the same crowd as Malcolm and Hal. I don't mean it personally," said Betty. "The Pattons are crazy and cheap, and the likes of them won't even let the *World* die a decent death."

"Who's talking about death?" said Simmons.

Nobody answered. The silence was becoming embarrassing. Then Malcolm rose slowly, and Hal did the same. Malcolm said, "Well, I guess we'll be going. I have to meet some students, and I have some errands."

"I have to go, too," said Hal. He hesitated, then said, "Some of you may not wish to see me, or either of us, again. That's all right. We're not here to sell anything or buy anything. I'm not mad, and I don't think Malcolm is, either."

"Oh, no," said Malcolm. "Not personally, but I am a little perturbed that decent people like you don't see certain things. It's a question of perspective, of philosophy. We are moving away from our historical roots, the roots that nourished us to our present position. That's what hurts."

"That's why I brought these two people here," said Simmons with an air of triumph, "but you jumped on them. I've never seen the likes of it. I apologize to both of you gentlemen."

"And as for the radicals being a minority," said Hal, "that's true, but it's minorities that have caused most of the trouble in the world. Were the Bolsheviks the majority at the time of Kerensky? My eye. They were a small minority, but they made the most noise, and now Russia is in a state of slavery. I repeat, a minority did it. The same is going on right now; well, it was truer two, three years ago, five years ago, but it's still true. The same is going on in the literary world. And the lady over there brought up Patton. Well, he's not my kind of man, I admit, but he has done valuable work in ferreting out Communist influence, and I guess the only thing to do is to make intelligent use of him. On balance, I should say he's a good man. You don't throw out a barrel of apples because one of them is rotten, would you?" He looked directly at Betty.

She hesitated, then said, "I've said all I'm going to say. There's more than Patton, more than one rotten apple. But I've said all I'm going to say."

Malcolm and Hal left.

"They took plenty from you people, and they were decent about it," said Simmons, as he walked out.

five

When David went home that night, he recalled both Malcolm Dowd and Hal Peters clearly. The encounter with Dowd occurred at a dentist's office during his early days on the *World*. David had been having some dental problems. He mentioned the fact to Slack, the publisher at the time, and Slack suggested Dr. Alfred Saterstein. Slack, who had studied dentistry himself, said, "He's a crackerjack, the best dentist in America. I knew him at dental school, and for a long time I went to him myself. I wouldn't go to anybody else. Then I stopped. My wife didn't like him. I'll be damned if I know why. She yipped and yapped about this and that—who the hell knows women?—so I started to go to a nephew of hers, a good dentist, but no Al. Go to him and tell him I sent you. He's married to a *shikse,* but he's all right."

Dr. Saterstein really was a good dentist, but he was more than a dentist. He had a rather large office. The room in which he treated patients was not too large, but there were two other rooms, where he lived during the week. His home was in Connecticut. He slept in his New York "apartment" week days, and he spent the weekends with his wife and children in the country.

The recollection of this man brought back to David's mind a somewhat painful episode. Al had a dental assistant named Eunice, and David thought now and then that she spent an unnecessary amount of time near him when Al was treating him. On a couple of occasions Al had said, "Eunice likes you. I told her you're a fine man, and would make a fine mate." Then he gurgled, to take off the serious implications of what he had said. Eunice merely said, "He only wants to marry me off. Jewish men are as bad as Jewish women, they're *schadchens*."

"*Schadchonim*," corrected Al, but he quickly added, "but she's an intellectual just the same. She knows all about Proust. And Dreiser, too, and Anatole France."

David liked Eunice in a vague way . . . she didn't offend him, but neither did he yearn for her. He recalled she had a rather pointless face, a normal female, but not much else. David had to see Al about seven or eight times, and toward the end Eunice held his hand a little longer than was necessary and she also smiled at him with more meaning than courtesy required. Then, one afternoon, Eunice called David and said, "I'm having some people over the house, writers, doctors, you know, professional people, and I wondered if you'd like to come over. I'd love to have you."

David, in his naïveté, was completely nonplused. He hemmed and hawed, and said he was busy that particular night. She was disappointed. "My mother and father will be as sorry as I am," she said. "I've told them so much about you. How gentle and sweet you were."

"I'm sorry," said David, "but I am busy."

Eunice called him again three weeks later. This time she asked if he wouldn't like to go with her to a friend's house next Saturday. "Some very nice people will be there, and I believe you would like it." Again David told her he was busy that night. He knew that she knew he wasn't busy this time, as he wasn't busy the previous time. David was disturbed on both occasions. He had hurt a pleasant girl, whose only offense was that she liked him . . . and the memory of that bit of callousness bothered him for years. He regretted that Malcolm had revived that memory.

Al liked the company of intellectuals. Once, twice a week he would invite three or four of them to come to his apartment after supper to "shmoos" about books and plays and general cultural matters. The very first time David came to see him professionally he invited David to join the "club." David came to several meetings of the "club." There was a professor of humanities at Cooper Union, who had written a good book on Emily Dickinson; there was an architect who had one complaint: "Why do the *goyim,* ·so many of them, ask me to design their churches, and why hasn't a single synagogue asked me? I'm not an anti-Semite. I really like Jews. What a life! The *goyim* trust me with their Jesuses, but the Jews don't trust me with the Ten Commandments, and me a good Jew." There was also a professor of psychiatry at Columbia University who was quite unusual in that he liked martinis in preference to Manischevitz wine and who, when in his cups, said that he was terribly worried that the "goddamn Christian Scientists, in the long run, might win out with their basic principle of mind over body; it's an old principle, medicine has known about it for centuries. We call it psychosomatic medicine, but this three-times married Mary Baker Eddy will get all the credit, because her brand of distorted and superficial truth has a religious aura. Mind you, I'm not anti-Christian, not much, anyway, because I despise the Jewish Scientists as much as I despise the Christian Scientists." There was also a businessman (he was in "textiles, the crappiest crap in the clothing business"), who hated business, his wife and children ("Boy, are they cheap?"), but who loved music. He had an enormous record library, and his favorite was Brahms, who, he claimed, was "greater than Beethoven or Bach or Mozart, the only exception being Schubert, who was not human, anyway. He was a Jewish angel, as a matter of fact. I think research will reveal that Schubert was Jewish, his mother or his grandmother, or his grandfather, or further back—no, it was some male; splendor comes down the male line, the female line is just a subway." And there was Malcolm Dowd. David learned a good deal about him through Al, who was fascinated by Dowd's *tsores.*

Malcolm Dowd twenty years before was Morris Denzer. His brothers and sisters were still called Denzer. Shortly after Morris was graduated from the College of the City of New York he changed his name to Malcolm Dowd and he also notified his parents and the rest of the family that he had renounced Judaism and was now "just a human being."

The elder Denzer did not leap into a fury when Malcolm made this historic announcement one Friday night, nor did his mother. The brothers and sisters seemed unconcerned.

Then his father said quietly, *"Meshuggeh.* All I can say now is that I hope you live long enough to realize how *meshuggeh* you are."

His mother said only, "I don't know what to think, I don't know, I just don't know. Changing names I have never understood, never. A name is a name, and that's all. Changing a name changes nothing."

His father said, "Didn't you have a professor at City College— Morris Cohen?"

"Yes," said the newly coined Malcolm.

"A big professor, eh?" asked his father.

"A great professor, a great philosopher," said Malcolm.

"So tell me, Morris," said Malcolm's father, "tell me: If Professor Morris Cohen keeps his name, why shouldn't you, tell me, why shouldn't you?"

"He belongs to an older generation."

"And a wiser one," said his father. "Nu, so my name doesn't suit you. Denzer is not good enough for my son, and Morris is not good enough. It's good enough for Morris Cohen, but not for Morris Denzer. And as for giving up Judaism, you've never been much of a Jew anyway. Smart ones like you we have always had, and they all realize before they die how foolish they've been. So now, we have to have two names on the mail box, Denzer and Dowd."

"It will be a shame," said Malcolm's mother. "I'm a Denzer, not a Dowd, that's a *goyish* name. Besides, there's no room on the mail box for another name."

"I'll get my mail elsewhere," said Malcolm, "so you don't have to worry."

"Are you moving some other place?" asked his father. "It's bad enough our name isn't good enough for you; now our home isn't good enough for you."

"Who's talking about moving?" said Malcolm. "You invented that yourself."

"Ah, from you we've only had disappointment and heart-ache. An enemy in our own house. That is a son! What sins have I committed to deserve this curse, what have I done, tell me?" With that, his father got up and walked out of the room.

Malcolm, who was rather deficient in character, had a good mind. He took graduate courses at New York University, where he got his Ph.D. *summa cum laude*. His thesis was a truly brilliant piece of research: "The Jewish Metaphysic as Reflected in Spinoza's Epistemology." Columbia University printed the thesis as a book, and it was well received in the scholarly journals. Malcolm gave a copy to his parents. Father Denzer looked at it and looked at it. He was proud and troubled. "Our Morris is still a Jew, but he doesn't know it. Spinoza also was a Jew and didn't know it. But Spinoza went to *shul*, our Morris doesn't, at least he doesn't tell us. Nu, I should *shep naches* (literally, drink in contentment), but I feel there is a hole in my heart. So we'll see what we'll see. In America everything is mixed up, joy and agony."

Father and Mother Denzer had plenty of both as Malcolm progressed in his career. In a most unusual move, New York University appointed Malcolm assistant professor of philosophy on its own faculty, skipping the rank of instructor. Malcolm was a good teacher, and his course, "Introduction to Philosophy" was one of the most popular in the whole College of Liberal Arts. Malcolm also published regularly in the philosophical journals. After three years he asked to be promoted to the rank of associate professor, but the chairman of the department refused. His reasons were vague: "Your advancement has been phenomenally rapid. Remember you skipped being an instructor, and we've had people on the faculty who've been assistant professors for ten years before becoming associates. Be patient, don't be so aggressive."

Malcolm told this to his parents. "You know the reason without asking me," said his father.

"Anti-Semitism?" asked Malcolm.

"What else?" said his father. "Your chairman would be astonished if you told him this, but it's true. When you get older and get some sense into you, you will learn that nearly all Christians are anti-Semites, and Christian professors are jealous of Jewish professors. You've done more in three years than your chairman has done in fifteen years. There you have your answer. It's very plain. Look for another job."

That's exactly what Malcolm did. He looked for another job, and he got one quickly at Columbia University. No less a person than John Dewey urged that Malcolm be made an associate professor, with a promise of a full professorship not long after. Malcolm was an immediate success as a teacher at Columbia, as he was at New York University. Having the friendship and blessing of John Dewey naturally helped him enormously. Within a few months Malcolm did three things: he became openly active in the Communist fellow-traveler movement; twice he told the Jewish Students Society at Columbia University, in Earl Hall that he had no religion; and he got married. While in City College, Malcolm had been involved in "liberal" activities on and off campus; he had spoken in favor of this or that aspect of life in Russia, but he had not openly espoused the Russian government as a whole. Now that he was an associate professor at Columbia he did come out "in favor of Russia." Some said he had joined the Communist party, others said he had not, but he definitely defended the set-up in Russia, and he did denounce "American imperialism, American capitalist colonialism, black slavery in the South and in Harlem, the robber baron lobbies," and the other familiar "curses" of life in America.

Malcolm was not satisfied to preach this sort of leftism off campus and on campus, but, according to some of his colleagues, he also preached it in the classroom. It was said that he dragged in Marx and Engels and Liebknecht and Plekhanov at every opportunity. Soon a group of alumni issued a public denunciation of Malcolm: "Dr. Dowd is distorting the function of the classroom, turning it into a place for political propaganda, and we think this is wrong. We think this is a gross violation of academic freedom. A teacher has a right to teach as he pleases within his own area of competence. He has no right to introduce extraneous ideas or facts or alleged facts. We call upon the administration of Columbia University to enforce genuine academic freedom and to see that those who violate it cease and desist from their unprofessional activities."

What ensued became known, for a while, as the Malcolm

Dowd case. Some members of the faculty defended him, others agreed with the alumni group, but nearly sixty percent of the faculty took no sides. It was this last fact that hurt Malcolm most. As he said to the girl who became his wife: "These leaders of culture, these paragons for youth, these men who teach the virtues of courage, are afraid to show some courage themselves." But there was something that hurt him even more. A member of the alumni committee had unearthed an article that Malcolm had written for a purely educational magazine, in which he discussed the problem of politics in the classroom. The article included the following passage:

"A university is a forum of free discussion. That discussion must be absolutely free, unimpeded by the political-economic climate of opinion that happens to be dominant at a particular time. We live in a capitalist society, but in a classroom the defense (or, indeed, the refutation) of capitalism has no place. Capitalism, in a class of economics, for example, should be scrutinized objectively and impartially along with socialism and communism and syndicalism and the single tax. Further, a teacher's personal predilection should not influence his mode of teaching. It should not influence him to withhold facts or criticisms. He should not try to impose his own views upon his students. He should merely try to help the students make up their own minds, and the best way to do this is to present all the facts and all views, however conflicting, before them. Teachers who incline toward 'liberal' economics or politice often, alas, forget this. It is as wrong to preach socialism in a classroom as to preach fascism. The philosophy of the *New Republic* has no more rights, to speak educationally, than has the philosophy of the National Association of Manufacturers. Teachers of either persuasion may, by intricate feats of logic, justify their adulteration of the atmosphere of the classroom with their private points of view, but in their hearts they will know that they are guilty of this adulteration. Logic can never still the voice of conscience. It can be a dangerous snare and a blinding delusion."

Malcolm was hard-pressed to deal with this section of an article that he had written a few years before and had almost forgotten. "The enemy knows how to dig up one's past," he said to his future wife. "They have their researchers, who know where to dig." But he had to deal with it, because some of the "arch-reactionary and conservative" newspapers and magazines persisted in asking how he justified his present actions with his "former philosophy." Malcolm addressed student groups and union groups and "broad, liberal" groups. Making speeches before these groups was a hardship for Malcolm, because in his deep unconscious he wasn't too sure of his ground: he still felt as he did in that article, but, at the same time, he felt driven to do something "for the cause, and in the place where it counts so much, the classroom." It had reached Malcolm's ear that a "reactionary" professor of history at Columbia had said at a party, about the fix Malcolm was in: "Malcolm wants to be a prostitute and a virgin at the same time. I'd hate to sweat that one out." Then came probably the hardest blow of all: the liberal weeklies and a goodly number of the liberal newspapers, at least in the East, while supporting Malcolm's desire to bring another point of view into the classroom, at the same time doubted that a classroom in metaphysics or epistemology was the right place "to preach Marxism in any way, shape or manner. We urge Dr. Dowd to reread his own article of some years ago and try to abide by it himself. What made sense then, still makes sense to us. There is no question of free speech or academic freedom involved. The old cliché holds: there's a time and place for everything. The sooner Dr. Dowd stops making an issue out of an aberration on his part, the better will it be for himself, for his university, and for university scholars in general."

"They let me down," said Malcolm to his future wife. "This I didn't expect." Yet one corner of his mind told him that these liberal publications were right. His heart had gone out of the battle. The Communists and Trotskyites continued to hold protest meetings "to defend academic freedom against capitalist imperialists and exploiters using colleges and universities to spread their criminal lies against the people." Malcolm had appeared at some of their meetings in the beginning, but he was uncomfortable at them, he didn't know exactly why, and then he stopped attending them. He told the leaders of these protest meetings: "You are doing so well, I leave it to you. When I can come I surely will come." He never came again. His future wife, who seldom spoke, agreed with him that "there really is little point in spending your energy, dear, in going to these meetings along with the others." Malcolm wondered exactly what was going through her mind. He wondered whether she didn't, deep down, agree with the liberal publications. He didn't dare to ask her outright. He was afraid of what she would say. He was even more afraid that she would evade answering him by holding his hand and then kissing him.

The administration at Columbia, so far, had said nothing to Malcolm. This pleased him and troubled him. He had, on one occasion, attacked Columbia as a "haven of capitalist propaganda." At the time he regretted making this remark, but he knew of no acceptable way of retracting it, especially in view of the Communist and other left-wing protest meetings. Now he was embarrassed that this "haven of capitalist propaganda" had not interfered with him, had allowed him to go his own way. "They've really been pretty decent to me," he said to his future wife. "They could have suspended me, pending investigation; they could have brought up the matter of putting the university in a bad light, damaging its reputation, all kinds of things, but they did nothing. They've been really decent."

"They have, dear," she said. "I've been thinking the same thing."

Malcolm wondered what else she'd been thinking, but again he didn't dare to ask. He wished he were not practically engaged to her, so that he would not be burdened with these questions he didn't ask her. At the same time he was grateful to her for being with him in these very troublesome times. He got little enough comfort in his home. His father merely said, "This you needed like a hole in the head. Here's a fine university that is good to you, and you bring up all kinds of things that you know are not true. You got yourself in, now get yourself out." Malcolm looked at this man, his father, whom he had considered old-fashioned, narrow-minded, and even a bit foolish, and he was astonished how intelligent he was. But he said nothing.

Suddenly the whole "Malcolm Dowd case" stopped being news. The papers and magazines ignored it. Three or four months of commotion—and now this arid silence. Hardly anybody talked about the case. On the Columbia campus students did not turn around to look at this "celebrity." They passed him by. Malcolm continued going to his classes, but now he brought up Marx and Engels less and less, and pretty soon his philosophy classes were no different from others, as to subject matter. Then one day a minor administrative official of the university called Malcolm in to his office. Malcolm was not troubled, but he was puzzled. He was also a little bit ashamed, not quite knowing how much of his real feelings he should tell this official. If he told him too little he would be dishonest with himself; if he told too much he would be disloyel to all his "friends" who had fought so hard for him . . . and at the moment he wondered what actually he had fought for. A fine position for a professor of philosophy to be in. . . .

The administrator was courteous. Smiling, he said, "I hope you don't mind my asking to have a chat with you."

Somehow that smile cut deep into Malcolm's soul. "Oh, no, not at all," he said, with greater calm and assurance than were actually in him.

"Thank you. Some of us here, recently, have been called academic exploiters, or is it academic capitalist exploiters?"

"Oh, that. Don't take that too seriously," said Malcolm.

"We haven't taken it seriously," said the administrator, and this also hurt Malcolm. If only this man would have the decency to shout at him. The administrator continued, "Some of us here have thought that perhaps we ought to let you know where we stand. We have not interfered with you, we have made no statement. We believe in letting an issue be talked out, the market place of ideas, Justice Oliver Wendell Holmes says somewhere, doesn't he?"

"Yes, something of the sort, a very good phrase," said Malcolm, who thought to himself, This is a kindly, good man.

"Yes, a fine phrase. Well, no real harm has been done by the recent, oh, excitement. We sort of trusted you to right things with yourself, with your classes, with your university. And speaking for myself alone, I would like to tell you, first of all, that you are a good teacher, and second that I did read that celebrated article of yours"—he smiled, not out of malice, but out of sheer courtesy—"and I liked it. There's good sense in it. I subscribe to the ideas in it. Well, I hope I haven't taken up too much of your time. This is really all, and thank you for coming."

Malcolm thanked him, shook hands, and left. He was relieved, and he was also ashamed of himself. He couldn't even discuss his exact state of mind with his future wife. She asked him what the administrator had said. Malcolm said, "Oh, only that I shouldn't worry."

"Is that all?" she asked.

"Just about," said Malcolm.

"Really?"

"Yes."

"That's funny, calling you for that, just for that."

"That's what I thought. Only one thing, though . . ."

"What?" she asked.

He didn't answer. His mind was wandering.

"Darling, tell me. Only one thing? What did you mean?"

"I didn't like the way he talked to me."

"Was he mean, insulting, you know, threatening, anything like that?"

"Oh, no, not at all. He was all gentleness, really decent."

"So what do you mean, dear?"

"Oh, nothing. Do you mind if we don't discuss it any more? I've had enough of this whole business. I only want to assure you he was very nice, but let's not talk about it any more."

"As you say, dear."

Malcolm was now in a state that troubled him constantly. He was not merely ashamed of his recent actions at Columbia, he also began to question his allegiance to the "leftist" movement the world over. His experiences at the protest meetings of the Communists and fellow travelers and "general liberal" people had depressed him: he didn't like their shouting, their obvious lying, their aloofness—always he had the feeling that these liberal people, especially the extreme left-wingers—were not too deeply interested in his own plight and ideas, but in him as a tool for "broader" plans for the world. Malcolm resented that. He thought it was vaguely immoral. He didn't feel he could trust these people. He was fairly sure that they would abandon him if it suited their "broader" purposes.

Then there was the matter of the junior administrator at Columbia whom he had seen only a few days ago. That man had, unwittingly, humiliated him, made a mockery of Malcolm's whole ideology, indeed, of a good deal of his life. Yet Malcolm liked him—he liked his courtesy, which was almost totally absent among the radicals and liberals he had lately encountered. Malcolm also liked what he stood for: orderly, patient academic procedures . . . and David began to wonder whether the very system that this administrator represented, that is, the system in the outside world, capitalism, was really as bad as he had been saying. Malcolm had the feeling that he would enjoy the company of such people far more than the company of the radicals and liberals. Finally, there was Malcolm's father. He couldn't get out of his mind the quick, sharp wisdom that he had imparted: "You needed all this like a hole in the head. The university has been good to you, and you are doing and saying things that you know are wrong." His father had repeated this two, three times, in more or less the same words, and each time Malcolm felt a dagger go through him. His father, his foolish and parochial and backward father, had more sense than his Ph.D. son, more ordinary common sense. . . . And, who knows, perhaps the Judaism that his father was so deeply attached to had more to it than Malcolm had realized.

Malcolm had nobody with whom he could discuss his problems and his doubts. In his climb up the academic ladder he had abandoned his boyhood friends; they knew him, they knew his quirks. Some of them were very intelligent, though they had no college education and not one of them had any notion of epistemology or metaphysics . . . yes, they had common sense, and he had the feeling they would be of far greater help to him now than any of his Ph.D. acquaintances at Columbia or at any other university. But he didn't know how to renew his relations with these old friends. He would hardly know what to say to them, how to explain his long neglect of them . . . no doubt they thought that he considered them not good enough for him, he a Ph.D.; that he was snobbish; and they were right, of course. They wouldn't trust him now. They wouldn't say so outright; they were better mannered than some "more educated" colleagues of his. . . .

There was Ruth Goodson, to whom he was "informally" engaged. She was loyal to him, the only human being, actually, who saw him whenever he wanted to see her, who did not argue with him, who held his hand and caressed him and kissed him when he needed comforting. She taught history in a junior high school, and knew enough for her job. She really was sweet, "mature" politically, agreeing with him all the way in his recent activities at Columbia. He himself now was not sure about his rightness in these activities, but he was glad that she had agreed with him: that's what a woman was for, to agree with her man when he wanted her to agree, never to argue with him. . . . My God, he said to himself, this sort of thinking ran counter to what he had been saying in and out of class about the moral and intellectual and spiritual equality of women with men ("They are not second-class human beings, as our ancestors had said, they are full first-class human beings, with the same rights and privileges as men"). Well, he didn't believe this any more now, either; as a matter of fact, he wasn't sure he had ever believed it, though why he had said so puzzled him. Probably he merely repeated what a "mature, intelligent man" was expected to say about "the woman problem." But why was he expected to do this, who expected him? Social pressures apparently had mysterious origins and the reasons for their persistence were also mysterious. Well, he had done one thing right: he had taken Ruth to his home a few times. He was glad that she made a good impression on his parents and on his brothers and sisters, but it was the impression on his parents that interested him chiefly.

"A fine girl," Malcolm's mother had said. "A very fine girl. I hope it's something between you two. How much longer will you drag yourself as a bachelor? A man needs companionship, a man needs a woman, a wife, a mother for his children. You know each other for a long time. I know her parents, fine people. We talked about it."

"Talked about what?" asked Malcolm.

"We talked. Mothers talk. He asks what we talked about."

"What did you talk about? Can't you tell me?"

"Morris"—his parents refused to call him Malcolm, and while Malcolm had been annoyed by this years before, now he was rather pleased—"you know what we talked about. We both said it's time already. That's what we talked about. You have your Ph.D.; you're a professor, you have a fine girl, Ruth is quiet, so *haimish,* a diamond, so what do you want? I don't understand. A lot of things about you I don't understand. Sometimes I wonder if I'm your mother."

Malcolm's father was brief and to the point: "Ruth is a good girl. She has more sense in her little finger than you have in your whole head, with your Ph.D. and everything. Marry her. What else is there to say?"

Malcolm still wasn't sure that he should marry Ruth, but he really didn't know why he wasn't sure. He wished she wasn't so quiet, but then if she had turned their relationship into a debating society, as was the case with some of his friends, he would be unhappy. She was pretty in a modest way; she obviously was very fond of him, she was very passionate as a kisser. Yet there was something about her that troubled him. He would see something in her eyes, on occasion, that seemed to say to him there were parts of her being that were unknown to him. He wanted to discuss the matter one more time with his mother alone. He was a bit afraid of his father. He felt that his father had some contempt for him, and that he couldn't forgive him for changing his name from Morris Denzer to Malcolm Dowd. Actually, there were times when Malcolm wasn't so sure any more that he had done the right thing. His youthful rebellion made less and less sense as time went on. His mother didn't like what he had done any more than his father, but her attitude was more resigned; she was kinder.

"What is really bothering you, Morris?" she asked gently.

"I really don't know," he said.

"My son, marriage is a serious thing. Nobody is ever really sure. But who is sure about anything? If you're more than a little bit sure, that's good enough. With a woman, there's not much to know. A man is different. He has more parts, business, character, hopes, after all; a man has to run his home, the children, his wife; make a living. With a woman it's different. If she loves you, and is willing to sacrifice herself for you, and you like her, that's enough. I can't tell you what to do. You're a grown man. And remember, Ruth is a grown woman, too. What you're doing now is not right. With a woman a year is more than a year, much more. So that's all I have to say. You know I wish you only happiness, and so does your father, you know that."

"I know that."

Ruth became a different woman almost from the moment she agreed to marry Malcolm: a fresh color came to her cheeks, a new brightness came to her eyes, and a general excitement spread through her whole being. Malcolm would never have imagined such changes in her. He was startled by her first suggestion, namely, that they be married by a justice of the peace "in some other state, it would be romantic, or maybe by a judge ‚in New York, or by the city clerk."

"But we can't do that," Malcolm said. "My mother and father and the others, we can't . . ."

"But why not?"

"And your parents, too, they're no different from mine, you know what I mean, they will expect some sort of wedding."

She looked at him, with a look in her eyes he had never seen before. "I must say I am surprised," she said, "but we'll do as you say. I hope it won't be one of those huge, vulgar affairs."

The word "vulgar," said with that slight bitterness, seemed strange coming from lips that had said so little all these many months—rather, years. The wedding was in a little Orthodox *shul,* with about fifty people present. A rabbi, of course, performed the ceremony. There was the usual dinner, and the dancing, and the "few remarks" from this and that *mechut'n* (in-law). Malcolm was glad it was this sort of wedding, but he wasn't quite ready to say it even to himself. He was sure that Ruth was not pleased. He had overheard her say to a girl friend, whom he had seen at several of the progressive and liberal meetings called in his "defense," "I hope you're not too embarrassed. It's not what I wanted, but Malcolm, you know . . ." Malcolm was so shocked he quickly moved out of her sight so she wouldn't know he had heard. For a few seconds he would have called the wedding off, but it was too late. Besides, too many people, especially his parents, would be deeply hurt. He would say nothing about it to Ruth . . . and maybe he could "straighten" her out. She seemed pliable, despite her recent show of determination . . . and suddenly he recalled a passage in Samuel Butler's *The Way of All Flesh,* he didn't recall the exact place or the exact words: "There is no lonelier time in the life of a man than the minute after the minister has said the fateful words: I now pronounce you man and wife."

Ruth was soft and loving and agreeable during their honeymoon (it was during Malcolm's Christmas–New Year vacation at the university). Especially the first three days. Malcolm was content, and he regretted that they hadn't got married a year before, e.en two years before. Now and then he wanted to talk about some current event, some matter at the university, but she wouldn't let him, saying, "Oh, darling, let's forget the outside world and just be together, saying nothing, like this," and she would cuddle close to him and kiss him and kiss him. He was very happy, except that now and then he recalled her remark at the wedding, and it was in such sharp contrast to her present loving self that he wondered if he had heard correctly: Ruth just couldn't be the same person who had made that remark and was now so close to him, so sweet, so eager to give everything of herself to him.

Then certain changes began to take place. On the fourth day, during lunch, she said, "Darling, I know this is our honeymoon, but there are some practical things we have to discuss. We got married so suddenly, well, sort of, that we had almost no time to talk about things that, well, we have to talk about. Now, I gave in to you on the matter of a religious wedding. Frankly"— there was a slight hint of chiding in her face, even before she said the words—"I don't want to run a kosher house. I don't believe in it. I don't believe in all this superstition. Besides, I happen to like bacon and lobsters, and I know you do."

"That's all right," said Malcolm. He wanted to add that while he agreed with her, he was disturbed by her vehemence and by her use of the word "superstition." He saw little logical sense in *kashruth,* but he rather liked the idea, now, that his parents kept a kosher house, and he didn't like to hear his wife of four days call his father and mother, by implication, superstitious. She could have said it differently, more gently, in an offhand, semi-jocular way. He hoped that Ruth was not one of those "outspoken" women: "I say what's on my mind. I believe in being honest." Honesty, honesty, thought Malcolm, how cruel it can be.

"Good," said Ruth. "Now, there are some other things. What I'm about to tell you is really confidential. I promised I wouldn't tell anybody when I joined; everybody promises, I promised. But you are my husband and I feel I should tell you everything. I don't like secrets. I'm a member of the Communist party. I belong to the Roger Williams cell, and we meet way up in the Bronx, the Kingsbridge neighborhood. I can't tell you where because I know the house but not the number. It's on Woollcott Place, but sometimes we'll meet here. Now, I have to come to the meetings alone. You can't come, because you're not a member of the party."

Malcolm was almost breathless with astonishment and even dismay . . . this quiet, soft-spoken woman was a member of the Communist party. "How did you know?" he asked.

"I had somebody look up the records. I knew it anyway."

"How?"

"Well, you don't remember, most likely, but shortly after we started going steady, I asked you if you had a pen-name. You looked at me surprised. Then I knew. When you're in the party a pen-name means your party name. My party name is Anne Hutchinson, and that's also my pen-name."

Malcolm was beside himself with befuddlment. He wished he could run away from this creature in front of him. But he couldn't. She was his wife. They were on their honeymoon. He felt sweat running down his face.

"You look so pale and funny, dear," said Ruth.

Malcolm barely heard her.

"Are you ill?"

Again he didn't answer.

"Tell me, darling, you look strange, I hardly recognize you." She touched his hand across the table, but he pulled his hand away.

"Anything wrong, dear?"

"I don't like it," he said faintly. "I don't like it at all. The next thing you'll be telling me is that you're a spy."

"You can't mean that," Ruth said haughtily. "You just can't. What do you think I am?"

"That's what I want to know. What are you? Who are you?"

"Look me straight in the eye, Malcolm. Do I look like a spy?"

He didn't answer.

She raised her voice, and there was the beginning of a shriek in it. This only added to his worries. Ruth a shrieking woman!

"You've made a serious charge against your wife. I demand an answer."

He looked at her. He was in better control of himself. "Don't you talk to me about demanding anything of me. Don't you ever talk to me again this way."

"Bourgeois morality," she snapped.

"You don't even know what that phrase means. You're just repeating what your bosses told you in your stinking cell. You're a monkey, mimicking, imitating. You're just jabbering phrases."

She looked at him sternly, then said slowly, "Don't you want me to be honest with you? I didn't have to tell you what I just told you. As a matter of fact, I did something wrong by telling you, but I wanted to start off our marriage by being honest, truthful. Would you want me to be otherwise?"

He said nothing, his head in his hands.

"Tell me."

"I don't know what to tell, what to think. I loved you, you don't know how much, these last three days. I congratulated myself for having married you." He stopped. He wondered whether he should tell her what he had heard her say at the wedding. He decided not to tell her. "I don't know what to say, Ruth, I just don't know. Things are different."

"They're not different, Malcolm, they're not different. Let's go up to our room in our hotel. I want to talk to you." They went to their room. On the way Malcolm was worried about the fact that she seemed so sure of herself, so efficient; she seemed to know what to do, what to say. He wondered: Is this part of Communist discipline? He trembled at the thought of this possibility.

In the room, they sat down on two chairs with their knees touching, Ruth holding his hands in hers. She looked at him, kissed his hands, and said, "Malcolm, listen to me, please. You've just made me lose ten years of my life. Malcolm, please listen to me. I have loved you longer than you know. My only complaint is that you waited so long to ask me to marry you. We've just had three wonderful days and nights. I am delirious with joy when you make love to me. You know that, Malcolm, you know that, don't you?"

"Yes."

"I am delirious with delight because I love you, because I want you in me, all through me, you know that, don't you, Malcolm, don't you?"

He looked at her, and he was touched by the sorrow on her face . . . for a few moments he felt guilty . . . this lovely face that he had kissed so passionately was now streaked with tears and with lines of worry. Her lips trembled, her hands felt a little clammy, but he was glad that she was holding his hands. He was still filled with doubts about her, but now, in some vague way, he felt closer to her than ever before. If he knew how to do it gracefully and honestly, he would pull her into bed, undress her, and make love to her for hours, but then doubts entered his mind. He had read so many things about the diabolical ways of the Communists; he hadn't believed them; he had thought they were all capitalist propaganda, the invention of the capitalist-imperialist press, but since he was in the office of the Columbia administrator, he wasn't so sure about all that he had believed about the capitalist-imperialist press. Lately, indeed, he had begun to doubt the materialistic interpretation of history, which he had labeled only a few months ago, in his classes, as one of the major contributions of modern philosophy.

"I know that," he said, squeezing her hands slightly.

"Darling, I am your wife, and I want to say things to you now that women seldom tell their men, even their husbands. But I want you to know, I want you to know everything. May I tell you?"

"If you wish."

She looked at him, a little disappointed. "Well, I will tell you, darling. I love the very smell of your body. I love the feel of your thighs, I love the taste of your mouth. When you ejaculate in me, I am stunned with joy, I just don't know how to tell you. Malcolm, Malcolm, I want you, I want to be your wife. I want to be honest with you. I want you to know everything about me. But listen, darling. Is it wrong for me to want to help the poor and the oppressed?" She looked at him.

He trembled inside. He didn't like this kind of talk, certainly not now. But he said nothing.

"That's why I joined the Communist party in the first place.

It was about the same year I got my job in the school system. You know I'm not much of a scholar. Look, you might as well know. I have an A.M. in secondary education, but my overall grade was B minus. I get mixed up when ideas get too complicated. But I do know there is poverty in the world, it breaks my heart to see a family of seven living in three rooms and the wife looking haggard and the husband sick from working fourteen hours a day, at two or more jobs. I think of my own family. That's why I joined the Communist party. I go to meetings, darling, I do the reading, but I don't always understand what I'm reading. I still want to belong to the party. You're not a member, but I know you're sympathetic, and maybe sometime you'll join. Darling, darling, I don't know what else to say. I'm proud to be your wife, I'm thrilled even to think about it."

Malcolm suddenly became dubious. "Did your Roger Williams cell ask you to try to get me to join the party?"

She turned her face away.

"I want to know," he said.

"They did."

"And what did you say?"

"Darling, this was at the beginning, I mean when we first began to see each other. In our cell we tell whom we've met, and so on, and I told them I met you, and that we were seeing each other, that I liked you very much, and that's when they asked me."

"Were you behind all those demonstrations in my defense?"

"Not I, by myself, no, Malcolm. But I did bring the matter up, and I did recommend that we do something about it, since you were fighting our battle, even though you were not a member of the party. As a matter of fact, I was rather angry that they didn't follow my suggestion right away. I think they looked you up, investigated you. I don't know what they do. All such matters go to some kind of headquarters. Darling, I don't understand all these things, but I did keep on asking what they were going to do to help you, and then the word came down, as they say in the cell, that they were going to help you, and they did, didn't they, darling?"

Malcolm was in a turmoil of emotions. He was angry with Ruth, he was sorry for her, he was disturbed by her obvious

73

innocence, and yet he was even more disturbed that he had entered into a marriage with this sort of innocent girl, who loved him yet who caused him all this anguish now.

"Are you sorry for any of the things you've done?" he asked, and felt strange for asking this inquisitorial question.

A hardness came to her face. "Sorry? For what?"

"Do you think I am happy about everything you told me?"

"You seem to be saying I did something wrong, Malcolm. What did I do that was wrong? I joined an organization that I think wants to help poor people, that is helping a country where poor people have rights and privileges and are not the slaves of exploiters, where there is liberty of all kinds, political and economic and religious. What's wrong in joining such an organization? I thought you were for the same things."

Malcolm looked at her . . . his wife of three days really was simple-minded, and she had swallowed everything that was taught her. Truth to tell, he had swallowed it, too, but he had always had some doubts, and now he had many doubts, but this is not what really bothered him. What bothered him was that his wife clearly was putting loyalty to party above loyalty to him as her husband . . . and he didn't understand her as a woman: a few moments ago she was all love and eagerness to give her entire self, body and soul, to him. He had actually felt guilty for making her feel the need to say all she said. Now she was talking like a Communist functionary . . . and there was the feeling, deep in Malcolm, that somehow she had been acting a treacherous part throughout their entire courtship . . . he couldn't put his finger on the specific acts of treachery, but he sensed them. How could he now trust a woman—his wife, at that, who has just told him that for months before their marriage she had been trying to do something, involving him, namely, to join the party, without having told him? Her cell was discussing him, investigating him; she knew this, yet didn't tell him; and now she was his wife, and she insisted she loved him. How was all this possible? And she herself saw nothing wrong in what she had done.

"Aren't you listening to me, Malcolm? You seem to be thinking of something else."

"I am thinking of something else, but they all have to do

with you, with us"—the *us* seemed strange to Malcolm, he didn't feel any more a part of her, or that she was a part of him—"with lots of things. There are so many things wrong, dead wrong."

"You think so?"

"Yes, I think so, and what hurts me especially is that you don't seem to think so. You know, something just occurred to me."

"What?"

"I don't mean to hurt you, Ruth, even though you've already hurt me enough. But I have the feeling that you throw out these phrases, about capitalist exploiters, imperialism, and so on, sort of mechanically. You don't especially mean to say them, you don't really know their full meaning or lack of meaning or bogus meaning that the Communist functionaries have put on them, you just spill them out. So maybe I shouldn't be angry with you. But now something else has come to my mind—this is the worst."

"Tell me."

"Here we are on our honeymoon, and already we've had very serious battles, and both of us have been hurt."

Ruth looked down at her lap, clasped her hands, and Malcolm saw tears trickling down her cheeks. He looked at her, thinking what a confusing, complicated, innocent, conniving, sweet, offensive, soft, lovable creature she was, how little he really knew her.

"It's all my fault," she said, still looking down at her lap. "But I meant well. I thought I was doing the right thing by telling you. Actually, there are some other things I wanted to bring up."

"I hope they're not as bad as what you already have brought up."

"Not bad, just different."

A rush of tenderness for her impelled Malcolm to come over to her, embrace her, and kiss her. "Let's not talk any more about any of this. This is a honeymoon, not a debate."

She looked up at him, and her tear-streaked face touched Malcolm. "You've said some horrible things, darling, terrible things."

"No more discussions," he said, smiling, and kissed her. "No more." He kissed her again.

"But can I say one thing, please, darling?"

"Only one thing, no more."

"I love you with all my heart."

"Me, too," and he kissed her long and vigorously.

The remaining week of their honeymoon was truly sheer bliss. The bitter words seemed like a bitter dream to them, and neither made any mention of them. One night, while they were in a passionate embrace, Ruth whispered to him, "Sweetheart, I want to have a dozen boys who look and act and think just like you do."

In his infinite gratitude for these words he said, "And I want our children to look all like you."

Neither had imagined that married love could be like this. The last night of their honeymoon was even sweeter than the earlier ones, and Malcolm, with his philosophical training, tried to reason out the explanation. But he got nowhere—and he began to wonder how good reason was, after all, since it seemed of so little help now.

The cooling-off period after their honeymoon began almost the very first day. One morning at breakfast—this was only three days after their return—she said, almost shame-facedly, "I have to go to the meeting tonight. You know the one I mean."

"Do you have to go tonight? After all, we've just come back."

"I'm afraid I have to, darling. I have a perfect record of attendance, and I don't want to spoil it."

"Since it's so perfect, your record, I should think you could spoil it a little. After all, you're a newly married woman, and I think your cell-mates would understand." He wondered what she'd say about his use of the expression "cell-mates." It came out of his mouth automatically, but he was glad. There was a certain aptness about it.

"No, I'd rather not," Ruth said.

"You're not answering my argument. You're merely handing down a decision." Malcolm was beginning to be annoyed. The party was interfering with his home life. Would he never be able to escape its influence?

"Darling, please let's not argue. I'll try to be home as early as I can."

"So that's it," said Malcolm.

76

"It's not so sad. Many married women do it, have done it for years. Most of them come with their husbands, because their husbands are members too. Each cell has a good deal of autonomy, and makes its own rules—anyway, some of them. So let's not argue about it, dear, please."

Malcolm was puzzled by the quick change she could make from being a loving wife to being a loyal Communist party member. He didn't like the second at all, and he hoped it wouldn't spoil the first. Ah, he thought, how much he had learned in less than two weeks! At times he thought he had lived with Ruth for years . . . and sometimes the thought would rush through his mind: Did I really need all this bother and worry and bewilderment? The loving part was good, very good, Ruth was a superb bed-mate, but the memory of the loving nights was no match for what was going on right now at the breakfast table. This was not a table of love, it was a small battlefield.

"So, suppose I pick you up after the meeting," offered Malcolm.

"No. You're not supposed to know where we meet. Oh, I guess people know, and maybe some girls have been picked up, but the rules say no."

"So who'll take you home? It will be late, won't it?"

"It could be eleven or midnight, most likely eleven, and one of the men will probably take me home. Besides, I'm a big girl, and I can come home by myself."

Malcolm was uneasy. This whole thing was getting more and more unpleasant. "Oh, hell, why don't you skip it this one time? They'll understand."

"We've already gone over that. Let's not argue about it any more, darling, please. You're making a mountain out of a molehill. It's only a meeting, just a meeting. You'll get used to it."

Malcolm wondered if he ever would get used to it, but he decided to say no more. It was difficult for him, however, to control himself. It was even more difficult for him to control himself when Ruth returned after midnight. He was waiting for her to say what went on, but she kept silent. He asked, "So what did you jabber about?" He was sorry he used the word "jabber," but he wasn't going to take it back. My God, he

77

thought, do I have to measure every word when I talk to my wife? She didn't answer. She went to the kitchen to make coffee. He tried again. "How did you come home?"

"Marty took me."

"Who's Marty?"

"A member."

"But he has a name, Marty something, doesn't he?"

"We're not supposed to reveal the names, the full names, the real ones of the membership. We've had too much trouble with informers. One tells another, then the other tells a third, and then the FBI has the information."

"But I'm your husband."

"That's one of the things we discussed tonight."

"Me?"

"Yes, you. They really made it miserable for me, especially this same Marty, who can be very objectionable."

"Objectionable, how?"

"He's been trying to kiss me for two years."

"Doesn't he know you're married now?"

"Of course. He's married himself. He thinks fidelity is a shibboleth, that's what he calls it. So he asked why I didn't get you to join, especially after what the party did for you, and he wondered if I wasn't lax in my duty. I said I tried and will try as much as I can to have you join, but I wasn't going to do any more, that you're a grown man and will do what you want to, and when. Marty was really mean."

"If he was so mean, why did you go home with him?"

"Oh, he insisted, he said he was going my way anyway, so I said all right."

"Did he try to kiss you?"

"Yes. He can't be insulted. He put his arm around my waist, and I gave him a push."

"Is that why you seem so upset?"

"I'm not upset," she said, not looking at him.

He remained seated and tried to catch her eye, but she evaded him. He looked into his cup of coffee, sipped it. He became angry. "You are upset," he said, "and I want to know why."

"All right, I'm upset," she said. "I'm confused, about lots

78

of things, and frankly I'm tired and feel like going to bed. If you want to stay up, you'll have to do it by yourself."

"Is Marty upsetting you?" he asked.

She turned to face him squarely. There was anger around her lips. "Don't be foolish. You're being immature."

"When are you going to start trying to get me into the party?"

"You'll join when you want to join," she said. "Frankly, I don't see why you haven't joined before. Sometimes I think you act like a confused liberal."

"Ha, another one of your clichés that you picked up among your friends, Marty and the others. Well, let me tell you right now, so that there'll be no misunderstanding. I will never join the party, never, and I have other things to tell you, but not now."

"Tell me whatever you want to tell me, or don't tell me, it's immaterial to me. I meant to tell you tomorrow, but I might as well do it now. The next meeting of the cell will be here. In a case like that, you, as my husband, can remain, but in another room, you understand. Our cell is pretty strict. It's my turn. I forgot it was coming so soon."

"I'll make it easier for you and Marty and the others. I won't be here when the gang comes."

"That's nice of you, real nice. And please don't mention Marty any more. You're trying to make something out of nothing. I sometimes think my trouble is that I'm so honest and believe in telling my husband everything. Marty doesn't mean a thing to me. How else do you want me to say it? Give you an affidavit?"

"Did he ever kiss you?"

"Malcolm, are you serious? In the past two years he probably did kiss me a few times. He chases me, and it was the easiest way to get rid of him. It meant nothing. So please stop this about Marty. I'm sick of it. For a professor of philosophy you can be very childish." And she walked off.

Malcolm had to agree with Ruth in her last remark. For a professor of philosophy he certainly was acting irrationally. But he had been hurt, confused, and humiliated. He was sure there was nothing between Ruth and Marty, yet he resented his taking her home tonight; he resented his having kissed her in the past. Malcolm himself had said in class that one of the marks of the civilized man is that he does not pry into the premarital secrets of his partner, and she doesn't do it, either, yet here he was prying . . . he was actually jealous. Now that he thought of it, why did Ruth permit Marty to take her home, knowing what she knows? Why did she act so guilty when Malcolm asked her about him? And why should he leave his own home when the party cell meets there? And why did the cell make things difficult for Ruth, by insisting that she try to make him join the party? Above all, what had happened to his marriage. . . .

The day of the meeting, Malcolm did not come home at all. He called Ruth and told her that he would work at the library on a paper for a philosophical magazine, that he would have dinner out, and would be home about midnight. She said, "That will be all right. See you then." He was puzzled by this brief statement. Why didn't she insist that he come home early and have a home-cooked supper? The cell members were not coming till after eight. Why didn't she apologize for making him stay away? Why didn't she behave more like a loving wife? For a while the thought ran through his mind that perhaps he should go to his mother's for the evening, but how could he explain things to his parents? They would hardly believe him. They surely wouldn't believe him, for they often had spoken about Ruth's quietness and gentleness and common sense. He wouldn't tell them, for that would be a form of snitching on his own wife. If he did tell his parents that Ruth was a Communist party member, he could almost hear his father exclaim, "This I don't believe, I just don't believe it, not Ruth!" And he could almost see his mother look at him, bewildered, her hands folded in her lap, and saying barely audibly, "I don't know what to say, I don't know. Such crazy things happen to children these days. The world is crazy, the whole world. But Ruth a Communist. . . !"

So Malcolm did work in the Columbia Library till about seven, then he had dinner in Times Square, and decided to go to a motion picture theatre on Forty-second Street. He saw a double feature, *What Price Glory?* and *A Star Is Born.* At first he felt ill at ease with the kind of people who were in the theatre (derelicts, vagabonds, prostitutes, lonely old men), but then he felt at ease, he didn't know exactly why. Perhaps, he thought, it was because they seemed so simple and genuine and earthy, and there was no nonsense in them about communism and cell meetings, and they probably knew nothing about the materialistic conception of history, about Marxism, about the proletariat. For a while Malcolm wondered if he wouldn't be happier if fate had deprived him of his Ph.D., made him forget his whole past life, and deposited him among these people, to live their life and think their thoughts and be possessed of their dreams.

Perhaps it would be pleasant to be married to a simple woman, a graduate only of elementary school, who understood having children, keeping a tidy house, and fulfilling her husband's needs. Really, what was wrong with that way of life? Here, in less than six months, he had been through what was really a kind of hell. A junior high school teacher had upset his whole life, so much so that he was unable to work on the article he had promised to write for one of the philosophical journals. After all, wasn't this the life his parents were living? What was wrong with their life? They struggled economically, they could use more money, have a better apartment, wear better clothes, go to the country in the summer, possibly have a car, but they were not too unhappy . . . and they didn't have his problems now. God, if only he could have married a girl like his mother! What loyalty was in her, what dedication, what a sense of decency, what sheer psychological and emotional health. Ah, thought Malcolm, education is a trouble-maker, and it really doesn't fit people to deal with life's real problems, the sort he was now having with Ruth. He had a hunch that almost any one of the men and women who were now in the theatre with him would be of more help to him than any family counsellor or psychologist.

The two pictures were really not bad, he thought. *What Price Glory?* was a little melodramatic. Still, Sergeant Flagg was a real character, and the French cutie was, well, cute, and sleeping with her would have interested Malcolm. Ah, thought Malcolm, how wonderful it must be to sleep and have breakfast and take a walk with a woman who didn't go to meetings of a Communist party cell. How wonderful it must be to kiss a woman, to suck her lips, sure that these same lips didn't snitch at him before a secret political gathering. Some people were lucky. What was his rush in marrying Ruth anyway? Yes, his parents urged him, true enough, but it was he who did the marrying. After all, he knew or should have known Ruth better than they did. No, it was all his fault, entirely his fault. . . . *A Star Is Born* wasn't bad, either. Rather saccharine, yet acceptable. This was the original version, with Janet Gaynor in the female lead. She was sweet way back, a little too sweet; nevertheless, a full and real and uncomplicated and loyal woman. Janet was loyal to her drunken husband to the bitter end and beyond. Loyal. How bitter that word now sounded to Malcolm. He wasn't sure of Ruth's loyalty, he wasn't sure whether he came first in her heart or the party. No, he was sure. The party came first, or he wouldn't now be where he was.

When the picture ended, it was a little after eleven, too early for Malcolm to go home, so he dropped into a cafeteria for coffee and a doughnut. He was even lonelier now than when he was in the theatre. He also realized that, now that he was married, he was lonelier in a cafeteria than before his marriage. He was going home soon, and he dreaded it, but being here alone in this cafeteria was miserable, too. A middle-aged woman came in, evidently a prostitute. She was alone, and ordered only coffee, and looked around and into the street. Malcolm wondered what he would say if she came to his table and asked him if he wouldn't "like to have a good time" with her. He had never been with a prostitute. He wondered what it was like. He recalled that one of the great figures in Marxist history, Moses Hess, had married a prostitute, or at least had lived with her as man and wife. Then there was Van Gogh, who lived for a while with a prostitute. And didn't Pericles—or was it Alcibiades—marry a courtesan? They seemed to have found pleasure and comfort with their women. Certainly more so than he was now finding with Ruth. Suddenly Malcolm noticed that one of the men who had been sitting alone in the cafeteria had walked over to the woman's table and sat down. They talked for a while. The woman seemed to have gentle lips, and there was charm in her smile. Now she and the man walked out. Malcolm felt strange. He was glad for both of them; he was also sorry for them. What genuine pleasure would they get in each other's arms for a space of a half hour or so, all the time knowing that this was bought love? Well, thought Malcolm, what about his own love, his own Ruth? Oh, she was a "fine" girl, but who is to say that this woman who had just walked out with a stranger isn't a fine woman, too? After all, what makes one woman fine and another vulgar?

When Malcolm came home, Ruth was putting away coffee cups and dishes. She greeted him pleasantly. "Was it a good meeting?" he asked.

"Yes, I should say so. Like any other meeting."

"Was I discussed?"

"No, they only asked what you were doing. I said you were at the library and would be home later."

"Aren't you interested in where I was?"

"If you want to tell me. I don't pry the way you do."

"What does that cryptic remark mean?"

"Marty," she said.

"Was he here tonight?"

"Yes."

Malcolm deeply resented Marty's presence in his home. The resentment burst upon him suddenly. "Did he try to kiss you?"

"That's what I mean by prying."

"Did he kiss you?"

"Yes."

"You let him?"

"Of course. He was in my own home. Other men kissed me good-night, and he did, too. I couldn't say yes to the others and no to him alone. It meant nothing."

Malcolm was still furious, but he hesitated to say anything for fear he would say something he didn't mean.

Ruth sat down. "I would like to talk to you, Malcolm. It concerns both of us very much. The other things we have talked about, the party and Marty, are minor matters compared with this. I am pregnant."

Malcolm was stunned. He felt trapped. In a few weeks he had lived more than he had lived in all his thirty-seven years. He had never realized that life could be so confused and com-

83

plicated. He wondered why he had ever got himself into this appalling situation. Way back in his subconscious he was wondering whether he should persist in his marriage to this strange and ever-surprising woman, and now he was given a sentence of eternity. All his training and reading in philosophy was of no help to him. Nobody was of any help to him. Only his parents could say anything of help to him, only they had his interest truly at heart. How lonely he was now, how bereft and bewildered he was. There was nobody at the university he could talk to. Many of his colleagues were jealous of him. They would probably be delighted just to hear of his troubles; besides, he couldn't tell them, anyway, even if there were friends among them, because it was all so intimate. . . . God, life really was a snare and a delusion . . . he felt his face getting hot, he felt his heart beating fast, he felt a pain in his chest.

"Well, aren't you going to say anything?" said Ruth.

"Oh, yes. I'm glad. I guess I didn't expect it."

"What did you expect, after the way we acted on our honeymoon?"

"Yes, that's true."

"These things happen. Nature."

"Yes. Nature. But . . ."

"I know, you didn't expect it, but it's true."

"Are you sure?"

"Absolutely. I went to Dr. Gerlach, a gynecologist, and he gave me a rabbit test. If you want to know all the details, I gave him a sample of my urine, he tested it, and said I was pregnant. Are you sorry?"

"No, not exactly."

"Then why are you acting the way you're acting?"

Malcolm felt completely enslaved to the female species. Ruth had conquered. Eve had conquered. Man had lost, Malcolm had lost. Who said this was a man's world? God, what a terrible mess!

"Why don't you answer me?"

He looked at her, and he was appalled by the look of triumph on her face. He had gone into her and now she had him in her clutches. He recalled the Biblical phrase, "And he went in unto her." What a surrender of the male sex!

"I don't know what to say," said Malcolm. "I'm glad, of course, I really am."

"You don't act that way. What did you expect from what we did on our honeymoon?"

He was offended by her matter-of-fact way of talking about their lovemaking. It sounded like a business deal: This is what you did, this is what you get.

"No, I don't know what to say. Sure I'm glad. Now, I guess we have to begin to plan all sorts of things."

"I've done that already."

"What do you mean?"

"Well, I'm due in November, November fifteenth, Dr. Gerlach says, a few days before or a few days after. He figured from the time we had our last intercourse."

Malcolm squirmed. How could women talk this way?

"Oh," he said, his stomach sinking at the physicality and even vulgarity of it all.

"And he felt my breasts and he felt my womb; he said it was swollen a little bit. He had no doubt."

"He felt your breasts and your womb—how did he do it?" He felt foolish as soon as he said it, but the words came out of his mouth mechanically.

Ruth answered him simply: "What do you mean? He felt my breasts with his hands, yes, with his hands, and he put his fingers up my vagina and felt my womb. Is that so difficult for you to imagine? It's a part of his profession."

"I never heard of this Dr. Gerlach. You didn't tell me about him."

"No, I didn't. You don't want me to tell you all about my female problems, do you?"

"I guess not, still . . ."

"Still, what?"

"Ruth, I just don't know what to say. I'm trying, in these few minutes, to get adjusted to the idea of my being a father. You've known about it for a few hours or a day or two. I haven't. You really should try to sympathize with me." He felt humiliated to be talking this way. He had just had a bitter, lonely, befuddled, hurtful evening, and now this. Life really was difficult, very difficult. And this woman, his wife, in front of him, wasn't helping him. He wondered if she didn't enjoy seeing him suffer. Is this the way all women felt when they told their husbands they were pregnant? Why hasn't the male sex done something about meeting this menace of the female sex? Oh, God, another thought occurred to him. Was the child his? Was it Marty's? He must know. But how could he ask Ruth? She'd think he was crazy. Well, perhaps he was. But he didn't like Marty . . . he didn't like what she had just said, that she had permitted him to kiss her ("What could I do? The others kissed me, I couldn't say no just to him") . . . well, kissing, sleeping with one, the whole free atmosphere of the Communist world, it all meant so little to them. God, what a mess he was in!

"You seem to be hesitating, Malcolm. You're not being very complimentary to me. I'm carrying your child, and you say nothing."

This somehow made him feel better: "I'm carrying your child." No, Marty had nothing to do with it; yes, it was his, Malcolm's child. But did Marty ever sleep with Ruth? Malcolm wasn't sure. He was pretty sure that Ruth was a virgin when he married her, but then he wasn't so sure. There was a little blood on the sheet, but not very much. He never would have thought of this unless she had mentioned Marty. God, what a life! And why was he using the name of God so often—he an atheist? He was completely confused, helpless, and hopeless.

"I'm very happy, darling." The mechanical use of the word "darling" gave him a strange reassurance. Of course, it was his child, oh, sure. He looked at her. He was filled with a sense of miracle, and suddenly he was filled with a sense of importance, and with a desire to embrace this woman who was carrying his child. This really was wonderful. His child. It was in her, growing every second, it would be part of him, part of both of them; yes, that was a miracle, and he was acting in a foolish, intellectual, professorial manner . . . life was a mixed-up thing. He didn't know what to do about it, about his present state, about life in general, about anything. Yes, *What Price Glory? . . . A Star Is Born . . .* what glory? what star? He looked at Ruth, and she did look very attractive, very desirable. Suddenly he got up, went over to her, hugged her and kissed her, and whispered in her ear, "I'm so happy. Our own child. I love you. I was just overwhelmed. After all. . . . It's wonderful, really wonderful . . . and we did have a good time on our honeymoon . . ."

She looked at him, blushing a little. "Malcolm . . ."

He felt playful. "Well, we did have a good time, didn't we?"

"Malcolm." She threw her arms around him and whispered in his ear, "I love you, I love you. We'll have a beautiful child. I don't care if it's a girl or a boy, as long as it's healthy."

They made love passionately that night. In the midst of it Ruth said, "We better do this as much as we can now."

"What do you mean?"

"The doctor said that after the fourth month, intercourse can be dangerous for the baby," said Ruth.

Malcolm squirmed inwardly again at the physicality of his wife's conversation. Were all women this way? Malcolm imagined they were . . . but he didn't like it. It took away so much from the romance and the spiritual delight of love and marriage. Suddenly he recalled that somewhere he had read (was it in Stendhal, or Schopenhauer, or Samuel Butler, or Havelock Ellis?) that women were deeply attached to the physical, to the body and its functions, especially to their own bodies and to physiology and anatomy in general. Well, that was good, there was sweetness and delight and profound joy for a man in a woman's body, but why did women have to finger-point at their bodies, so to speak? Didn't they sense how it offended men? Or didn't they care? Did they, subconsciously, continue to offend men in order to show their basic conquest of men, even though, in many respects, it was a man's world?

"So we'll do what the doctor said we should do and what the doctor said we shouldn't do," said Malcolm.

"You're a good boy," said Ruth playfully, as she dug her face into his chest. "Make love to me again right now, I want you so much, so very much, darling."

Later that same night, Ruth said, "If he's a boy, I want him to be a great social leader, a fighter for human rights."

"Well . . ."

"Wouldn't you like that, too, darling?"

"Yes, I suppose so."

"And if she's a girl, Malcolm, I want her to be married to a social fighter. The whole future will be a struggle for civil rights, for economic rights, for political rights; the whole future will be the future of the so-called common man, don't you think so?"

Malcolm didn't know what to say. He didn't like this sort of talk. It seemed like a stranger in the house, an intruder.

"Oh, I only want them to do what they want to do, I mean, if it's a boy or if it's a girl, as long as it's a good thing. I'm talking funny, but that's what I mean. Suppose the boy wants to be a physicist or a chemist or a mathematician or even a philosopher, and suppose the girl wants to be the same; you know, women are now in physics and in chemistry, too. I read the other day that a very eminent physicist in Europe is a woman—a Jew, as a matter of fact—a Dr. Leitner. So if our child should want that, that will be all right with me."

"I know, I know, Malcolm, but I'll be happier if he or she joins the struggle for the rights of workers and, well, the common people. Oh, darling, hold me, hold me tight, I'm so happy, so very, very happy. Give me your mouth, darling, I want to drink it in."

Malcolm was astonished at Ruth's sensuality. He was also pleased, but he was worried, too. Being sensual, perhaps she had slept with Marty or with some others . . . not that she loved them as she loved him, but because she simply couldn't get along without sexual intercourse. He was ashamed to think such thoughts. This was no way for a philosopher to carry on. He struggled to stifle these thoughts but he did not succeed.

Freud, he haid to himself, obviously was right: Reason is the figleaf of the emotions. Freud himself, he recalled, was a jealous man. Whenever, on a walk together, his wife would smile at a man, an old acquaintance, all sorts of ugly thoughts would run through his mind. Freud would not permit his wife or any of the children to use "indecent" words in the home or elsewhere. Malcolm smiled to himself. He wondered if Freud's wife had ever uttered the same kind of talk in bed as Ruth did since they were married. That kind of talk didn't bother Malcolm. He rather liked it. It added spice to the lovemaking; it added spice to Ruth's personality, and the spice seemed to spill over into the daytime, and Malcolm could almost smell it; in fact, he thought, this spice was more alluring to him than the aroma that came from a perfume bottle.

The recollection of Freud's remark also brought up Freud's attitude to Jewishness. Freud's philosophy in this regard was pretty much like Einstein's later. Einstein is reported to have said, "I have no religion, but I am a Jew." Now that this phrase came back to Malcolm, he liked it more and more, and he wondered whether he hadn't been wrong before in his belligerent non-Jewishness. Even his vaunted atheism began to look silly. Freud had never claimed he was an atheist, Dr. Weizmann hadn't, Dr. Herzl hadn't, Ben-Gurion hadn't. Believing was not a matter of reason, it was a matter of symbolism. It was the ritual of logic. It was an acceptance of legends, in which there was some factual truth, how much he didn't know, but it didn't matter. There was more to truth than factuality. Meaning, significance, overtones, aromas of the mind and soul—these have truth, too, very powerful truth. Malcolm was thinking in vague terms, in partial circles, but this activity seemed to be giving him greater enlightenment and insight and more maturity. He felt liberated from a past in his thinking that now appeared embarrassingly adolescent. He was sure that his father and mother, especially his father, would be pleased to know what was going through his mind now, but he wasn't sure he had the courage to admit the error of his former ways. He was still against going to *shul,* he was still against *kashruth,* against not wearing cloth made from a mixture of cotton and wool or whatever the forbidden mixture was . . . *against,* but not the way he had been against, violently, discourteously. Now he would only refrain from going to *shul* but say nothing about it openly, especially to his parents and others to whom these matters were important. Now he would be more dedicated to the values of Jewish culture and history and Jewish *peoplehood.* He recalled having read somewhere— was it in Dr. Shmarya Levin's writings?—that Judaism was a peculiar religion: it had no clear body of creed or ritual; it was an amalgam, or the efflorescence, of Jewish history and *peoplehood;* Judaism was a whole body of experience, involving history and ethics and philosophy and poetry and a deep feeling of psychological and spiritual *togetherness.* Malcolm would like to say all this to his parents in some indirect way, but a worry came to him, he sensed that Ruth, who came from the same type of family as his, remained belligerently atheistic and non-Jewish and, he feared, also anti-Jewish. Since she was so devoted a Communist she had to be anti-Israel and pro-Arab. She had thrown out hints in this direction. She didn't say so openly, and he suspected it was because she didn't want to upset him too much so soon after their marriage; she saw how upset he was by what she had already told him about herself, and these were relatively minor matters.

Malcolm's worries in these areas came to a head soon enough, when Ruth was in her fifth month, and had just begun to "feel life." Both of them had a glorious time, especially at night, when they put their hands to her stomach and felt the "kicks."

"A powerful little boy," Malcolm said.

"A strong little girl," Ruth said, smiling. "You men always want boys. I'm afraid women want boys, too."

"But I wouldn't mind if it's a girl, like you," said Malcolm.

"You're sweet."

A Sunday afternoon not long after, as they were lazily reading the huge newspaper, she brought up the matter of religion in connection with the baby. "Darling," she said, "if it's a boy, I don't want a *briss* (circumcision), with a dirty *mohel,* and wine, and blessings and all that superstition. It's all so barbaric. I hope you agree."

Malcolm was more shocked than surprised. He had just been going through a somewhat agonized reappraisal of his attitude to Judaism, he was getting closer to it culturally and psychologically, and his thinking implied at least an acceptance of the *briss* ceremony. He looked at Ruth, and suddenly she became a bit ugly in his eyes; there was a hardness around her mouth, the kind of hardness he had seen around the mouths of other female Communists. Women, he thought, showed this hardness more often than did men. Hardness in itself offended Malcolm, but hardness in a woman's face offended him especially.

"You agree, don't you dear?"

"Well, in the first place, doctors think that circumcision is a good thing anyway. Jews who are circumcised have almost no cancer of the penis, whereas uncircumcised non-Jews do have cancer of the penis. I think that's a pretty established fact."

"Actually, it isn't. It's only a tribal custom, a fetish, of no real medical value."

"That's surprising. Where did you read this?"

"I don't remember exactly. It was in some magazine I picked up at one of our meetings. It was by a doctor, the article. But if we agree to do it, if it's a boy, I want a regular surgeon to do it, not one of those filthy *mohels.*"

Malcolm smiled bitterly. "In the first place, the *mohels* are not filthy. They're professionals, and I read somewhere that they know how to do it far better than surgeons. They're experienced. In the second place, if it's going to be done, what's the harm in having a prayer at the same time, and some wine? It would please my parents, and I think it would please your parents, too. I don't see any harm in doing this."

"It's a matter of principle."

"Pleasing our parents is a matter of principle, too."

Ruth became incensed. Malcolm was bewildered by her abrupt change of mood, from softness to hardness, from rationality to fanaticism.

"I thought you had given up all that," she said. "I sometimes think some of the others in the party were right when they said you have one foot in the capitalist world still, that you're a confused liberal, that people like you sometimes end up Senator Taft men." Senator Taft, at the time, had the reputation, in Communist and liberal circles, of being an arch-reactionary, "the worst kind of Republican, a McKinley Republican."

Malcolm was annoyed. "That's name-calling, that's not arguing rationally. And as for Senator Taft, I would trust him with human liberties and human values more than I would trust Stalin or Malenkov or Khrushchev, or any of your other Jesuses."

"Now, you're name-calling. And what you say does not surprise me, by the way. So-called liberals like you the workers can do without."

"Can you do without me?" Malcolm was stunned by his own question. He wanted to soften it, but he let it go. Now he was hurt because she was not offended by the question. So her party was more important to her than her husband.

"That question or remark was uncalled for. I'll let it go for the time being. Anyway, I don't want to go on arguing. I don't even know why I brought up this matter of the *briss.*" Now a different look came to her eyes, a helpless, sad, and almost trapped, hopeless look. Apparently she was trying to keep back crying.

"What is it, Ruth?"

"I'm terribly worried. I'm beside myself with worry, Malcolm.

91

I'm staining. I didn't tell you, I didn't want to bother you. I've been staining for several days. At the beginning it wasn't much, now it's getting more. We have not been having intercourse for more than a month, so it can't be that. Malcolm, I don't mind telling you I'm frantic." She lowered her head and cried.

"Did you see Dr. Gerlach?"

"Yes. He said it wasn't good, but he didn't seem to be too worried. He gave me some injections, hormones or something, and he told me to stay off my feet as much as possible."

"So why are you sitting up?"

"But I'm not standing. I'll lie down soon."

"Are you in pain?"

"No. Just terribly worried. I wanted to keep this worry from you, but I can't any longer. Darling, I so want this baby, more than anything in the world."

"Go to bed right now. Lying down is better than sitting up," said Malcolm, deeply touched by what he was beholding. Ruth was a Communist, but she was also a woman, and the woman in her was dominant now. Besides, he himself was very much concerned. He had looked forward to the baby, imagining all sorts of things he would do for it.

Ruth went to bed. She stretched out and closed her eyes. Malcolm sat on a chair nearby. Soon he noticed that his wife put her hand to her stomach. He knew why. "Did you feel the kick?" he asked.

"Yes, thank God," she said.

The use of the word "God" impressed itself upon Malcolm. But he said nothing.

"So it's good," he said.

"Yes." She still kept her eyes closed, and a flood of pity went over Malcolm. "Darling, you don't know how much I want this baby, more than anything in the world. This kick I feel is what's keeping me sane. Dr. Gerlach said that so long as there is life, it's good. He told me that if I don't stop staining in three days I should see him again."

"I want to go with you when you see him. I mean I hope you don't have to see him."

"I know, darling. I hope so, too."

"Try to sleep."

She didn't answer him. He held her hand in his, and then he noticed that she had fallen asleep, her hand still on her stomach. He wanted to touch her stomach, but he was afraid he would wake her. He got up slowly and went out of the bedroom.

He called up Dr. Gerlach at his home. Dr. Gerlach said gently, "Dr. Dowd, I don't mind at all your calling me at home, not at all. I know how you feel. Is your wife listening? I mean, is she in the room? Just answer yes or no."

"It's all right. She's in another room, in the bedroom, sleeping, and I have the door closed. Please tell me the situation."

"What did she tell you, Dr. Dowd?"

Malcolm told him.

"Well, I'm sorry to say, it's a little worse, and I'm not blaming her for not telling you everything. It's her first baby, and it's a terrible thing for a woman to go through what she's going through. I'm doing all I can. The hormone injections I'm giving her may work, and they may not. I trust nature more than these hormones; I mean, we still have much work to do in that regard. Your wife is in good general health. I told her to eat lots of meat and eggs and fish—proteins. I don't like the sound of the baby's heart. It's a little faint. I also don't like its position. Then, the staining is getting more copious. Two days ago, she called me up in the middle of the day, crying and crying, some thick pieces came out. Well, that need not be too serious. The staining seems to be down now. I can only say that the next few days will tell. But I have to prepare you, Dr. Dowd. If she loses the baby, it will be for the best. It will only mean that the fetus is not healthy, and what seems to be happening is that nature is trying to get rid of an unhealthy fetus. I hope I'm wrong. But remember, many women have miscarriages at the beginning, and then go on to have a half dozen perfectly healthy children. Why these things happen we don't really know. As long as the sperm and the ovum are healthy, and as long as the womb is healthy, healthy babies are possible. So, we can only hope and pray. The longer I'm a doctor the more I find it necessary to tell people to hope and pray. There's a lot more that medicine *doesn't* know than otherwise. Try to comfort your wife, to keep her spirits up. It's far from hopeless. She's a remarkable woman. She thinks the world of you."

Malcolm was sorry that the doctor had made the last remark. It was the routine thing for him to say; it didn't report a true remark, of that he was sure. At the same time he was sorry for Ruth, though his deep love for her had cooled a great deal. She was simply causing him too much anguish, and he had not written a line of any value since their marriage. There was hardness and meanness and conniving in her, and too often he was troubled about her sexual morals, and he also had doubts about her loyalty and love for him. At the same time, there was something dreadful about what God or nature or whatever you want to call it was doing to her and to him. Why, why, why all this agony? He found himself asking the old questions that he had thought were simple, but now he knew they were not simple; they were eternal, and they had no answers. All his philosophy was of no use to him now. Ruth was a human being, Ruth was a woman, Ruth was his wife, Ruth wanted a child; Ruth, for all her preposterous logic and misinformation and fanaticism, had a right to the happiness of having a child of her own. It was all so cruel and ghastly, and he himself felt trapped within a maze of traps.

One late afternoon when Malcolm came home Ruth was out. This surprised him. He expected to find her resting in bed. A half hour passed, then another half hour, and still she did not come. He called Dr. Gerlach's office. No answer. He called Dr. Gerlach's home. His wife said that as far as she knew he was at the hospital. He called the hospital and was told the doctor was there but could not be reached. Malcolm went to the hospital, and after considerable questioning was told the doctor was attending to Ruth in the emergency section. He was asked to wait. Dr. Gerlach finally came out.

"Dr. Dowd, your wife called me. She had passed thick bloody pieces in the toilet bowl. I told her to come to the hospital at once. I didn't tell her, but I am telling you that the outlook is very dim. I barely hear any heartbeat. I believe the baby is gone. We should know very soon. My own honest belief is that since she's had so much trouble, it would be best if she miscarried. A fetus with all this difficulty is almost bound to be deformed. I better go in now."

In less than an hour he came out, and Malcolm knew what

he was going to say. He felt both relieved and appalled. "We did what we could," said Gerlach. "Your wife will be fine, but you'll have to be kind to her. This is a terrible shock to any woman. I wish I could do something, but I'm afraid I can't. You'll be able to see her in about three hours. She should be able to go home in three days, maybe two days. As far as I could see and feel, everything is all right. She'll bleed a little for a while, maybe for a day or two, but then it will subside. Nothing to worry about. I'm sorry."

Malcolm saw her in the hospital bed. She was awake. Her eyes were closed. He held her hand, he kissed it, but she did not respond. "I'm terribly sorry, Ruth."

She did not answer.

"I spoke to Dr Gerlach. He said he did all that could be done. He said you would be ready to come home in two, three days."

She said nothing.

"He said you are all right. And he said that there is no reason why you shouldn't be able to have a half dozen healthy children."

She opened her mouth as if to speak, then closed her mouth.

"Dr. Gerlach said it's for the best. If you had delivered it, it probably would not have been healthy. He told me that."

Still she said nothing, and still she kept her eyes closed. At home she was virtually just as uncommunicative. She would ask for a glass of water and thank him, or she would ask for some orange juice and thank him. She ate almost nothing except a bit of roll with butter and jam. Dr. Gerlach said she must eat much more, but she persisted in her virtual fast. Malcolm saw Dr. Gerlach in private and asked for advice.

"It's not unusual for women who've lost their first child in a miscarriage to act this way. It's a terrible blow, as I've told you. But she'll get out of it. Nature will take over. Show her as much love as you can. That's what she needs most of."

But Ruth seemed to be offended by his every attempt to show love. She wouldn't let him hold her hand, she refused his kisses, she pushed aside his hand in bed. She was equally uncommunicative with his mother and with her own mother. The only people she talked to at all were her colleagues at the junior high school where she taught, and also some others who, he suspected, were members of her Communist cell. Suddenly she snapped out of it. She dressed and took care of the house and went to school. She also went to her meetings. But she acted toward him in a cold and sisterly manner. He tried to embrace her on several occasions, but she rejected his attentions. Then he decided to talk to her.

"How long will this go on?" he asked.

"What are you referring to?" she answered, evading his eyes.

"Ruth, don't play games. You know very well what I'm talking about. Are we married or aren't we? Ever since the miscarriage you have acted as if I were to blame. You haven't treated me with ordinary courtesy, not to say love. I have a right to know where we stand."

"Well," she began, "I think we ought to stay apart for a few weeks or maybe longer. I have to think things through. It will do us good."

"Why? We're not married even two years—what am I talking about, it's only a little over a year and a half. And I don't mind telling you that it's been hell for me; plain, unadulterated hell. You act as if you don't like me as a husband. I must know."

"Let's take a vacation from each other for a while. I may have something to say sooner, perhaps."

"Aren't we going to discuss this, like grown people? You are giving me orders again, like before. I don't like it. My mother keeps on asking me what's wrong with us, why do you act the way you do, why you are so rude over the telephone."

"Oh, your mother. That's all you think about. You're a mother's boy, bourgeois morality, bourgeois emotions."

"You're just using words, Ruth. You're a stupid monkey." He got up. "I'll get myself a room somewhere. You can stay here." She said nothing. He walked out.

Malcolm and Ruth didn't get in touch with each other for three weeks, almost a month, in fact. He didn't tell her that he was living in a small hotel in the neighborhood of Columbia University, but Ruth was thoughtful enough to forward his mail to the philosophy department. One evening he had to go over to pick up some books he had forgotten. He still had a key, and he used it. As he came in he heard people talking. About fifteen men and women were present; some of them he recognized as having visited Ruth when she was ill. Ruth greeted him politely but coldly. She introduced him, not by his name, but simply as "my husband."

"I only came in to pick up some books I need," he said to Ruth, as he excused himself from the others and went to their bedroom. He found the books at once, and was on the point of leaving.

"You might have called," Ruth said.

"Called? This is my home, too, isn't it?"

"I thought you said you wanted to live elsewhere?"

"I did. Because you said you wanted a vacation from me."

"That wasn't quite the way I said it, but the meaning is the same, I guess."

"So what are you complaining about?" asked Malcolm, who thought Ruth's face had become harder than he had ever seen it before.

"I still think you should have called."

"I don't think so, unless you have a lover." He knew he had made a cheap remark, but he didn't care.

"Oh."

"Yes, oh. Do you?"

"You've given me an idea, my dear husband, my dear absent husband."

"This was your idea."

"I guess it was."

"Well, I better be going, you have company. Cell-mates, I imagine."

"Malcolm, your mother has been here twice. She called a couple of times right after you left, and finally I had to tell her about our arrangement. Did she tell you about it?"

Malcolm was surprised. He had spoken to his mother on the telephone, but she had said nothing. "No, she didn't, I feel funny about the whole thing."

"She didn't tell you because I asked her not to. I never knew what a marvelous woman she is, Malcolm." He had never before heard Ruth say anything so complimentary about his mother. He didn't know what to say. "She really is, Malcolm."

"What did she say?"

"You know what she said, Malcolm. She cried. She said we should try to get together again. She told me lots of things about you."

"Nice things?" He was glad they were talking this way.

"Yes. Malcolm, there are people there. I was wondering . . ."

"What?"

"Could you come in later?"

"Come back?"

"We'll see, Malcolm. I would like it if you came back later, in two hours, two and a half hours. I can't just chase them out."

"No, of course not."

"Good," Ruth said, and moved close to him. Then she threw her arms around him, and buried her face in his jacket. He held her tight. He was thrilled and bewildered and at a total loss what to do or say. He wanted to come back, he didn't want to; he wanted to get a divorce, he didn't want to. Only a few minutes ago she seemed so undesirable, now he could make love to her.

She lifted her head and took his face in her hands and kissed him hard on the lips. Suddenly she became businesslike, brushing her hair back and smoothing her blouse.

"Later," they both said.

That night was profoundly delightful for both of them. They made love and they talked and they made love again, and then they talked some more, and they hugged each other and whispered endearing words into each other's ears.

"Darling," she said. "I learned one thing, the most important thing. I need you, without you I just can't be anything. I have to tell you this, you know how frank I am; that's what got me into trouble with you at the beginning"—she smiled and kissed him hard and long—"I have to be frank with you, I'm that way. I love your smell, your touch, the taste of your mouth, and I love so much the way you love me, oh, darling, we must never fight again."

Malcolm was thrilled—and puzzled. Her switches and about-faces bewildered him. Perhaps, he thought, in spite of her mouthing of Communist clichés, she was, at heart, a simple girl who wanted to be a wife and mother, and really was not a violent radical or a conniving Communist; she was just eager for love and she really was touched by the privations of the poor, and some Communist man (Marty perhaps) or maybe it was some older woman had told her that she ought to join "the movement." Now that he thought of it, Ruth had brought home all sorts of magazines and handouts and books and pamphlets from her meetings, but he didn't recall that she did more than glance at them and put them in the bookcase. Still, he was confused. She had said some terrible things to him, but then he had said terrible things to her. He wondered whether she realized how terrible her remarks were. She reminded him of the seven-year-old son of a friend who used four-letter words to his father and mother, but he really had little idea what they meant. Ruth belonged to the vast number of men and women, some high up academically, who repeat phrases they don't understand the full meaning of. They repeat them because they seem plausible at the moment, or they repeat thm because their friends do, and if they disagreed they would be ostracized, so to speak, among their friends and acquaintances. Then there is the other reason: repeating these phrases gave some people a sense of intellectual maturity, of being involved, of being well-informed, of keeping abreast of world affairs.

No doubt Ruth belonged to this huge group. Malcolm wondered now how good a Communist she was. She belonged, she carried a card, but did she really care the way genuine fanatics cared? Malcolm was quite sure now that Ruth was not a fanatic. He had no evidence, really, but he did have a strong hunch. How could a real Communist behave toward him the way she had tonight? Malcolm smiled to himself: After all, Communist women were women, too, with sex urges, with yearnings for love . . . but, no, this was different, with Ruth. Yes, it was different . . . he smiled to himself again, and thought what strange thoughts the students in his logic class would have if they could hear him reasoning now about Ruth. Ah, thought Malcolm, logic was one thing, and life was another. Maybe all logic was good for was mathematics . . . who knows, who knows. . . . The heart has its own reasons, most of them are probably closed to human understanding. One must only be patient when these reasons of the heart begin operating . . . and right now these reasons of the heart were operating between Ruth and himself. Despite all his heartache and his loneliness and bewilderment and all his anger and despair, he wanted to be back with Ruth and try again.

Ruth embraced him and kissed him again and embraced him again. "I'm so glad we're together again, right here in bed, where we belong. Am I being awful for talking this way?"

"No. Maybe I should tell you, I like it, the way you say it, and, well, I might as well be frank, too"—she kissed him again —"I feel flattered when you talk this way. After all, men like flattery, too, men like to be liked."

"But, darling, you haven't said anything."

"About what?"

"About us."

"About us? You haven't let me. Every time I. . ."

"I know, I know, Malcolm," she said, kissing his hand.

"You know what I want to say. Let's forget everything in the past, and go back to where we started. Let's—"

She took his face in her hands and then buried her face in his neck: "That's all I wanted to hear." Then she said, "There's something else I want to tell you."

"Oh, my God," he said. "More trouble."

"No, silly," she said, as she kissed his neck. "No more trouble."

"I can believe that?"

"You can believe that. You really are sweet, Malcolm. But maybe I'll talk about it tomorrow."

He put her down on her back, and rested himself on his elbows above her. "Now, my dear wife, you are trapped and you have to tell me."

"Only if you let me kiss you once before I talk."

"You can kiss me twice, if you wish."

She kissed him twice, then she said, "I wonder if God arranged it, I mean our fights, so that we could have all this. Do you think so, Malcolm? you're a philosopher."

Malcolm wanted to bring up her use of the word "God"— she an atheist—but instinct deterred him. "It could be," he said. "I'll have to figure it out logically. Now tell me what you were going to tell me. You're not going to evade. Tell me." He took both her breasts in his hands. "I love them both."

"I'm glad," she said, as she put her hands on his. "So this is what I was going to say. I told the party I was going to take some time off from the meetings. Others have done it before. I told them I wasn't well, but that's not the real reason."

"What's the real reason?"

"You."

"Ruth, you're wonderful. I'm glad we got married."

She pressed her hands harder on his. "Yes, the reason is you, us. Malcolm, you have no idea how much I missed you the past four weeks or whatever it was. It seemed like years. You don't know how much I cried. Only my mother knows. She was with me every night the first week. I don't know what's wrong with me. I was so bitchy with you, so terrible. I said things I didn't mean. You are right, I'm a stupid monkey about certain things I said."

"Oh, I didn't mean. . ."

"You did, Malcolm, and I'm glad you did. It's true. Darling, don't laugh at me, I'm only a simple-minded woman, but I liked the book *Kitty Foyle*. One of the things in it I'll always remember is where some character, or maybe it's the author, says that women are lost without men, that they learn good manners and sense in general from men. And darling, that's true, and I want you to teach me. Darling, teach me, everything. That's what I wanted to tell you."

"When did you tell them this, Ruth?"

She smiled, and kissed his two hands, finger by finger.

"When did you tell them, Ruth?"

"Tonight."

"Tonight?"

"Yes. We women are so tricky, I mean we do things men don't understand. Darling, forgive me. I'm not really tricky. I did it all because of you, because of us. Early in the evening I wasn't going to do it. I told you I'm frank, though it's terribly true I missed you and cried, all that is true. But I didn't mean to ask for time off at the beginning this evening. But then you came, darling, and when I saw you, my heart melted. If I could, I would have chased them all out and thrown myself at your feet. I was worried you'd never come back. But I saw that you still loved me, and I was glad, and I knew it would work. I mean we would get together again, and we would love each other. I could tell by your eyes and the way you kissed me. So I decided

101

right there and then I would tell them. I think they were surprised, but I didn't care. So that's what I was going to tell you. Now, are you satisfied?"

"Very much, Ruth."

"I knew you would be. Darling, I talk like a sixteen-year-old girl, but all I want in this world is that you love me. All women are always sixteen years old, darling. I have just told you a secret about women. Anyway, I don't care, I want you, everything about you."

"And I want you," said Malcolm, thrilled and bewildered by this woman who was so different from the woman he had known during their courtship days and for a time afterward.

"Darling," she said. "Let's go to sleep. It's so late, and I guess we could use sleep."

Life for the Dowds now took a new direction, and the fact never ceased to puzzle Malcolm. He, the rational philosopher, felt he was being carried along a stream, almost entirely guided by Ruth, who knew nothing about philosophy and who appeared to operate according to rules that were mysterious to him. She reminded him of Bergson's *élan vital,* which obviously had a logic of its own that not even Kant had been able to penetrate . . . he probably knew nothing about it; being a bachelor, he had never encountered it. As time went on Malcolm was all the more puzzled, but he had decided to let himself be directed almost entirely by Ruth, who became more and more delightful in his eyes. The hardness around her lips had vanished, her cheeks became fuller and softer, her hips appeared more and more desirable to him. He loved her aroma, her smile, the curve of her breasts . . . he loved the occasional earthiness of her speech. At night she would sometimes say, "My womb is yearning for you. You have a darling fanny, it just fits my hands, and it's firm." Then, when she told him she was pregnant again, their joy barely knew any bounds. Malcolm was fearful of another miscarriage. But Ruth, at least outwardly, had no doubts. "This time I'll make it," she said one afternoon, with her hands on her hips, and then patting her stomach. "I know it. I feel it. When I'm sure, I'm sure."

One Friday evening Malcolm came home from school, and to his surprise and delight and puzzlement, he saw two lighted candles on the table. He looked at Ruth, and she returned his look, smiling.

"I like it, but—" began Malcolm.

Ruth kissed him. "That's all I wanted to hear."

"But I mean . . ."

"I'll tell you something now that will please and maybe surprise you. I told your mother and my mother that as soon as I reach my fourth or fifth month, when I can feel life, I'll light candles every Friday night and get *chaleh* for the Friday-night blessing. I wanted to bless the candles when you came, but I wanted to surprise you with the candles all lighted. But there was another reason."

Malcolm smiled. Ruth always had "another reason." He liked this quirk of hers. The sight of her blooming body added to his delight. He saw she was waiting for him. "What's the other reason?"

"You. I knew you'd be pleased."

"I am pleased, very pleased, but how did you know?"

"I knew, and I wanted to please you, is there anything wrong in that?"

Malcolm had noticed that several letters from the Roger Williams Liberal Organization, a euphemism for the Communist cell that Ruth belonged to, remained on her night table unopened. Then he saw magazines there, also unopened. A bit later she did open them—they were in bed together, and he was reading the newspapers, and he noticed that she had opened these letters and torn the magazine wrappers, but that she had put them back, having given them little of her time. He was tempted to talk to her about this, but he refrained. He had had so much good luck "letting nature take its course" that he decided to let nature do the same now. He was sure that she had not gone to a meeting of the cell for months. There were some strange telephone calls that she didn't tell him about; he suspected they were from members of the Roger Williams Liberal Organization. Again he said nothing. He was glad he had enough sense, at those times, to leave the room. He hoped that this would sit well with Ruth.

One Sunday afternoon, when she was already "bulging luxuriously," as he told her, and she was happy about the phrase, she served him *tsimmes,* a thick, sweet concoction of beef fat and potatoes and plums and carrots and raisins and molasses. His mother always made it for him, since he liked it so much, and he had often missed it since he got married.

"Just marvelous, darling. How did you know I loved it? Mother used to make it for me at least once every two weeks. It's fattening, but I don't care. You must have extrasensory perception. Just wonderful. Do you like it?"

"Yes, very much. I don't care about it's being fattening. A little more weight now won't make any difference to me."

"So tell me," he said.

She smiled. "You talk like a Jew." She smiled again and touched his hand. He was puzzled by her remark, which a few months ago she probably would have considered "a display of chauvinism and parochialism," and God knows what other phrases she had picked up among her cell-mates.

"I'll tell you," she said, "but before I tell you I want to say that I added the molasses on my own. It's a little different from the usual Jewish recipe for *tsimmes,* if there is a usual recipe. I added molasses because molasses has iron, and one book on prenatal care for mothers said that there is a new theory that carrying mothers are sometimes deficient in iron, and that they should have lots of meat and liver and molasses, all things that have iron. I like molasses; I can almost taste the iron. I even like the smell of rusty nails." Playfully, she added, "Is that bad? Will our baby chew nails?"

"You amaze me, darling," Malcolm said.

"I love you, I love you. Oh, about the *tsimmes.* Remember, I'm frank."

"There we go again."

"I got the idea from your mother. As you know, she drops over quite often; so does my mother. They're both wonderful, and you just don't know how they love both of us, and how happy they are about the baby. Am I being childish, the way I talk, Malcolm, am I?"

He took her hand and put it to his cheek. "Darling, you are being childish and I love you this way. Now back to *tsimmes.*"

"I've made such a big *tsimmes* out of the *tsimmes,* that I'm embarrassed there isn't really so much to say. Your mother happened to mention that you like it so much, so she gave me the recipe, and I worked and worked on it, and here it is. That's all there is to it."

Malcolm became thoughtful. The whole aura of his home rushed into his heart. Then he said, "Mother is an amazing woman. So is Father, once you get to know him. I've been pretty terrible to both of them."

"And I've been terrible to you," she said.

"That's the past. I told you we mustn't go back to all that."

"I won't. But your mother and my mother talked a lot to me, when they were here, every time they come, and they've set me to thinking. I have to tell you this. Oh, no, don't worry, Malcolm, it's all good. Why is it, darling, that when you come from school and other times, when we're together, I want to talk to you so much I'm afraid I don't know when to stop? I jabber and jabber. It's not just my pregnancy, I just want to talk to you, and be with you, and hold you. Oh, so about the other things. Your mother especially told me about the persecution of Jews in the Soviet Union. They read me things from the *Jewish Daily Forward* and from *The New York Times*. I know the papers have been full of this anti-Semitism—these anti-Semitic reports, for a long time. I even brought them up at our meetings, you know, but they made light of them, said they were capitalistic lies. I believed what they said, but I must say that I didn't believe one hundred percent. I always doubted a little bit, but in a meeting you mustn't doubt too much, or they say you're a reactionary. But now I believe everything the *Forward* and the *Times* say. The Soviet Union is viciously anti-Semitic. And your mother, especially, said, 'Say what you will about the United States, it's not anti-Semitic, like in the Soviet Union. There are some anti-Semites, but the federal and the state and the city governments are not anti-Semitic, the way they are in the Soviet Union.' And a few times your mother said other wise things to me. You know the way she talks, slowly; I adore her, she's very wise. She said something like this: 'Here, it's not Paradise. It's not Paradise anywhere, except in Israel, of course. But people can talk. They don't get arrested for talking. They can print papers and say anything about the government and nothing happens to them; policemen don't come late at night and take

105

them away and nobody ever hears about them any more, like in Russia. It's a democracy here. There's good points about our democracy and bad points, but what the Communists say about this country, enemies of the workers and all that, it's better here, much better. In Russia, where it's supposed to be so good for the workers, the workers can't strike. Here they strike all they want. Even Senator Taft is for strikes, I mean he isn't against them. It's free here, anyway, much freer than anywhere else, much freer than in the Soviet Union. There, it is a slave camp, like the *Forward* says. And about Israel, this country is for Israel. The Soviet Union is for the Arabs. Well, I'm for Israel. I tell you, an expert I am not, but some things can be understood with common sense.' That's what your mother said."

"I can hear her say it," said Malcolm.

"And, Malcolm, I want to say now that your mother is right, and please don't ask me too many questions right now. I'm a little tired and I want to lie down."

"Oh, sure, sure."

The baby was a girl. Much to Malcolm's surprise and pleasure, Ruth suggested that they name her Deborah. "I like the name Deborah; besides it's your grandmother's name, your mother told me. Deborah Dowd, it sounds just fine to me. Do you like it?"

"I think it's just fine."

The two grandmothers hovered over the baby, day and night, as the saying goes. Fortunately, there was no serious problem with her. Ruth had had an easy delivery but the two grandmothers insisted she rest, that they would take care of the house. "You just rest and be happy." Once Malcolm's mother said, "I think to myself, can anybody really be happier than your father and I are now? Such an angel she is, little Deborah, such a diamond, I could eat her up."

One evening, while Deborah was sleeping, Ruth gave Malcolm a letter to read. It was from Marty, who now was the chairman of the Roger Williams cell. It was brief: "Dear Ruth: You have not paid your dues for over a year. You have not answered our letters. You have been discourteous to comrades who have called you on the telephone. There is nothing left for us to do but to expel you from our ranks. I personally never thought that the day would come when Comrade Ruth would go over to the camp of the capitalist exploiters. I personally never thought that you would believe the dastardly lies in *The New York Times* and the *Jewish Daily Forward,* which is an even greater enemy of the workers and of the homeland of the downtrodden, the Soviet Union. Yours truly, Marty Biedemann, chairman."

Malcolm was delighted, but he was at a loss what to say. Ruth was so unpredictable that he didn't dare provoke her into any argument with him. One could hardly argue with Ruth. Her decisions were often made on illogical grounds, and what commences with irrationality cannot be dispelled with rationality. "The letter sort of surprises me," he said, and was immediately sorry for saying it. It was not the right thing to say. He looked at Ruth with fear as to what would happen.

"Why?"

"It's hard to say. I guess I'm not prepared to say anything rational about it. Perhaps I might as well tell you now that I've divorced myself completely from Marxist philosophy. It was an intellectual plaything when I was young and less patient. Now I see it for the one-sided, uninformed, inhuman thing it is. Above all, I cannot tolerate the Communists and their dupes. They're even more brutal and uncivilized than their theory. The Communists in Russia are just the worst sort of Tammany politicians—far worse than Tammany has ever produced. The Tammany politicians are grafters, some of them, and they fake votes, but they wouldn't dare to stifle free speech completely, and they wouldn't dare to oppose a clear public mandate. And of course, there is the United States Constitution, and Brandeis and Holmes. In this country decent things don't always win, far from it, but they have a chance, a very good chance. In Russia they have no chance. And I'm beginning to have a liking for such arch-reactionaries as Senator Taft. I'm not so sure that Stalin and Khrushchev and Trotsky have not been worse reactionaries. He does believe in freedom. He may be wrong in his ideas as to how freedom is to be maintained and achieved, but he's for freedom, and he doesn't look upon himself as infallible. You can disagree with him without being afraid he'll get you killed or sent to jail, or that your family will be tortured." He stopped. "Whew! I didn't mean to say all this, Ruth, a speech for no reason."

She touched his hand and squeezed it. "Don't apologize. Don't ever apologize, darling, when you talk to me this way. I have so much to learn from you. I showed you the letter because I want you to know everything."

"Because you're very frank," he said smiling. She patted his hand. "Well, I'll be frank, too. I love that letter. I'll come right out and say what I want to say. I hope it means that you're through with them."

Ruth looked down, then straight at Malcolm. "Darling, it's taken me a long time, too long. Communist talk is a drug, especially for a simple-minded girl like me, who really doesn't know very much about anything. It sounds so good when you don't know all the facts and what's behind the facts, and when you believe the lies they tell you and that they print, and then there are the threats all the time. If you don't agree, you're an enemy. They don't allow for discussion, for real discussion. I used to play a game with myself. When some new proposal came up for discussion, as they called it, I would look at the chairman and listen to him, to see which way the wind was blowing, and naturally when the vote came up I voted the way he wanted. I guess we all did, because the vote was always unanimous. That's what made me think right at the beginning. Some times I felt like asking questions that sort of disagreed with the chairman, you know what I mean, but I didn't. I was afraid I'd be called a traitor, an enemy, God knows what. Malcolm, this may surprise you. I've had doubts for a long time, and I guess I was waiting for some logical reason to kind of move out. With us getting together, I mean, at the beginning, with the baby now, I sort of let matters slide. Now what's happened is what I wanted to happen. I hope you're not worried by what Marty says and implies."

"No, of course not, but I'm sorry you have to be the butt of the vicious talk that must be going on at the meetings."

"I suppose I am, a little. But one thing I won't do, I won't snitch on anybody. That, never. Most of the people there, I really mean it—I mean most are like the way I was. They're not enemies of this country, they're just, well, misguided and afraid. That's the worst thing of belonging to the Communist party. You're afraid. Fear, yes, plain fear."

"That's how it is all over Russia, all over Poland, in all the Iron Curtain countries."

"I believe it."

"Only one thing, darling, bothers me."

"What, Malcolm?"

"Well, it's only human nature that when you give up one position you incline to move way over to the other extreme. We must watch out for that, but we mustn't compromise. For a while, anyway, we may do it."

"I suppose there is that danger. So what shall I do about the letter, darling?"

"Put it away and forget it. There's no point in arguing with such people."

"But it makes me sad. I won't be able to see some of the people there. There's a girl, Esther, who's married to a dentist; and there's another girl, Matilda, who's single, but very sweet. I honestly think she comes because she's lonely; it's a regular place to go to. You might ask why she doesn't belong to Hadassah—by the way, I may join them, it's the least I can do for all the foolish things I've said about Israel, the usual stuff about it being reactionary, controlled by American capital, and the rest—as I say, you might ask why she didn't join some other organizations, even the League for Women Voters, and organizations like that. Well, it's hard to say. I suppose she comes from a poor family, wanted to help out poor people. She met somebody who belonged to the Communist party; their slogans sound good, and before she knew it, she was in, and that was that."

"We'll have to make new friends. It will take time, but we'll make them." He smiled.

She smiled in response. "I like what happens to your mouth, Malcolm, when you smile."

"Something happens?"

"Yes. I noticed that the same thing happens to Deborah. She's your child all right. You, both of you, get two little dimples on both sides of your mouth."

"My mother would say you won't break up the *shidach* (engagement) on account of that?"

"No, I won't. Malcolm, the Jews have such wonderful sayings. I read somewhere the other day, a man was talking to another about doing something foolish, and he said, 'It's like giving a drink of water to a drowning dog.' "

"This happens to be a favorite expression of my mother's."

"Is there a book of such expressions?"

"I suppose there is. Some *goy* will begin using them, and

then the Jews will be proud of them. The Jews are the most snobbish and the proudest people known to history, but at the same time they are the most modest and most insecure. They need a *goy* to tell them that what they've always done and will continue to do is right. That makes it kosher. My father used to read out loud sometimes, on Saturday night, stories by Sholom Aleichem, and his writings are full of Jewish sayings. I remember a couple. A man is wearing rims without lenses, and another man asks him what's the point, and the man answers, 'It's better than nothing.' The other is this: One poor Jew asks another how he's doing, and the other says, 'How am I doing? With God's help I starve three times a day.' "

"They're wonderful, the Jews. How Jews can be against Jews, like the American Communists and how they talk about Israel, I mean the American Communists, I just don't understand. I used to want to ask what the Arabs have ever done for the Soviets, what the Arabs have ever done for their own people. Some of these Arab countries have real slavery, real human slavery, even now."

"That's all in the past," said Malcolm. "Oh, this is what I started to say before. I'm a little ashamed to bring it up. I've been reading the *New Republic* and *The American World* in the library. I like them both, the *New Republic* more than the *World*. The *World* used to be better, but it's still worth reading, anyway. What I want to say is that I kept from subscribing to them and having them come to the house because . . . you know."

She smiled. "Remember what you said; that's past. By all means let us subscribe. And we'll tell each other everything."

He touched her hand. "You mean we'll be frank with each other." She slapped his hand playfully, then squeezed it.

"This reminds me," he added, "I've been seeing, now and then, a very nice guy in the library. He's a critic, a writer, I think he sometimes writes for the *New Republic*. I was thinking we might ask him and his wife over some time. He was with the party way back, he admitted to me—I mean he told me in an offhand way. Anyway, I like him."

"Sure."

"His name is Hal Peters, a couple of years older than I am. Very nice guy."

"Good, you arrange it."

six

The Dowds and the Peterses liked each other at once. Three of them had gone through the same saddening experiences with the radical left. Ruth and Hal had been members of the party. Malcolm had never actually belonged, but he was so close intellectually and emotionally he could have. The only one who had been merely "sympathetic" was Gladys Peters. She was roundfaced, a bit chubby, open-hearted, and ready to smile for almost any reason. At one point during the first evening at the Dowds' she said, "I guess I was too simple to be too concerned, I mean, to join the party. I suppose I never was more than a Socialist, a Norman Thomas Socialist, but I was afraid to say so. You know, Norman Thomas was a dirty word for a long time. My father was a Congregational minister—that's how Hal and I met. Hal was a minister for a while, as he told you, and went to a regional meeting in Cape Cod, Edgartown, a beautiful place. I was with Father, I don't remember the reason now."

Hal interrupted her. "You were going to the Burdett Business College in Boston, remember? You came down to visit your father, that was when he had his church in Worcester, I think."

111

"No, he had his church then at Springfield," she said, smiling, as if asking her husband's forgiveness for disagreeing with him. "But you are right, absolutely right, that I went to the Burdett Business College. It was on the same street."

"Dartmouth," Hal reminded her.

Again she smiled. "That is right. Hal has such a remarkable memory. And the college was only a few doors away from a lovely old Congregational church called, strangely enough, the New Old South Church. I liked to sit there, it's so quiet and comforting."

She looked at Ruth, who couldn't imagine that this gentle, placid woman ever needed comforting.

Gladys continued, "I used to go to hear John Havnes Holmes and a Boston Community Church leader, I think his name was Skinner, and I liked their kind of interest in social questions. I guess being a minister's daughter, I appreciate references to the Bible and religious writings in general. Some times Scott Nearing came to the Community Church meetings and I liked what he said. He wasn't extreme, and, frankly, when the Communists denounced him as a lackey or something like that, I knew I didn't want to be with them. I did vote for Norman Thomas several times, and I thought Jasper McLevy of Bridgeport was a good man, and I think I handed out leaflets for him once in Boston. I don't know what good that did, he was running for office in Bridgeport, not in Boston, but there were some people at this New Old South Church who were interested in Mr. McLevy. They asked me if I would help, so I said yes. I guess I'm not the philosophical kind. That's Hal's strong point."

"Well," said Hal, "she's exaggerating my competence and underestimating her own understanding. Her common sense sees things more clearly than all my reading."

"Oh, shush," said Gladys. "I haven't read a book on politics or economics all the way through in all my life. I sort of try to grasp things like a woman, don't you, Ruth?"

"I think I do. I don't always understand what Malcolm is saying, but I guess at it, and I know he's right. This may come as a surprise to Malcolm, but I, too, have never read a book on economics or politics all the way through. They're so dull. Malcolm, is that a terrible thing to say, in company, too?"

She seemed genuinely disturbed, so Malcolm went over to her and kissed her. "It wasn't a terrible thing to say. Most of those books are dull."

"Isn't that a fact?" said Gladys. "Right after we were married, Hal gave me a book by Bertrand Russell, *Roads to Reconstruction,* I think it's called, is that right, dear?"

Hal shook his head. "I'm afraid I don't remember."

"Well, Hal told me he was clear and sensible, but he kept on saying the same thing over and over again, and, as I recall it—this may sound strange—while he was clear he made many really complicated things too clear, I mean he didn't answer difficult questions. He was for premarital sex, and he gave reasons: women are as free as men and should have the same privileges. But that's not true. Women are not the same as men, and women can't do all the same things as men do. Every woman knows that; his own wife could have told him."

"Which wife?" asked Malcolm.

"As a matter of fact," said Hal, "it was Gladys who made me rethink my position. I did a terrible thing. I used to tell Gladys what went on at our meetings, how there was little real discussion and how I was afraid to disagree with what was being said about the Soviet Union, and I didn't like Stalin's brutality. The first time I questioned Stalin's wisdom I was called naïve and juvenile, but I was forgiven. I had just become a member. I didn't like what they said about all the Christian churches. I knew my own church, the Congregational Church, was doing a great deal for the poor and for clean politics, but again I didn't dare to talk. And I didn't like the anti-Semitism in Russia. Russia always was anti-Semitic, and the part of the Constitution that guaranteed freedom of worship is a joke, of course, and the Jews are oppressed and killed, but I didn't mention these things. Gladys, God bless her, used to get outraged. She would say, 'Then why do you stay on? That's plain fascism or dictatorship, or whatever you want to call it.' Well, I was hesitant, but Gladys kept on arguing with me, I mean giving me her own ideas, and I'm glad she did. So, you know, that's how it happened. I finally got up enough courage to do what, subconsciously, I always wanted to do, and that Gladys always wanted me to do."

Gladys looked affectionately at Hal, then she turned to Ruth:

113

"Women don't know as much as men do, but they're more direct, don't you think so? I guess they don't respect authority so much; isn't that so, Ruth?"

"Yes and no, Gladys. I really don't know much. Malcolm and his mother helped me out of my lostness, if there is such a word. He put doubts in my mind, and his mother did, too."

"I sometimes think," said Hal thoughtfully, "that it was the Communist attack on the church, I mean all religion, not just the Christian Church—I mean the Jewish synagogue, and all religions. Having been a minister for a short while, I saw how really socially conscious the Church, in the main, always has been. Oh, some elements of the Church, in Russia, where I think it is accurate to say it always was anti-Semitic. And the Catholic Church, of course many of the popes have been anti-Semitic, and many cardinals and ordinary priests, that's true; and I am obliged to say that the Protestant churches have often worked hand in hand with exploiters. All that is true, but always there was a strong element, at least in the Protestant Church, that fought evils in society. After all, it was the Congregational and Universalist and Unitarian churches in New England that were among the first to come out against slavery. Norman Thomas is a minister. Oh, yes, Rabbi Stephen Wise was in the forefront in the fight to get Mayor Jimmy Walker out of office, and he also organized marches and help for the strikers in Gastonia and in Paterson and in Passaic. I think he also did a good deal for the Scottsboro Boys. The Protestant Church is always mindful of the social gospel. Jesus was a revolutionary. There's no doubt about that. Every Christian minister or priest always has this on his conscience. And the Old Testament is an outline for profound social reform. Deuteronomy is full of socialism, for the protection of the rights of laborers, against all kinds of exploitation of workers and of women, and it is for community welfare. One of the things that I always remember, it's strange about such things. This, I think, is not actually in the Old Testament. But it is in the Talmud or in the writings of one of the great rabbis, anyway, it flows naturally out of the Old Testament. This rabbi said that if an orphan girl is about to be married, and she hasn't the wherewithal to arrange her wedding, it is the obligation of the community to arrange the wedding for her, and also the dowry, I think. It calls that a great *mitzvah,* isn't that what they call it?—a good deed, Malcolm?"

"A *mitzvah,*" said Malcolm, "is more than a good deed. My father once explained it to me this way. He said a *mitzvah* is a good deed done with music, with a glad heart."

"Another thing I remember," said Hal. "I heard Rabbi Stephen Wise himself say it once, from the pulpit in Carnegie Hall, where his temple used to be. I used to go there even in my wild Communist days—toward the end, I must admit, and even then I went sort of secretly. I took Gladys there when I was courting her."

"I just loved Rabbi Wise," said Gladys. "I know some people called him overdramatic, sensational, but I didn't think so. I spoke to my father about him. My father liked him a lot. When I brought up the matter of sensationalism, he said that a preacher sometimes has to be sensational. After all, the Hebrew prophets didn't mince words, and they used pretty strong language."

"One of the things I especially remember Rabbi Wise saying is that among the Jews there is no word for what 'charity' means to us. The word *tsedokeh,* I somehow remember the word, doesn't mean charity, it means justice. And that fact alone says worlds about the Jewish concept of social justice."

"The one thing my father used to say about the Communists," said Gladys, "the thing that riles him a great deal, naturally, he being a minister, is what they didn't say about the Psalms and the stories of Ruth and Esther. Father called the Psalms the most beautiful poems ever written, in any religion, in any language, but the Communists never mentioned them. He said, if they want to be against religion, well, they can be, but you can't ignore the Psalms and the Song of Songs."

"Oh, in literature," said Hal, "the Russian critics of today are pretty terrible, and the censorship there is just dreadful. There's no such things as honest literary criticism there. But I'm not one to talk," he quickly added. "I remember saying one day, in a little restaurant in Greenwich Village, to David Polonsky, a classmate of mine at Harvard, who was or still is on the *American World,* sure, he still is, I saw his name on it somewhere. I told him that Flaubert's *Madame Bovary* was a bad novel because it was a glorification of middle-class values, and—

listen to this—that Gustav Flaubert was a bad novelist, an enemy of the workers, and all that. This is hard to live down. David is a quiet sort of man. He only looked at me with his myopic eyes and said, so that you could hardly hear him across the table, 'You can't mean that, Hal, you can't mean that! you're too intelligent.' "

"That worries him a great deal," said Gladys.

"It should," said Malcolm. "I have plenty to forget, too."

When the Dowds left, Ruth said, "They are the most wonderful people. After the sort I've known at meetings, they're a joy, a real joy. We can say anything we like, whether we agree or not, and we don't have to be afraid. I realize more and more in what a prison I've lived. They're so easy to talk to, just to have around. I think I'll call up Gladys in a couple of days, for shopping or something. I could have your mother or my mother come over and baby-sit, just for a couple of hours."

"I'm glad," said Malcolm. "I knew you'd like them."

David recalled a great deal about Hal from their Harvard days together and also later. As a matter of fact, David had accepted two or three articles for the *World* from Hal, before he became a Communist. Shortly after graduating from Harvard, he had stayed on for a master's, then went to the Union Theological Seminary. He got a post as a minister at a small Congregational church in Worcester, where he taught English for a while at Clark University, and later at Northampton, where he taught English for a while at Smith College. The two had corresponded right along. They became friends at Harvard, where they attended some classes together. David remembered especially the class in metaphysics that both took in their sophomore year. The instructor was Professor William Ernest Hocking, an eminent Roycean idealist. David took the course for no special reason. He was pretty much a lost soul at Harvard during all his four years. At one time in his stay there he thought of becoming a professor of philosophy, and that was how he came to take the Hocking course. He soon learned that he had made a mistake. Professor Hocking was a poor teacher. He mumbled into his mustache so that nobody was quite sure of what he was saying. David was also disappointed by Hocking's attitude: He

116

seemed to want to rush through the class, and didn't answer questions fully. David at the time was inclined toward the views of Kant and Hegel and Bishop Berkeley in the realm of metaphysics, but he thought that Hocking was unfair to the realists, especially to Bertrand Russell, whom he called sneeringly, "a common-sense metaphysician." David once asked Professor Hocking, "The human race has been assuming the existence of physical matter, without a Perceptor or Divinity, for hundreds and thousands of years, well, at least five thousand years, and the assumption has proved correct. Why then can't we assume that matter exists independently of a perceiver? What more proof do you need? I think statisticians would say that was pretty good evidence."

Professor Hocking said, "Mathematically, you are right, Mr. Polonsky, but logically you are wrong. It's possible for people to live by a wrong assumption for eternity and yet for that assumption to be wrong, as I have said."

David became a little angry at this cavalier answer. "But, Professor, isn't that stretching logic a little too far?"

"Logic is logic," snapped Professor Hocking.

After class Hal and David discussed the matter. "That was no way to answer a fair question," said David.

"He probably had a tiff with his wife this morning," said Hal, smiling. "I hear she wears the pants."

Another time Hal asked David, "Do you know what you will do after you get your degree?"

"I have no idea whatever. Actually, all I want to do is read and write, but I'm afraid to tell my father. I know what he'd say to me."

"What would he say?"

"He'd say, 'From that you can't make a living.' As a matter of fact, I don't even know what to major in, and it's getting late to decide."

Hal said he was torn between a desire to teach English and entering the Congregational ministry. "It's an easy faith to tie up with; the creed part is pretty loose, but the social gospel, the ethics part, rather appeals to me. I might become a Unitarian, though, but I'm not so sure. They're too bland. I like a little magic in my religion, and Congregationalism just has enough for me."

Hal and David took a seminar together dealing with "Social Problems in a Troubled World," conducted by Dr. Niles Carpenter, a young instructor in the social ethics department. Dr. Carpenter was rather green as a teacher and not overly blessed with sympathetic insight into the problems he was dealing with or with the yearnings for social reform among young students. There was an evening—the class met once a week between six and eight—when the question of "justice of property ownership" came up. Dr. Carpenter stated that the concept of ownership of property had gone through a long evolutionary history; that at the beginning all property was communally owned; that later, with the rise of the family, it became family-owned; that still later it became "power-owned," that is, "those who were stronger took what they wanted, and kept it, and those who were weaker were, in effect, the slaves of these stronger ones"; that during the Middle Ages especially the Roman Catholic Church was one of the largest property owners, laying claim to its right by both conquest and "spiritual privilege"; and that with the rise of capitalism there emerged for the first time, on a large scale, individual ownership: "people owned what they had a so-called right to—the right of purchase, the right of bequest, or the right of discovery or invention."

All this looked like a simplification of something far more complicated, but the students were stumped as to how to phrase their questions. Hal and David, however, were not so much worried about the accuracy of Dr. Carpenter's rapid historical survey; they were more concerned with the "morality of property ownership." Hal, who was far better informed on the subject than David, asked simply, "What right has anybody to any property?"

Dr. Carpenter smiled. "That is in line with Proudhon's epigram: All property is theft."

David couldn't help smiling at this concept as it applied to his own family. He said, "Take a family with two parents and seven children, where the father has property totaling maybe $100—the shoes and clothing and furniture of the house, plus the savings account, if any—and this obviously is very little property for so large a family. The father is a decent man and works hard, but he can never really make enough for his family,

118

especially when, in the work he does, tailoring, he is unemployed a total of about ten weeks a year, at the very least. Now would you say this man's property is theft?" David, of course, was describing his own father's situation.

"That's an extreme state of affairs—" began Dr. Carpenter. Hal interrupted him. "It's not extreme at all. I've been reading the latest edition of the department of labor statistics of the United States Department of Labor, or maybe it's the Census Bureau, and there it says that nearly one-third of the families of the nation, where the adults are all working, mind you, one third of these families live on a below minimum subsistence level."

"How do they live then?" asked Dr. Carpenter.

This naïve question riled Hal and David and the rest of the class. Hal took up the cudgels for them. "How do they live? They live the way the poor have lived down the ages. They eat potatoes, they eat bread, they eat rice, they have almost no entertainment, they wear the same clothes year in and year out, patching and refitting and mending, and they wear hand-me-down shoes and clothes. That's existing, not living. Now, in line with what David said, would you call their property theft? Isn't the theft the other way around?"

Dr. Carpenter was a bit hurt by the implication that he, the instructor in the class, was uninformed. He had been trying to open up the subject for class discussion. Obviously he had done it crudely. Unwittingly he had turned the discussion into a none too subtle personal attack upon himself. He decided to try another approach: "You have now raised an important social question, Hal, a very important one. It is, of course, the basic question of what the individual contributes to the acquisition of his property, what the community does, or if you will, whether all private ownership, I mean, of course, private ownership on a large scale, the kind of property that the Rockerfellers have and the Astors and the Carnegies, I don't mean the few sad belongings of the silent majority of the poor and destitute. The question is whether any large-scale property isn't illegal and immoral and antisocial."

A third student brought up the question of the philosophy of the Single Tax.

"Henry George thought profoundly along these lines," said

Dr. Carpenter. "I'm not ready to say he had the solution to all the problems of present-day society, but he did bring up many new questions."

Hal was still annoyed by what he considered Dr. Carpenter's basic evasion of the central problem: the morality or immorality of ownership per se. "Of course, Henry George was important," he said, in a tone that was a bit exasperated. "The Astor family long ago bought a small piece of land where the Grand Central Station in New York now is. Through no effort on their own, the location boomed into one of the most valuable pieces of real estate in the world. Of course, the Astor heirs shouldn't reap all the profits of that land. I go further than Henry George. We don't need a Single Tax. We should confiscate all the profits. The City of New York created these profits, the City of New York has a right to all of these profits."

A fourth student asked, "That may be so, but would this kind of confiscation, this kind of enlarged Single Tax solve all our problems? Would the income to the state got this way be enough to give the minimum of civilized life to all the people?"

"I doubt it," said Hal. "I doubt it very much. That's why the Single Tax concept is only a drop in the bucket, a palliative. We need something more radical, more drastic."

"Like socialism?" said David.

"Or communism?" put in the third student.

"Those are good questions, too," said Dr. Carpenter.

The whole class was annoyed by the patronizing tone of Dr. Carpenter's last remark. But Hal was annoyed with the whole class, including David, who had never before seen him so perturbed. "Well, yes, why not socialism or communism? They are not the invention of the devil. There's plenty of socialism in the Bible. Read Westermarck and Briffault. There's been plenty of socialism in primitive societies and in many societies now, in some parts of Latin America, in the South Sea Islands."

"In some of these islands there's also social ownership of wives," said a fifth student.

The class smiled, but not Hal. "Wives are different," he said glumly. It suddenly occurred to David that Hal was not overly blessed with a sense of humor, that he was obstinate and possibly also a bit discourteous. Dr. Carpenter was not a ball of fire as a teacher or as a scholar, but he was their teacher and he deserved ordinary respect, which Hal appeared reluctant to give him.

"Wives certainly are different," said Dr. Carpenter. "Ask the man who's been married two or three times—"

The fifth student interrupted: "I read in a book of psychology that when a man marries more than one wife, or more than two, he is really marrying the same woman under different names. Men incline to marry the same kind of neurotics or slobs all the time, and women marry the same kind of, well, men, you know."

Hal would not be put off any more. He plunged right in; he must have his say. "I don't like the words socialism or communism. They're inflammatory words. They're like the color red to a bull. I prefer the word collectivism. What's wrong in the collective ownership of public utilities? Why should we have to pay exorbitant rates to Boston Edison and the Western Union? In France and Italy the government owns the public utilities and the telephone and telegraph. There's also the railroads, of course. The government should own those, too. The Scandinavian countries are way ahead of us on all these points; they're way ahead of France and Italy and England. As a matter of fact, they have something even more revolutionary. They have social welfare. Roughly, this means that medical care is provided by the state, in many cases, and there is old age care. The state takes care of a lot of this, and will probably take care of more in the near future."

"It might interest you to know, Hal," said Dr. Carpenter— "I mention this only as an interesting sidelight, I'm not sure of its significance myself—that the suicide rate in Sweden is the highest in the world."

Hal was angry. "What does that prove?"

"I don't know that it proves anything," said Dr. Carpenter. "I only meant that it's something worth keeping in mind. I can participate in this discussion, can't I?" He realized at once that this was the wrong thing to say, but he also realized that if he apologized he would only intensify the atmosphere of the class.

Hal made things still worse by ignoring Dr. Carpenter's comment altogether. "The basic theory of what's going on in Russia

121

now seems sensible enough. Give everybody, that is, have the state give everybody the minimum needs for existence: a roof, food, recreation. If anybody serves the state in a special way, as a scientist, as a teacher, as an inventor, he gets more. The important thing is to make public service honorable and rewarding."

"Doesn't that put a money tag on public service? A person discovered something, so he gets more fruit, or an extra suit. Isn't this a little—well, degrading is the wrong word—but is there something wrong there?"

For the first time Hal smiled. "I guess that's what the theologians mean by original sin. People want some reward for extra effort. Honor, I suppose, isn't enough. But that is a special problem. I'm talking about the basic idea. I think it's sensible. Much more so than having multi-millionaires, a handful of them, and millions and millions of sharecroppers and city paupers and sickness and hunger. Anyway, I think it's a lot better."

"What about civil liberties?" asked Dr. Carpenter.

"What about them?" said Hal.

"The newspapers are full of instances of censorship and suppression of views opposed to the present rulers, especially Stalin and his gang. Trotsky appears to be in disfavor, but he is no better philosophically. Criticizing the government in Russia is a risky business."

Hal sighed, as if to say he had heard all this stale stuff. "Civil liberties? I've read about it in *The New York Times*. I don't believe everything in the *Times*. Besides, what sort of civil liberties have we in the United States? Did you read Upton Sinclair's *The Brass Check?*"

"What about it?" asked Dr. Carpenter.

"What about it?" echoed Hal. "There's very little real freedom of speech over here. Take the department stores. If there's a fire in one of them, and that store advertises a lot, you'll see no mention of the fire in any newspaper. And if the son of any other big advertiser, or the son of the president of any big department store, any relative of a big-money man, gets into trouble and is arrested or found guilty, the newspapers will say nothing about it. Is that what you would call a free press? And what about the partial covering, the biased covering of strikes and union matters in general? Capital is treated with respect but labor is treated with contempt or ignored completely. So we ought to be careful when we criticize Russia on this issue. We're just as guilty."

David felt he had to say something, even though he knew that Hal wouldn't like what he had to say. He hadn't known till this very night how deeply involved in radical thinking Hal was. David said, "I didn't read all of *The Brass Check*. I thought it was pretty dull and shrill. But I am willing to grant the basic truth of his central thesis. The press has been corrupt to a great extent, maybe a very great extent. But I do think it is getting better, thanks, in part, maybe to Sinclair's book. Yes, he deserves much credit, and thanks also to the growing number of schools of journalism. Whatever the reason, the press is improving. But the point I want to make is that even with this far-from-perfect press, there is room in this country for newspapers and magazines that do print news about big department store fires and the trouble that the children of the rich get into. And there are *The Nation* and the *New Republic* and *The Appeal to Reason* and many other magazines; yes, there used to be *McClure's* and *Everybody's* and the early *Cosmopolitan* where some very severe criticisms have been made of big companies, like Standard Oil and the Rockefeller moneys in general, and the Robber Barons of the railroads. And the newspapers did expose the Teapot Dome scandal of the Harding administration, and it did come out that Harding had a mistress in the White House and that Albert Fall, the Secretary of the Interior, was a bribe taker. I could go on and on. Bad as we are in this country, in journalism, we are a lot better than it is in Soviet Russia."

"These are all minor matters," said Hal.

"Minor, my left foot," said the third student. "They're very important."

It was obvious that David's remarks had shaken Hal. So he decided to try another argument. "Granted that democracy is not perfect in Russia, we must take into consideration the fact that it is surrounded by enemies, and has to protect itself from the lies of the capitalist countries."

"That's a dangerous argument for any government to use," said David. "Mussolini is using pretty much the same argument to suppress free speech in Italy, and the Catholic Church makes the same claim in insisting that its faithful not read the books on its Index. Only those who are afraid of the truth object to having it published. I'm for complete freedom of expression at all times. Oh, you brought up the matter of Russia now being surrounded by enemies. Others have claimed it needs time to get its house in order, and so on, and so it has to restrict freedom of expression. Apparently the principle there is that disagreement is disloyalty, that disagreement is treason. This is not only nonsense, it is a threat to all freedoms. You may call me a chauvinist, a naïve patriot, and things of that sort. Well, so I'm a chauvinist. But during the American Revolution the new country of the United States, what became the United States, had plenty of troubles from all over, especially England, and the other non-democratic countries were not too anxious to see a new type of government start over here. I know that France was friendly. My point is that there was trouble from abroad, insofar as the United States was concerned, and there was plenty of trouble right here. The minutes of the Continental Congress reveal what dissension there was. After all, Hamilton wanted a powerful central government while Jefferson and some others wanted little central government. I'm no authority in this area. But we all know there was serious disagreement. No one, I repeat no one, dared to muzzle the other point of view. The press was wide open, reporting everything. And the country not only survived, it flourished and grew and grew. That's the way I like it, and I don't see why it can't be the same in Russia now."

Hal was exasperated with David. "This is all so unrealistic."

David sensed that the friendship between him and Hal had suffered a severe jolt. Hal was moving more and more in the direction of "positive action" in the social realm, and his sympathies were clearly with Soviet Russia, with all its faults. He also appeared to be ready to overlook basic evils (evils in David's eyes, but relatively minor errors in Hal's eyes) with respect to civil rights if only "the greater public good" would be served and "practical results" would be achieved. To David this kind of approach was alien. He was "for the poor," of course, but he also was adamantly for democratic processes, and "prac-

124

tical results," to him, were of only temporary good. In short, Hal was moving in one direction, whereas David was moving in another. But they still saw each other.

At the time there was a department of Social Ethics at Harvard, of which the leading spirit was Dr. Richard Cabot, a former medical man who had come over to the study of the social welfare aspects of medicine. He was a kindly man, who, like so many New Englanders down the years, wanted "to do some good" in this world. Hal and David visited some of his classes and also attended some of his public lectures. David was not impressed, nor was he offended. Hal was deeply offended. He said, "This kind of palliative preaching only patches up evils. It doesn't get at the root of the problem of social living in the United States today, in the whole world, in fact. More serious measures are needed, if the world is to get anywhere."

"Serious measures like what?" asked David.

"Along the lines Russia is following. They're pioneering, so all kinds of rough edges are to be expected, but they have the right idea, I should think. Socialism is too tame for the world of modern capitalism."

Norman Thomas made one of his periodic lecture visits to Harvard and David wanted to hear him. Hal wouldn't come. "He's an innocent tool of the capitalists," said Hal, "and sometimes I'm not sure he's so innocent. In any case, what he says is hogwash." David did go to hear Thomas, and he was very much impressed by the man's knowledge and the persuasiveness of his views. He liked especially one part of his talk, which went something like this: "They say there is security in Soviet Russia. I am sure there is. There is also security in a prison. No amount of security is worth anything if you pay for it with the loss of civil liberties." David repeated this to Hal. Hal didn't even give David the courtesy of a rebuttal. "I knew he'd say that. He lives in the nineteenth century. Anyway, he's not worth talking about."

Cooling in their friendship began at once. They'd meet now and then in the college bookstore or in the campus, but did little more than exchange greetings. There were two exceptions. David used to find solace and comfort at Appleton Chapel, even more so when there was no service. The quiet seemed to be saying to him what he wanted to hear. All his college days, all his adolescent days he had an abiding fear of poverty, and especially of what would happen to the family if his father suddenly died . . . what would happen to his mother and to his brothers and sisters . . . what would happen to their education—all wanted to go to college—what would happen to his own education. Then there was David's bewilderment at Harvard. It was a disappointment to him in almost every respect. Nearly all the professors were mediocre teachers and revealed little genuine scholarship. Moreover, they seemed to lack the excitement of learning, the poetic joy in merely knowing. And there was the lack of deep friendship. David had looked forward to making friends with students who had his same general outlook and shared his yearning for the music of the mind and the delight of the heart, to whom the Harvard yard and the Harvard libraries and the Harvard lecture and concert halls would be a miniature paradise. He also missed female companionship. The Radcliffe girls appeared to be too shrill (at least that was so of those he met), or they belonged to wealthy families and behaved in a manner foreign to David. He wanted the company of girls who were young Queen Esthers or young Ruths and Naomis, and he had not met any.

There was, further, the matter of Jewishness. He was deeply drawn to it, he could almost hear it sing in his blood vessels, but some of the dogmas troubled him, which he didn't dare to discuss with his father, who already had many grave doubts about David's orthodoxy. The questions that coursed through David's mind were the old ones: Is *kashruth* essential to being a Jew? Is praying three times a day essential? Is Reform Judaism truly a form of "covered-up" Christianity, as his father once said? Does the wearing of *tsitses* make one a better Jew? What sense is there in the rule that one must wait six hours after eating meat before partaking of dairy products? There was one aspect of Jewishness that David never had any doubts about, namely, Zionism. He accepted it the way he accepted his breathing, his walking, his digestive processes. But even here there was a problem. His home was divided on this issue: His mother was ardently Zionist, while his father looked upon it as a form of atheism, not exactly atheism, but surely not genuine Judaism. David sided with his mother, but it was disturbing to know that his father was against it. Father, more or less, waited for the Messiah to come in on a white donkey, as tradition would have it. When David wanted to discuss some Zionist news item, he waited till his father was out of the house, and then discussed it with his mother. He didn't like this evasiveness, nor did his mother, he was sure. Yet neither knew what to do about it. Just being in Appleton Chapel in the middle of the day or in the evening made David feel more at ease with himself and with the world.

One afternoon David went into Appleton Chapel and sat in a back pew. Only three other persons were present, up front. Two soon departed, leaving only one. David couldn't see who the person was, except that it was a man. Then, when that person turned, David recognized Hal. He was glad to be alone with Hal in the quiet chapel, though he didn't know why. Hal appeared more his old self; his belligerency seemed to be a matter of the past, and in spite of all that had happened between them he felt close to him now. Both sat there for another fifteen minutes, then Hal got up and walked back, up the aisle. Their eyes met, and David joined him.

Outside, they looked at each other shyly. They were glad to see each other. They hadn't met in weeks. "Let's sit down on the steps of the physics building," said Hal.

"Fine."

"I made up my mind about something in that chapel," said Hal.

"About what?"

"I'll go in for the ministry, at the Union Theological in New York. It's freer there, more concerned with the social gospel. Harry Ward's there; you know him, don't you?"

"Yes. He's involved with all sorts of causes."

"Very much so. To him religion is not merely believing in things, it's in doing things. I like that."

"Yes. I'm afraid I didn't make up my mind about anything," said David. "I don't really know what I want to do, as I've told you before. But I like that chapel. I go in all perturbed about many things, some of which are not even clear in my own mind, and I go out feeling fine. I try to go there Friday afternoon, late Friday afternoon, when the organist rehearses for the Sunday services, I suppose. It's wonderful then. The music seems to float all around and come down from the sky and go right into me, and then glide out." David began to smile.

"Why are you smiling?"

"Oh, I didn't mean to smile. I was thinking about my father. He wouldn't like it if he knew I went into a church to get rest and peace. He'd like it if I went into a synagogue, not when nobody is there, but when services are going on. Well, I don't know of any synagogue nearby. The Jews have yet to learn from the Christians—I don't imagine there are synagogues that stay open all day for rest, prayer, and meditation, as the signs say outside the churches. That's a good idea. Then, this church, this chapel is not Christian, in a sense. It's nondenominational; rabbis and priests and ministers have preached there."

"That's true," said Hal, "but I guess you could say it's sort of Unitarian or Congregational, at least so it was two hundred years ago, or maybe longer, but it's just a house of worship for everybody, I guess. Anyway, I like it for the same reasons you like it. It's restful." He stopped. "My radical friends wouldn't like it that I went to church for rest and meditation. And I guess they wouldn't like it either if they knew that when I go to chapel I sometimes pray silently. I see nothing wrong in it. I confess I have a need for it."

David was glad to hear this. This is the Hal whom he was drawn to at first, but he wondered which Hal would win out in the end: this gentle, honest, warm person, or the storming belligerent one. "I can't say I pray silently," said David. "But I do sometimes pick up a hymnal and read two or three of the Psalms. They're tremendous. And sometimes I open up the New Testament, not often I must say, and read the Sermon on the Mount. That's fine. But I have to add that some parts are violently anti-Semitic. If I remember correctly, St. John's Gospel refers to the Jews as the sons of the Devil, and Matthew teems with anti-Semitic phrases."

"I know. All who ever took the trouble to read the New Testament carefully have noticed this. I believe somebody has counted at least a hundred anti-Semitic references in the New Testament. What can be done about it? I don't know. These references are horrible, naturally, and should be repudiated. But there are some wonderful things in the New Testamnt, too. The Gospel of Luke is really very good; so are some of St.

Paul's letters or epistles, as they are called. It's these parts that have appealed to the poets and the other great writers. You know Donne?"

"John Donne. Of course. His sermons are marvelous. With a few changes here and there, Jews could accept them."

"Of course. And William Blake and Dean Swift and the Bishop of Chichester. They were drawn to the Bible, to both parts, but I guess I have to admit that it was the sheer warmth and humanity of the Old Testament that drew them most. I tell you frankly, David, that I always feel a little strange with my radical friends—and you probably know by now that I see many of them—when they talk about helping the workers and raising wages and improving working conditions. All this is fine, but doing something for the soul is also fine, and there's so much good in the Bible and in what the churches do, but they don't see it, they don't even discuss it. And if I used the word soul in front of them they'd laugh at me and think I belonged to the Middle Ages. You know something, David?"

"What?"

"I'd like to be like some of the old New England preachers, especially a man like Theodore Parker, one of the principal thinkers of the Community Church movement in the United States, a really marvelous man. Well, I'd like to be a sort of combination of Parker and Ralph Waldo Emerson. That's why I'm going to the Union Theological Seminary."

"I wish I were as sure as you are, Hal, about what I want to do. I'm so mixed up and worried about so many things."

Hal smiled. Then he said, "You have all the qualifications for being a writer: confusion, sensitivity, bewilderment. You'll be a poet and fiction writer. I can see it. I want to be that also, I admit, but I want to be more active, out in the field. I may end up as a minister and an English teacher. That's what my parents said to me only recently. You're a two-engine man, said my father."

"Maybe I shouldn't say it, but I hope you do become a two-engine man, as your father says. Why be a one-engine man?"

"That's right, why?"

"Right now, I'm a no-engine man," said David.

"There's no such thing," said Hal. "You may be one of those late developers, or late finder-outers."

"Well, we'll see what we'll see," said David. "That's one of the pleasures of being young, and one of the pains: you don't know what's facing you."

There was the time, a month before commencement, when David was walking along the Charles River, not far from the Stadium. He had time on his hands, but as usual he was troubled by all sorts of vague fears and yearnings and hazy memories. He saw a man in the distance, sitting on the shore, not far from the water. He was throwing pebbles into the river. David approached and saw it was Hal. He came to him and sat down by his side. "Are you trying to upset the tides?"

"I wish I could," said Hal, "though I don't know why I want to upset the tides or anything else. I have a fear, though, I'm going in for a life of upsetting people and organizations. I feel compelled to do it, and I also feel something else."

"What?"

"Well, to put it simply, I feel drawn to the life of contemplation. I guess I can't have it both ways."

"Some people have done it," said David.

"Who?"

"Charles Darwin and Sigmund Freud and Karl Marx." David almost said "your Karl Marx," and he was glad he didn't.

"Yes, that's true. But there's one trouble. I'm not Darwin or Freud or Marx. I'm in a smaller league, a very much smaller league. It has just occurred to me that if I could be anybody, even remotely, it would be Bertrand Russell. But that's out, too. I can't write as well as he does, I'm not a mathematician, and, well, he's really superficial. I think it was Lenin who called him an elementary school teacher. He's better than that, but not very much. Then there's something else. I want to be out on the picket line and read and teach John Donne at the same time. What a combination that is!"

"I have one advantage over you, Hal, and one disadvantage. I'm not pushed any way. I'll just drift along, I guess."

"Oh, you'll get your bearings."

David felt playful and glad that Hal was in this non-Marxist, nonbelligerent mood. "Maybe I don't want to get my bearings," he said.

130

Hal smiled. "You may be right."

"Now that I think of it, what's wrong in drifting?"

Hal looked at him, only a little startled.

David continued. "Take this Charles River, a fine old river, of long duration. Would you say it's five hundred years old?"

Hal joined the playfulness. "It could be even older, say five hundred and ten years old."

"Very good. I'll settle for 150,000 years. Actually, it's probably much older, as rivers go in this world. Rivers live a long time, they just go rolling along, paying no attention to anything."

"Good. I'll settle for 150,000 years," said Hal, "give a few years either way."

"And this grand old Charles River has been drifting all this time, and yet it's doing all right, isn't it?"

"I guess it is, come to think of it."

"So what's wrong with drifting?"

"Nothing, I guess," said Hal. "But seriously, I got other problems. Very ordinary ones, even commonplace, and I am puzzled. My mind is clear on them, but the heart . . . My parents are involved . . . and a girl."

"A girl?"

"Yes, a girl, a really fine girl. In her foolishness, she thinks the world of me. She's the daughter of a doctor that my father knows, and I have been seeing her now and then, when I get home to Amesbury—that's old John Greenleaf Whittier's home. She's going to some normal school, is a substitute teacher now, and will become a full-time teacher next year. My parents think she'd make me a good wife. I'm stumped. I have nothing against her. Well, I have, I guess. She knows nothing—you know what I mean? She likes everything I like, and if I change my mind she changes hers. She's not stupid, though. I suppose she's a good cook, will probably make a good mother. And another thing— I don't imagine my parents overlooked that—her father is rich. His doctoring is only a sideline. He's in real estate, and has stock in all sorts of things. She's an only child, too. Oh, she kisses well. But tell me this, David, why should I get married?"

"I don't know why or why not."

"I suppose eventually I'll get married and so will you. But this is too secure, too safe, and there are days and weeks when

I don't think of her. She writes me two letters a week, like a clock, and I write her one letter in three weeks, and I don't know what to say to fill more than one page. I think I'll give her the cold shoulder, slowly, of course. But I can just see her face when the truth dawns on her. She'll ask me, 'Don't you like me? I thought you did.' And my parents will want to know why I won't marry her, and what can I tell them? If I tell them the truth, they'll think I'm crazy. She'll probably come for Commencement, and I suppose her parents will come, too. My parents will probably invite them, probably already have. Only as friends, of course, nothing more. Do you blame me for being worried? But I've got an out."

"What?" asked David, who now saw an aspect in Hal that he had not known before, and he liked it.

"As I told you, I'm going to the Union Theological Seminary in New York. I'll be away from her, and maybe things will cool off, eh?"

David smiled. "You don't believe that, do you?"

"I guess not."

"So what are you going to do?"

"Well, David, one thing I won't do, I won't marry her. What would I do with a wife now?"

"Have you given a hint to your parents?"

"I have, but what do you think my mother and father say when I hint to them?"

"What?"

"They say every young man is full of hesitations as he approaches marriage; what do you think of that?"

"I don't know what to say, Hal."

"So that's what's worrying me now, one of the hundreds of things. Of course," Hal said, hesitating, "I could tell her that I'm thinking of joining the Communist party, which I may do, and she would then run away like from a case of leprosy. What do you think of that for a way out?"

"Are you sure she'd run away?"

Hal smiled. "I'm not. She would probably only lower her eyes, and say, 'If that's what you want, darling, then that's what you want.' Of course, she wouldn't mean it. But a wife's love, you know. What I want to know is how I got into this mess.

I'd see her because I didn't know how to say no, and she is pleasant, and one thing led to another, and here I am. There's no engagement, nothing of the sort, but the two sets of parents are acting as if everything is set. And I know Geraldine, that's her name, is seeing nobody else."

"Did she tell you that?"

"No. But I know. She's that kind of girl."

"Oh."

"I feel hemmed in, with walls all around me. Trapped."

"I can see that."

"I just can't hurt the girl. Geraldine is really fine, but not for me, and not now. Last Thanksgiving I was at her home, and my parents were there too—the families have been friends for years. So on the surface it looked nothing out of the ordinary, nothing special. But what do you think she said to me when we were alone after dinner?"

"I don't know. What?"

"Guess."

"That she liked you?"

"She tells me that all the time, but this was something different. She said, 'Darling, we both have something to be thankful for, haven't we?' I was stunned, really. What could I say? My face got hot and sweaty. I said yes, and I felt terrible. Now you understand."

"I'm afraid I do."

"Well, we'll see what we'll see," said Hal.

David met Geraldine at Commencement. She was short, slight, with a bland face. David wondered how this creature could be causing Hal all the anguish. He also met Hal's and Geraldine's parents, and again he wondered how these decent-looking people could have acquiesced in a developing situation that had placed Hal in a "trap." Hal appeared to be indifferent during the exercises. He said hardly anything to David. In fact, Hal's mind seemed far away from Cambridge, Massachusetts.

Hal did go to the Union Theological Seminary, taking the first degree in divinity. He got a post as Congregational minister in a small town in New Hampshire, then in a small town in western Massachusetts. From his brief letters, David got the impression that Hal had not been happy at either post. He continued to complain about his parishioners' lack of interest in social affairs. "They seem to be living in a vacuum, and from this come explosions." He added this ominous note: "The way I feel now I want to participate in these explosions." David knew what that meant.

A few months later David got a letter from him in which he cleared up two points that kept on disturbing David's mind. Hal wrote: "Perhaps I should tell you that Geraldine and I are not seeing each other any more. It was a painful thing, but as a minister I could not see myself entering into a relationship that would have been a lie from the very beginning. I did not tell her any of the fibs I told you I might use. Thank God for that. At least I can live with myself on that score. I don't like deception. And because I don't like deception I have to tell you something else, though you probably have suspected it right along. I am now a member of the Communist party. I hope this doesn't shock you too much. Much of what you said about the party is true, all too true. But parties, like religious organizations, are run by human beings, and human beings are fallible. I do believe that basically the Communist party is on the right track, and that in the future it will rectify many of its mistakes. I did have a struggle with my sense of ministerial obligation. The good Dr. Harry Ward, however, pointed out to me that there was no conflict between true, genuine Christianity and the movement for social betterment that the Communist party stands for. I intend to tell my parishioners, wherever I go, of my affiliation with the Communist party. My parents, I need not tell you, are heartsick about this, but they are decent people and are sticking by me. I am terribly sorry I am causing them worry on this score, as I caused them worry in connection with Geraldine—I cannot in all truth say that my conscience is entirely at peace with respect to her, a very lovely human being, indeed. But a man must live according to the truth as he sees it. I shall try to do this, come what may."

He added a postscript: "I must tell you that in the small towns of the United States, at least in Massachusetts and New Hampshire and Vermont, where I have served as a full minister or as an assistant minister, there is an undercurrent of what, I am sorry to say, has to be called anti-Semitism. They are all good people, and they would all be outraged if they were called basic anti-Semites, but they are. There are few Jews in these small towns of New England, but those few are living in an in-between world of acceptance and implied rejection. In one town, a bit of a place, the general store is owned by a Jew, a fine, decent man, with a fine, good wife. They have four daughters of college age, all very pretty. There are five other Jewish families, and all the socializing these families engage in is among themselves. I got to talking to the Jewish gentleman who runs the general store and he said that when they first moved in, the Christian neighbors were very kind, invited them over once, twice at the most, and no more. They're polite in the street, and in public matters, school committee meetings, town meetings, and so on, they greet each other warmly, and that's all. As he said, 'We Jews always have a five o'clock curfew, as far as social-izing with Christians is concerned.' Well, there are no such troubles in Soviet Russia. There the record is very good, you have to admit that yourself."

David was annoyed by this letter. It was friendly, but it also revealed a naïveté on the part of Hal who was, after all, a Phi Beta Kappa man. The Stalin purge of the Jewish doctors in the late thirties indicated to the whole world that Stalin, a former seminarian in the Russian Orthodox Church, was violently anti-Semitic, that Jewish seminaries in Russia were entirely abolished, that all Jewish education was virtually also abolished, that Jews alone were listed according to religion on their identification cards. David hesitated writing this to Hal. He didn't want to start an argument in the mails. Then he did write to him, admonishing him for his lack of information and lack of intelligent evaluation. A month later he got a curt note from Hal. The key sentence in it was, "I think, David, we better not go into the matter of the situation in Soviet Russia. You think I'm naïve, obviously, and I think you're duped by the capitalist press, and you're probably also oversensitive on the Jewish issue. You have a right to be concerned, naturally, but you must view things in proper per-spective."

They did not correspond for years. Indirectly David heard that Hal had given up the ministry entirely: he had lost interest in the church as an instrument for social betterment, and there was also the fact that no congregation, however "liberal," wanted to accept as its spiritual leader an admitted Communist. For a while he taught English on the college level, and indeed had hoped to make this his vocation. But he preached communism so openly and denounced the United States so violently that he found his academic standing jeopardized. He was refused reappointment at one college, and it was then, after all the years of silence between them, that Hal had written to David, who at the time was on the *Globe,* asking him to write an editorial in defense of academic freedom. "What I am going through now is a brazen example of capitalism's control of the intellectual activity of the institutions of higher learning." David did write an editorial, but it was merely factual, urging the colleges not to be afraid of fresh ideas but at the same time calling upon "left-wingers to exercise a greater regard for the fact that colleges and universities are a market place for ideas, not a place for the indoctrination of one body of ideas. Free and open discussion is one thing, and propagandizing is another."

Hal was dissatisfied with this "mealy-mouthed" editorial, but he did suggest that they meet again the next time he came to New York, "which I may make my home very soon." They met, and both were glad. David sensed that Hal already had some doubts about the discipline in the Communist party: "I sometimes say to them that they act like Jesuits, and they don't exactly like that." He also mentioned that he would probably be married soon. "She's no Geraldine. Her name is Gladys, and she's the daughter of a Congregational minister. Yes, I still belong to the church, though I must admit that I don't stress it at meetings of the party. I'll never leave the church. And I know I can trust you, so I'll tell you that Gladys is urging me to leave the party. She doesn't think they're democratic. Well, she has a right to her opinion. But I may marry her. I like her." Later, when David went to the *World,* he accepted two articles by Hal. Both were well-written, well documented analyses of the activities of some of the southern churches in the Ku Klux Klan movement. The evidence of involvement was appalling, and the articles brought forth good mail.

Though Hal was now living in New York, and though he

136

wrote frequently for the liberal and radical periodicals, he and David seldom met, except by accident on Fifth Avenue. Then he began to see Hal's name signed to reviews in *The New York Times Book Review* and also in the *Herald Tribune Books*. About this time he met him in a radical meeting place, a restaurant actually, called Moshe's Cubbyhole, and it was here that Hal had called Flaubert a lackey of capitalism and "a spokesman for decaying middle-class morality." David looked at him in dismay. He didn't believe he meant it, and he said so. Hal looked a little shame-faced, and he said, "I guess I am exaggerating a bit; still there's some truth in what I'm saying." David now was ready to believe that in the not too distant future Hal would leave, openly or otherwise, the Communist party. When David learned that Hal had married Gladys, he was sure that he would leave the party. Then, one morning, he read in *The New York Times* a violent denunciation of Hal by the American Communist Party. The moody, troubled, basically gentle Hal was called "a vicious betrayer of the cause of the working class, a snake in the grass, an enemy of all decency, a liar, a notorious example of intellectual expediency. It's quiet people like him who are most to be watched." Not long afterward, Hal published a novel about small-town life, dealing with his experiences as a minister. Then he published a book of literary criticism. Both were not too well received. Then Hal became a roving reviewer of books, a lecturer, and a teacher in the adult education division of Columbia University, where he met Malcolm Dowd.

seven

Simmons, of course, had his way with Malcolm Dowd and Hal Peters—and also with Langston Caxton Patton. The results of the writings of these three were pretty much as predicted by the other members of the staff of the *American World.* Actually, the articles by Dowd and Peters were not too bad; but the articles they had others write ("in line with our ideas") were pretty shrill. The articles by Patton were disastrous. Dowd contributed two sober analyses of "the American spirit," in terms of the "basic principles" of Samuel Adams and John Adams and "the early Alexander Hamilton," his general theme being that "all forms of collectivism for whatever ulterior laudable purposes" in the end worked against the common good. He wasn't too sure about "the long-term" value of the Income Tax or of any "form of government regulation beyond the rudimentary one of protecting the public from, let us say, tainted food or bad air," and he also was inclined to the minimum of social welfare activities, such as "caring for those who have no relatives to minister to them in their old age, or even extending the area of public hospitalization." Dowd called himself "a democratic

138

anarchist, with utter and unalterable emphasis upon civil liberties and individual freedoms." He was opposed to the New Deal "utterly [a favorite word of his] and for the same reasons used by the United States Supreme Court to outlaw the National Recovery Act." He was against the Fair Deal of President Truman, though not so violently. Dowd pointed out that "President Truman fought John L. Lewis, the Labor Baron, whereas President Roosevelt knuckled under to him. Therein lies the difference between the two deals, though both basically run counter to the direction of the American spirit."

Betty Gard didn't object too much to some points in this line of reasoning, but she did add that "it fails to take into account the whole trend toward the state taking over more of the functions formerly left to rugged individualism. Life is just too complicated now for the system of a hundred years ago. The idea of democratic anarchism is just a phrase. You can't have them both, democracy and anarchism; coupling them is a trick, a verbal trick, nothing more. I see nothing wrong in Social Security and Federal Deposit Insurance. I'm no historian or philosopher, as Dowd is, but I have a hunch the Adamses and even Hamilton would have applauded the New Deal and the Fair Deal, and would have thought Senator Taft was an old fogy, which is what I think he is; his whole school is old fogy. I don't see any diminution of civil liberties in this country because of the New Deal and Social Security. People who say that are just crazy, I mean it, just crazy. I don't mean to be personal, but it's crazy to think all this. As crazy as the New York *Daily News* that predicted that FDR would close down all the newspapers. They kept on being nasty to Eleanor Roosevelt and their dumb kids, and FDR didn't put them into jail. It's all so crazy."

The mail on the Dowd articles disturbed Simmons most. Even some of his "conservative" friends said that Dowd was "very learned, but he really makes no sense. He's talking about a dream world, and he's raising red herrings. America is still America, New Deal and all. The man lacks political imagination. His philosophical learning may be all right in the classroom, but when applied to the world of everyday it is pointless."

Simmons rather liked the Dowd articles. Deep down, as Peter

said, Simmons "would have felt most at home in the days of Adam Smith. The man is not heartless, he's just stupid. I sometimes wonder if he isn't afraid, deep in his unconscious, of the government taking away his money and his comforts. There's something very petty about him; he's shriveled through and through." But Simmons was a realist, and he sensed that the Dowd articles were not "doing the trick." The articles Dowd got others to do, along his line of thinking, were far worse. One man pleaded for a "return of technocracy," a silly philosophy that appeared to favor the rule of "technocratic cadres," meaning, it would seem (no one actually understood the technocratic jargon), the rule of scientific groups "guided and directed by men attuned to the needs of twentieth century society," as one of them said. Peter called this "a fancy word for simple and unadulterated fascism."

Betty said, "Who wants Mussolini in the United States? Even the Italians couldn't stand him."

Still another man that Dowd got favored abolishing popular suffrage and returning to "suffrage based on property, for that kind of suffrage brought forth the best brains and abilities. People with a stake in society vote more intelligently than people who have never been able to find a place for themselves in life." Betty's one comment on this was: "This kind of thinking is from the Ice Age or before." Even Simmons thought this was going too far.

Peters contributed two articles reappraising proletarian literature. Apparently his purpose was to confess to his critical mistakes in rating so highly novels by "proletarian authors who did not distinguish between a desire to help people and the ability to put down on paper the inner hopes and aspirations and despairs of the eternal man and the eternal woman, who have only fortuitous connection with proletarian status." It was unnecessary to say much about these articles. Simmons said it well: "We print this kind of stuff a little longer, and we'll have a dozen readers, all related to Hal Peters and his wife." David said hardly anything while discussion about these Dowd and Peters pieces was going on. He made it clear, however, by turning up his nose or silently assenting to what Betty and Peter said, that he saw no salvation in the Dowd-Peters articles. He thought to himself

140

that there was no salvation for the magazine at all. He began to wonder whether any editor, however great, could save the magazine. He became fatalistic about magazines. He was slowly developing a theory about magazines: They were like human beings, they had their childhood, adolescence, adulthood, senescence, and death, and no amount of medication could stave off the end. But he was greatly disturbed by the writings of Patton.

Everything that Betty and Peter had said about Patton seemed to be all too true. He was a man apparently without principles of any kind. He was widely published and widely condemned. At no time in the preceding three years was he without the threat of a libel suit hovering over him. Simmons had met him at one of the many parties he attended. Simmons was a great believer in the "usefulness" of parties. "That's where you meet the right sort of people," he claimed. "People get relaxed with a drink or two, they talk freely, and it's at parties, I believe, that you learn more about the state of the country and the whole world than anywhere else. Certainly you learn more at parties than you do out of books." Simmons was drawn to smooth talkers and ready smilers and those who simplified complex problems. Here, too, he had a theory: "I don't believe there's a problem in the world, in politics, in finance, in science, in any field whatever that cannot be solved quickly once all the facts are known, and I believe that the relevant facts are not many. Most problem-solvers get bogged down in too many facts."

Patton was a glib talker *par excellence*. He seldom hesitated when asked a question, and when he did answer he would bring up a "fact" that the listener had probably never heard of before. If the listener took the trouble to check the "fact" he would often find that it was totally wrong or only partly true, and that Patton's interpretation was based upon the assumption that it was totally correct. He was once asked by an instructor in psychology at a New York City college what he thought about the prevalent belief in psychological and anthropological circles that Negroes, as a group were not inferior intellectually to whites. "You come from the South," said the instructor, "and I wondered what your pragmatic judgment on this would be; after all, you have lived with Negroes, so you should know."

Patton smiled as usual, and said, "I know that theory. It's

only a theory, and not too well based on fact. It's a theory based upon a wish or a hope. I subject myself to being called a reactionary, I don't really care what people call me, but I believe in facing facts. My own experience leads me to think that Negroes are perfectly nice people. We've had them work for us for years; they're absolutely reliable, much more so than many white people we've had work for us. But about their higher intelligence, so to speak, I don't know. Have you ever talked to graduates of Tuskegee or of Southern University in Baton Rouge or even Howard University in Washington? Well, I have. They're bright, but their brightness stops at a certain point, and then you feel you're talking to a, well, ordinary man. I looked into this. I came across a study made of Negro intelligence as compared to white intelligence, published by the University of Manchester in England. I don't remember the name of the author exactly— he was a doctor of science—and his first name was Leslie, and the magazine was called *Royal Anthropological Abstracts,* or it may have been *British Anthropological Abstracts.* The issue of the magazine was the last one, so you should be able to get it in some good library. Well, this Dr. Leslie worked on his study for more than five years, making all kinds of tests on Negroes, in Jamaica, in Nigeria, in the Bahamas, in the smaller islands of the West Indies, and among some Negro people in southern Georgia. As I say, it was a very well-documented article, you don't expect me to remember the tables or the charts, but the conclusions I remember very well, and I give them to you in substance. He said unequivocally that Negroes reach a certain plateau of intellectual development and go no further as a group. And he said, in view of this, that it is no accident that Negroes the world over have produced nothing really superior in any of the arts in the past 150 years, as well as can be learned from available records. I believe that he says—no, I am sure, now that I think of it—that similar conclusions have been reached by other investigations by Germans and especially by French psychologists and anthropologists, who have had considerable dealings with Negroes in their widespread colonial empire, that is, their former colonial empire. I know this is not a pleasant conclusion, but science is science."

The instructor was surprised by this testimony. "I think I

know this journal you are speaking of, but I admit I haven't seen it for some time. I'll surely look it up. Columbia or NYU probably has it. I'm doing a little research in that area myself, and I might make use of the tables there." The instructor found several British journals with titles like the one Patton had given, but found no such article in any issue published in the past ten years. Then, to make doubly sure, he looked up all indexes dealing with studies of racial psychological quotients and with all aspects of Negro emotion and mentality, and nowhere did he find any such reference. The instructor still didn't let go. He wrote a letter to Patton, but he never got a reply.

Then there was the occasion, at a gathering, when Patton came out with the flat statement, "The rate of homosexuality among men and women prisoners in the North is greater by nearly twenty percent than in the South. Investigators attribute it to corn liquor, which is a sexual depressant."

A newspaperman present asked, "Where did you get those figures?"

"The Commissioner of Correction, or whatever you call him, in the State of Louisiana, who holds a Ph.D. in penology."

The newspaperman said, "Now that's strange. I saw this commissioner, Phil Hagerby, only two weeks ago. He has no Ph.D. in penology or in anything else. As a matter of fact, I don't think he ever went to college, not even in one of those fly-bitten Southern colleges."

"Now, now," said Patton. "We have some very good colleges, especially the whites have, if I stick my neck out on this matter of races. Have you ever heard of the University of North Carolina? Have you ever heard of the Southern Methodist University? They have a fine football team, but they also have a very good liberal arts college and a fine physics department, and, I believe, a good medical school, too. Then there's the University of Texas, a very fine school. So be careful when you talk about Southern schools. We have some bad ones, I grant you, but we also have some good ones." He smiled. "You know, there's such a thing as Yankee parochialism. There's more to the United States than New York and Boston and Philadelphia. I just want to set the record straight."

The newspaperman persisted. "I know all that. But I also

know that there are more poor colleges in the South than in the North or the West. And I'll tell you how I know. I just finished a survey of the colleges and universities that are accredited and that are not accredited, and the results of that survey, which will be published in virtually all the Scripps-Howard newspapers in the country, is that the percentage of poor, non-accredited schools of higher learning in the whole country is shockingly greater below the Mason-Dixon line than in the North or the West or the Northwest. Now, I want to tell you something else. I have been studying figures of the Census section of the Department of Commerce, and the revelations are, really, revelations, and very disturbing. By percentage there are far fewer—I say far fewer advisedly—telephones and books purchased and automobiles and radios owned in the South than anywhere else in the country. But to come back to this matter of homosexuality and Phil Hagerby. What you say is all rubbish. Hagerby wouldn't be able to read any kind of report, and it is a disgrace that he is the head of the prisons of a big state like Louisiana, a downright disgrace. But I do want to tell you this. Have you ever heard of Dr. Harry Elmer Barnes?"

"No," said Patton. "Who is he?"

"He's one of the greatest penologists in the country, not like Hagerby, who's a dope, a real, ignorant dope. I'm not mincing any words. I'm giving you facts, real facts, not made-up facts, and I don't mean to be personal. I've had a few drinks, but I can carry my liquor, and I know what I'm talking about. Now, this Dr. Barnes—"

"By the way, where does he come from?"

"He is, or was until recently, professor of history and sociology at Smith College."

"Where's that?"

"Well, even a Southerner should know about Smith College. It's one of the best colleges in the country, a women's college, but very good."

"What state is it in?"

"It's in Northampton, Massachusetts."

"Oh, well . . ."

"What do you mean, oh, well . . . ?"

"It's a Northern college," said Patton, "and that's all I want to know."

"That's a bigoted point of view, if you will permit me to say so. A man like Dr. Barnes is a real social scientist. He is not a Northerner or a Southerner or a God-knows-what when it comes to his scholarship. He calls 'em as he sees 'em. And if you are hinting that he is influenced by the fact that he teaches at a Northern school, then you're crazy, and I don't mean to be personal, I only want to say that you're dead wrong. Now, about homosexuality in prisons. I have read reports by Dr. Barnes and others, real scientific reports, and they all say that homosexuality is rampant in Southern prisons, absolutely rampant, and the wardens know it and don't care. Up North, there's homosexuality in prisons, sure there is, but it's far less than in the South, and one reason is that there are no Hagerbys up North, even in crummy states like West Virginia, which is a sort of border state; up North they have educated and trained wardens, people who can read and write. Now about this corn liquor. What kind of funny stuff is that? Where did you get it? Tell me exactly. I know the prisons very well. I've visited a great many of them, and I've done a lot of reading in the field. I don't remember ever reading a single line about corn liquor being a deterrent to homosexual desires. That's nonsense. You've heard that in some saloon or in some whorehouse, and I don't mean to be personal. Mister, I don't want to make a pest of myself, but I do want to tell you the facts, real facts. You'll read all about them, the homosexuality and other things, in the Scripps-Howard newspapers all over the country. I think they got it scheduled for a couple of months hence. And I don't mind telling you myself that what I write is so. No imagination. Straight facts."

The hostess gently put a stop to the argument, but it was clear to all that the newspaperman had shown up Patton. Simmons had been at this party and had heard Patton and the newspaperman, and later that night he said to Clarice, his wife, "The newspaper man was a smoothie, and he did get the better of the argument with Patton. But I like Patton. He didn't get flustered. I believe he had facts that could have refuted the newspaperman's arguments, but Patton is a real Southern gentleman and didn't want to offend a fellow guest at a party. You noticed that the newspaperman slung all the mud, but Patton just took it."

145

Clarice was not so sure. She didn't like Patton at all. In fact, she was positive that he was a very shabby person, especially after she had read some of his sensational articles in the popular weeklies. But she was a loyal wife, and all she said was, "Well, they were both a little drunk, and it's hard to say who was right and who was wrong."

Simmons called Patton and the two met a few times. The more Simmons saw of Patton the more he liked his general frame of mind. As Simmons said to a doubting Clarice, "You can't fool that man. He doesn't get taken in by any foolishness." And, of course, he was influenced by the fact that Patton agreed with so many of his own ideas and assumptions. There was an occasion, at lunch, when Patton said, "You know, I am getting a little tired of the farmers, they're always begging money from the government, begging for handouts. I know they have plenty of troubles, the weather and all that, droughts, thunderstorms and caterpillars. But other businessmen have troubles, too, the people who sell cars and the people who have hardware stores, and grocers, yet they don't ask for handouts. What is there so special about farmers that we should help them? This is a free democracy, and people go into whatever businesses they want and take their chances, and if they succeed, that's just fine, and if they fail, well, that's too bad and they try something else. That's what a free economy means. But farmers have always been beggars."

Simmons thought that this line of thinking was very perceptive, and he thought that something else Patton had said was profound. Patton saw little sense in the movement that was beginning to spread over the country to provide medical care for all people who couldn't afford it, and for all over the age of sixty-five. "Plain nonsense," Patton had said. "Utter and absolute nonsense. It will make out of the American people a nation of malingerers, who will use the hospitals to get free meals and free entertainment, and maybe free female company. Now I mean this last. I know, down South, for example, and this is the truth, as much as I dislike it, but what is true of the South is as true of the North and other parts of the country. Women get older faster than men, wrinkly, and smelly, and hair on their faces, and bulges around the belly and the neck, you know. Men keep on being romantic late into life, and they like the looks of fresh young things. Nature is nature. And the idea of going into a hospital for a checkup and just a rest appeals to men, especially when they get waited on and felt all over by pretty things that are dressed all in white. Besides, who'll pay for all this free so-called medical care? The New Dealers say that every man and woman has a right to free medical care, free welfare funds, you know, and free schooling, that's where the state universities have been such a menace. They've been milking the public. This free college education is very expensive, and for what? If we live by a free enterprise system, let's live by it; if we don't, let's admit it. I think we should live by a free enterprise system. It has stood us in good stead. Charity for those who truly need it, sure! But that is not the state's concern. That's the concern of local communities and churches and private charitable organizations."

Despite the opposition of his editors, Simmons put Patton to work on some "lively" articles for the *American World*. The first one they agreed on—Simmons merely notified the other editors, without discussing the idea with them, since they were so vigorously opposed to any dealings with Patton—was on "the truth of prostitution in the United States." After all, Patton had told Simmons, "prostitution is a fact of life; there are houses all over the country, and right here in the great city of New York, some very fancy ones, and everybody wants to read about it. The *Atlantic Monthly* is squeamish about it, and so is *Harper's*. But that's sheer hypocrisy. Hell, if it was important enough for the Bible to discuss, it's good and important enough a subject for an American magazine to discuss."

The prostitution series was planned as three articles. Simmons gave Patton $750 for expenses, and promised him another $750 for the articles themselves, if they were accepted. The first article was accepted by Simmons himself, which shocked the editorial board. On the basis of this acceptance Patton asked for the whole $750, because he claimed he was in need of money. "You now know what I can do, so you have no risk," said Patton, and Simmons didn't know how to answer this point, though he did want to see how the first article would be received. He gave it to his editor, who sent it to the press

147

without changes. Betty saw the manuscript and labeled it "the godamndest garbage I have ever seen. This will kill us." The others just didn't care, and remained silent. David told Simmons that he did not like the Patton article, but Simmons sneered at him, "Hell, you're a liberal like the rest of them, only you have the decency to admit it, and you're one of these ivory tower men. You wait and see what a commotion the article stirs up."

"But it's cheap," said David.

"Why is it cheap?"

"It doesn't state facts, it scandalizes them."

"What does that mean?"

"It means he doesn't just state facts, he goes into irrelevant details about the girls' scanty clothing, the Oriental perfume of the actual bedrooms, the full breasts of the prostitutes, the wobbly behinds—my God, do I have to spell it out for you? Tell me this, Lester, do you like this sort of stuff?"

"That's a dirty question," said Lester. "You know damn well I don't like it. But there are a lot of things in this world I don't like and I put up with them. I think this stuff will sell magazines. It's valuable, it's fresh; nobody else will print it, as Patton says; it's in the Bible, as Patton has told you, or maybe as I have told you, so what's cheap about it, and why do you sneer at it?"

"All right, I'll come right out with it," said David. "Do you feel good about printing this sort of stuff? Wait a minute, wait a minute. One more question, and I hope you don't get angry about it. Does Clarice like it?"

Simmons looked away. "No, she doesn't. But I think she's wrong. I'm not ashamed of the article. We'll see what happens."

In the first article Patton painted lurid pictures of the bagnios in various parts of the United States: in New York, in Chicago, in Los Angeles, in San Francisco, in Dallas, in Boston, in Kansas City, in Butte, in Santa Fe. He said, "I give you the background of these houses of ill fame. They have a color and an atmosphere of their own." Then he went into describing the various odors of incense in different bagnios. He also described the bedrooms of the girls—"in five-dollar rooms, in twenty-dollar rooms, and in hundred-dollar rooms." He also distinguished, in their capabilities, between Southern girls and Northern girls, and Far West girls and Middle Western girls. Then he went into a discussion of the capabilities of girls of different racial and religious origins: "It is true that Chinese girls are more lax in their bedroom practices. It is true that Jewish girls are, in the opinion of many, the most luscious and most satisfying. Mohammedan girls, strangely enough, are rather dull, at least in the view of most men who have availed themselves of their favors." He said that perhaps the most revealing comment ever made by a madam—and this, he said, "tells why so many men, married even more than unmarried, go to prostitutes—was that "my girls are no different than wives, only they give the men more for their money." He quoted another madam, a Jewish woman, who said, in answer to a question from Patton about Jewish prostitutes, "Well, there are not so many Jewish prostitutes, though many start out that way, but they don't stay prostitutes. They become madams, and they service only those men they really like. And I've never known a prostitute who didn't make a good wife."

The mail that came in after this article was on the stands less than a week was stupendous and devastating. One subscriber wrote, "I have read and subscribed to the *World* for twenty years, almost or thereabout, and it hurts me to ask you to cancel my subscription. This article by Patton is an outrage. What he says is sheer pornography."

Another reader wrote: "Are you trying to compete with *True Stories* or *True Romances?* What has happened to taste in the offices of the *American World?*"

A woman wrote: "I must cancel my subscription. My dear, late husband subscribed to the *World* from the very first issue. He was an admirer of Mr. Brandt and Mr. Jennings, but I do feel that his ghost is very unhappy about what has happened to the *World*. I've had doubts for the past few years. The Woman of the Month feature, The Mother of the Month, and all those chiropractic and natural hygiene articles troubled me. Then came a time when I found myself spending less and less time with the magazine. There just wasn't anything to stimulate me. So many of the articles seemed to me to be so ill-mannered. I know I speak like an old fogy, but I have to tell you what I think. But

149

this last article on prostitution is really the limit. This is pandering. This is not editing. I know a little about editing. For a while, before I married, I was an editor of *The Nation,* a fine magazine with a sense of mission; it was right even when it was wrong. So I do know something about editing, and I must say that this prostitution article is a new low for the *World,* and much as I hate to say it, I think the management of the magazine is more eager for the run-of-the-mill readers than for respect from selective readers. With sorrow."

Another letter was more to the point and brief: "Please cancel my subscription at once. I believe in freedom of speech and freedom of the press. But I have some doubts about the freedom of pointlessness and the freedom to be needlessly pornographic. I resent that you have now deprived me of the one magazine that I thought would maintain some principles of civilized decency. You have lost a friend. You have lost a whole family of friends. I cannot believe that this sad fact means nothing to you. The *American World* which I used to be so proud to display on my living room table will not be there anymore."

Simmons was depressed. As he told Clarice, "I think I pulled a bad one again. Frankly, I didn't think it was such a bad article. I rather liked it. I thought it was amusing and would get us readers. But what I thought and what readers thought are not the same. What surprises me is that we got so few letters saying they liked the article. Actually, these letters, I must admit, were not much. They came from crackpots or just people who like to read this sort of stuff. Maybe we should tell Patton to hold off on the next article, but how can I tell him that?"

"Just tell him," said Clarice curtly.

Simmons looked at her. "So you were against me, too."

"No, dear, not against you, and you shouldn't say that. But I was against the article and the whole idea. I tried to talk to you, but you went right ahead like a bull in a china shop. And the editors, the people you hired to edit and to give opinions, are angry. You were not even courteous to them."

"Well, I knew they were against it," said Simmons.

"You should have let them talk about it. They might have changed your mind, and we would have been saved all this mess, loss of subscriptions and sales and, worst of all, these terrible letters from old subscribers and decent men and women, that's what worries me most."

"Well, maybe it's not so bad. Besides, the issue is on the stands only two weeks, a little more."

"But subscribers have had it longer. Frankly, I'm worried also about the libraries, especially the public libraries. The college libraries are a little more independent in this respect." Clarice was justified in her fears. Very soon cancellations began to come in from public libraries in smaller cities, then from big cities. Not one of them, at first, explained the cancellations. Simmons decided to find out. He wrote to three public libraries in sizable cities. They all answered. One said, "In reply to your letter asking us why we have cancelled our subscription, we inform you that parents of children who brought the latest issue of the *American World* home were outraged, and complained to us. We took the matter up at a meeting, and since our subscription will expire soon anyway, we decided to cancel it now." Another library wrote: "We have long been troubled by the *American World,* chiefly because so many regular readers have complained about its deteriorating quality. We're not a wealthy community and the budget for magazines and books is limited, so we decided to cancel." The third library wrote: "One of the trustees of our library, president of one of our banks and long chairman of the Four Feathers annual campaign for local charities, happened to glance at the latest issue of the *World* when it came in, and he was angry that we 'spent good money for this sort of trash.' He brought it up before the board, and they requested us to stop it. Perhaps it is not amiss for me to say, and I love to read magazines, that I do think that the *World* of recent times is not what it was under the editorship of Mr. Brandt. I say this not to criticize, only to be helpful."

After reading these letters Simmons said to Clarice, "That does it. I was wrong, Patton hasn't finished his next article. I'll have to talk to him. There's no sense in pouring good money into a project that got us this response. I inquired at some key newsstands in the city, also at the two terminals, and the sales are pretty bad. I guess what one of the dealers said is true: The prostitution article is tame for those who enjoy all the lurid

151

details of this kind of subject—there are lots of really dirty magazines on the stands that spell this out in greater detail, and the other people really don't care about this sort of stuff."

Clarice had to control herself from repeating what she had already told him. "You better tell Patton soon. He may be working on the stuff now."

"I will. Now I'm sorry I paid him all the $750. It will be hard to get half of it back, or any of it back. He doesn't seem the sort of man you can get money back from."

"He doesn't look like the sort of man who's for us, anyway," said Clarice.

"I know you don't like him. I admit I have some doubts about him, but he's a good reporter. He has several other ideas."

"I hope they're better than this one."

"Well, they're about promotion, and he is talking about helping out financially."

Clarice was depressed by this news, but she desisted from pursuing the matter. Simmons did not have much difficulty in getting Patton to "postpone" the second article on prostitution. He did, however, promise to let him do a series on "wild spending by the Federal government" on projects that are "worthless, pointless, and make for a population of beggars." Patton convinced Simmons that too much money is being spent on colleges and on "milk for babies . . . most of these babies are illegitimate, and in many cases the mothers drink the milk and give only a little to the babies. And many of the public parks and playgrounds that the government is spending money on are just garbage heaps, of no use to anybody." Simmons felt that he had at least to tell his editors about these ideas. He knew they would object to them . . . and he knew he was running the risk of having the entire staff leave him . . . but he thought he could stave this off for a while. He wasn't too worried, because Patton had hinted to him that if he was editor of the *American World,* he could get somebody to put money into the magazine: "I know a big oil man in California—he also has some wells in Oklahoma—who is loaded, and fifty thousand or a hundred thousand means nothing to him. I have to warn you ahead of time, though, that he'll probably want to write an article or an editorial now and then, but don't worry too much about that, because I can help him out; you know what I mean. Besides, he thinks along our line, so there'll be no difficulty on that score." Simmons was not too happy about giving up the editorship—he liked the title of editor—but then he thought this might not be such a bad idea. If, God forbid, the *World* died, the blame would be put on the last editor, Patton, not Simmons. So he gave his word. He wondered whether he should tell Clarice, who, he was sure, would be opposed to the scheme. Well, he thought, no need to sink into a barrel of trouble with her now. There'll be time enough to argue with her when the deal is consummated, which he hoped would be soon.

Then something happened that Simmons hadn't counted on. Clarice apparently was clairvoyant. She suspected that something was going on between her husband and Patton. One evening, after supper, she confronted him with her suspicion. "Is Patton going on the magazine?"

He was taken aback. "What do you mean?"

She smiled at her husband of many years, troubled that he was revealing himself as devious, who when in difficulties with his conscience sought refuge in legalities and logic. "I don't know how else to say it," she said. "Is he going on as an editor, as a part owner, as the full owner? There's something going on."

"Well, nothing definite, actually, which is why I haven't told you. But we have been discussing things."

"What things?"

"All sorts of things. I did tell you he didn't mind about the second article on prostitution. He was real nice about that."

"But did he return any of the money you gave him?"

"No."

"So what's so nice about him?"

"Well, it's not quite the way you think. He did propose several other articles, and I guess the money he owes me will be taken into account."

"Did he say it would?"

"No. But I assume it."

"I wouldn't assume anything with that man."

"Boy, when you get mad on a man, you won't budge, Clarice."

"I don't like him. He's no good for the magazine. Is he thinking of putting money into the magazine?"

"In a way."

"I thought so. It won't be his money. I know him. Lester,

why do you continue to have anything to do with Patton or with any of his friends? No possible good can come out of it. Believe me." She stood up, looked bitterly at her husband, and walked out of the room.

It took longer for the Patton-Simmons deal to go through. Patton also was rather slow in doing his articles on the waste of government money. All the editors objected to the idea. Simmons felt he had to mollify them till the deal went through; naturally, he told them nothing about the negotiations. He would, of course, have to tell them in the end, but there was time for that. He did promise his editors that before the first article appeared he would show it to all of them. "You'll find Patton willing to compromise. He's a reasonable man. But that's still a long way off."

Not one of the editors said a word. They knew and he knew what would happen. Just about now David got his first teaching position, and his mind was on that, not on the *World,* which offended him almost physically.

eight

David was elated, bewildered, and depressed. He was elated because he had obtained a position as a teacher of "nonfictional writing and markets" at a writers' conference in Intercity Community University in southern Missouri for two weeks at the end of July, plus a promise of a full-time position teaching English in Rye University in New York State. Teaching was to be a new career for him. Helen had managed to get him both positions. He wondered how he would make out as a teacher. Helen had no doubt about his ability. "You're a born teacher, darling, I know it," she said.

"How do you know?"

"I know. I can feel it. I'm sure. So don't worry about it anymore. There's nothing to worry about."

"I've never taught before, Helen."

"That makes no difference at all. You know your subject and you're an exciting talker, and you have patience, and I love you."

Somehow this exuberance encouraged David, and when a mood of doubt engulfed him he remembered Helen's complete confidence, and he felt better. But he was depressed about leaving journalism. He had had such high hopes for his career on magazines, he had been so delighted when he had met Brandt and got his first job on the *World,* and now the *World* had become a shambles and Brandt an unpleasant if sorrowful memory. He had been full of hope when he got a job on the *Globe,* but he was quickly disillusioned. Indeed, the whole field of journalism now seemed to him to be in a low state. If it was true—and David believed it was—that a powerful and crusading press was essential to a healthy democratic society, then the future of American democracy was clearly in jeopardy. The major periodicals didn't seem to have a sense of mission, their editors seemed to be more interested in increasing circulation than in digging into corruption in the cities and in the states and in Washington. There was a blandness about the writing that was to be found in these periodicals. The "big" magazines now were *Reader's Digest, Time, Life, Newsweek,* all money-makers, all sorry examples of noble journalism.

Then there was the journalism of the radio that was spreading like wildfire. Men with tenor or baritone voices read off bare news reports written by others, and what the people actually got was the bare bones of news, not the flesh and blood of everyday life. More people got their "news of the world" from these brief radio reports than from their newspapers. "Interpretation," which was the function of periodicals, was pushed aside. Periodicals no longer had any leadership in the world of opinion. The good weeklies had, in the main, in one way or another been blemished by their flirting with the shibboleths of communism and other forms of totalitarianism. The Trotzkyites and the Lovestoneites and the other splinter groups claimed to correct the prevarications of the Communists in their own press, but their press too was not to be relied on. Besides, the writing in it was largely dull and shabby. Finally, of course, there was the sheer emotional wrench of leaving a profession that you had given about twenty years of your life to. David sought for comfort from Helen on this score. Her arms and her lips and her breasts and her common sense were a haven of refuge to him—and an unending delight.

"Darling, you wouldn't be human if you didn't feel sad about leaving magazines. When you leave an old house you've lived in for twenty years you feel sad. Leaving anything or anybody is sad. Forgive me, darling, for mentioning Mordecai again. You just don't know how sorry I felt when I left him. But I had to, and soon it didn't hurt so much, and then it hurt only a very little. Ah, maybe I shouldn't have brought his name up now. I do it only, darling, because that is so much in the past. So forget it. But you'll get over being sad for leaving magazines. Wait and see. You'll make such a good teacher that you'll wonder why you've never been one before. Wait and see. I know it, I know it."

These words did not make David's sorrow vanish, but they did make it easier to bear it. He still thought about it now and then, every day. One week, much to his delight, he met Orson Bourne Winter, former editor of the *Globe* and also Paul Jennings, former music critic of the *World*. Jennings called him to go to a concert with him at Carnegie Hall "and maybe we could have a bite of supper at the Blue Ribbon . . . yes, Friday, good, good." David looked forward to this, and as a present to himself he dropped into the Oyster Bar in the Grand Central. David was fond of their New England fish chowder and home-baked apple pie. Inside, he saw a familiar face not far away, and the man waved to him to come over. As David approached him he saw at once it was Orson Bourne Winter (or OBW, as he was affectionately called), former editor of the *Globe*. "If you're not too occupied with something, perhaps you'll sit with me," said OBW. David was delighted.

"Lately I've been coming here once a week or once every ten days for the lobster stew," said OBW.

"It is good here, but I generally order oyster stew and steamed clams," said David.

"They're good, too. I hear they get their fish delivered every day from up Maine and Long Island. Very good and very reasonable." He smiled. "My wife, Sophia, you remember her?"

"Of course. How is she?"

"Very well, thank you. Women are funny. She used to be fond of sea food, especially lobster and clams. In fact, it was she who got me to like them, but now she can't stand them. At first she said the fish here wasn't fresh, then she said that she had decided to concentrate on shrimps. Now she says outright she doesn't like lobsters and oysters anymore. I love them. Women are funny."

"Well," said David, a little bored with the subject, "tastes change. By the way, didn't I see an announcement of a new book you are putting out?"

"That is true. It took me almost five years, and I hope it's good. It's a book on Horace Mann, a very great educator and a very great social philosopher. Actually, I hadn't meant to write on him. I started out with a book on Theodore Parker, but I got sidetracked. And it's the strangest thing how I got shunted off. I came across references to him in my researches into New England history, naturally, but he didn't register in my mind. You know how such things happen. Then I came across his last words, just before he died in 1859: 'Be ashamed to die until you have won some victory for humanity.' Isn't that a noble statement?"

"It is."

"That moved me very much. And then, you know how such things happen, I passed the Boston State House—I've passed it hundreds of times, thousands of times, and thought nothing of it, you know, very beautiful, but I guess I took it for granted. Then, for the first time, I saw the marvelous full-height statue of Horace Mann. A wonderful face, such strength, such determination. Well, that's how I got to do the book on him. A very great man. The father of American education. Very sensible and balanced. He was in politics, as you know, in Massachusetts and in Washington, but he was not a politician; he was an educational statesman, using politics to further worthy aims in education. And what have you been doing, David? Still on the *World?*"

"No. I'm going into teaching."

"Congratulations. Frankly, and Sophia will bear me out, I always thought you really belong in education, not in journalism, which is becoming more and more a jungle."

David smiled. "I don't know whether to say thank you, or otherwise. But I'm a little sad about leaving journalism. I've put some twenty years into it. It's a wrench."

158

"I know, I know," said OBW. "That's how I felt when they pushed me out of the *Globe*."

"They didn't actually do that," said David politely.

"They did, of course they did, but that's past. At the time, however, it hurt. But slowly I learned to live with it, and you will learn, too. Besides, you're a bit younger than I am. And I'm not so sure you belong in it now, anyway."

"What do you mean, OBW?"

"Journalism has become a business. It's hardly a profession any more. Moral crusading has largely gone out of it. Oh, in some respects it's better. There is less corruption in the daily press, but the weeklies and monthlies of interpretation are virtually dead. I don't see much chance for the liberal weeklies. *The Nation* and the *New Republic* are having hard times, and their difficulties will mount. *Time* and *Newsweek* and that other one in Washington, *World Report* or something, will take over the weekly market; *Life,* too, in some ways that's the worst—a glorified, pretentious tabloid, out to get the readership of the *Reader's Digest,* who are lost without pictures. These so-called magazines will take over on a big scale, no doubt of it, and then they'll die; people will get tired of them. Don't you agree?"

"I'm afraid I do. It will be a sad time for America when they do take over."

"Yes, David, it will. But, strangely enough, as I get older, I get both more conservative and more optimistic, a peculiar combination. These weeklies are silly and super-conservative and they have little straight news, largely biased. They will gain in circulation, but they will decline in influence. What will happen then? Oh, there'll be a period of adjustment. Then people will come back to first principles. They'll ask for weeklies and monthlies that appeal to mature people, not to those who get snippets of news between radio advertisements of cures for athlete's foot and constipation. Nothing can take the place of the intelligent, well-informed printed word. Good times will come. Silly times don't last forever. The United States still, thank God, has enough vitality and health to withstand even the *Reader's Digest* and *Time* and *Life* and the radio. The United States survived Harding and Coolidge, and it will survive these shabby periodicals without purpose and without vision. The making of

159

money is a temporary thing. So good luck to you on your teaching. Sophia was saying to me only the other night that I should have stuck to my teaching from the beginning. You know, I taught at Harvard, and I gave it up for some silly reason. But the past is the past. May I ask, are you married?"

"No. Unfortunately."

"Permit an old married man to advise you. Find yourself a worthy woman, and cling to her. A good woman is an enormous comfort to a man. I thank God for my Sophia. Forgive me for talking to you this way."

David wondered what OBW would say about Helen. David had considered marrying Helen for months now, and it plagued him that he hadn't asked her . . . he was sure she would leap at the suggestion. But while a future with her held many delights for David, it also held possibilities of something else, and David couldn't quite put his finger on that something else. She had occasional lapses of taste, and he knew himself too well to overlook the fact that such lapses of taste in marriage would disturb him terribly, far more than they disturbed him now, when they were only friends. Among other things, he was fearful that she would bring up her relations with her late husband Mordecai . . . whenever she did it he would look at her and marvel at her lack of sensitivity. David would try to overcome the shock by staying away from her for a few days; but if they were married he would have to see her and listen to her, and that would aggravate his distaste for her. And David wondered what Helen would think of OBW. She would like him in a tolerant way, but in the end she would find reasons for not seeing him. She might even say, "Oh, he's such a dull *goy*." Well, OBW was that, but he was many other things, a great many good.

"I suppose I will get married some time soon," said David.

"It's best to do so in your younger years. The man and woman have a chance to get accustomed to each other, and I do say that some adjustment is necessary, some give and take. With love, all this is not difficult. Oh, I do wish to say, I am glad for you and your people about Israel. That was a historic achievement."

Somehow David was disappointed in this cool, logical, obvious statement. He had long wondered about OBW's attitude toward the Jews. In all the years he had been his colleague on the *Globe,* he recalled OBW saying pleasant things about Italian immigrants and German immigrants and Norwegian immigrants, and about Negroes, but he did not recall similar statements about the Jews. OBW's rare remarks about Jews, he remembered, were merely polite, but there were other occasions when they were rather strange, to put it mildly. David once suggested an editorial on the *Jewish Daily Forward* and Abraham Cahan, its celebrated editor, who also wrote a fine novel, *The Rise of David Levinsky.* At the moment David forgot the reason for this editorial. The entire editorial board of the *Globe* applauded the idea, and that David should write it. OBW was among those who agreed; he could do nothing else since he wrote such a laudatory chapter on him in one of his books. Now he said, "Naturally, Cahan was an influential man. I cannot read Yiddish, but others have described its contents to me; his newspaper has a vast influence in the Jewish community. But I wish to say in the confines of this office some things I didn't say in my book, solely because I wasn't clear about the issue at the time, and I'm not sure I'm clear about it now. That is the question of racial separatism in the United States, what Theodore Roosevelt, a little crudely, called hyphenated Americanism."

David remembered how aghast he was at this statement, and how disturbed he was that none of the other editors felt it necessary to say anything to OBW. David didn't know whether he should say anything or not . . . a Jew had to think twice before saying something that a non-Jew would probably not hesitate to say, especially when it had to do with correcting somebody who said something openly anti-Semitic, or that was anti-Semitic by implication. David said slowly, "I'm not sure I follow you, OBW. America is by definition an amalgam of races. Every strand in our nation contributes to the strength of the nation: the French strand, the German strand, the Dutch strand, the Jewish strand. No one speaks of hyphenated Americanism when one thinks of Presidents Martin Van Buren or the two Roosevelts, whose forebears were not Anglo-Saxon."

"I'm afraid you misunderstand me," said OBW, who clearly was disturbed by the implication of what he had said. "I'm not anti any segment of our population. My record, in print too, is clear on that point. I'm proud of my writings on that score. But there is such a thing as separatism, as I call it. By that I simply mean an overemphasis on the splinter group as distinguished from the overall group, the large community—well, the nation."

"But I don't understand you, OBW," said David. "What Abraham Cahan did was to Americanize the splinter group, as you call it. Frankly, I object to that term. It seems to imply that Jews are foreign to America. They are not. They are integral to it. In the realm of government, there was Oscar Straus, Secretary of Commerce and Labor, who was a very distinguished American. And, of course, there was Louis D. Brandeis, a United States Supreme Court Justice, and I think I can truthfully say, objectively, too, that he has been a very good judge. So what do you mean by splinter groups?"

"You are too sensitive," said OBW. "I meant no harm. I repeat, my record is clear on that, open and clear. I was for Brandeis for the United States Supreme Court. I told President Wilson I was for him. My record is clear."

David was perturbed by all this, but he wasn't clear as to how to answer OBW. He was sure he was unconsciously anti-Semitic, but he couldn't prove it, and he wouldn't dream of labeling him an anti-Semite. He would be shocked.

All this went through David's mind, as he sat with OBW. "I feel as if I were an inch, or maybe two inches, taller as the result of the establishment, or maybe I should say the re-establishment of the State of Israel," said David.

"I can understand that," said OBW.

"Thank you," said David.

"But I must add something. I hope the conquering Israelis are not unmindful of the rights of the Arabs."

"Just what do you mean?"

"Well, I mean the rights of the Arabs. There are many thousands of them in Israel, they were there for years, and they have rights."

Again David was annoyed. "Of course they have rights. But the Arab countries told them to stay in Israel, as a bargaining point. Besides, the Israelis have many times offered to repay them for the loss of their homes, they have offered them full citizenship. I believe there are about five or ten Arab members of the Knesset, the Israeli Parliament."

"Well, I guess that is true. But the Arabs have rights."

"Of course they do."

OBW sensed that the discussion was becoming a little bitter. He said, "Well, let's go back to journalism. It really is pretty bleak. And I want to repeat that I wish you the very best in your new career, teaching."

David left OBW with mixed feelings. He was attracted to him because of his dedication to the highest principles of journalism, but he was also offended by him because of his attitude to Israel. He wondered whether there wasn't a trace of anti-Semitism in OBW. And he recalled again, as he had done so often in the past, whether it was true, as his grandfather had said, "Scratch any Christian, and you find an anti-Semite." The recollection frightened him, but he had no reasonable way out. He never saw OBW again, though he thought of him often. But almost always when he thought of him he also thought of Henry James' remark about "the Hebrew conquest of New York," and about "the destruction of English culture in America."

The more David thought of OBW the more was he offended and depressed. If the OBW's could be so anti-Semitic, what hope was there for the Jews, in the long run or the short run? But then he recalled the anti-Semitism of men on the order of Knut Hamsun, the Norwegian Nobel Prize winner in literature, and Richard Straus, the composer-conductor, and Wilhelm Furt-wängler, the German conductor, and Willem Mengelberg, the Dutch conductor . . . and, coming closer to home, Harry Brandt, former editor of the *American World* and clearly an anti-Semite. He said all this to Paul Jennings when they met for dinner. Jennings seemed troubled, as soon as David spoke about OBW, and said, "Let's talk about this afterward. I want to enjoy my lamb stew and my apple strudel and my coffee. One thing the Blue Ribbon has never fallen down on is coffee. Sometimes their soup is good, too, but their coffee is always good."

The concert they went to had as its feature Mahler's Ninth Symphony, the Earth symphony, as Jennings called it. The opening and only other number was Beethoven's Coriolanus Overture. As they went to the concert, Jennings said, "Mahler mystifies me. Sometimes I think he's glorious, sometimes I think he's a long-winded bore. As for the Coriolanus Overture, what can anyone say, except that it's Beethoven, and he's never bad, only sometimes he's better than other times."

"I feel the same," said David. "But I have to say that sometimes I am deeply moved by Mahler. He seems to write music the way Gertrude Stein writes prose, or the way James Joyce writes prose. And now and then Mahler can be most movingly lyrical."

The concert was superb. The conductor was Bruno Walter, a missionary for Mahler. Both Jennings and David agreed that Walter was at his topmost heights during the concert. Said Jennings, "Love is important to interpretation, I guess. I have to say that I have never liked Mahler so much as I do tonight."

"I know the theatre a little better than I do music," said David, "and maybe what I'll say is rather far-fetched. Mahler tonight reminded me of Eugene O'Neill, the O'Neill of *Long Day's Journey* and *The Iceman Cometh*. Long and involved and wonderful. I guess there's something sometimes, not always, in being prolix."

"Yes, if you have something to be prolix about. Verbosity in music as in literature does not mean too many words. It means too many words for what you have to say."

"I like the way Walter played the Coriolanus. It sounded like a whole symphony, not an overture."

"Beethoven was cryptic, and he wrote close to the bone. Whenever I think of him I think of muscle, yet he could sing. Everything about him was gigantic, even more so than about Bach or Brahms. Bach and Brahms were superhuman, Beethoven was gigantic. I am not sure I am wholly clear about what I'm saying. He smiled like a giant. He kissed like a giant. He cried like a giant; remember the grand, glorious funeral march in the second movement of the Seventh Symphony? But then again, here I am arguing against my own point of view; recall his piano piece *Für Elise,* like a woman singing to her child. Beethoven is always arguing with God. He is like Job that way."

"Your mentioning Job brings up a question with respect to Mahler." David was sorry he had begun to ask the question in his mind. He knew that Jennings was Jewish but that he made little of it—he was neither ashamed nor proud; perhaps the accurate thing to say about his attitude toward his Jewishness was that he was uncomfortable about it to the extent that he didn't accept his Jewishness so openly that he never hesitated to talk about it or to make Jewish jokes or even to use an occasional word or phrase.

"What is the question?" asked Jennings.

"About Job and Mahler. Mahler was a Jew. I know he was converted, but no Jew is ever converted. You remember what Heine said: 'There are two classic ways of wasting water; one is rolling it uphill and the other is baptizing a Jew.' "

Jennings smiled. "That's really funny. But remember that he himself never got unconverted. I have often wondered why."

"I know. I mean I don't know why. But his whole attitude was Jewish, I feel, I mean his love songs, his patient cynicism, his humor."

"I guess so."

"Wouldn't you say that one can find a great deal of Jewishness in Mahler? Frankly, I think I sense it in nearly everything he wrote, especially in his long symphonies. His depths of despair, his flights of song, his talking to himself, so to speak, his sharp onslaughts on heaven—all Jews always argue with God —these seem to be Jewish, to me, at least. Before I knew it for a fact, for instance, I was pretty sure that Rossini was a Jew, at least of Jewish origin. His William Tell Overture, his *Barber of Seville* could almost be sung at Jewish weddings. I mean it. I can hear them at Jewish weddings, or even at some of the synagogue services on some holiday nights, especially Simchas Torah."

"It's hard to say about such things."

"I know," said David, who was now glad that he was driving home a point. "But I think it's true. What is in the chromosomes must come out on the printed page and the music paper. Now, there is Proust. He was Jewish, and I think I can see the Jewish spirit on every page of *Remembrance of Things Past,* his introspection, he is digging into the innermost recesses of the souls of men and women, even his nervousness is Jewish, I believe."

"Well, it's hard to say," said Jennings.

"What do you mean?"

"Who knows about such things? So many mysterious things go into the composition of a work of art, so very many."

David was annoyed at this evasiveness. "But you yourself

have said that Berlioz is typically French, and Massenet is typically French, and Sullivan was typically English and Boccherini was typically Italian. Why can't somebody be typically Jewish?"

"Well, it's a little different with the Jews. They reflect themselves, their Jewishness, but they also reflect the countries they resided in, they came from. A Jew is an amalgam."

David saw sense in what Jennings said, but at the same time he resented his disinclination to come right out and admit a Jewish influence. "Yes," he said, "a Jew is an amalgam, but the dominant strain in him is Jewishness, wouldn't you say that?"

"I don't know, I just don't know. I don't understand what the phrase 'dominant strain' means."

"But you have used it, not in these words, but in essence. When you say Massenet is French in spirit, you mean that the dominant strain is French, isn't that what you mean?"

"Yes and no."

David was exasperated with Jennings. He looked at him and was disgusted. Here was a Jew who was ashamed of his Jewishness, though he probably didn't know it consciously. What is wrong with these people? Jennings was a good music critic. There was no doubt of that. He was a critic of integrity, with an eye for shabbiness in composition and in interpretation, and an eagerness to denounce both. Yet this same man was himself a shabby person, who was ashamed of his origin. David suddenly decided to "give it to him." He said, "I have to disagree with you in your hesitations and doubts. If a man can have a French soul and be moved by a French spirit, then a Jew can have a Jewish soul and be moved by a Jewish spirit. I see no sense in being sure about one and dubious about the other. I go further. Now that the Jews have Israel as their own national homeland, the Israeli spirit, in time, will express itself more fully and more openly, and that is the chief importance of Israel. It makes Jewishness easier and deeper, and it takes away the shame of some Jews of their Jewishness." David looked at Jennings to make sure that he got the full import of what he said. Jennings gave no sign of how he felt.

There were a few moments of hesitation on the part of Jennings. Then he said, "You are a little too hard on me and the hundreds and thousands who feel as I do. We are the largest of the lost generation, the most unhappy, the most depressed and bewildered. I appreciate what you said about the importance of Israel. I see it intellectually, but emotionally I'm neutral. You see, in my home, there was little Jewishness, there were only vague memories. That's where you Russian Jews have it over us German Jews; yes, I come from German-Jewish stock, it's a little mixed up, but a little Jewish blood makes all the difference. The Christians don't let you forget it. One of my great-grandfathers was called Janowitz, he came originally from Poland, I believe, or that part of Russia that is close to Poland. Somewhere along the line, one of the Janowitzes got converted to Lutheranism, but the man in my line, I don't really know exactly who, he wouldn't convert, and so that part of my family remained Jewish, but not so much Jewish as non-Christian. I have done some reading in Jewish history, but it hasn't meant much to me, because, I assume, I did this late in life, after forty, and after forty you don't learn anything. Oh, it's all so difficult and so complex. I met Artur Rubinstein, the pianist, only a few days ago. He's wonderful as a pianist. Just wonderful. We are good friends. As you may know, he comes from wealthy Polish Jews, not very Jewish, but far closer to it than the Janowitzes were, very much closer. He's married to a non-Jewish woman, as you probably know. He lets her do what she pleases about her religion. I really don't know what she is, some kind of Christian. But Rubinstein himself is profoundly Jewish. He has said time and again, 'I am proud I am a Jew.' I wish I could say that. But I can't. I'm a Johnny-come-lately. My tragedy is that I'm not proud of being anything. I mean I have no pride of the sort that Rubinstein has, and don't for a moment think that I don't feel that lack. But there's nothing I can do about it. My kind shouldn't be denounced or even sneered at. We should be pitied."

David was shaken by this confession. He didn't know quite what to say. "I never realized," he finally said, "the complexity of the whole Jewish problem."

"Oh, it's complex and sad," said Jennings. "Now, you told me you're going into teaching, yet you're depressed about leaving journalism. That is natural. I still, after all these years, have a hankering for having my own magazine, where I could print whatever I wanted. When I quit the *World,* I was in the depths

167

for days and weeks. I just can't stand that man Simmons. He's a cheap and vulgar man. But these are the people who are taking over the magazines, who are the magazine kings. There's nothing we can do about them. We just have to let them hang themselves. Oh, there's nothing wrong in teaching. I couldn't do it. I don't have enough patience, but you do. And, of course, you'll have a lot of time to do your own writing. I think you've made a good move." He touched David's hand, and added, "And don't be too hard on me and others like me. Let's have a nightcap on that."

They had a nightcap—and David was filled with a deep sense of pity and affection and gratitude—and also determination.

nine

Helen was touring with a company producing the shorter plays (some ordinary one-acters, others long one-acters) of Chekhov, Andreyev, Gorki, and Pirandello. She was very happy, because this was the first time in years that she had obtained sizable parts in any plays: they were not American plays, but they were certainly major foreign plays. She got fine notices and was exuberant. She wrote three, four times a week to David. After her first review in St. Louis, she wrote to David at length.

". . . Darling, there is only one thing missing now to my joy, that you are not with me. You will see from the review in this envelope how well I was received, with what big, round, singing words! The audience was big and huge and wonderful. Many young people, too, and that I liked. I don't want people to forget the simply great plays of the Russian writers and the other writers. We're going to other cities, Detroit, Kansas City, Peoria, Seattle, Los Angeles, San Francisco, Portland, many other cities, and it will be wonderful, only I wish I could see you for one minute. Darling, I could walk and walk miles and miles just to be with you and kiss you, and make sure you're not worrying too much.

You always worry about the wrong things. You're so sensitive that sometimes you worry when you don't have to. I think I've given you some reasons for worrying, and I don't want to mention this again. But whenever you worry on account of what I say or do, it's all wrong for you to worry. I talk too much, darling, sometimes I say things that mean nothing to me, but to you they probably mean lots of things, all of them not true, just wrong, wrong. Anyway, you will be around here when you start your teaching, and that makes me feel nearer to you. Now, the Jews. In St. Louis, there is a big Jewish community. Darling, a committee came to see me, they knew what Mordecai did for Hebrew, and what some of us actors did, they were very nice, they asked me to talk at one of the homes, they gave us supper, and I talked, and it was just wonderful. I learned that they have been buying lots of Israel bonds, the Hadassah organization here is very active, and the children are studying Hebrew in the Hebrew school, and I met some of the rabbis, they are very nice people, all of them can speak Hebrew, some a great deal, and many have been to Israel already. That is very good. I never knew there was so much Jewish life in this part of the country. I hear for a little while there was some anti-Semitism, from an organization called something like the Minute Men, and a man called Gerald Smith, or something like that, he is no good, when he comes here he speaks terrible things about Jews. But it's better now, my friends here tell me, much better. Ah, my darling, it's so wonderful to be with Jews. I was afraid there wouldn't be any where I went. That was foolish for me to think. Of course, Christians come to see the plays, many of them come, but sometimes I think the Jews appreciate these plays more, I really do. Jews understand the soul better, don't you think, the soul and suffering? Maybe I'm wrong, but I know I'm right, and I know you will understand what I mean. And please remember not to worry, and never forget that I love you. That is all you have to remember."

Later, she wrote: "Please go to a party that Mrs. Lois Scannell is giving next Friday night. She wrote to me, I have known her for a little while, and she is friendly, and is interested in Russia, and if I was not here I would go. I wrote to her you would go. It will be a good party, she knows everybody, and she is interesting. I think you have heard of her, everybody has for

170

a long time. Now she is not so big in the public, but she is still important. I want you to go, darling, because it is good for you, make you feel relaxed, and keep your mind off worrying. And I want to be friendly with Lois. So please go. Don't think about anything, darling, think only about me and how much I love you."

Actually David knew a great deal about Mrs. Lois Scannell, though he had met her only on a very few brief occasions. Graciously, she wrote to David shortly after he heard from Helen, "I am so glad you will be coming to my party. Please come early so that we can talk about some mutual friends, especially Brandt and Jennings, both of them half-men." David was startled by the last phrase; it was rather harsh coming from someone whom David barely knew—and to put this comment in a note!

Mrs. Scannell, at the moment, was the wife of a Jew—she was Christian—a Baptist, her father having been a Baptist preacher in Kansas. The Jew was her third husband, and there were rumors that this marriage, too, was a bit shaky. Lois was born in Independence, Missouri, but at an early age was taken by her parents from one small town in Kansas to another. Her father was an outspoken man from the pulpit, and his flock was seldom happy with him. He did not agree with the dominant Baptist view that drinking was intrinsically evil. He was for moderation in drinking, though he himself was not a drinker: "I don't even drink beer, and I don't permit my wife to use Lydia Pinkham's beverage, because I have heard it has port wine in it. My principle is that we have no right to control the living habits of others, so long as they don't invade the rights of others. The drinking of beverages, especially wine, is almost as old as the human race, and in moderation it is known to be of little or no harm. In fact, some doctors say a little wine is beneficial for the heart and the digestion, though I find I don't need it."

Many of Pastor Jackson's congregation drank whiskey, gin, wine, and beer, but they didn't want their preacher to defend drinking. "What we do is one thing," some of them said, "but we want our preacher to defend the principle of prohibition. Some people engage in adultery now and then, unfortunately, but even these very people would not defend taking out the Commandment against adultery. People are human, but principles must be held sacred."

171

There were other things about Pastor Jackson that annoyed devout and loyal Baptists. He was a bit too free on doctrinal points. As a Baptist he preached total immersion, but he publicly stated on several occasions that baptism by sprinkling is no less valid than baptism by total immersion. "It's all symbolic, anyway," he would say, "and a little water more or less means nothing." Then there was the matter of the doctrine of the Virgin Birth. No one dared to say that Pastor Jackson didn't subscribe to the doctrine, but several revealed that they had seen on his study table books by Harry Emerson Fosdick, Percy Stickney Grant, and John Haynes Holmes, every one of whom was known to be a "liberal" on this doctrine. Pastor Jackson also did not hesitate to defend labor, and it was reported that as a seminarian he had marched in a picket line, though no one knew when this was or what the picket was about. Finally, there was Pastor Jackson's wife, Emily, a tall, stocky, open-faced, richly-breasted woman, who always appeared happy and who admitted that she was a Lucy Stoner, that is, she believed in women's rights. "For women," she said, "are more than females, they are also citizens. Women are not and must not consider themselves second-class human beings. Marriage is a partnership. A wife is a helpmate to her husband, and he should also be a helpmate to his wife."

Actually, Emily behaved pretty much the way the other wives did: she cooked and sewed and took care of the house. Her "freedom" was almost entirely theoretical, and, in fact, she had not spoken about herself as a Lucy Stoner for years, except on brief occasions, and even then only if she was provoked by someone who had heard about her activities as a Lucy Stoner some twenty years before—and even then she was not very active; she merely belonged to a local chapter and attended a few meetings, nothing more. But the gossip about her mounted and mounted. No one ever dared to question her morals, but some of the women did say, sadly, "Well, you never can tell about such women, you never can tell. It is a sin to spread evil and malicious gossip, but facts are facts." All these rumors about her and the strange notions about her husband led to the general feeling in the communities they went to, that "Well, our new preacher is a strange one, and his wife is uppity, too good for us or whatever." Thus Pastor Jackson's one-year contract was seldom extended. On occasion he complained to his Baptist seminary, but the seminary could do almost nothing, first because the Baptist denomination is a very democratic one, each congregation is virtually in total control of its activities; and second, because the seminary professors, as a group, were embarrassed by him. He seemed to be toying with dubious "modernistic" ideas, and the vaguely questionable reputation of his wife didn't help. However, eventually he did settle down in a small Baptist parish in Pittsburg, Kansas, where the people took to him and his wife. The words his congregants used for him were "stimulating and lively, and he sure is a good talker." The young men and women spoke favorably of him, too, and that solidified his hold. He remained in Pittsburg for the rest of his life.

Lois Jackson was their only child, and was a replica of her mother. The young men called her "juicy and kissable" and the slightly older men called her "statuesque." All sought her favors, but they only got a smile that coursed through their being, leaving traces of deep regret. They were all her beaux, but not one was a favorite. She was a good student in school, and went to the University of Kansas for her education. She did well, majoring in social studies, with English as a minor. She didn't quite know what she wanted to do. She thought of teaching elementary or secondary school, and her professors told her she would easily get a position. She also thought of going into journalism; the only reason she thought of journalism was that the field seemed to offer opportunities, eventually, for her to go to Europe. Her father's finances were such that going any other way to Europe was out of the question. Finally, she played with the idea of becoming a field worker for the Department of Labor or the welfare department in Kansas. With a recommendation from one of her professors she got a job as a reporter on the Topeka, Kansas, *Capital-Journal*. She saw at once that this was the life for her: it was exciting, she met people of influence, even as a mere reporter, she was a good deal in the company of men (her interest in men at this period was intense and mounting), and she was in a big city, the biggest she'd ever been in. She earned $30 a week, which was far more than she needed for her room and board and incidental expenses. She spent much time in the local library reading the national periodicals, from the *Atlantic Monthly* to the

Ladies Home Journal, and from the *Virginia Quarterly Review* to *The New Yorker.*

Her mother, Emily, strangely enough, despite her Lucy Stoner leaning, was chiefly interested in seeing her daughter married. She suspected that her daughter had strong sex urges, so far hidden, dormant, but only God knows how much longer she would be able to keep these urges under control. Emily recognized in her daughter a great deal of her own qualities. She herself had had powerful sex urges as a young girl, and thoughts of sin had gone through her mind many times—sweet, fearful, and forbidden sin. She recalled a picnic she had gone to when she was only seventeen; it was a picnic from the local high school. One of the boys had begun kissing her, and she had encouraged him, and liked what he was doing to her mouth and her tongue, and she pressed her body close to his, thrilled by what she felt, but when he put his hand to her thighs she suddenly pulled loose—exhausted and thrilled and ashamed and delighted and ashamed again. She never told her mother about this. She saw the boy many times after that, and she let him kiss her as much as he wanted, but she made sure that she did not press her body against his ever again . . . she was afraid that she wouldn't always be able to resist him. The most she allowed herself was to kiss his lips passionately and to pull at his tongue. She remembered that she was frantic to get married and had more or less resigned herself to marrying anybody at all presentable. There were many candidates for her favors, but none she liked. Then a young preacher came to town, Donald Jackson. He was handsome, well-proportioned, and her parents liked him. She was at first a little cool to him, wondering whether his being a preacher would interfere with his lovemaking—she was in desperate need of a full, unhesitating, virile man who would enjoy uninhibited lovemaking. Slowly she learned that her doubts were unfounded. The Rev. Donald Jackson had hands that wandered all over her body and that thrilled her, and he could kiss, and she also knew he was virile. He was as eager for marriage as she was, and within a few weeks after he had come to town as the new preacher, they were engaged. She was worried that the engagement would be long, and her suffering equally long. She didn't know her fiancé. He wanted a quick marriage: "I need a helpmate in my work," he told her parents. She smiled, knowing what she wanted to know. During their brief engagement she permitted him liberties she had not given the young man at the picnic—except, of course, the ultimate. Her fiancé said, "That I leave to our wedding night. I respect you as well as love you." On the wedding night he was superb in bed. But Lois was troubled. She liked being loved, but she got less thrill out of it than she had hoped. Perhaps, she thought, with time, she would get to like the lovemaking more than she did, and in time perhaps she would get to like it as much as her husband did. Unfortunately, that time never came. She liked her husband, she liked his company, she liked his work, she sympathized with his general views, but she could never respond fully to his lovemaking.

She was troubled by this, and secretly went to a gynecologist. The gynecologist examined her and said she was perfectly all right physiologically. "As for the other thing, that is a psychological matter, outside my area of competence. Perhaps you should see a psychoanalyst. I don't imagine you will need more than one or two meetings with him." He recommended a psychoanalyst. He quickly added, "I probably should tell you that I put little stock by this psychology business. My own view of your case. if you wish to hear it, is that some women are slow in rising to the occasion of sex. A lot is determined by your background, and I know your background. Your husband is a fine man, and as you yourself admit you love him and he is satisfactory in the basics, if I may put it that way. My own belief is that in time you will learn to enjoy your lovemaking as much as he does. Meanwhile, I think I ought to tell you, as a pleasant surprise, that I think you are pregnant. I still have to make another test or two, and we'll see. Are you late in your period?"

"Well, as a matter of fact, I have been thinking about it. I'm three weeks late, almost a month, maybe longer."

"I'm not surprised. The tip of your womb is a little firm, and your breasts are quite firm."

"I noticed about the breasts myself."

She was pregnant. She was pleased, she was bewildered. Her husband was even more pleased, and not at all bewildered. He now made demands upon her almost every night. She was flattered, but she found she had to feign pleasure. In her third month she told him that she had read in a book that intercourse then became dangerous for the fetus. To her surprise he said that he had seen her gynecologist, and he said that with care they could have intercourse for another five, six weeks. "Some women are more eager for intercourse during their pregnancy than before," said the doctor, who, recalling what Emily had told him, had some doubts about the applicability of this general statement to her. Emily was nonplused. She said, "Then he must know better than the books." They continued to have intercourse, and she continued to feign pleasure. When the six weeks were up, she was relieved; though she hardly said so even to herself. She made her regular monthly calls at her gynecologist's office. He said everything was coming along fine, but he asked, on one occasion, "I don't understand you, Mrs. Jackson, you seem depressed at times."

She was startled. "Depressed? Oh, no. I guess it's my morning sickness that sort of lasts into the late morning and early afternoon."

"Morning sickness in your sixth month? Most unusual."

She felt trapped. "Oh, I guess I meant just a little dizziness."

"That is possible. Some women feel a little dizziness at times almost till delivery."

Her delivery was very difficult. It was a breach delivery, the baby's feet coming out first. The doctor hadn't expected it. Surgery was needed, but he assured her that her daughter was perfect.

When the child was six months old, Emily continued to go to her doctor, who finally had to say to her, "Mrs. Jackson, I am obliged to inform you that I doubt you will be able to have other children. Your womb was injured during delivery. It was tilted and a little shriveled. I am sorry."

Emily was silent. She was sorry, and she wasn't sorry. She didn't really enjoy bearing her child, and the possibility of having more children had troubled her. She mocked concern, sighing, and said, "I don't have to tell you how I feel. But I don't see that there's anything that can be done, is there?"

"I'm afraid not, but I would suggest you see some other gynecologists. I can give you the names of two or three very good ones."

She took the names and thanked him, but had no intention of seeing them. She still had to see the doctor for some minor repairs in her genital organs. At one such visit she met a somewhat younger woman, who was having problems with conceiving. She and Emily took to each other at once, and they went out together for coffee. The other woman touched Emily's hips a couple of times, and Emily liked that. Then the other woman, when the two crossed the streets, took hold of Emily's hand, and this too Emily liked. In the restaurant Emily breathed in the other woman's scent. She said so to her. The other woman smiled. "I don't use any special scent, just a little cologne, in the morning." Then she touched Emily's hand across the table and said, "It's so sweet of you to say this." When they parted, they held hands for a while, and both of them were delighted. For the rest of the afternoon and the evening Emily could smell that other woman's smell. They met two more times for coffee. They felt closer and closer, and very happy with each other. Emily called the other woman a third time, but she excused herself. She excused herself a fourth time. Emily didn't call her again. She was troubled by her, she was drawn to her. She occupied her dreams. In one dream the other woman was lying on the floor of Emily's bedroom, naked and motionless, but with a strange look in her eyes. Emily tried to talk to her, but something kept her from doing so. She didn't tell her husband. She told nobody. Her husband continued to want to have intercourse with her. She resigned herself to his wishes, but there were times when she lay passive on the bed, allowing him to do as he pleased. He noticed this, and thought he knew the reason. He said, "I know how you feel, Emily, about what the doctor said. A woman takes this terribly. But we do have a lovely daughter, and the doctor could be wrong. I know of many instances where women were told they could have no more children, and then they had a slew of them."

"I know, dear," said Emily. "You are very sweet."

The two of them established a routine whereby they would

sleep together twice a week, with hardly any conversation going on between them. The husband thought it was strange, but he recalled what the gynecologist had told him: "It takes women a little longer to snap out of such situations. Be patient. You will be rewarded." He was patient, but he was not rewarded.

At times Emily did become more passionate, she displayed the same intense desire she had before they got married and at the very beginning of their marriage, but before the night was over she gave up and lay there exhausted, dismayed, and bewildered—eager to please her husband and to feel the rapture of old, but she didn't know how. So it went on for the rest of their days—with Emily yearning for she knew not what, and her husband accepting what he resigned himself to accept. Once a month he thought that his wife had "recovered," but by the following morning, and sometimes sooner, he realized that no recovery had taken place.

Emily buried her bewilderment in church and other activities. At first she was at a loss how to feel about Lois. Slowly she became deeply attached to her, and then she became her chief concern. She was pleased by her good mind as shown in school, but as Lois blossomed out as a woman, Emily became more and more worried. She thought she saw the same eager look in her eyes that she herself had had as a young girl. She wondered if Lois would have the same experience that she had on that picnic back in her youth. Above all she was troubled as to how Lois would take the "new morality" that was sweeping the country: chastity before and after marriage was being questioned, the purely physical appetites in all areas were being stressed, young boys and girls of college age were drinking and smoking openly, and some of the language they used was just horrid. Would Lois exercise control? Emily wasn't sure, she wasn't sure at all. Her worries would be over if Lois got married—even though Emily's own married life left much to be desired in a strange, vague way. Still, she thought, marriage was good for a woman; it kept her from mischief . . . and young girls, alas, were prone to mischief at all times, more so now than ever before. Boys, of course, were also prone to mischief, but girls had to pay for their mischief dearly, at times, very dearly.

Emily's fears were fully justified. The professor who had recommended her for her position had long had a desire for Lois, though he was fifteen years older than she. He found it difficult enough to be in her presence when she was a student in his classes; now that she was away he was in a turmoil for want of her. He visited her in Topeka for a series of week-ends, and one Sunday evening they went to bed together, to the dismay of both but also to their great pleasure. . . . How strange it was, thought Lois, I, a daughter of a Baptist preacher, should do this, feel virtually no guilt, and find such delight in what I have done. She barely knew the professor, she wasn't especially attracted to him physically (at school she had once called him a "fossil") . . . true, they had petted a little, but she had done this with other boys, particularly fellow newspapermen . . . some had asked her to sleep with them, but she had merely shunted them off . . . and here was a man who hadn't asked her, come to think of it, but had undressed her and then they were making love to each other. She must have been in a stupor, she thought. The professor, John Prince, knew that he had deflowered her, and he was a bit worried about this, and also about the fact that Lois wasn't worried. He had heard of girls who were careless and even stupid about such things; some girls with high grades in college took little care of themselves sexually. He didn't want trouble, especially since he was married—actually he was separated from his wife, they had not discussed the matter of divorce, and there was a tacit understanding of late that they would make up. At this very moment, after he had had his pleasure of Lois, it surprised him that he wished to be with his wife. What had just taken place was fine, but now that it was over it seemed to have vanished into thin air. He looked at Lois, who was smiling to herself in a silly manner, and he began to think what a gulf in years and in experience there was between them. He had pretty much exhausted what he could discuss with her . . . she was, after all, such a little girl.

There was something else, a secret thing, that was giving him grounds for worry. He was partly Jewish—according to Jewish law he was wholly Jewish, since his mother was Jewish. His father was a Campbellite, which is to say he was a member of an offshoot of the Baptist denomination: the Campbellites did not have to accept the divinity of Christ, though many did; they did not have to accept the doctrine of the Virgin Birth, though many did; all they had to accept was the binding nature of the Ten Commandments and the other ethical precepts of the Two Testaments. John's father almost never went to church, but did not formally leave the church. John had been circumcised and was given a rather brief *bar mitzvah,* at the insistence of his mother (the father saw no sense in it, but didn't feel too strongly about the matter, so he had agreed), but beyond that John had no religion. He occasionally read Jewish history and philosophy—he was a professor of psychology—but he did not go to synagogue even on Rosh Hashonoh and Yom Kippur. When he accepted the post at the university where he met Lois he lied about his religion, as he had lied at the previous college: he called himself a Unitarian, merely because he was sure that if he said he was Jewish he'd have greater difficulty in getting a position. Most Middle Western institutions of higher learning, especially in small communities, had unannounced quotas for the acceptance of Jewish members of the faculty. John didn't like what he did; he was ashamed of it; but he calmed his conscience by telling himself that the blame was not really his, but that of the Christian community which practiced discrimination based upon anti-Semitism. Still, he never got over the shame. He called himself Unitarian because the girl he married was Unitarian, "a real Unitarian." He told her the truth, and she merely smiled. "It means nothing to me," she said. "I am marrying you, not your religion or lack of religion." He wasn't sure this liberal attitude made any sense; there was something juvenile about it, but he liked her so much that he didn't dwell upon the matter.

However, after they were married, she began to say things that annoyed him and also to do things that were annoying to him—nearly all of them in the realm of religion. She went at least twice a month to a local Unitarian church, she was a dues-paying member, and she was also "active" in the church in a minor way—she helped catalogue the modest library, she gave them used books and magazines, and she helped adorn the

Christmas tree. Finally he decided to discuss these matters with her.

"I thought religion didn't matter to you," he said.

"It doesn't," she said with a firmness that disturbed him. "It depends upon what you mean by religion. If you mean rituals and all sorts of magic and all that, of course it means nothing to me. But if religion means a desire to belong to the community, to do good to people, to help the poor, and things of that sort, then I'm for it, and I am surprised that you are not also interested."

"Wait a minute," he said. "Not so fast. The Elks and the Odd Fellows and the Beavers and the Moose and the Rotarians and the Kiwanians are also interested in doing good. Why don't you join them, or the women's sections? I think nearly all have women's chapters or something. Why join the St. Luke's Unitarian Church, with a minister who was ordained in a Christian seminary, and readings from the New Testament, and a Christmas tree, and Easter celebrations? I ask you, why all this? I'm baffled, I don't mind my telling you."

She was surprised by his outburst, but she controlled herself from answering in kind. "It only shows how narrow-minded you are," she said. "What counts is not the form but the substance."

"And what does that profound remark mean?"

"It means that I prefer doing my good work through the Unitarian Church."

"Why?"

"Because I like it. I feel at home in it."

"Why?"

"Well, I like it. My God, do I have to go into details?"

"Yes, because I don't like it. To put it bluntly, you lied to me when you said that religion means nothing to you. It means a lot to you. And I don't like it, that religion means all this to you, Christmas trees and all that rubbish."

"I resent that crack about Christmas trees and rubbish."

"I resent the fact that you resent it."

"So you do. Actually, I thought of talking to you about something else, but your attitude being what it is, I guess I better not."

"Tell me."

181

"You'll start arguing, John, and I just am not in the mood. I thought we were civilized beings."

"Tell me."

"I was going to suggest that you join the Unitarian Church. There are many Jewish people in it."

"You can't mean that! Do you think I'm crazy? I'm not much of a Jew, but I'm not going to become a Christian. No sir."

"Nobody is asking you to become a Christian. Unitarianism is not a form of Christianity."

"Don't give me that. Only dumb Jews believe that, and all the Jews who gave up their Judaism for Unitarianism are dumb."

"They didn't have to give up anything to become Unitarians."

"So why did they join your church and not a synagogue?"

"I don't know. I guess they wanted to."

"For an intelligent woman you're very dumb. They joined the Unitarian Church because they wanted to as a way of not being called Jewish. In simple language that even you should understand; these dumb bastards were ashamed of being Jewish, that's why they joined. I'm not ashamed of being Jewish, and don't you forget it. I don't practice it, but I'm a Jew. Some intelligent Jews will not practice Judaism, the ritual and so on, but no intelligent Jew will ever leave Judaism. He knows that all forms of Christianity, at best, are only third and fourth carbon copies of Judaism, and the rest is hogwash, the Virgin Birth and all that."

"You're being rude."

"I know it, and I meant to be, because you lied to me when you said religion doesn't mean anything to you. Like the rest of you Christians, and Unitarians are Christians, Jesus is something holy to you, and the New Testament is also holy. Jesus means nothing to me. If he ever existed, he was only a minor figure in the Jewish history of his time, a mere human being, with a digestion and a chest and legs and the rest of it, like you and me. And the New Testament is just a dull book, full of magic and fairy tales."

"You talk like a hooligan, John. I am hurt."

"You are right. I am talking like a hooligan, and I apologize not to you, but to myself. You forced me to talk this way. And don't you ever for one second think I will ever join the Unitarian Church or any other church."

182

That night they "made up." She nestled up to him in bed, crying, and said, "I don't know why I talked as I did. You're a psychologist and you must know what happened in me."

He smiled. She often talked as if he were privy to more secrets of the human soul than the ordinary person just because he taught psychology. Sometimes this innocence attracted him, sometimes it offended. At this time it attracted him.

"And I was a little rough, too," he said. "I guess I was angry. I'm sorry." He kissed her.

"You had every right to be, darling."

But she didn't let up on what he called her "Unitarian binge." A few days later she said, "The least you can do is come to one of our services and one of our cultural meetings. As a matter of fact, the committee wants me to ask you to talk some evening on Dr. Albert Schweitzer, who, by the way, is a Unitarian, or what we call a Unitarian in this country; he is a philosopher and a psychologist. I said I couldn't talk for you, but that I would ask you. We've had people from all faiths talk to us, Catholics, Buddhists, Taoists, Jews."

For a moment John thought that this was a subtle form of missionizing on her part, but he decided it wasn't, since he was sure she had little trickiness in her . . . he had come to realize that she was quite simple-minded, far more so than he had ever imagined. This actually was troubling him, lately . . . her simple-mindedness was beginning to bore him. She was only trying to be "cooperative and helpful."

When he came to deliver the lecture on Dr. Schweitzer, less than a score of people showed up. Their questions were mostly superficial, though well-meaning, and the coffee-and-cake afterwards was rather pathetic: total strangers smiled mechanically in an attempt to be friendly, and their small-talk was forced and ludicrous.

He also attended a service. He was astonished at how many Jewish faces appeared at both the lecture and the services, a fact that depressed him. His professional instinct told him that no matter what the dominant principle was (tolerance and understanding and equal respect for all beliefs), the Jews were always on the defensive, however unconsciously. A non-believing Christian, he was sure, nearly always acted in a condescending manner

183

toward non-believing Jews. A non-believing Christian discussed Jesus and the Virgin Birth openly and with no hesitation: after all, no one could call him a bigot, since he was a born Christian. A non-believing Jew could not afford such a luxury. He could never talk about Jesus or the Virgin Birth lightly, much less slightingly, for he knew that the little boy or the little girl in every non-believing Christian would resent it. A Jew must always be on guard in the presence of a Christian, no matter how vigorously he expressed his lack of belief in the faith of his parents. To John, this was a powerful reason for a Jew to remain always a Jew. He could always go back to his people, and it was only among his own people that he felt totally at home.

There was another reason why John was ill at ease at the Unitarian services: they were so orderly, so unpoetic, so "reasonable," and so dull. John recalled his Jewish upbringing and his visits to the synagogue: the singing was freer, there was conversation (sometimes louder than it should be, but it was warm and human), and there was poetry: the words of the prayers were so often based upon the Psalms and the sayings of the Fathers, and they often spoke of glory and eternity and mercy and loving kindness—and, now that he thought of it, that was what religion should be concerned with: glory and eternity and mercy and loveing kindness. Ah, he must visit a synagogue again soon . . . he had been away so long! No point in asking his wife to come; she would feel as if she were slumming, it would all be so "strange" to her . . . she wouldn't get the symbolism. He would have to explain every detail of the service . . . the ark, the Torah, the chanting, the function of the *chazen,* the meaning of the weekly reading of the Torah . . . not that he knew all the answers, but he felt the essence of the answers, and he did react emotionally to the sight of the Torah and he did react to some of the chanting. How could he explain what the lighting of the candles on Friday night meant to him, even in his most rationalistic and atheistic moments, how could he explain to her what the sound of Kol Nidre meant to him? He and she were worlds apart . . . yes, this was the price that he paid for being "rational" and "independent" of the rituals of the religion of his upbringing. But she was sweet, and he felt comfortable in

184

bed with her . . . at the same time he had to admit to himself that some of the magic of her body and general bearing were wearing off, and this new Unitarian business was something he hadn't expected. It bothered him.

She didn't ask him directly what he thought about *her* church, now that he had spoken there and attended a service, but wished him to come again for a talk—"not now, but in a few months. I'm sure the people would appreciate it."

He decided to be at least a little honest. "Well, I hope it will be a long time before you ask me again."

To his surprise she asked, "Do you mean the lecture or to the services, or what?"

"To both the lecture and the services."

"Oh. Did you find them . . ."

"I found them, well, to put it politely, uninteresting. The questions were mostly stupid, at the lecture, I mean, and I wasn't sure the few people there knew what I was talking about. Besides, the looks on their faces—"

"What was wrong with their looks?"

"Dull, just plain dull."

"You don't have to be so belligerent about it, John. These are decent people."

He looked at her and realized that there was so wide a gulf between them, such a lack of basic assumptions, that he decided to glide out of the growing controversy as gracefully as he could. "I'm not belligerent, and if I sound that way I'm sorry."

They had been married for nearly six years. The first three or four were truly lovely, and John congratulated himself upon his choice of a wife. But then these Unitarian arguments began and continued, and they ate into his liking of her. He suggested a separation for a few months, so that they can find themselves. "We've been arguing too much. I confess I'm a bit unhappy about various things, this Unitarian business, among them, but there are other things, and please don't ask me to specify. I'll move to some hotel, and of course we'll meet now and then, and, naturally, we don't have to tell anybody, unless there's some special reason."

She said nothing, merely looked at him with stricken eyes.

He was sorry for her. For a moment he wished he hadn't made the suggestion. He said, "Don't you think this is for the best?"

Again she merely looked at him.

"Don't you really think if would be for the best?" he asked again.

She looked down at her lap, and said, "If that's your wish." She began to cry softly. He came over to her, put his arm around her, and kissed the top of her head. Somehow he was offended by her aroma; she seemed so childish, unpleasantly so. He patted her head. "I'll call you," he said, hardly knowing what else to say. At the moment he was all the more eager to be on his own for a while. The first night away from her was a delight. The second night was a bit lonesome, and he also wondered whether he had done right. The third night he called her and they had supper out together. Across the table she seemed very desirable, and they spent the night together. In the morning, however, she did not seem so desirable, and her forced chatter annoyed him. They remained apart for a few days more, and then met again. So it had been going on at the time he recommended Lois for the position on the newspaper. There had been growing up between him and his wife a feeling that they would get together again as man and wife, though neither was definite. At times he wanted to come back, at other times he liked it the way it was. The notion of divorce was slowly leaving his mind. He just didn't dislike her enough for a divorce.

But now that he and Lois had made love he wished he were back with his wife. Childish as she was, she was more mature than this smiling girl. He wondered if she knew what she had done. He looked at her generous breasts, facing him in all their indifferent nakedness, and he wondered what comfort he had found in fondling them only a short while ago, and he looked at her white, somewhat thick neck—he hadn't noticed this before—and he didn't know exactly what to feel or think. She had white teeth; they reminded him of the teeth of a three-day-old calf he had seen as a boy on a farm in northern New York—the calf's teeth were large, white, a little slimy, and a trifle repulsive, exactly the way Lois's teeth looked now.

Suddenly she said, "I like you, John. You're a good lover,"

He wondered how she knew. She was a novice, he had deflowered her only a short while ago. Should he offend her or shouldn't he? He quickly concluded that she probably couldn't be offended anyway. She looked all female animal as she lay in bed, her legs apart, a bit of the sheet on her stomach, her breasts bare. She had not put on a nightgown for her first night of sex. Too hot for modesty and politeness, he told himself.

"Are you comparing me with somebody?" he asked.

Instead of objecting, she only smiled and said, "Come to me, darling, I want to feel you close to my body."

They made love again. She said, after a sigh, "You're really good, sweetheart. Now I can call myself a veteran."

That wasn't what his wife had said the first night. She had kept silent and merely whispered, after a while, "I love, I love you." He wished he were with her now.

They explored each other's bodies, especially their lips and tongues and drank of each and made love a third time . . . then she said, "Time for breakfast."

She went to the bathroom. Now smelling of soap and cologne, she kissed him on the lips, touched his genitalia, and went off to prepare breakfast. Again he was displeased. There was no graciousness. Again he recalled the first morning with his wife. She had held on to him far into morning, and then whispered, "Would you like something to eat, sweetheart?"

He recalled his answer: "Yes, you."

She kissed him, saying, "And I would like to eat you, sweetheart, but I think cannibalism is still illegal. I wish it weren't."

"I do, too."

Out of the bathroom, she looked much cleaner and more desirable and lovelier than Lois, who had been in the bathroom only about two minutes . . . God, he thought to himself, why had he been so eager to go to bed with Lois? . . . she's so vulgar and common and so dull, dull, dull. Was this another of nature's dirty tricks? But there were some questions he must ask her, and tell her things . . . and he must do it after breakfast.

Lois's breakfast was makeshift. She poured orange juice from a can and left the can on the table. Her bacon and eggs were hastily prepared. The bacon was too crisp, the eggs were too scrambled, and the toast was so black he wondered how he could eat it. There was no butter on the table and he had to ask for it. The only truly tolerable thing was the coffee. Then she began to smoke . . . she finished more than a half dozen cigarettes, and doused them in the saucer. Then she said, "I'll wash these later. I feel deliciously tired. Let's go back to bed." They did, and John wished he were five hundred miles away.

He asked, "Lois, did you use a diaphragm or something?"

"Of course not, silly. This is the first time for me, as if you didn't know. And you can't get a diaphragm while you're a virgin."

"Oh, but did you take any other precaution?"

"Oh, John darling, don't worry. Nothing will happen."

"How do you know?"

"I know. I'm not worried, so why should you be?"

"But I *am* worried, Lois. After all . . ."

"After all, what?"

"I mean in case something should happen. You know, things happen, and we're both healthy specimens."

She smiled. "You are very healthy. The first time I thought you'd tear me apart."

He wished he could slap her face. "When are you due, Lois?"

"Due?"

She began to count on her fingers, like a backward elementary school child. "In a week, I think, maybe six days."

"Isn't that a dangerous time?"

"How should I know?" she said. "Don't worry. Let me hold you, and don't worry, don't be such a worry bug. Everything will be all right. I know everything will be all right."

"I hope so," John said.

"Let's not talk about it anymore, John. I only want to tell you that I'm very much in love with you. You're gorgeous."

"You make me feel like a chorus girl," said John.

She hid her face in her hands, and for a few seconds she was very appealing and innocent and sweet. "You—a girl!"

He said nothing.

"Darling, I hope you don't mind what I'm going to say. While you were making love to me, I was thinking of *Fanny Hill.*"

"What do you mean?"

"The book, silly, written by some preacher, a preacher like my father, but a little different, I guess. But then, I'm not so sure. I've had intuitions about my father."

John was bewildered. "I don't follow you."

"Oh, you a professor of psychology. *Fanny Hill* is the dirty book a preacher by the name of Clelland wrote. My God, haven't you heard of it?"

"I think I have."

"You think you have! Really? Are you telling the truth?"

"I am telling the truth."

"It's a novel, not much of a novel, I guess, about a whore, or a prostitute, I don't know what the difference is, who has one man after another. The one thing I remember is that she talks of the male organ as the machine. I don't know why, but it made me laugh, and even now I feel like laughing. All the girls read the book. You men don't know what girls read, what they think about, what they talk about. You have a marvelous machine, darling." Again she hid her face in her hands. John didn't know what to make of this girl. She was vulgar, she was desirable, she was stupid, she was perceptive, she was appealing, she was repulsive.

John decided he might as well talk to her about some important matters. "Lois, there are some things I have to tell you."

"Big secrets," she said.

"First of all, I'm a married man."

"I know it, knew it all the time."

"How did you know?"

"Now, John. Girls in college know everything about the faculty. One of the girls, I won't tell you who, had a big mash on you. When she found out you were married, she stopped chasing you."

"Who was it?"

"I said I won't tell you. But I will tell you that I told her to go after you anyway. You know why?"

"Why?"

"Because I saw your wife once, and I think she's not much as a lover. I said to this girl that you were dying for some good loving, and being married had nothing to do with it."

John was astonished at this rudeness and invasion upon his privacy. He was also amazed to learn what girls talk about . . . and above all he was amazed at this girl into whom he had gone four times in the last four hours—to his delight and bewilderment, and obviously to her pleasure, but there was something about her pleasure that troubled him. Her delight in him was so different from the delight that his wife got from him. Lois's delight was more physical, almost physiological . . . and there didn't seem to be any music to what had gone on between them. Lois, he began to fear, really was what is generally called "common"—yet, as he looked at her, he was attracted to her, and he wondered if he couldn't have both his wife and this strange, sensual, indifferent, satisfying, disappointing girl.

"Lois," he said, "there's something else I have to tell you." He stopped, and looked at her, and was offended by the smirk on her face. "Why that look?"

"I don't know, John."

She seemed to be enjoying a sense of power over him. She certainly was victorious over him. Her professor had made love to her. Her professor was a married man and had risked his position for her. Her professor was more than a professor. He was a man. He was a male. He was a gorgeous male, as she had told him.

He decided to tell her at once, no matter what was going through her fantastic mind, far more fantastic than he had imagined when she was in his classes, and was looking up at him, and making notes in the notebook in her lap, with her legs crossed . . . those legs that had first attracted him, and that, once he had seen them exposed, were really nothing much, just shafts of goose pimples. "Lois, I'm Jewish. Did you know that?"

She thought a minute. "I didn't know it, till you went to bed with me. You know."

By this time he was accustomed to her vulgarity. "Does it make any difference to you, being the daughter of a Baptist minister?"

"Why should it make any difference?"

"Well, I thought, your father a Baptist preacher . . ."

"I like you, John, you know that, and that's all there is to it. If you were Japanese I'd feel the same. The religious thing means nothing to me. My being a Baptist is, well, nothing, really. My father had me baptized, and that's all. It all seems a little silly to me, John. Some of the girls at school spoke about what you were, a Methodist or a Unitarian or something. It never meant a thing to me."

John was disappointed, in a way. He had thought there would be discussion, even a little dismay. But there was nothing. She really was tolerant—no, that was the wrong word; tolerant implied condescension. She was truly civilized in this respect, far more so, he thought, than his wife, with all her Unitarian leanings—and Lois, the daughter of a Baptist minister, had no prejudices whatever. The thought occurred to him that perhaps it was the so-called common people, even the "immoral" ones, who were most decent in their attitudes to people of other creeds and races. He recalled, in his field studies in psychology, that there was far more interfaith and interracial marriage among the lower strata of the population than among the upper classes. Then the notion came to him that perhaps that is one of the reasons why so much genius comes from the lower strata and not from the upper. Beethoven's parents were plain people, so were Shakespeare's, John Milton's, Michelangelo's. The upper classes admired these geniuses, but they sneered at their parents and at all of the same social class as the parents.

"A penny for your thoughts," she said.

"Oh, I was thinking about all sorts of things, nothing important."

"Were you thinking about your wife, John?"

"Not exactly."

"I have been thinking about her," Lois said.

"You?"

"Yes. First, I wanted to tell you that you have no worry about my telling her. It's none of her business. I'm better for you than she is. Don't get worried. I don't want to marry you or anybody else for a long time. But it would be nice if we met occasionally. I like you. I like you a lot. Your wife doesn't have to know a thing. You probably think I'm not so smart. I saw the look in your eyes, as you were going over my breasts and thighs and throat. I liked it. I want you to like everything about me. You're a psychologist, so I think I'll tell you something. I feel as if I've grown—you would say matured—in the past few hours, since we made love to each other. I feel better, I mean I feel richer, you know what I mean?"

"I think I do," John said, again astonished at Lois. An amazing woman indeed.

"But I also have to tell you—and this would shock my father even more than what you and I have done—I have no sense of moral guilt. You gave me pleasure, I gave you pleasure. No one has been hurt. I agree with Bertrand Russell. Making love to one person night in and night out must be very dull."

John agreed with this notion intellectually, but emotionally he wasn't so sure. He knew he was unreasonable, but he had to face the facts with himself. He wasn't too troubled with his affair with Lois, but if he discovered that his wife had been to bed with another man, he would be horrified. He was sure his wife hadn't; but then, who knows? This girl in front of him had appeared so quiet and gentle and soft-spoken in class— at times, indeed, she seemed to be clam-tight in her opinions and emotions, yet here she was revealing herself as an immoral and, above all, a totally amoral woman insofar as sex was concerned. He wondered whether this was true of all women. Back in his college days he remembered someone saying, "Every man has his price, it is said, but every woman can be made to go to bed by any man. Every woman is a whore at heart. A man has some qualms about his adulteries; many men do, but I doubt there are one-tenth as many women who have such doubts. Woman really is the root of all evil, as the Bible says." At the same time, he couldn't imagine his own wife going to bed with another man . . . he just couldn't imagine it. Now he wasn't so sure he wanted to be with his wife . . . this mere girl was fascinating, she was evil incarnate, but she was also sweet and very satisfying in a strange way. At this moment he was yearning to make love to her again . . . she seemed to be oozing sweetness and juiciness and warmth and delight.

"What are you thinking of, John? Your mind seems to be far away. You weren't thinking of your wife again?"

"No. I was thinking of you."

"What were you thinking of me? That I'm a bad woman?"

"No, not exactly."

Lois burst out laughing. "How can I not be a bad woman *exactly?*"

He looked at her. Her first act of love, yet so mature in wisdom and in amorality. She was truly a strange creature. He told her so. "That's what I was thinking of," he said.

"Well, then I'm a case. So are you. So are we both. You know, darling, I am puzzled about myself. It seems to me as if I've had lots of affairs, but you're the first and you know it. I don't understand it, I really don't. Is there something precocious

192

about me?" She smiled. "Or was I a bad woman in an earlier life?"

"I don't know, Lois, I don't know. I do want to say, though, that I want to see you again."

"As a case study?"

"Of course not. Because I enjoy you."

"Very much, or just average?"

"I enjoyed you very much."

"That's what I want to hear. Come closer to me, and I'll kiss your ear and your nose and your lips. They appeal to me. I was watching your lips and your nose as you were talking. Did you know your nose makes motions as you talk?"

"No."

"It does."

He came to her, and she threw her arms around his neck.

He visited her every other week, or every third week, and their lovemaking was "just gorgeous," in her words. Then came a time when Lois told John she was busy, and she repeated this excuse two weeks later, and two weeks after that. The last time he asked her directly, "Anything wrong?"

"No. I really am busy."

"I don't believe it."

"Well," she said, "if you insist on the truth, I will tell you. I am interested in somebody else, a newspaperman from another city."

"Oh."

They never met again. Actually he had been getting a little tired of her, and he suspected that she was getting tired of him. He found less and less to talk to her about. Discussing each other's prowess in bed had lost its fascination. Her thighs and her breasts became mere objects. What he had thought was profound intuition on her part was a sort of female cunning, mixed with some sharp observation and wisdom gained reading books on the man-woman relationship and married love. Lois had almost no gentleness, little tenderness, and her endearments in bed were physical expletives rather than emotional affirmations. Yet he was hurt that she had rejected him for another man. His hurt lasted but a short time, however. He went his way, and Lois went her way.

Lois's way was a rather spectacular one. What John heard

about it did not surprise him. As he told his wife—they had made up soon after Lois had rejected him, "That girl is a comer, I saw that in class. There's something aggressive about her, aggressive in a female way. I'm not sure I know what I mean by this. Then, I suspect she's a little coarse."

"Oh, darling," she said, "aren't you being a little harsh? After all, you knew her only as a student in college; you haven't seen her since."

"Only my intuition, I guess. You wait, she'll be all over the newspapers for a long time, and then she'll collapse."

"Why do you say that, dear? Isn't that unfair?"

"Well, a teacher gets feelings about students. I think she will sell herself well, and she can repeat phrases that sound like profound thinking, but deep down she hasn't got it, at least I don't think so. She's hard and brittle and hollow."

"I think I have to defend my sex, John. I don't know her at all, but I hope she makes a brilliant career in journalism, and that you eat your words. What terrible things for you to say about a woman you probably wouldn't remember if you met her on the street."

Lois did appear often in the newspapers. She became a reporter on the Kansas City *Star,* where she achieved one scoop after another. She unearthed a minor bit of corruption in City Hall, resulting in the forced resignation of an official. She was promoted to City Hall reporter. Her news accounts were crisp and highly readable. Then she married an assistant managing editor by the name of Scannell—and so Lois Scannell was the name she kept the rest of her life, though she married twice again. Pictures of the couple appeared in newspapers in surrounding cities. The caption read: "Two Great Journalists Make It One." Then she was sent to Europe to cover "the woman's angle in European diplomacy." She changed this assignment on her own, telling her managing editor that "diplomacy is diplomacy, women have little to do with it except romantically, and that is only by-play." The managing editor agreed, and let her make her own decision. He told her husband, the assistant managing editor, "One thing I learned long ago: if you have a good person and you trust him, give him free rein." Lois sent in some good though not brilliant dispatches. The woman really could write—

so well, indeed, that she gave the impression of having more to say than she actually did. Then she wrote a series of three articles entitled, "The Junkers Are Still Around," pointing out that there were former Junkers high in the German government, that they were preparing for another war against the democracies, and that "if the democratic world isn't more alert, it will have grave trouble on its hands in less than twenty years." The articles were syndicated and widely quoted. Lois asked to be allowed to stay in Europe indefinitely, and she was quickly granted this permission. Her husband back home became disturbed. She was writing him less and less frequently, and her letters were becoming brief and indifferent. Rumors reached him that she was seen frequently in the company of a Viennese psychiatrist. He asked her if these rumors were true. She answered in her usual blunt fashion: "I was hoping to tell you myself before you asked me. Yes, I have been seeing Dr. Kurt Prezmysl, a top German-Polish medical man. We feel comfortable in each other's company. Perhaps I should tell you also that we have been contemplating marriage, although he's married. More on this later. Love and best wishes, Lois." The manner as well as the content of this letter hurt him deeply.

Before he could collect his thoughts he received another letter, in which Lois informed him that Kurt has "happily managed to get his divorce, and I am sure you will grant me a divorce, too. I would appreciate this. If you wish, leave all the details to me. Kurt knows a lawyer in Vienna who can get it done quickly. He will write to you. All he wants is a letter saying that you agree to the divorce." Lois married Kurt, and again her picture, this time with her new husband, appeared in major American newspapers. Her former professor-lover, John, looked at her picture, was a little surprised at the additional weight she had put on, and said to his wife, "She's rising higher and higher. That analyst husband of hers looks as if he weighed 250 pounds, and something tells me he's short, too."

"Oh, John, what have you against this girl? She isn't the first woman to get a divorce and remarry, and her husband is rather stout, I'm sure, but he doesn't weigh much more than you do. Leave the poor girl alone."

"I'll leave her alone till she appears in the newspapers again."

He looked and looked at Lois's picture, and asked himself how he could ever have found any satisfaction in bed with her . . . so hard-faced, tight-lipped, such cunning eyes, and so unwomanly . . . well, he wasn't the only one to be rejected by Lois; now there's a second, and a hard-headed newspaperman at that. He smiled to himself.

"Are you analyzing the poor girl?" asked his wife.

"No. I'm just puzzled."

"About what?"

"Oh, she was a good student, but at the same time she was hardly one I would have predicted would make her way in the world, as I believe she will for a while. The world is a strange place."

"I don't understand you, John. You probably wouldn't know her if she came into the room now, yet you keep on talking about her."

"So it goes," he yawned.

Lois's rise in the world, after her second marriage, was truly meteoric. She came back to the United States with her new husband and began a syndicated column in one of the Chicago newspapers. The column was bought up within a year by a hundred other newspapers, and the next year still another hundred newspapers bought it. She became one of the leading columnists, second only to Walter Lippmann in popularity and in influence. She wrote on virtually every subject: politics, economics, literature, education, religion, marriage. She lectured widely, and it was said that she received $1,000 a lecture. Her columns were collected into two volumes. The reviews were mixed. Women reviewers applauded her, but some of the men pointed out that while "Mrs. Scannell is facile, and does know her way around European politics, and to a lesser degree, American politics, she is rather weak in her history and political theory. Her columns, it is to be regretted, held up better individually than they do in the aggregate. After all, there is a distinction between journalism and history, between facility and perception." Another critic pointed out several errors of fact. One error impelled him to sarcasm: "Doesn't Mrs. Scannell know that a man cannot be a son and a grandson of the same father? I would suggest that she consult any encyclopedia and read about John Adams. It is likely that she will learn that John Quincy

Adams had a closer relationship to John Adams than that of grandson. That, at least, has been my impression." Still another was annoyed by Mrs. Scannell's comparison of President Hindenburg with Bismarck: "Bismarck was a diplomat, with humor as well as ruthlessness. Hindenburg hides his humor very well, as well as his diplomacy. The first led Germany to eminence. The second very likely will lead Germany to destruction."

She made a quick trip to Spain and Portugal, and on the basis of a few days' visit to each country she wrote a series of articles on "The Approach of Democracy to the Iberian Peninsula." She predicted that General Franco wouldn't last another year: "The revolutionary spirit among the Spanish workers is mounting daily, and it is not at all unlikely that Madrid will fall into their hands before Christmas. Catalonia is already lost to the Falangists. All that remains is a formal declaration of independence from Madrid. The Archbishop of Monserrat is at this minute composing the Catalonian Declaration of Independence." As for Portugal, she said, "Salazar is more firmly intrenched in Portugal than Franco is in Spain, but he is sitting on a volcano. In all my days as a journalist I have never heard such open and violent criticism of a government as I heard in Lisbon. The Portuguese army and navy are by no means in the hands of the dictator. If a showdown should come even now, the army and navy would side with the revolutionary workers. The Iberian peninsula is a cauldron of unrest that will soon erupt."

These observations created a great deal of discussion. No commentator, in the United States or abroad, agreed wholeheartedly with Lois, though a few saw "some truth in what she has to say. There must be some underground dissatisfaction in the Iberian peninsula, and Mrs. Scannell apparently has managed to get the confidence of the leaders of the Iberian underground." European commentators were almost uniformly unfavorable and even hostile to her ideas. An English writer said, "I regret to say that what Mrs. Scannell has to say—and I have only the highest respect for her competence—runs contrary to what I have observed in seven separate trips to Spain and Portugal. I cannot for the life of me see that there is any appreciable anti-government force in either country, and, much as I dislike to say it, I fear that the two dictators are firmly entrenched in power." A French analyst was less kind: "Mrs. Scannell could not be more wrong if she tried. I have spoken to many labor leaders and political revolutionaries in both Spain and Portugal, and I cannot see any ground whatever for saying that revolution is, as the Americans say, around the corner. This is simply not true. Can I prove it? No, I cannot. But I place thirty years of political observation on the line as the earnest of my conviction of the accuracy of my remarks."

Mrs. Scannell was not at all disturbed by these hostile comments. The American public continued to read her. Indeed, more newspapers subscribed to her column, so that she now appeared in nearly three hundred newspapers. She was, indeed, the Woman of the Year, the Woman of the Decade. Her name was on the lips of hundreds of thousands of men and women who followed foreign affairs, and those who didn't had surely heard of her, by way of the radio and word of mouth. Mrs. Scannell then undertook a heavily publicized trip to the Orient, and sent back dispatches that were truly sensational. What she had to say ran counter to what American observers had been saying. In one column she said, "All talk about an imminent conflict between Japan and the United States is, as they say in the Midwest, pure hogwash. The Japanese need our trade and friendship, and we need theirs. To be practical, Japan has designs on China, not honorable designs in terms of personal or even international morality, but the designs are there. Japan knows that if she should alienate the United States she could not realize these designs. It's as simple as all that. Japan will not go to war with the United States. In all international politics there is nothing surer than this."

As for Russia attacking Japan, Mrs. Scannell said, "That, too, is out of the question. The Russo-Japanese trade is increasing phenomenally, and will continue to do so. Why should Russia attack Japan, or vice versa? China? Russia has Outer Mongolia, and that is all of China she can now digest. What Japan has in mind is no concern of hers. What logic, then, is there in a conflict between the two countries. Diplomacy is often difficult to understand, but it is not irrational." These remarks aroused widespread and almost hysterical controversy. Right wing commentators in the United States practically accused her of treason. One said: "To say what Mrs. Scannell says is to lull the American public to sleep insofar as the Oriental danger is concerned. At this very minute Japanese spies are scouring the Hawaiian Islands and photographing military installations on the Pacific, as our Intelligence well knows." Another commentator said, "What the busy lady says must give the Japanese military a big laugh. Their military plans against the United States are nearly complete." And from still another. "Russia is the implacable enemy of the United States. For anyone, especially with the influence of Mrs. Scannell, to say that Russia will not attack the United States or Japan, and the United States can sleep in peace, insofar as the Orient is concerned and insofar as Russia is concerned, borders on the criminal."

John, Lois's professor-lover, read these comments. He had been following his former love's career closely. He could now be objective, or so he believed. He had long ago made up with his wife. Now father of three children, he had resigned himself to what he called a low-key marriage, chiefly because all the marriages he knew of were either disastrous, horrendous, or plain dull. Lois fascinated him. The same kind of world that put Harding in the White House and Jimmy Walker as the mayor of New York City, had put Lois Scannell where she was. He might do an analysis in depth on her—a study of mob psychology, bringing the work of Le Bon up to date. He said to his wife, after he read the latest unfriendly comments on Lois's writings, "This is it."

She was mystified, "That is what?"

"Lois Scannell is finished."

"Darling, you must be a little mad. Why do you keep on thinking about her? Fifteen years ago you had her in class, you haven't seen her since, yet you think and talk about her. Have you a secret desire for her? You know she's probably changed several times since you saw her. Women change, just as men change. What is it now?"

"Well, she says the United States has nothing to fear from Japan or Russia, and the boys who know, really know, say she's crazy. She said that Franco in Spain and Salazar in Portugal were through, and the boys who ought to know also said that she was crazy. Well, I think she's crazy, too. She said this two years ago."

"But you don't know a thing about politics."

"That's true, I don't know a thing about politics, but I have a sense about things."

"And John, I have a sense that you're crazy. I begin to think you're jealous. A student of yours has made good, and you can't take it. Come clean, isn't that so?"

If his wife had said this years before he would have been offended by her poor taste, lack of diplomacy, and sheer stupidity. But he had resigned himself to all this in her. He had come to accept poor taste, lack of diplomacy, and sheer stupidity as things a husband must suffer from his wife. Women became that way as part of their privileges of being married. The marriage license, to many women, was a passport to discourtesy, vulgarity, and sheer stupidity—God, he thought, there was no limit to wives' stupidity.

"No, I'm not jealous. I'm only fascinated. This woman is finished. My prediction will come true."

It did come true, and in the not too distant future. Slowly people began to question Lois's omniscience. More radio commentators began to question the validity of her remarks, not only on foreign affairs, but also on domestic affairs. She had made some friendly remarks about Thomas E. Dewey as "a brilliant statesman and political visionary," which struck many as rather excessive. She also began to make friendly remarks about the Arabs in Israel and in the countries surrounding Israel, asserting, on one occasion, "The Arab people have a case, and their flouting of the United Nations vote creating the State of Israel must be understood against the background of several hundred years of history." One radio commentator labeled this remark "sheer ignorance and outrageous, uninformed partiality. Someone should tell Mrs. Scannell that it is usually a good thing to know what one is talking about or writing about."

Then some newspapers, especially in the big cities, cancelled their subscriptions to her column . . . soon more did the same . . . and before the end of a year she had only fifty newspapers, most of them of small circulation. Her column had disappeared from almost all the large, truly influential newspapers. She got fewer lectures, and she was paid far less than before. Now she had to bargain for $500 or even $400 . . . and soon the time came when she was offered only $250. Then her personal life deteriorated. Her psychiatrist husband, Kurt, achieved a full professorship at New York University, but found that he had to go to social functions alone, since his wife was on the road lecturing. He complained to her: "Lois, I feel like a bachelor. I want to be a husband, but I can't be a husband to a traveling and always-busy wife." She pooh-poohed him. "As a psychiatrist, you're an old fogy. I am your wife, but I am also a human being. Are you sure you're not jealous?" Kurt was thunderstruck. All he said was, "I choose to disregard what you just said. Please be a wife." She did not change. Kurt spoke to her again, but she wouldn't even discuss the matter with him, since she had to catch a train for a lecture.

He asked for a divorce. Moreover, he told her he wanted to marry someone else. "I am in love with a young nurse at the Psychiatric Institute. She is willing and is even glad just to be my wife, stay home, come with me to meetings and parties, and talk to me, not run off to meetings and lectures, and who knows what. You are a civilized woman, as you have told me often, so I am sure you will give me my divorce. You can have everything in the apartment, except, of course, my books, papers, and other things of that sort. I am sorry this has happened. I like you, Lois, but I am a man, and I need a wife. I have found one now, someone who is willing to be a wife, and even to take my name. You wouldn't even use my name."

Lois looked at him. All she could say was, "Oh."

"I am sorry, but so it has to be."

"Can't we talk it over? I was thinking about what you said, and I had some plans."

"I'm sorry, Lois. My friend is waiting for me."

News of the divorce appeared in the major newspapers, but now less space was given to Lois's doings than heretofore . . . and slowly people began to talk less and less about her, far less than before. Her telephone rang less often . . . her lecture agent and her column agent seldom called her—she now called them, something she had not done before, demanding to know why she hadn't heard from them. She spent more time by herself. She called people for lunch, she invited them for dinner. To her surprise few of the people she had invited to dinner invited her back. There was something about those who did that disturbed her. They seldom invited many other people to come to the same dinners, and those who were invited were "merely friends," not people distinguished in their fields. Lois had become just a friend, no longer a celebrity. Actually, the situation was worse with her. Now she was a lonely former celebrity, twice divorced, childless; a failure. She was in her late forties. She wanted company. She did not especially want sex. She was amazed how little she wanted sex. Yet the company she wanted was male company, not women. As she told a friend, not long before—a man she had met only once, but he had filled her with liquor, and she became talkative: "Women are malicious. They are jealous of other women who get into the limelight, and they wait for the moment when these successful women will slip. The world of women is a battlefield. Besides, they have nothing to say. They only repeat what their husbands say."

Lois still had a way with men. At one of the parties she had been invited to there was a huge man, about her own age, who was a painter, hailing from Prague but now an American citizen. He rather liked her and patted her rear end. Having been in Europe for a considerable time, she knew what that meant. She immediately made a play for him. They spent the rest of the evening together, and he took her home. She invited him in for coffee. They made love the same night. She liked it, she didn't like it. The important thing was that he liked it. In the morning she doused herself with a cologne she imagined he would like: 4711, a favorite of European men. He did like it. She made a splendid breakfast. She liked him more in the morning than the previous night. She had the feeling that before long they would be married, if only he wasn't married already. It was difficult to tell about European men: that they went to bed with you was no guarantee that they were bachelors. She was puzzled by his name Brent Karlbuss. "How does a man from Prague get that kind of name? Brent?" she asked.

"Many people wonder. My real name is Bogdan. My people first came from Jugoslavia. My last name used to be Karelich. Somebody, when I became a citizen, said I should change the name, both of them. He suggested Brent Karlbuss. I agreed. So I am Brent Karlbuss. Now you know everything. Is it a bad name? Maybe ugly, as you say?"

"Oh, no. I was only wondering."

"But there is something else I have to tell you. It is maybe important, but to you, a European, maybe no."

"I'm not a European, Brent, I'm an American."

"I know, I know, but you know my meaning. I am Jewish."

"Why do you tell me?"

"Forgive me. But in Europe you learn to think this is important."

"It is important," said Lois, who immediately recalled her first lover, and she marveled at the mysterious ways of life and history. "But it is important not the way you think. It tells me a great deal about yourself, the way if a man tells me he is French or German I know something about him. In the United States things are different. Much different."

"I know. That is good. But I wanted to tell you." He smiled lasciviously. "You knew it before, last night, yes?"

Strangely enough, this offended her, even though she had hardly been a model of reticence in this area. She ignored his remark. "So your being Jewish is only a fact, and as a fact it is important. I suppose you lost some people in pogroms years ago. There used to be much anti-Semitism in Jugoslavia and Russia and Poland, in the whole Slavic world."

"There is still anti-Semitism in Europe. The Europeans, as a whole, don't like Jews. For this the Catholics are most to blame. They teach anti-Semitism. But what can you do?"

"Nothing, I suppose."

He continued, "But here in the United States it is different. I had a wife—she is dead now; she was Catholic, and she hated Jews. So you see how deep anti-Semitism is, a man's own wife. In Europe you learn things. That is why I said what I said."

A feeling of relief went through Lois. She could have this man. He would be a good companion. She made inquiries about his standing in the painting world. He had a good reputation, it seemed.

They slept together during the next few days, then decided on marriage. The news of her third marriage was reported in a back section of the press. The two moved into an apartment on the East Side of New York City. It was a huge apartment—seven rooms. He used two rooms for his painting, and she used two rooms for her writing. More people came to visit him professionally than came to visit her. He boasted that since he married her he had done more work, and more good work than for a long period before. He also got more commissions: he was a portrait painter, and apparently society women and their husbands liked his work. Lois kept on writing, but little of it saw print. Her column was now almost nonexistent. In the New York area only a paper in Staten Island accepted it, and one of the papers in Newark, New Jersey. She began to drink, and soon she was drinking heavily. Brent gently suggested that she shouldn't drink so much. There were periods of ten, twelve days when she did not drink at all, but then she would plunge into it again. Lois knew she was on the road to ruination. She wondered whether socializing more might help her. Brent wasn't much of a party man, but then he agreed to having parties. These did less for Lois than she had hoped, because she found herself drinking more in the space of four, five hours at a party than she would have drunk alone in a day. But now she had to continue as a party-giver, at least for a while.

It was to such a party that she had invited Helen. Helen had urged David to go, while she was on the road. At the time Helen made the suggestion David had somehow forgotten that, years before, he had accepted two articles by Lois for the *World,* and another for the *Globe,* both dealing with foreign affairs. Of course, David had known about Lois's rise, fall, and decline. He was eager to go to the party.

As he came in he was surprised by the number of people and by their state of intoxication. Lois spied him as he moved towards her. She threw her arms around him as if they had known each other for decades. Actually they barely knew each other. She kissed him on both cheeks, on the forehead, and straight on the mouth. "Now," she said, "I've given you the full treatment. My, you're young! How is it we haven't met more often? Come, I want you to meet my husband."

Brent looked huge, with a sweaty face, thick wrists, baggy pants, and stumpy fingers. He held a highball in one hand, and it was obvious that, like Lois, he had been drinking. He had apparently spilled some of his drink or some other liquid on his shirt and jacket. "Lois has told me a great deal about you, David," he said.

"Good?" asked David.

"Nothing but. Lois, bring our friend something."

David had a Manhattan, and then wandered among the guests. He knew no one personally, though he had heard of many of those present. Most were from the publishing world, but there were also lecture bureau agents, actors and actresses, male and female dancers, and a few men from Wall Street. As he moved about he overheard some Yiddish words: *ganif, chazer, nafke, mumzer, goy* (crook, pig, whore, bastard, gentile). He looked at the faces of the people using them, and was astonished; they didn't seem to be Jewish. As usual he was most offended by the behavior of the drunken women: they slobbered, cigarette ashes were on the skirts, their faces were red, and several had difficulty connecting their words. One had her arms around the neck of a middle-aged man. She kept offering him her drink, but he refused.

"Are you afraid of my lips on the glass, you swine?" she asked affectionately.

"No, darling. I just don't want to mix drinks. I'm having a brandy and you're offering me a Martini. That's dynamite. Besides, I'm not a swine." He kissed her.

"Right, absolutely right," she said. "You're not a swine. You're a kosher swine." And she burst out in a raucous laugh. "A kosher swine, my darling," She poked him in the stomach, way down, and said, "I know you're real kosher, don't I, darling?" She kissed him. She repeated, "Don't I, darling?"

The man obviously was embarrassed. He had not had as much to drink as his friend, or he could carry it better. But she still had her arm around his neck, and she kept on nibbling at his chin. "Don't I know, darling?" she repeated.

"Yes," he said, a bit disgusted.

"That's better," she said. "Much better. I know a good deal about you, you lunk." She turned around, her arm still around his neck. "Friends, this man is my lover, and a mighty good lover he is, too. And I'm lucky in another way. He's Jewish. Hear that? He's Jewish. Complete, hundred percent Jewish, and that's what I like about him. Jews make good husbands. Family. Yes, the family. My mother is a red-hot Presbyterian, and she doesn't like my lover, not that she knows that we . . ." She snickered. "Presbyterians! But she's a good woman, a real good woman. She's only old-fashioned. She wants to know why I didn't tie up with what she calls 'your own kind.' Well, this kosher man is my own kind."

"Oh, quit it," said the man. "You're drunk. Quit it."

"Why should I quit, darling?"

"I said quit it. You don't talk about such things in public. You know that."

"So you're ashamed of me, eh, my Jewish lover is ashamed of me. The Chosen People, eh?"

"I said quit it." He became stern. "Now quit it."

She looked him straight in the eye, and realizing he was serious, she mumbled, "All right. I'll quit it, as you say. I was only trying to be complimentary. But if you don't like my compliments, then I'll stop. If I have hurt you, I'm sorry, darling. Let me kiss you." She kissed him. "Forgive me?" He didn't answer her, but moved away. She remained standing bewildered. She burst into tears. "I've lost another man. Oh, my God!"

Another group was discussing Eisenhower. They all seemed to be aghast at him. One, apparently on the faculty of Columbia University, said, "It is incredible how stupid that man is. He sits there, in a faculty meeting, and asks where he should stand on any issue. In all the time he's been here he has never offered a single idea of his own. He's a smiler. He does what committees decide he should do. He wouldn't dare to go against any committee decision. He works by the chain of command system, like in the Army."

"That's called administration," said a younger man. "An administrator follows vigorously, or he leads meekly, and when he leads meekly it's only on very minor issues."

The first one said, "Nicholas Murray Butler was no Aristotle, but he had ideas in education, he could talk theory, he was stupid in a learned way. This Eisenhower is just dumb, plain dumb. But the real blame is to be put not on him. He took on a nice job that was offered to him. The real blame falls on the heads of the trustees who appointed him. They are the real enemies of the university."

The younger man said, "You have just given the chief qualifications for his being elected President of the United States. The people can't take a Jefferson or a Cleveland or a Wilson too often. They want someone more like themselves: ignorant, easygoing good guys."

A third group was discussing the new breed of columnists.

A woman said, "I know everybody says Walter Lippmann is brilliant. I think he's childish. He writes clearly, but he has nothing to say, not a damn thing. He always has good reasons for the wrong things. I feel about him the way some people, including me, feel about Senator Taft: a very brilliant man until he makes up his mind."

Another said, "Bad as Lippmann is, George Sokolsky is worse. There is a man utterly without principle. And ignorant! He predicted once that Japan would never go to war against the United States. He predicted once that Russia and the United States would be the best of friends. He predicted that Franco would bring real democracy to Spain. He praised Mussolini as the best friend the common people of Italy ever had. I could go on and on. He's a devout Jew, I hear, but he's married to a Chinese girl, and someone told me he belongs to a Protestant church and a Jewish temple and some Buddhist organization. I can't believe this, but Sokolsky would probably have some very powerful reasons for belonging to these different organizations. He's fat, sloppy, and untrustworthy."

A third, an elderly woman, said, "I like Sam Grafton in the New York *Post*. He's so vigorous in a quiet way."

Those nearby tried to control their laughter. Finally one of them said, "Grafton is the *Nation* at its worst: belligerently wrong-headed, and moral in the manner of a livewire city editor. He fawns on you. His words melt, his ideas vanish. I must say that paper, the New York *Post* is worse than its columnists. It is the poor man's *Manchester Guardian*. It is the intellectual's tabloid. I don't see how an astrology column in the *Post* is any better than an astrology column in *Daily News*. Cheap is cheap, vulgar is vulgar, ignorant is ignorant. These columnists nowadays have no style. Heywood Broun was an amateur radical, but he had style, personality. And"—he turned around to make sure she wasn't listening—"Lois Scannell had style. No doubt of that."

"No doubt at all. She just had hard luck with the things she said about Spain and Portugal and Japan and Russia and the United States. It's funny, though, Lippmann and Sokolsky made the same mistakes, but their columns persist."

"Just hard luck."

David heard someone orating in high voice not far away. People were approaching to hear him. David went over. A man and a woman were standing on a table and carrying on a dialogue. The woman was apparently in her mid-thirties and very pretty in a way that David liked: a bit plump around the hips, a constant twinkle in her eye, a slight touch of gray in her hair, and with cheeks just becoming chubby. In short, she looked like Helen, and his desire for Helen leaped to his heart. The woman was in the role of the "straight man." She said, "Where do you stand on the recognition of Red China, Mr. President?"

"A very timely question. Timely, indeed," he replied. "I believe that this great nation should recognize only those nations that, by deed as well as by precept, subscribe to the principles of decent international life. Having said this, I must add that the door is always open to Communist China, and we certainly are not at odds with their people, but with their government. Speaking for myself, I, personally, am always ready to reconsider the position of the United States on this pressing issue, as indeed on all other pressing issues. And let me add that the issue of Communist China is truly and indeed pressing. I hope I have made my position crystal clear."

"You have, Mr. President," she said. "Crystal clear."

"Thank you. I believe in letting the American people know exactly where I stand on every vital issue. In a democracy such as we are, and I dare say we are the greatest and the most genuine democracy in the world today, bar none, the people have a right—and I insist on it—to know where their leaders stand, where they are leading."

"Thank you, Mr. President. The other day one of the large Western newspapers took you to task for not presenting the case of the United States—I mean, of course, your Secretary of the Interior, Mr. Shortlip Blabbermouth—in the matter of the ownership of offshore oil in California and Oregon and Washington, but especially California."

"Yes, I do know the commotion that has been caused. I regret it, naturally, but I am also glad about it, if I may put it in the vernacular. I regret it because there is so much misunderstanding, and I want to say here and now, and without equivocation or qualification, that Secretary Shortlip Blabbermouth has made the government position crystal clear, yes, crystal clear, and I stand a hundred percent behind him. But it is good, yes, good indeed, in a democracy, that these pressing matters, and I want to say here and now that offshore oil is a pressing matter, it is good that these issues are openly discussed. This discussion will surely help us to come to a clear and positive determination as to what to do. And, finally, I do wish to state here and now, and without equivocation and qualification, that my administration, as long as I have the privilege of guiding it, will do everything, in this instance and in all other instances, that accrue to the broad, general, all-inclusive interest in this country. And may I add, now, that if this be super-patriotism, I plead guilty to it, and gladly so. I hope I have answered your question. I try to be open and aboveboard."

"Thank you, Mr. President."

"Pardon me for interrupting. If at any time I have not made myself crystal clear on any issue, please do not hesitate for one minute to ask me to elaborate. I shall be more than happy to do so."

"Thank you, Mr. President. You have made yourself crystal clear. I hope we are not detaining you too long from your duties, after all . . ."

"Oh, no, not at all. Nothing is more pressing than my duties to the American people, to explain to them clearly and without equivocation my stand and the stand of the administration on every major issue. I want to make it perfectly clear, here and now, and without any equivocation or qualification, that I consider myself a servant of the American people who elected me to high office. I consider it a privilege to be their servant and spokesman, especially servant, and I know of nothing, absolutely nothing that takes precedence over my duty to the good men and women who elected me to the high office of President of the United States, which post, if I may say so, I consider to be the greatest, the most wonderful in the whole world. If this be super-patriotism or chauvinism, as some of our intellectuals say, then I plead guilty to it, and gladly so."

"Thank you, Mr. President. Before I ask my next question, with your permission . . ."

"Ask whatever questions you wish. I consider it my duty

and privilege to try to answer all questions involving the public weal, than which, if I may say so, there can be no higher concern or involvement insofar as our duties or prerogatives may be concerned. Have I made myself clear, here and now, and without equivocation or qualification?"

"Thank you, Mr. President. You have made yourself perfectly clear. Now, as I said, forgive me, I wish to collect myself and I hope I am not wasting any of your valuable time. Oh, yes, you spoke of intellectuals in a rather, shall I say, uncomplimentary manner. May I ask, if you wish to answer this question, naturally, you will answer or not, as is your pleasure, how do you stand on intellectuals, I mean on their participation in government and in general public matters? You know what I mean, and I hope I'm not presumptuous."

"That is a very good question, and I am grateful for the opportunity to answer it, and to state my position in a crystal clear manner, without equivocation or qualification. My friends, and I hope the American people take this to heart, it is important, it is really important. Now, the intellectuals. Yes, that's what you asked. How I feel about them. What is my position on them. What is my attitude on them. Do I interpret your question correctly?"

"You do, Mr. President. Crystal clear."

"Good. Now, I am the last one to say that intellectuals have no place in government, or, indeed, in public life. The intellectuals comprise a significant section of the population, I haven't got the exact percentage in front of me, but I believe it is sizable. After all, let me see, there are fifteen hundred fully accredited colleges and universities in the country, oh, no, I gave you the wrong figure, I believe it's nearer to three thousand. Now, people go to these institutions. That's a fair assumption. Where there are institutions, people go to them. Would you say I am being a little far-fetched in this assumption? Is it too bold? Too extreme?"

"No, Mr. President. That is reasonable enough, if I may say so."

"Thank you. Now, the people who go to these institutions may be called intellectuals. I think that is a fair and reasonable supposition or assumption. Well, in a rough way, as a general conservative estimate, these intellectuals, on a reasonable basis or ground of figuring, you understood my line of reasoning, these intellectuals, I mean the teachers and the students—after all, where there are teachers it is safe and reasonable to assume that there are students, too, would you agree to that statement?"

"I would, Mr. President. A perfectly reasonable assumption. As usual, you are being crystal clear."

"Thank you, thank you so very much. Now, I believe it is safe to say that intellectuals are, or, rather, compromise, I mean comprise, I guess, a significant element or cross section of the population, at least, significant in number. Now, I make bold to say that where any segment of the population, any segment whatsoever, I do not discriminate. Here and now, without equivocation or qualification of any kind, I believe in being forthright on every issue, that is the least the American people can expect of their elected officials, and on this matter I am perfectly willing to be crystal clear. Now, where was I? Oh, yes, the intellectuals. They are important in the body politic. I have no doubt on that score, none whatever. I am being a little long on this issue, but I want to make myself crystal clear on it, because it is that important. I have no doubts or hesitations on that score whatsoever. None at all. Now, since they are that significant, as I have just shown, amply I hope, wouldn't you say that?"

"Absolutely, Mr. President. Absolutely. Crystal clear."

"That's my aim in my public statements. I don't wish anybody to say, at any time, that I am vague or evading. I am not one to evade, I am not one to be vague. A public official has a duty to be crystal clear, wouldn't you say that?"

"I definitely would, Mr. President. And, if I may say so, I do believe I speak for the entire body of press correspondents here today, or, perhaps, I should say, this afternoon."

"Oh, that's all right. I consider the afternoon as part of the day, wouldn't you agree to that?"

"I would, Mr. President. I definitely would."

"Thank you. Now about the intellectuals. I wish to be crystal clear. I consider intellectuals important. I say this without any qualifications whatsoever. After all, intellectuals are in colleges and in universities, and that is important enough for me, and for the American people, too. After all, I am the spokesman for the American people, right?"

"Yes, Mr. President. You are, and crystal clear, too."

"Thank you. I am glad the nation's press fully appreciates my position on all issues, and my desire to be clear too."

"On that, Mr. President, I can give you complete assurance. We appreciate you completely, and we realize that you are being crystal clear."

"Good, now I want to get to the heart of the matter. I believe in being clear, but I also believe in getting down to the roots. Intellectuals are important. I state that categorically. But they must play their proportionate and integral and interrelated part in the body politic. Indeed, every segment of the population must do the same. We all belong to one big family, without let or hindrance, wouldn't you say that?"

"I definitely would, Mr. President. You are being crystal clear."

"Thank you. Now, intellectuals are people, and people are the same throughout the entire nation. Yes, people are people. I don't think there is any doubt on that score. None whatsoever. Good. Now, intellectuals are people. I don't see, for the life of me, how anybody can hold an opposite view, even in the opposition party. I know what I am saying is unpopular in the present political atmosphere, but I must express my convictions. We must all live with ourselves, wouldn't you say that?"

"I would. I definitely would, Mr. President. And I believe I express the views of the entire press corps on this issue, and we realize how vital it is, how significantly vital it is. As usual, you are being crystal clear."

"Thank you. So now you have my position on the intellectuals spelled out to the last decimal point. I imagine I am risking my political future with these pronouncements, but one must live with oneself. I am against vagueness. I am against shilly-shallying. My friends, and I am sure I can call you my friends, I must tell you I live by very basic principles, which I got at my mother's breast, so to speak, and at my father's knee, you know what I mean. One must live with oneself. I try to do that. I make my position on all issues crystal clear, in every way, shape or manner, bar none. Am I being clear?"

"Yes, Mr. President."

"The recollection of my mother and father recalls to me, I mean I remember, all the wonderful lessons in life I got from my parents, my father and mother, if I may particularize in this instance, and I confess it is a rather personal reference, but all of us, I dare say, now and then do make personal references, and I do so, in this instance, without apology."

"May I say, Mr. President, and I run the risk of interrupting, that the press corps, and indeed the whole country, appreciates your basic humanity. This, indeed, if I may say so, is what makes you so beloved of all. People call you a father image. Speaking for myself, and I dare say I am a woman, and I want to make myself crystal clear on that issue, I am a woman, I also think, if I may so, look upon you, as a glorious mother image, which indeed you are. You comprise the whole gamut of American life, the fathers and the mothers especially."

"Thank you, thank you. I am pleased deeply to hear this. I always have been a champion of fatherhood and motherhood. I believe these two great institutions, fatherhood and motherhood, if I may particularize, are among the most important institutions in the country, and, perhaps in the world, though here I am stepping on territory where I am not an authority. I am a mere amateur in the realm of these matters, and I am the first to admit that they are important. I like to look at the Big Picture in Public Life. It is the only way to get perspective. Wouldn't you say that?"

"I definitely would, Mr. President. You are being crystal clear."

"Thank you, thank you so much. One thing I do wish to be is crystal clear, if I say so. The American people have a right to expect this of their public officials. I look upon public office as a public trust. It is a holy thing, as my sainted mother and my sainted father taught me. I hope I never reach the stage of sophistication when I will repudiate the teachings of my parents, I mean my father and mother. It has just occurred to me that no matter what our station in life, economically or socially or in any other way whatsoever—we all have fathers and mothers, I believe the opposition party would go along with me on that— and I do believe further, I wish to be crystal clear on that, what one gets at the breast of his mother and at the knees of his father, are important, I would go so far as to say, very important. We are now down to fundamentals, basics, I might even say basic fundamentals. I don't believe in being superficial.

213

I simply don't believe in it. Life is too short for that. We must live by fundamentals, by basics, by basic fundamentals, or, if you prefer, fundamental basics. I believe in personal choice or likes or inclinations. That is part of democratic living. I take my stand on that, in every way, or shape, or manner, interpret it as you wish or please."

"Thank you, Mr. President. One final question. There is the troublesome Middle Eastern situation. The conflict between Israel and the Arab states. It appears that the Arab states do not wish to accept the decision of the Security Council that Israel be established as a legitimate independent state. There is war now going on between the two groups of nations. The United States, through its ambassador to the United Nations, supported the establishment of the State of Israel. Now, what is the position of the United States on this important issue?"

"I'm very glad you asked this question. It is an important question. Indeed, I would say it is seminal, though it could be this is an overstatement. But you get the general drift of my position, and also that of the government of the United States. Now, I want to be perfectly clear, crystal clear, as to what I say on this issue. It is important, very important—indeed, morally, politically, internationally, in every way, indeed. We support the United Nations as the chief agency of peace, the world's last hope for the realization of the concept of Christian brotherhood, perhaps, in all fairness and in the interests of accuracy, I should say, Judeo-Christian brotherhood. We people of the world belong to one big community. We are men and women, all created in the image of one Maker. We must learn to live with each other. If we don't, there will be no agreement among us, would you say that?"

"I definitely would, Mr. President. You are being crystal clear."

"Thank you, thank you very much. I therefore would say, without equivocation or qualification, that the decision of the United Nations has been made, I don't see, in all frankness, how that can be denied. It's in the record. That decision I respect, and the government of the United States respects. But I want to go beyond that. I am for peace. I am for peace first, second, last, and always. I would venture to say that I think the peoples of the Middle East, and we are friends with all of them, without regard as to race, creed, or place of origin, you know what I mean, we are friends to all of them, without let or hindrance, in every way or manner or shape. I do hope, and I say this fervently, with all heart and conviction, and I do believe this, believe me, all of you here, and all the American people, I am for peace. I hope the various conflicting nations and communities and people of the Middle East will learn to live in peace and harmony, without fighting in any way, shape, or manner. I do believe that the United States, throughout its entire history, has made its position clear on peace. We are for it. I wish the whole world would hear this. The government and the people of the United States are for peace, absolutely, without equivocation or qualification. I, as President of the United States, am for peace, in every way, shape, or manner, without any hesitation. We live by principles and other important standards, and on that I am willing to state my stand and position. I hope I have made myself crystal clear. Public office means nothing to me except as an opportunity to service the people of this great and glorious nation and the world, too, because I believe we citizens of the United States, are also citizens of the world. The world is one big community, and I do believe we should belong to it, willy-nilly."

"Thank you, Mr. President."

There was an outburst of applause, as there had been during this dialogue. David had to put his hand to his mouth, he could barely keep from laughter. The same was true of many of the others. David walked about listening in on various conversations. There was really little that was worth hearing. Mostly personal gossip about people that David didn't know. Then a woman stopped him, looked him straight in the eye, and said, "Aren't you David Polonsky?"

David was a bit startled. "Yes, why?"

She laughed and said, "I won't bite you. I was told to look out for you, chaperon you."

He looked at her. She was about Helen's age, a little plumper, perhaps, but with the same openness of face. There was a smile on her face. She was holding a glass, half full.

"You seem to be thinking about someone or something," she said.

Suddenly he liked her. A fine, comforting womanhood seemed to be coming from her breasts and her mouth and around her eyes. "As a matter of fact, I *am* thinking of someone, someone I like very much. You look just like her—well, you know."

"I am complimented, David. By the way, my name is Goldie Krantz. But call me Goldie. And I think I ought to tell you I'm not an Arab, nor even a Lebanese or an Iranian. Now tell me who you were thinking of."

"Do you know anyone whose first name is Helen?"

She burst out laughing and kissed him on the cheek. "You're adorable. Helen will be glad to hear what you said about her. I thought it was you, from the very first moment I saw you, it must have been two hours ago. Come on over in some corner so that we can be by ourselves. Want to?"

"I do."

"Don't you want a drink?"

"I've had one. That's enough for me. What I really want is a coffee, but there doesn't seem to be any."

Goldie said, "You hold this drink for me. It's the same one I was given when I first came in. I took a few sips, and I've been holding it ever since, to keep anybody from giving me another. You know these *shikoorim* (drunkards). So please hold this, and I'll see if I can't get two coffees for us. No harm in trying."

David watched her walk off. She was firm and fine—and a woman such as he liked. How much like his Helen she looked. She was back with two coffees. "See," she said, "Goldie finds everything, except what she really wants."

"What do you mean by that?" David asked, and immediately apologized, "Sorry. I didn't mean that question."

She looked at him, smiled, and said, "You had a good idea. Coffee is better than all their *schnapps*. These *goyim* drink like fish, and some of our Jews, I am sorry to say, are learning to drink just as much. I don't like it. It used to be said of Jews that, say what you will about them, they are good family men and don't get drunk. That's not true anymore. Jewish men get divorces, just like the *goyim,* they have their little *shikses,* and they drink their Martinis and God knows what else. I'm so glad to see you. Lois invited several of us Russian actors. We have met her, her new husband; frankly, we want to get some money from her for a Russian theatre of our own. If she won't give any money, maybe she knows others who will. She knows everybody, or used to. So I went. Helen wrote to me from the road that you would be here. She adores you, and I can see why. By the way, many people have felt as you do, that there is a resemblance between us, Helen and me. Actually, I'm older."

"You don't look it, really," said David, surprised at his diplomacy.

"That's sweet of you, David, but Goldie could be an older sister, a much older sister of Helen's. I love her like a sister. She has had her troubles, well, so do we all. But she's a diamond. She's told me about you."

"Oh."

"Oh, yes. You know, she's a very outgoing woman, very warm and affectionate. Men have been after her—you can imagine, a woman like that. Opera impresarios, theatrical managers, bankers, college professors, even one college president, and plain dull rich people. But you are the only one she loves, you just don't know how much she thinks of you. It's a pleasure to hear her talk about you. It's not my business what's between you, or what will happen, I only want to congratulate you, both of you. You live, you get older, you get aches and pains; for a woman all this is very hard. You get married, it's not much happier, with a stranger in the house it's not a marriage, it's a concentration camp; you get divorced, you don't get divorced, what's the difference? A concentration camp is a concentration camp, because a bad marriage lasts much longer after a divorce, it lasts and lasts, all the bitterness and all the loneliness. So you get older, and then you sit down a Sunday afternoon or evening and you realize how few friends you really have, especially among men, and a woman needs a man, a man to love, a man to love her, and if a woman hasn't got such a man when she already has lots of gray, it's a hard road for her to the grave, a very hard and lonely road. Love doesn't come late for a woman. Only regret. Only bitterness. Of course, when love comes to a woman who's over twenty-one, it's a miracle, and then it can be so beautiful. Love in the middle or late summer of a woman's life is a miracle and a blessing and a joy and it lights up the day

217

and the night and the whole year. It's like a holiday all day long and all season long. And that is why I congratulate you and Helen." She stopped, touched his knee. "Forgive me, David, for talking this way. I always get sad when I go to these parties, they're so *prost* (vulgar), and people shout and laugh aloud and are just not nice. But, David, I feel so good now, really I can't tell you how good I feel."

"Oh, that's good to hear, I mean . . ."

"David, we live in miraculous times. Future generations will envy us. Think of it. Israel after two thousand years, after all the killings and all the lies and the terrible things the churches have done. You know, people talk about the terrible Arab countries, what they are doing to destroy Israel. True, too true. But the Christian countries, first of all, were quiet and silent all the time the Nazis were killing us, all the time the Russians and the Rumanians and Poles were killing us. And before, who has done more to kill Jews, to make life miserable for them than the popes and all the Christian countries? A Jew, even in England and in France and in Italy, was dirt, plain dirt, mud, worse than a dog or a cat. A cat or a dog could go out of the ghetto, but a Jew couldn't; no, he must stay in. He had no rights, no rights at all. The bitterest anti-Semites are the Christians. So I say nothing when I hear a Christian or two say the Arabs are terrible; the Christians are worse. But listen, David. Have you been to Israel?"

"No, I'm sorry to say. Not yet. But I will go, that I will do."

"You must. Listen, David. I just came back from there. I say just, I mean three months ago, maybe four months. We went by plane to England, a group of us actors. We got off in Athens, a beautiful city, a beautiful place to live in, the Acropolis, the square where Plato and Socrates taught students—such a place. Then we took the plane to Lydda airport. It's not a long ride by plane from Athens to Lydda, maybe two hours, maybe a little less. I had never been to Israel before. I don't know why. In life, foolish things happen, you have foolish reasons for not doing what you want to do. Anyway, I went. It was a good ride. The Greeks run a good air line. I hear they also have a good shipping line to Israel. Anyway, we were flying. Then the pilot said, 'We'll soon be over Tel Aviv, an all-Jewish city.

218

Look down in a few minutes and you will see the lights of Tel Aviv.' I just don't know how I felt. My heart leaped back two thousand years. I thought of my parents' home in Russia, of my father praying, of the *seder,* of Rosh Hashonoh, of Yom Kippur, of my whole youth, of everything, you know. Then the pilot turned off the lights, and we looked down on Tel Aviv. I tell you, David, I got tears in my eyes—I wanted to cry so much, I couldn't cry. Then, suddenly, someone got up in the plane and sang *Hatikvah,* and we all stood up and joined him. As I think of it now, I can cry again. Oh, David, it was wonderful, so terribly wonderful. That's what it means to be a Jew. That's what Judaism means. We Jews always get together on such occasions. We are all Jews." She stopped, looked at David, and then said, "I told this to Helen, and do you know what she said, David?"

"What?"

"She said, David has to hear this, he has to, absolutely. And you must tell it to him sometime, when you meet. Maybe you can tell it to him when you see him at Lois's. That's what she said, David. Isn't Helen wonderful?"

"I envy you your experience," said David.

She looked around. "We're almost the last ones here," Goldie said. She smiled. "It's nicer this way."

Lois and Brent and two other men came over, and soon they were sitting with Goldie and David. "Whoops!" said Lois. "Did you like the party?"

"Very much," said Goldie and David.

"I'm glad you didn't leave," said Lois. "We hardly had any chance to talk to you. I didn't mean to be so rude, but you know how it is at such gatherings." David was amazed how much she had sobered up. Brent kept silent. He only smiled in a rather foolish fashion. Then Lois introduced the two men. "This distinguished-looking, mature gentleman is Dr. Felix Link, the world's greatest historian, and this is Mr. Jim Silver, the world's greatest journalist." The two made polite disclaimers. Lois continued, "I'll bring some sandwiches and peanuts and things, I'm a little hungry, and I hope you are, too."

When she was back she said, "Wasn't that take-off on a presidential press conference simply delicious?"

All agreed it was. She added, "It's so true, really, astonishingly true. But I was thinking there are no such things in Europe, not to this extent. In a way it's hard on our officials. The newspapermen catch them off guard, and they make fools of themselves often, especially when they have nothing to say even if they had more time."

"Hitler never gave press conferences," said Brent.

"Oh, darling, he did, but not often," said Lois. "He *was* too clever for that."

"A very clever man," said Dr. Link.

"I heard him a couple of times in Berlin," said Jim Silver. "I thought he was a terrible fool, but I suppose I heard him on his day off."

"He had many days off," said Dr. Link. "But the people loved him."

"What people?" asked Goldie. "I know nothing about politics, but some problems are simple and one doesn't have to know politics. What people were fooled by him? What I want to know is why so many so-called intellectuals were taken in, so many professors and musicians and actors and bankers. I know that includes some criminal Jewish bankers, who didn't believe what he said he would do to the Jews. I just don't understand, this I will never understand."

"Jews are no better than other people," said Jim Silver. "I know several dumb ones. I'm Jewish by extraction."

"I am, too," said Dr. Link, "now that we are all confessing."

"So is Brent," said Lois. "My God, I'm the only *goy* in the crowd." She finished the drink she had been holding in her hand. "But these things don't matter to me."

"Jews tend to be clannish," said Dr. Link. "I'm Hungarian, and I used to go to the Jewish quarter now and then, and I noticed how they congregate together. I often thought they would be safer if they spread out more."

"I think the same," said Jim Silver.

Brent made himself another drink and brought a fresh one for Lois, who drank almost half of it at a gulp. Brent smiled and said slowly, "I wish the time would come when Jews and Christians would all be one family. Now next month, or maybe in two months it will be Yom Kippur, that's one day in the year, and Rosh Hashonoh, too, of course—these two holidays I know, from my home. We never went to a synagogue, but we knew about these holidays. Here many Jewish stores will be closed, some schools will be closed, many people will not work. I wonder why."

"In my university," said Dr. Link, "many professors will not come to class. I say there are two ways of praying. One of them is teaching."

Goldie could not contain herself any longer. David had noticed her clenching her teeth, looking down at her lap, staring at him, looking away. "I hope the professor will forgive me, but what he said just now about praying and teaching is foolish. It is not very intelligent. I really mean it. I'll try not to be angry. What is wrong with praying? Many intelligent people pray. Sometimes I do, alone, by myself. Oh, my God, there are so many things I want to say, and maybe I shouldn't say them."

"Oh, no, Goldie, say anything you want."

Goldie looked at David, who was also getting angry, and he was ashamed he hadn't said something himself. He looked at Brent, at his fat, sloppy, snickering face, and he recalled what he had just said about Jews and clannishness . . . and he looked at Dr. Link and saw his smugness all around his eyes . . . and there was Jim Silver who obviously was agreeing with Dr. Link and Brent. Suddenly David said, "I agree completely with what Goldie said. I go even further. It's the attitude of Dr. Link that has caused the Jews so much trouble. It's a form of self-shame."

"Oh, I'm sick of that phrase, self-shame," said Jim Silver.

"It's a foolish phrase," said Dr. Link. "Name-calling. Jews in America are the worst that way. In Hungary I never heard it."

"I did hear it in Hungary," said Goldie. "I heard it from many intelligent Jews about people like you, Dr. Link, and you, Mr. Silver. Why is it that so many intellectual Jews are so ashamed of their Judaism? I once heard a rabbi say, or maybe I shouldn't use that word in front of Dr. Link and Mr. Silver and you"—she looked at Brent, who continued smiling—"maybe I shouldn't say anything, I feel so full of things I want to say."

Lois put her arm around Goldie, "In this house, you can

221

say anything you want. We hold back nothing. Say anything you want."

Goldie looked at David, "Should I? I want to."

"By all means," said David. "If you don't, I will, and you can do it much better."

Goldie turned to Lois, "You won't feel angry?"

"Talk, say anything you want," said Lois, as she made herself another drink. "We are all mature people."

"This rabbi," began Goldie, who now seemed to be in better command of her feelings, and this worried David, because he was getting angrier by the minute . . . he felt almost physically repelled by all the Jews present, except himself and Goldie, of course . . . "this rabbi," Goldie was saying, "said that it is astonishing how Jewish intellectuals can know so much about French history and Chinese geography and what goes on in the Indian Ocean, at the bottom of the Indian Ocean, and God knows what else, yet how ignorant and childish they are about their own people, their customs and their literature and their philosophy and everything about them. Why do so many Jewish intellectuals feel so ashamed of their own history and religion? Believe me, I just can't understand it, I just can't." She caught her breath, and David noticed that she was getting excited again, and he was glad. "Listen. I'm an actress, a good one."

Lois patted Goldie's arm and said, "A very good one, isn't she, Brent?"

"Very good," said Brent.

Goldie said, "Thank you," and looked at Dr. Link and Jim Silver, who remained silent. "So, I get invited. An actress gets invited. People invite actresses. So I got invited to the home of this professor of social science, whatever that is—I used to study economics and sociology, now it's social science. He's Jewish, his wife is Jewish. It was Friday night. We Jews light candles on Friday night. It's a beautiful custom. I didn't know these people, but I could see they were Jewish. We sat down at the table, no candles, no blessing. So I said so, where are the candles and the blessing? Maybe I shouldn't have said it, but I did. So this professor says they are not religious, they don't believe in superstition. Later in the evening, he began to talk about Chinese religion and Japanese religion, and he showed me prayer wheels from India somewhere, and little Buddhas. Now, isn't that foolish? This man is so interested in all this Chinese religion and Indian religion, but his own religion he is ashamed of. Oh, I forgot the most important thing of all. He and his wife go to Chinese religious services sometimes, also Japanese religious services, and Bahai services; they say they are interesting, these services, colorful. But not their own religion. It is all so foolish, so stupid. I mean it, just foolish and stupid."

"That is all very true," said Dr. Link, "but I don't think it is necessary to accept theology to be a civilized man, and I don't happen to like any theology, including the Jewish. As a matter of fact, I seem to recall that Dr. Herzl himself was not an observant Jew, and the same was true of Dr. Nordau and several others."

This line of reasoning upset David. He had heard it before, and in his opinion it was entirely specious. "Listen," he said, "what you say seems so rational, but it isn't, it's actually irrelevant. Herzl was not an observant Jew, but he was well-informed in Jewish history and philosophy and he knew the beauty of Jewish religious ritual, its mystical significance, and he did not sneer at any form of ritual. You didn't even know that Yom Kippur was only a few days away. And let me ask you, what is the last book on any aspect of Jewish culture that you have read? The last article? Tell me."

"Now you're talking like a prosecuting attorney," said Jim Silver. "Why in hell should I interest myself in something that doesn't interest me."

"You're interested in knowing something about the stock you came from?" asked David.

"I'm Jewish only by extraction," said Silver.

"Then your father was a dentist," said Goldie. "This is all so childish. To be blunt about it, if you're born Jewish you're Jewish all your life, and the *goyim*, the whole world, won't let you forget it. If you stay away from them, you live in a ghetto. If you join with them in any endeavor and let your views become known, you're a pusher, aggressive. For God's sake, when will

223

you Jewish intellectuals face the truth and act like civilized people, truly civilized people?"

"I didn't know I wasn't civilized," said Brent quietly.

"Now that's unkind," said Lois. "Goldie wasn't talking about you."

"But she was talking about me," said Jim Silver. "I'm sick of all this pressuring of born Jews to be narrow-minded. I admit that Jews have something to contribute to civilization. The Bible and all that. But why in hell do they have to be clannish, always preaching this and that, and now nationalism? If any people should give up nationalism it's the Jews. The Jews have a civilization to give the world, and they can do it in this country and in France and in Italy. They don't need Israel, with all the killing and all the nationalistic hocus-pocus."

"Suppose," said David, "you told Winston Churchill that he is crazy in his insistence upon the glory of the tight little island, that he might as well join up with Albania or Italy or India or Ecuador. Suppose you made that suggestion to him. I tell you what he'd do, he'd spit in your eye, and he'd be right. The English need England. The French need France. The Germans need Germany. And the Jews need Israel. Not merely for humanitarian reasons, as a refuge for Jews who are oppressed by anti-Semites in Russia and Poland and Spain—all Christian countries, in one way or another, are anti-Semitic. Not just for humanitarian reasons, but for cultural survival. Jewish culture, all that is best in Judaism, grows and flourishes best in a Jewish climate, a Jewish atmosphere. Shakespeare needed England to be Shakespeare. Cervantes needed Spain to be Cervantes. And Bialik and Hazaz and Agnon need Israel to be Bialik and Hazaz and Agnon. You must breathe your kind of air to be your fullest self. This is so elementary, frankly, that I just don't see the argument."

"I don't believe it," said Brent.

"I don't either," said Dr. Link and Jim Silver. And Silver added, "Hell, Walter Lippmann is Jewish by extraction, yet he has done well in the United States. He didn't need Israel."

"I wonder about that," said David. "I don't want to drag this argument out, but I will say about him what Emerson said about Emma Lazarus. Emerson said about her poetry: 'I miss the voice of the prophets, I miss the poetry, the deep religious poetry of the Psalms.' This is what has kept Lippmann from being greater rather than occasionally talented. He has denied his origins, he has denied the call of his Jewish chromosomes, he is living between two worlds, and he is brilliant at times, rather than profound. He is a lost, wandering thinker."

"Oh, Jews, Jews," said Brent, barely able to enunciate his words. "Sometimes I get tired of hearing the word Jews, always Jews. They complain, they are persecuted. Maybe Arthur Koestler is right in saying that they should assimilate. I don't want to be selfish, but I suffered so much for being a Jew, and what did I get for it?"

"But were you really a Jew?" asked Goldie.

"What do you mean?" asked Brent, surprised.

"Well, then, I will tell you," said Goldie. "If you were really a Jew you wouldn't say, 'What did I get for it?' "

"What do you mean?"

"That also proves that you were not really a Jew. Forgive me. Of course, you are Jewish, even if you don't realize how Jewish you are. I mean, no Jew ever asks whether it is worth while being a Jew."

Lois interrupted. "Goldie, I think you've put your finger on the nub of the whole problem. A Jew is a Jew. A Christian is a Christian. You accept it. You don't argue about it. Brent is a Jew, and I wish he were more of a Jew. I wish I were more of a Christian. Being yourself is what is important. It's the business of being yourself that's important. While you were all talking, my whole past life was rushing past me. Forgive me for being personal. I've known many Jews, some I've known very well. I've always felt very much at home with them, and I've never really known why. Now, at this very minute, I think I do know. They are themselves, the good Jews, the really good Jews. They suffer for all mankind. They are the people of Jesus. And that's where I differ with Goldie and David and others. And that's where I agree with Brent and Dr. Link and Jim Silver. In their eagerness the Jews have become stark nationlists. They have done terrible things to the Arabs, pillaging their homes and driving them into miserable ghetto living. The Arabs have a case. I insist on it. Does that make me anti-Semitic? Well, if it does, then I'm anti-Semitic, though I don't see how I can be anti-

Semitic with a Jewish husband, and I have known many Jews in my life, a great many, and I have enjoyed their respect, and they have enjoyed my respect. But what is right is right."

Goldie could barely contain herself. "Lois, forgive me," she began, "this is terrible, what you are saying. The Jews have offered to indemnify the Arabs, they have offered to incorporate them into the Israeli state."

"But, Goldie, listen," said Lois, "didn't the Arabs have a prior claim to what is now Israel, since they lived there all these centuries? The Jews took their land, it's as simple as that."

"This is not true," said David. "The Arabs have no prior claim, they have no claim. At no time did they have any political claim upon Israel. Notice, I do not say 'what is now Israel.' Israel always belonged to the Israelis."

"Forgive me, David," said Goldie. "You are right, of course. Our friends here are falling for the Arab propaganda. Never, never did the Arabs have a claim to Israel. First the Romans had control. Then the Turks, then the English. The Arabs never had control. The Jews were so fair that they paid the Arabs for their lands, and the land they kept on buying belongs to them. It's terrible, the lies the Arabs are telling. The Arab states insisted that the Arabs remain in Israel, so that they'll have an issue in world opinion. Israel is a poor country, and they would not be able to give comfortable living to the Arabs, any more than they could give comfortable living to the Jews. The Arab states want the Arab refugees to remain in Israel, so that they would have something to talk about. The Arab states are terribly afraid of Israel. Israel is the only democratic state in the Orient. It is the only state where men and women are treated with dignity, where there are no slaves. The world may not know it, but in Yemen there is still human slavery."

"Well, I still think the Arabs have a case, a human case," said Lois. "Frankly, I'm too tired to go into the reasons and the facts, which are quite horrible."

Goldie looked at David for guidance. David sensed that there was no point in pursuing this line of talk. He felt that both he and Goldie were in an enemy camp, that no matter what they said, they would meet opposition. He was especially incensed by the fact that among their "enemies" were Jews, who claimed they were Jews "by extraction," which David interpreted as a polite way of saying these Jews were sorry they were born Jews.

Jim Silvers rose and said, a bit angrily, "What gets me is that Jews are always so conscious of their Jewishness, that they don't seem to be able to discuss anything else. When I'm with non-Jews—by the way I hate the word *goy* that so many Jews use for Christians, that's an insult . . ."

Goldie interrupted him. "I'm sorry, Mr. Silver. There is no insult. If you knew any Hebrew you would know that *goy* simply means a citizen of another country, a foreigner, a non-citizen. There is no insult in the word, no insult at all. It's all in your mind, the insult."

"Oh, God, let's stop this mutual attacking. Nobody wants to insult anybody," said Lois. "I'm tired. Let's all have a drink and a sandwich or something. I think, I mean, I still think the way I said. I suppose Goldie and David feel as they do, and that is their privilege. And Brent and Jim think as they do."

David said nothing. Goldie said nothing. Lois looked at them. "Have I said something bad, you two?"

David and Goldie still said nothing.

"I meant no harm, honest," said Lois. "But it is getting late. And this was a party, remember?"

Brent perked up. "Sure, it was a party, not a United Nations argument that leads nowhere. The world is crazy, that's what I think. I see it in all the faces I paint. I was thinking about myself and about David and Goldie. It all depends how you were brought up. I was brought up as a non-Jewish Jew, if that means anything. I have no emotions about Jews. I guess if a painter painted me he would see a lost man. I had no emotions as a young man, I mean as a Jew with roots. So maybe what I said was wrong, but I didn't know what else to say. All Jews like me, I guess, have no home. I confess it. I was silent because I didn't know what to say. Religion is roots. I had no religion, so I had no roots. Maybe that's why I don't want there to be more talk about Jews. I don't know what that means. I have to say that I was jealous of David and Goldie. They are excited about their past and their traditions. I am not. Why? Because I didn't have a past, except a broken, false, unreal past, and I had no traditions. A painter sees things in faces. I have looked at my face, and I have seen terrible things; I mean a lot of emptiness. So before I begin crying, let us have something to eat."

David and Goldie looked at Brent and were strangely moved. What Jim Silver felt was not clear. He kept silent, though he looked intently at Brent. Suddenly Lois got up and walked over to Brent and kissed him slowly and long. "I love you," she said.

Goldie hesitated, not knowing whether she should pursue this line of talk, but she felt she simply had to say something else. She said, "What Brent has just said is one of the saddest things I have ever heard. I have read about the lost generation in America, I mean in American literature. But the Jews have had a lost generation, not for ten or twenty years, but for more than two thousand years. And sometimes I think the intellectuals have been more lost than the rest of us. That's what my father used to say, and his brother, too. My father ran a bookstore in Kiev for a while, then he had a store in Minsk, where he sold not just books, but also *talaisim*."

"What's that?" asked Lois.

"Prayer shawls," said Goldie.

"Oh, I've seen those," said Lois. "I saw them in the big synagogue in Prague, the Alt-Neue Schule they called it. A very beautiful synagogue. Sorry I interrupted you."

"It's all right," continued Goldie. "This is one of the worst tragedies of the Jews. Really terrible. You see, the poor people, the poor Jews, they worked, they did whatever they did, and they were Jews. I mean they went to synagogue, they observed the holidays, they were content with their spiritual life, their Jewishness. Oh, I forgot to tell you what my uncle did, my father's brother. He was one of the few Jews in Kiev who was a school-teacher in a non-Jewish school, a *gymnasium*. The only reason was that he was the only one who knew mathematics, algebra or something, I don't know anything about these things. He and my father liked each other, they really were brothers."

Lois said, "Goldie, I love what you're saying, but I think I'll get some more coffee. So please wait a minute. I'll put the coffee on, and then I want to hear the rest."

When she came back, Lois said, "Before you go on, Goldie, I want to say a few things, just a few. As I was listening to you, I was thinking. You Jews really lead a very rich spiritual and intellectual and communal life. I envy you. I think all Christians should envy you. You have such a wonderful past, the Bible and the Talmud and the rabbis and the literature, I mean the secular literature. And then there were all the tricks you had to resort to to beat the executioners in Spain and Portugal."

"We didn't beat many of the executioners," said David.

"That is true," said Lois. "Too true. But, if I may be blunt, the whole thing made you very inventive. Yes, you've had terrible times, pogroms and all. I know about the Kishinev pogrom and some others. Shocking. The Christian world has so much to be ashamed of when it comes to its treatment of Jews. But, in a strange and tragic way, it has all enriched you people."

"Yes, that is true," said David. "But think of the price we have paid. Think of the millions of people that have been killed, not just by Hitler but by the smaller Hitlers before him."

"I know," said Lois.

"That is true," said Brent.

David and Goldie looked at Jim Silver, who remained silent. For a moment Goldie thought of addressing him, but then apparently she decided that nothing could be done with him. Then Goldie said, "Yes, we've been enriched, and we have also been made poor, very poor. As I said, my father and my uncle taught me a great deal. The poor Jews did not pay as much as the intellectual Jews. The poor Jews, as I have said, lived as Jews and built up a wonderful culture, especially in Eastern Europe, in Russia and in Poland and in Rumania—especially Russia and Poland. I know, I know, the Russians and the Poles are anti-Semites, their churches are anti-Semitic. The Russian Orthodox Church is terribly anti-Semitic. And the Catholic Church everywhere is anti-Semitic. My father and uncle told me about the anti-Semitism of the popes, nearly all of them, what terrible things they did to the Jews in Rome and in Spain and everywhere; it's a terrible church, the Catholic Church, for the Jews. But I think in Poland it is especially terrible to the Jews. Still, even so, the Jews of Eastern Europe produced a great culture, and this culture was the making of writers who wrote about the poor Jews, those who lived normal Jewish lives. Sholom Aleichem and Peretz wrote about them, not about the intellectuals. These intellectuals were really lost, as I have said. They were brought up as good Jews, like their poor parents, but they studied worldly books and became doctors and chemists and got Ph.D.'s in philosophy and in other things, and they looked for jobs as teachers and as professionals, you know—doctors, lawyers, and things like that. And being Jews, they couldn't get jobs. Germany was, still is, anti-Semitic."

"That is true," said Brent softly. "That, I'm afraid, is very true. Germans don't like Jews. Austrians are even worse. They always were more anti-Semitic than Germans. After all, Hitler was an Austrian."

"I wonder about all these generalizations," said Jim Silver. "I've heard them before, but how true are they?"

Brent looked at him. "How much time have you spent in Germany and Austria?"

"Oh, a few days now and then," said Jim Silver, a bit subdued.

"Well, I've lived there, especially in Germany, and I have spent a lot of time in Austria. Austrians hate Jews even more than do Germans, if that is possible. What is true is true. Goldie is right."

Goldie went on: "So these intellectuals couldn't get jobs, and they began to think maybe they should forget about their Jewishness, only a few got converted, but many just stopped being Jews, the kind of Jews they were home. And now they were not Jews and they were not Christians. They had no roots, no emotions. You know, people, what I sometimes think?"

"What, Goldie?" asked Lois.

"The saddest person in the world is the one who has no holidays. He is really lonely, really. I don't mean holidays like the Fourth of July. No. They are good. But religious holidays have more emotion. Especially to a Jew. Now, take me. I'm not a very good Jew, but I am a Jew. I couldn't imagine living without Passover and Rosh Hashonoh and Yom Kippur. They go back to my childhood. They add a holiness to my life. And these lost intellectual Jews had no more holidays. They lived cold lives. And, I hope you will forgive me, Brent, I hope you will, that is your tragedy and the tragedy of millions of other intellectuals. But, here, I have spoken for so long, and you said it so much better in a few words."

Jim Silver stood up and walked about the room. The others ignored him. Lois brought some fresh coffee and some left-over cake and nuts and cookies. "Now, really, no more talk. Enough of the intellectual life."

David took Goldie home. They said almost nothing about what went on in Lois's house. When he got back to his own apartment he had difficulty falling asleep. He was depressed by what he had heard and seen. There were so many non-Jewish Jews in the world. They looked upon themselves, as did Jim Silver, obviously, as emancipated, when actually they were lonely and miserable and without a home. They will probably learn the full extent of their misery when they are older and have been rebuffed time and again by a Christian world that, in the main, prefers to keep Jews at a distance. This was tragic. But there was also something uplifting about what he had witnessed. Brent realized the great emptiness in his life. And perhaps, thought David, other lost intellectuals also were realizing the emptiness in their lives. And there was something else. Lois. David hadn't seen her for years. He had heard many terrible things about her. And many of the things were terrible. This was especially true of her espousal of the Arab cause. She was clearly ignorant of the whole situation. She undoubtedly reflected the views of many intellectual Christians who looked upon themselves as liberal. At the same time, she did reveal, only a short while ago, that she was not wholly insensitive to the attitude of the Jews. She was dead wrong in her basic attitude to Israel. But she wasn't hopeless. A woman who could talk as she did about the richness of Jewish life down the centuries of time was not entirely hopeless. Something could be done to make her see all the facts. Was this entirely good? No, it was not. It was tragic that Jews always had to allow for such aberrations as Lois's and to look for ways to remedy her mistakes. Jews could not depend upon basic human instincts for Christians to be decent. Most Christians were poisoned, mentally, in Sunday school, at home, in church, by the anti-Semitic teachings of the New Testament and the priests and ministers. Jews, of all people, had to be cognizant of this initial poisoning. And Jews, of all people, had to look for ways to combat this violent anti-Semitism,

231

and this sort of anti-Semitism, inculcated in the Sunday school and at one's mother's breasts, was most difficult to deal with. One therefore had to look for the slightest means of combatting it. Nothing was too slight. And yet it was all so sad, and there was so much ground for Jews to despair. But Jews cannot afford to despair. Jews, above all people, must hope against hope. David thought of Helen. If only she were with him now, and he could hide his face in her breasts and gain comfort there.

ten

Goldie wrote to Helen about the Lois party, and so did David, of course. Both Goldie and David toned down the arguments that took place at Lois's party. Helen, however, sensed what had happened. She was disturbed, and wrote to Goldie to give her all the details: "I know my David. He is probably more upset than any of us realize. He probably is not sleeping on account of what happened. Please call him and do whatever you can to make things easy for him. How I wish I could be with him now. He suffers so much all alone, and he tells nobody." Goldie wrote back, saying, "It wasn't so bad. David gave a good account of himself. Lois wasn't so bad, though I could kill her for what she said about the Arabs and Israel. She's all for the Arabs. She's plain ignorant. But maybe it's worse. Maybe she's more anti-Semitic than you and I realize. All *goyim* are anti-Semitic. Her husband is just a good-natured drunkard, who is a little ashamed for not being more Jewish than he is. There was somebody else there, a terrible man, Jim Silver, the worst kind of Jewish anti-Semite I have ever met. I could have spat in his face, I hated him so much. Your David was wonderful.

He just didn't look at Silver. Maybe David was more right than I was. I got angry. David just ignored Silver. So don't worry. I will call David, and have him come over for dinner. I want to tell you that your David, whom I saw for the first time at Lois's party, is really wonderful, so gentle, so quick, and so sensitive. I could fall in love with him myself. Don't worry about anything."

To David, Helen wrote only enthusiastic letters, how glad she was he had "such a good time" at Lois's, how glad she was that he and Goldie had met, and urged him to go to Goldie's house for dinner once in a while: "She is a diamond, Goldie is. We have worked together so often, so many times, in so many shows, and we have never had a fight about anything. A diamond she is. There is none better. I suppose she was very strong in what she said at Lois's house, though she didn't tell me, but don't let that worry you. She is very frank about everything, but she has a heart of gold—plain, pure gold. And please, darling, don't worry about that writers' conference. You will be good, you will be very good. I know you will. And always remember I love you more than anything in the world, remember that, please."

After Lois's party, Helen wrote to David almost every day, long, warm, encouraging letters, and for a while he was wondering why he liked to get them, but he wondered if there was a special reason. There was a letter from Detroit that ran on for pages, which he liked especially, since it told him so much about the Jews in the United States. She wrote, among other things: "Darling, Detroit is a city like I have never seen before. I always thought all they did here is make Fords, and the only people here were people who worked for Ford. Detroit meant Ford. Well, was I surprised! When we were booked to play for a week here I thought there wouldn't be anybody to come to see us. But was I wrong! There are thousands and thousands of Jews in Detroit, so many, it's just a pleasure. There is a wonderful community center here, and so much goes on there, lectures, dance recitals, all sorts of things. I went there two days ago, just because I wanted to go there, and I went into a room, and I heard people singing songs, Yiddish and Hebrew songs, and I went into the room, and I saw that young boys and girls were singing, and older people, not so much older, and I was so thrilled. David, darling, I sometimes think that laughing and singing are the two greatest weapons of the Jews. Jews singing! Isn't that just wonderful?"

In a letter from Omaha, Nebraska, she wrote: "David, I thought that Nebraska was like Siberia. Who ever goes to Nebraska? I thought only Indians and cowboys and cows lived there. I never knew of anyone who lived there, I never got a letter from anybody who lived there. But was I surprised! There are many people in this state and so many Jews, thank God. And there are synagogues and community centers and there is a B'nai B'rith lodge and other lodges, and there is a Hadassah, and you should have seen how many Jews came to see us. It was just wonderful, just plain wonderful. I went to a Reform temple here. I had gone to a Reform temple before, in New York, other places. You know, I wasn't too happy, because, like you, I was brought up Orthodox. But again I was wrong. Reform Jews are Jews, too. It was a beautiful service, Friday night. Very beautiful. I liked especially the lighting of the candles, and the rabbi was good, and then the Oneg Shabbat was very beautiful, too. David, I just didn't know what was going on in this wonderful country, all over, and it's good for Jews here, very good. I hear now and then of this or that *meshuggene goy* saying something bad about Jews, but very few. Most of the people are real nice and friendly. But, darling, I'm becoming like you. Good as it is, it's not as good as it should be. We are still a small minority, a very small minority, and the air you breathe is not Jewish. We are tolerated, we are even accepted, but Jews don't want to be tolerated or accepted. They want to be part of the community, just like the trees are part of the community, just like the sky and the stars. Only in Israel are the Jews part of the community. In no other country. Only in Israel. Sometimes, darling, I can't blame some of the intellectuals who try to be part of the community by forgetting they are Jews. That is not too difficult to understand, but these intellectuals are wrong, all wrong. No Jew can ever forget he is a Jew. If he forgets for one moment, the *goyim* will remind him, not by saying so, of course, but by their silence. The Jews have always lived in a world of silence. That is the tragedy of living outside of Israel."

235

David was delighted to get these letters from Helen. They comforted him . . . about the state of the Jews in the United States, and about the fact that the United States west of the Hudson was not all wilderness, generally and Jewishly. Helen's letters also gave him comfort in his current state of bewilderment. He had given up journalism and was going into teaching, which he had never done before. He was writing a great deal of fiction, short and long, and also poetry. But he felt uneasy. He was at a crossing of the ways in his life. Coming home was a depressing experience. Home was not home. It was walls and silence. He caught himself talking to himself or listening to the radio, not because he was attentive to any program, but only because he wanted to hear a human voice in his unhuman apartment.

Helen was warm and intimate and devoted, but there was something that was holding him back from suggesting that they be married. He knew that this was troubling her, too. He felt that he was being unfair to her, and he wondered whether he wasn't also being unfair to himself. Could it be that he was a psychological bachelor? He doubted it. He was troubled about her occasional lapses from what he considered good taste, but perhaps, he thought, this was immature on his part. After all, she had been married before, she had given herself to another man before and had a child by him. It was reasonable that she should talk about her late husband and about her child. Helen was right. These references signified nothing except that she was human; if she ignored her late husband and her child she would be unnatural. All this was true. Yet, there was something that made him hesitate to ask Helen to marry him. Now he began to think of other matters in this regard. Was she too excitable for him? She obviously liked to go to parties, and he didn't. She liked to go out a great deal, to the theatre, to concerts, and he could get along with little of such excursions. And in the back of his mind there was the suspicion that she had slept with men other than her husband. He was ashamed of such thoughts, but he had to be honest with himself. Maybe the best thing, in this marriage business, he said to himself in despair, is to marry when you're in your early twenties and then you save yourself from many such problems. But he was no longer twenty; he was more than twice that age.

Then there was the news from home, in Boston. His father Moshe was ailing. He had been having pain in the middle of his stomach for three or four years now. He had gone to the clinic in the Massachusetts General Hospital. The doctors had taken X-rays and made various tests, but they seemed to be in the dark. One doctor thought there was nothing organically wrong. He suspected "sheer nerves. He appears to have stomach spasms of undisclosed nature. It interferes with the flow of bile, and there also seems to be a tightness in the lower intestine, and definitely in the colon. But surgery is not indicated, of that I am sure. I would suggest he go on a bland diet, milk, eggs, cottage cheese, and weak tea. He should try this for a month or so, and above all not worry, that surely will not help his stomach nerves." Moshe did try this bland diet for a month, but it did not help. Another doctor suspected something wrong in the liver, and he made various tests: "the liver seems to be all right, as far as I can make out. I see nothing wrong there." A third doctor wondered whether there was anything wrong with Moshe's metabolism, so he put him through various metabolic tests. The doctor said: "I wish my metabolism were as good as his. It's perfectly normal for his age. As far as I am concerned, he can eat whatever he wishes. He claims he has little appetite, but that is not terribly significant. What is significant is that whatever he eats he digests very well. I just don't know what to say."

Moshe continued to fail. He was losing weight, though not too alarmingly. He slept well. He did a normal day's work. But he did seem to be tired much of the time. Besides, there was the purely mental problem. He kept much to himself. He took long walks alone. He spent many hours in synagogue, more than ever. Even when he was at the table, or visiting, he appeared to be off elsewhere.

One of David's sisters wrote: "It's so sad. Father comes home, eats, and goes into the front room and sits there for hours, even after it gets dark; he just sits there alone, thinking. Sometimes I go in and ask him if he wants tea or something, and he just mumbles 'no,' he doesn't want anything. He isn't that way all the time. Sometimes he's very cheery and talkative, and you know his jokes, about people in his shop, about some of the *rebbes* (Chassidic spiritual leaders) that he sees, about the news. But then he shuts himself off from everybody and we just can't get to him."

One of David's brothers, the lawyer, wrote, "I tried to take Father to a movie or a show, or just a walk, the other day, but he said no. And right after that he went out by himself and didn't come back for three hours. When he came back we asked him where he had been, and all he said was the park. But what worries me is his physical health. I know the doctors say it's all right, but I don't think so. He eats all right, he sleeps all right, as far as we know, but he seems to be tired and weak. I don't really know what it is. He walks a lot, you know. He'd walk miles to save a streetcar fare, he's against the big corporations, he says, you know; and he is strong, he lifts things, and everything like that. But he still doesn't look right. I tell the doctors, and they ask for symptoms, and I tell them what I tell you, and they look at me as if I were crazy. Well, I hope I'm wrong."

The whole family knew that one of the reasons for Moshe's present state was the death of his wife, Nechame. The two had argued over the years, chiefly about Zionism—Nechame was pro-Zionist, he was dubious, subscribing mainly to the traditional notion of waiting for the Messiah to come of his own free will, very likely on a white donkey. The white donkey was not something he actually believed, it was only a symbol of the quiet way in which the Messiah would come into Jewish life, to redeem his people from all oppression and persecution, and to bring peace to the whole world. And they had sometimes argued about money matters. Moshe was a small earner, and the family was large, seven children, and sometimes he just didn't have enough money to pay for the bare necessities. There were also arguments about religion: Moshe was more Orthodox than his wife, and he insisted at first that the children eat nothing before the *seder* on the Passover, and since the Orthodox services at the *seder* generally lasted more than two hours, till nearly nine o'clock, the children would get restless from hunger, and Nechame would plead with him to let her give them a "piece of matzoh, with something, maybe fruit, maybe something else." He objected to this as a form of disbelief, but afterward accepted his wife's suggestion. In fact, he pretty much agreed to his wife's suggestions throughout their life together, but it took some persuasion on her part. She knew how to persuade him, and all arguments ended in peace. When she died he barely knew what to do with himself. Apparently he had depended on her to make up his mind for him on various matters, more matters than the children had known about. There was complete and absolute trust and love between them, such as existed among Orthodox Jewish immigrants from Eastern Europe. The husband came first to these women, and the children came second. The husband made decisions, and the wives carried them out. This didn't mean that the wives were "mere servants," as some of the Americanized children of these parents said. Not at all. Very often, as in the Polonsky household, the wife, in her quiet, persistent way, ran the household actually, but the husband thought that he was running it. This was all right with the wife. She didn't look for credit. She had no interest in being labeled a "first-class human being, just as you are; we are equal." All the wife was interested in was the health and well-being of her man and her brood. The matter of credit was not in her mind at all.

David had written to his father several times, but received no answer. He had not expected an answer. Hitherto, when he had written to his parents, he got answers, in time, from his mother, who wrote for Moshe as well as for herself. She was the correspondent as well as the housewife. David only wanted his father to know that he was thinking of him. His brothers and sisters reported that Moshe enjoyed David's letters: "He reads them over and over again, sometimes he reads sections to us several times. Of course, he lets us read the letters, but he insists that we return them to him. He saves all your letters. As a matter of fact, as you know, Mother did the same. They're in a shoe box in her bureau, and Father probably puts your letters alongside of the letters that Mother saved."

Then, one morning David got a long letter from his father. He recognized his labored, shaky handwriting on the envelope. It began with "My dearly beloved son," which brought a lump to David's throat. This is how his mother used to address him. Moshe thanked him for his letters, and wanted him to know how "deeply grateful I am to you for remembering your father. It is always good for a father to know that his children are still

239

his children, not just part of the outside world. A family should always remain a family. Your mother, blessed be her memory, is gone now to her well-deserved reward, and that is all the more reason why those of us whom the Uppermost has spared should stick together as a family, as a Jewish family should be. It is families that have kept the Jews together through all their long years of Exile, which now, thank God, is ended."

Then he went on, "I have been thinking about the Jewish state a great deal lately. Your blessed mother was right. As usual. You know, my dear son, that we did not always agree on this matter. I was a little old-fashioned. I waited for the Messiah. But I didn't think the matter through clearly. There are many guises to the Messiah. Our great rabbis have indicated that the Uppermost, blessed be His name, appears to His People and to the world in many forms and guises. The Messiah is the Messiah, but he could appear in the guise of Ben-Gurion or Dr. Weizmann, two wonderful Jews. And the donkey of tradition could appear in the guise of an airplane. Everything is possible to the Uppermost, blessed be His name. So God willed it that the Jewish state should now be ours again, in a way that He thinks best. And I thank God that I have lived long enough to see our land again as our own, as the prophets predicted that it would be. We of this generation are blessed indeed that we lived to see this happen. Nu, so I have not lived in vain. After two thousand years to see Israel ours again. I only wish there would be less trouble with the Arabs, and I only wish that so many fine Jewish young men would not be killed. Such a terrible thing it is to read about the killings. Terrible. We Jews are not war people, we are not killers, we are people of the Torah, but if strangers want to kill us, what can we do? But it's terrible, just terrible. I always think of the fathers and mothers of these fine young men. And young girls, too. So many of these girls are in the Army. Terrible. But I want to tell you that I have put an Israeli flag in our kitchen, right next to the picture of Dr. Herzl that your mother, of blessed memory, put there, and it does my heart good to look at both of them, the picture of that fine man, with that fine beard, and the beautiful white and blue flag, with the Mogen Dovid. I look at the picture of Dr. Herzl, and I am sad. Such a young man when he died; only forty-four,

I read in the *Forward,* only forty-four, think of it. But he will be remembered forever, with the greatest prophets of Israel. There is something else I want to tell you, my dear son. You have written to me, and your brothers and sisters have told me, that you are leaving the magazine profession and are going into teaching. I want to tell you that there is nothing in the world more wonderful than teaching. Jews are teachers. Jews teach the Torah. Every synagogue is first a *Bet Hamidrash,* a place of study. The rabbi is a teacher first and last. Always there is study among Jews, always there is teaching. So I am glad. I know you will be a good teacher. One of our great rabbis said, 'From my teachers I have learned a great deal, from my colleagues I have learned more, but from my students I have learned most of all.' So learn from your students. You must listen to them carefully. Of course, you must see to it that they listen to you, too, but you have very much to learn from them. Nu, so that is what I am writing to you about. One more thing, and you know it. Your mother of blessed memory and I have often talked about it, if only we would live long enough to see you married to a fine Jewish girl. My dear son, a man needs a companion in life, and there is no better companion in life to a man than a wife. I know. Nu, forgive me for bringing this up again. So be well, my dearly beloved son, and you know what wishes you have from me, and I would enjoy more letters from you, when you have the time."

David reread the letter, then slowly put it in his pocket. He was profoundly saddened by it, and he was profoundly elated. He was comforted and he was encouraged and he was inspired. His eyes filled as he began to read the letter again.

eleven

It was Friday night. David had a strong urge to go to the synagogue. He remembered having passed a synagogue not far from where he was living, and the sermon's subject had interested him: "Holiday Thoughts for Every Day." He didn't know what denomination the synagogue belonged to. It really made little difference to him. These days he had little interest in denominations. He had been to Reform temples that were more conservative than some Conservative synagogues, and he had been to Orthodox synagogues that could well have passed for Conservative synagogues, at least as far as he was concerned. He had noticed that the lines of demarcation between the demoninations were slowly getting thinner and thinner. He wasn't sure this was entirely to the good; differences in theology were good for growth in religious thought and tended to enrich religious life. In any case, what counted most to him in his present state of mind was the deep Jewishness of the service and the learning and religiosity of the rabbi.

As soon as he entered the synagogue he knew he was where he wanted to be. Men and women were sitting together, the men were wearing yarmulkes. The synagogue was virtually full. There was a fine Friday evening spirit. The *chazen* was good; his chants had *ta'am* (flavor), and he sang with sincerity as well as with professional skill. David always waited for the cantor to make the *kiddush* (blessing) of the wine before deciding, to himself, whether he was his kind of cantor. The cantor at this moment definitely was his kind of cantor. He had a powerful, melodious voice, and he pronounced the ancient words of the *kiddush* beautifully, word by word, syllable by syllable: "And it was evening and it was morning—the sixth day. And the heaven and the earth were finished and all their host. And on the seventh day God had finished his work which he had made; and he rested on the seventh day. . . . Blessed art thou, O Lord our God, King of the universe, who created the fruit of the wine." Afterward there was an *Oneg Shabbat* downstairs—a celebration of the Sabbath, a mark of delight in what God had done. Then the rabbi got up and began to talk. This was a little different from the usual procedure, as David knew it. Generally the sermon came just before the blessing of the wine. But it made no difference. Maybe the rabbi had the right idea, thought David. After some tea and cake the congregation would be in a better mood to hear a talk. Of course, there was the danger that some of the congregation would leave after the service and not stay for the talk. It apparently wasn't so this time. As far as David could make out, the entire congregation was present for the talk. This obviously spoke well for the rabbi.

The rabbi began quietly. "My talk tonight will wander a bit. I will say a few words about assimilation, about the differences between Jews and Christians in certain areas, and I will try to elucidate a concept that has caused some confusion in certain circles, especially among intellectuals. I refer to the concept of the Chosen, the Jews as a Chosen People. One sect of Jews, small but significant, the Reconstructionists, have eliminated the reference to the Jews as a Chosen People from the blessing made at the time of an *aliyah*—being called up to a reading of the Torah. I am not sure that was a wise move. I am not criticising them for doing it. The House of Judaism is wide and spacious, and there is room for a multiplicity of views, so long as the fundamentals of Judaism remain, and the fundamentals of Judaism certainly remain in Reconstructionism. The founder of the Reconstructionist movement was Dr. Mordecai Kaplan, who was my teacher at the Jewish Theological Seminary. I revered him then, I revere him now. He is one of the important men in American Jewish thought today." He smiled. "I have just unwittingly made a mistake, for which I hope my teacher will forgive me. I called him Dr. Kaplan. I should have called him Rabbi Kaplan. He once said that as the American rabbinate has declined, rabbis have become doctors. I guess there's something to that. I have never heard Maimonides referred to as Dr. Maimonides, or the Vilner Goan referred to as Dr. Goan.

"There was a great German philosopher, Rudolf Eucken, who said that there is, at bottom, only one question in life, insofar as man's relationship with the world outside himself is concerned, and that is: Is the world friendly? The simple truth is that there is much evidence that the world is not friendly, I mean that nature is not friendly. There are floods and sickness and hurricanes, and there is plain old age. But a wider view of the world, of life in general, leads us to think that there is more to the world than disease and hurricanes and old age. There is, first of all, sheer beauty of nature. My wife and I recently came back from Europe on a boat, and I used to sit outside in a deckchair, especially at sunrise and sunset, and watch the rays on the ocean and at night I would look at the stars and the sky and always marveled at all this grandeur. The world has hurricanes, but it also has the night sky, and the ocean, too. There is also love of wife and love of husband and love of children. And there is art, music, painting, and sculpture.

"Is the world friendly? The question can be answered in different ways. You can say yes, and you can say no. Religion has a simple and positive answer. It doesn't claim to have all the answers. Religion is not afraid of questions, any questions. Let me say that I mean one religion, Judaism. I cannot talk for other religions. Judaism insists upon people asking questions. After all, the Bible has two of the most atheistic books known to man: the Book of Job and Ecclesiastes. I say atheistic. I mean, of course, books that ask the most difficult of all questions, and Job argues with God. You will recall what Job's wife says, when he makes his celebrated complaints about what God had done to him. She says, Curse God, and die. And the people who compiled the Bible let that book in as inspired.

"No, Jews are not afraid of questions. As a matter of fact, there is a tradition that says that if a community has no atheist, it is incumbent upon the community to go out and hire an atheist. The theory is a simple one. An atheist asks questions, and answering him strengthens the faith.

"I said religion says that life is more friendly than unfriendly. Religion—I mean, of course, Judaism—does not deny the unfriendly aspects. But it says that in the end goodness does triumph, and this means that the universe is friendly, by and large. Bad people triumph, get big jobs, but history rates them as they should be, and their eminence becomes pathetic. Who here would want to change places with President Harding? I don't mean, naturally, where he is now. Seriously, I mean who would want to have his record—his cheap and shabby record, his disgrace, his terrible moral life? Who would want to be remembered by history, down the eons of time, as President Harding is remembered?

"This brings me to another aspect of Judaism. Judaism, more than other religions, is ever mindful of eternity. It says that all judgment must be viewed under the aspect of hundreds of years, thousands of years, forever. It is the only way to get perspective. This is hard to do, of course, but Judaism is not an easy religion. It is a religion for mature people. But, think, doesn't this reliance of eternity make sense? Let's get down to homey, everyday illustrations. Somebody does you harm. The first impulse is to get angry, raise your blood pressure, disturb your digestion, take it out on your wife. But what sense does this make? If you say to yourself, why should I upset myself about this bad man? What will what he did mean to me a hundred years from now, or ten years from now, or next year, or next week? Isn't it better to ignore him and forget him? Of course it is. But this attitude comes only from viewing things under the aspect of eternity, as the Romans said, as the Jews said long before them.

"Judaism goes beyond this. It not only views things from the standpoint of eternity; it says you are part of eternity. Why? Because you are made in the image of God, and God may be equated with eternity. In other words, Judaism dignifies man. Perhaps I should say that it continually affirms that he is not a mere speck of dust on the wheel of history; he is divine. He belongs, in terms of present-day psychology. And he belongs not just to a local club or lodge; he belongs to eternity, he is

245

made in the image of God. Now, there is a corollary to this. If man is part of eternity, made in the image of God, then he has an obligation to see to it that the world he lives in lives up to his divinity, to his place in the entire scheme of things. Perhaps I ought to say right here that this is a fundamental difference between Judaism and Christianity. Christianity says man is cursed with original sin. He is vile, unfit for the company of the angels. Judaism says that man is glorious, for he is made in the image of God, and the Psalms tell us that man is only a little lower than the angels. This is a critical difference.

"Judaism is a moral religion. Not just in the sense that it preaches decent relations between peoples and nations, and mercy and loving kindness. It says that such morals alone make social living possible, and it also says that such morals alone add to one's self-respect. A cheat is not only bad for society. He is also bad for himself. He lowers himself. A cheat, however far gone, really has difficulty looking into the mirror in the morning. There is no pleasure in looking at himself, for he is abominable. Rochefoucauld, the great French epigrammatist, stated it well when he said: Hypocrisy is the homage vice pays to virtue. A cheat who lies about his cheating thereby agrees that cheating is contemptible.

"But Judaism is moral on a global and on a cosmic scale. It says that morality not only works on earth, among human beings. It says the whole realm of nature obeys a moral law akin to man's moral law. Animals help each other. Planets are, so to speak, polite to each other. Planets do not disobey the laws of nature. That in itself is a form of morality. Man, then, belongs to the world of nature, and nature belongs to the world of man. Both are part of the family of Infinity. Both live by the same types of laws.

"The reason why Judaism is now having a hard time with the Jewish intellectuals is that their concern is with the now, not the eternal. If you view life from the point of view of the now there may be some sense in violating all moral laws. But man does not live by the now alone. He lives by the eternal. That is what is meant by conscience. Conscience knows the moral law, and it also knows that the eternal alone is the ever-present. The now vanishes as you talk about it. Man really yearns for the eternal, because, as I have pointed out, he is eternal. All emphasis on the now is doomed to failure. Human nature just cannot live by wine, women, and song, so to speak. Man must live by the eternal. He must live by Torah, which is another word for the eternal. To be brief, the trouble with the Jewish intellectuals is that they are really not intellectual. They have the insight of barroom habitués. They haven't got the big and wide perspective, and without that perspective no one can call himself an intellectual.

"I come back to morals, to contact with the eternal, no, to being part of the eternal. These are the cardinal aspects of Judaism. Now this is what is meant by the concept of the Chosen. There is absolutely no evidence whatsoever that this concept of the Chosen was ever meant to mean that the Jews are better than any other people. The prophets are always reminding them that they are not, that they are sinners, that they are abominators. And the prophets are always reminding them that God had chosen them to be the Way-Showers to the world in morals and in philosophy—that is, to be decent to one another, and never to forget that man is part of eternity, and that the same basic moral law that obtains among them also obtains in the universe without. The Nazis preached the superiority of Germany and Germans to all other nations and peoples. The French also have preached that in the past. The Jews never preached that Palestine and now Israel is superior to all other nations. They only preached the sublimity of the moral law in human relations, the grandeur of the concept of man's relationship to eternity. The Jews have never had a holy war to conquer nations who in their view are inferior. They have not been like the Spaniards and the Arabs, who have waged holy wars. The only wars the Jews have ever voluntarily waged is against their own transgressions of the moral law and the metaphysical concept of the eternal. The universality of Judaism is perhaps best illustrated by the saying of the great Rabbi Meir, who said that even a gentile who obeys the moral law and studies Torah is on a plane with the high priest himself.

"A final word about some of the things that the assimilationist Jewish intellectuals complain of; they complain they cannot accept the concept of an anthropomorphic God, of a monarchic God. This is all so naïve. When the prayer says God is King, all that is meant is that God is justice, and justice is supreme. God is not man. Of course, not man. God is referred to as possessing the attributes of man simply in order to make it easier for us to address Him. He is a Being who stands for Truth and Justice and Mercy and Eternity. Meteorologists refer to an angry wind. They don't mean the wind is like a man. Why don't intellectuals use the same logic, the same intelligence in their dealing with religion as with science? Why don't Jewish intellectuals especially do this? Isn't it a little silly to see Jewish intellectuals running away from what they think is an anthropomorphic God to what they do not hesitate to regard as an anthropomorphic nature? What is so superior about referring to a smiling sun to referring to a merciful God?

"I hope I have not gone too far astray in my brief remarks. I just wanted to say a few words tonight to the visiting students. We have invited many of them to be with us at the service tonight. I only wanted to leave a few thoughts with them. I don't have all the answers. Nobody does. But I do have some sidelights on the questions, and sidelights sometimes illuminate darkness."

David did not recall when he had heard so enlightening a sermon. He had never before heard so comforting a sermon. It made him enormously proud to be a Jew. He now felt he could cope with the problems that came his way. The spirit of the sermon would guide him in his new career of teaching. It would guide him in his writing. It would guide him in all his living. If only Brent and Jim Silver had heard it. If only Helen were with him now, had been with him in the temple. And now another thought came to him: a warm, deep-flowing thought: Judaism was truly invincible; it was based upon the soundest of all foundations, the human spirit, the eternal man and the eternal in all being, which were one and inseparable.

twelve

Goldie did as she was told. She called David shortly after the party at Lois's. He enjoyed going to her home at the beginning, chiefly because she spoke often about Helen, and she occasionally showed him letters from Helen. She also told him some experiences that Goldie had had with Helen, along with others of their troupe. "Helen used to love to travel. Wherever we went she would be the first one up in the morning, walking and walking, and sometimes she walked in very dangerous places, but she never minded. Sometimes she would even walk at night. late at night. Once, in Bucharest, Rumania, she came home, it must have been about two in the morning, and who do you think she had with her? A dilapidated woman, obviously a prostitute, and she sat her down and gave her a big supper. We had very little ourselves to eat, but Helen is always the big, glad giver, she has a heart of gold."

"Then what happened?" asked David.

"To whom?"

"To the prostitute."

"Oh, you know. She went back to her business. Helen saw

her later soliciting, and Helen was heartbroken. She thought she would save her. We argued with her and told her that such people can almost never be saved. They are what they are, because they like it, some sickness in them. Sometimes she would bring in old men, seventy or eighty years old, because they looked hungry. Sometimes I think if she could write she could really write something wonderful about all kinds of places. When she gets to a town, she knows it. But now she isn't so curious. I don't know what happened. She worries a lot."

This was news to David. He never thought that Helen worried about anything, certainly not for long. "Worries about what?"

"Oh, her son. How she'll take care of him. She has so little money. She paid the medical expenses for Mordecai, her former husband. You knew that, didn't you?"

"No, I didn't."

"That's the kind of woman Helen is. She was not in love with him, ever, I think. It was her good nature that made her marry him. He was after her for so long, and he was kind, so she agreed. But she never really cared for him. He was not for her. She needed a lively, younger man, who was excited as she was, a man who could take walks with her in the morning and at night, and go to all sorts of places, strange restaurants, lectures, you know. All Mordecai liked to do is sit and read a book or a newspaper or go to a friend's house and drink tea. That man would drink a dozen glasses of tea a night, maybe more. No, he wasn't for her. She was so in love with a theatre manager in Prague; oh, she would just raise her head and sigh, she loved him so much, but he had a wife, and I don't think he cared so much for her. Maybe I shouldn't have told you, David, I talk too much. Anyway, it was all so long ago, so it doesn't mean anything. Helen loves you. You don't know how she loves you. I've never heard her talk about anyone the way she talks about you. She loves you for everything, but one of the things she keeps on saying is that if anyone should ask her for the best, representative picture of a real Jew, in the best cultural sense, she would say right away, David Polonsky."

"That pleases me very much, Goldie. I like that. I can say the same about her. She is the ideal Jewish woman."

"I will tell her that, she'll be very glad to hear it."

David was disturbed by this last remark. He wanted Helen to know how he felt about her in every way, but he had the feeling that Goldie, a fine woman, was a tattle-tale. She was a good friend of Helen's, but he wondered how often she had said things, unwittingly, that were not all for Helen's good. For instance now. David wished he hadn't heard about the other man Helen was so in love with. He was sure that it was largely out of her mind and heart, but at the same time he wished he hadn't known about it.

"She certainly is," said David, a bit absentmindedly.

"But the whole thing is a little strange," began Goldie, and hesitated.

David was worried. Was she about to tell him something else that he would be happy not to know? At the same time, if she didn't tell him he'd be puzzled and concerned. "What is strange, Goldie?"

"It's about Helen. She's so Jewish now, so deeply Jewish, and that's good, of course. But she wasn't always that way."

"How do you mean?"

"She used to be a secularist once, you know what that means, of course. Maybe I can put it this way, she was more Zionist than religious. She even used to speak about the backwardness of religion, you know. Her father was very pious, and I guess she rebelled. But I don't know, maybe I'm making too much of this. It was only for a little while that she was that way. I guess we all were that way. I'm sorry I mentioned it, really I am. I mean we all go through changes of opinions."

David was even more troubled now about Goldie and her relationship to Helen. Why did she tell him all this, and then apologize for bringing it up? Is this friendship?

"Oh," said David, choosing his words, for fear of revealing his doubts about her, "that means nothing. After all, if you never change, you're not very much alive. I've changed my mind about lots of things, thank God for that. Only dead people never change their minds."

"Of course, naturally," said Goldie.

"Dr. Herzl himself changed his mind. You spoke of Helen being a secularist for a while . . ."

"Oh, please don't say that. She wasn't exactly a secularist.

I sort of interpreted it that way, but it was for a short time. Please don't even mention it to her. Not that it matters if you do, but it would be better if you didn't. Just forget it, it doesn't matter."

David looked at her, and he decided to tell her very little about anything personal. She was a dubious person. He wondered how Helen got to trust her . . . it was all so strange and disturbing. "Oh, don't worry, I won't say anything to Helen. As you say, it doesn't matter. As I was saying about Dr. Herzl— he was a secularist for quite a while, hardly practiced Judaism. Yet then, well, you know what he became, the founder of political Zionism."

"Of course. It's the same about people. One day you like someone, even love him, and then you change your mind about him. People are strange, believe me, I know. They say you never know anybody really until you go into partnership with him, in business, or marry him. Nobody really knows anybody. You live and learn."

David had the feeling that Goldie wanted him to ask her to elaborate, but he was so troubled by her that he decided to say nothing.

She interrupted his thoughts. "Helen told me you're going into teaching."

"Yes, I am. I've never done it before."

She laughed, then she said, "We all do lots of things we never did before. There's always a first time. Every day is a first time. Then, as I was telling Helen, when she spoke about you and teaching, it's good to change your line after a certain number of years."

David didn't like to hear that Helen was discussing him with this strange and dubious woman. "What do you mean?" he asked.

"You have a line of work, a business, or anything. After a while, say ten, twenty years, you get tired of it, and then you should have a change. That's what my father said. The funny thing is that he didn't change himself."

"Well, in a way I'm sorry to be leaving the magazine world. I've put twenty years into it." David was sorry he had revealed this much about himself. He disliked her more and more. She was good to him, inviting him to her home, introducing him to people, some interesting, but there was something quietly evil about her. Worse, he had to keep this thought to himself, for Helen was apparently deeply devoted to her.

"Eh, that's nothing. After a while you won't even think of it. That's the trouble with everything. Things happen and then you forget, and you wonder what you were so worried about. A Russian writer said, I forget his name, nothing lasts, little pleasures last just as long as big pleasures, and the memories of both fade away. Then you get older, and that's all there is to anything, rich and poor, famous and unknown. I think the same Russian writer said, with a woman it's different than with a man, she remembers joys and pains longer than a man does. Why do you think that is?"

"I don't know, Goldie. I never thought of this before. Never."

"But it's true, wouldn't you say?"

David smiled. "I'm not a woman. Really, I don't know. I've never thought of it before, one way or the other."

"Helen told me this. She also told me the name of the Russian writer. But I have a head like a sieve. I hardly ever remember anything. Helen is a real philosopher, she thinks so much about everything. And she has a golden heart. Isn't that a wonderful combination, a philosopher with a golden heart?"

"It is, very much so."

Goldie invited him to a party that he remembered for some time. About ten actors were there, five men and five women. All spoke either Russian or Polish, and all spoke broken English. The women were either large and big-breasted, or small and flat-chested. They all smelled of sharp spices. The men were large-boned and walked erect, as if they were ambassadors or plenipotentiaries. One of them came over to David and asked, "Are you David Polonsky?"

David said yes.

"I thought so," said the man. "Helen told me about you. She is in love with you." He smiled, then looked sad, then smiled again, "I should hate you."

"Why?"

"Because I love her, and she said she cannot see anybody since she knew you." He squeezed David's arm and said, "You lucky, lucky man." He put his fingers to his mouth and made a sucking sound. "She is a juicy woman, so juicy." And he walked away. David was offended by him. What, he wondered, was Helen doing even as an acquaintance of such a man? But then he remembered vaguely the tangy reputation of Russian actors.

Another man came up to him and introduced himself. "Goldie told me to come to you and present myself. I am glad to know you, Mr. Polonsky. As they say in America, a friend of Helen's is a friend of mine. You shouldn't feel so lonesome. We are all friends of yours. Goldie told me you are a professor in a university."

David was taken aback. "Oh, no, I'm not a professor. I'm going to teach in a university. For the first time, as a matter of fact."

"But you are still a professor, Mr. Polonsky. More a professor than I am." The man was satisfied with his joke. Abruptly he changed the subject: "Goldie is such a wonderful woman, so helpful, so thoughtful. She told me how much she has helped you."

David felt dismay at hearing this strange statement. He must tell Helen about Goldie, and he must warn her against the woman. But how? "Yes, Goldie has been very kind."

"And so many sufferings she has had, so many," said the man. "Really? I didn't know. I'm sorry."

"It would make a tragic play, more tragic than *King Lear,* believe me. But she's so brave. Look at her now, over there. If you knew what I know, you would wonder how she can be like that. But she's so brave, only like Russian woman can be brave. But she talks only to Helen."

"Oh."

"But we all know everything," said the man, mysteriously. "Very brave she is. You were at the party for Lois Scannell?"

"Yes."

"I know. Goldie told us." He made a sneering grimace. "She will not help us. I knew it all the time. I always knew it."

"Did you expect any money?" asked David. He was really indifferent but he felt he ought to say something.

"Well, yes, we did and we didn't. Some months ago a group of us met her, Helen was there too, and we told her about our project, to bring the Russian theatre to the people of America. Helen also wanted to bring the Hebrew and the Yiddish theatre to America, the American people, of course. You know, people are now talking about cultural exchange. It's a very good thing, only the right projects don't get the money. So Lois Scannell, she said she was interested, so excited she was, you know how excited she gets, and we all thought it will be, she will help us, herself and other people will help. She kept us, as you say, on the string. That's why Goldie went there the other night with you. And a few days later she called up Lois Scannell. Goldie told us she hardly remembered her on the telephone, isn't that terrible, cruel? Goldie had to remind her. Do you think Lois Scannell really drinks so much?"

"I really don't know."

"You are a fine gentleman. In Russia there is a saying that when a man doesn't tell if a woman drinks, he also doesn't tell if she makes love." He laughed, then resumed his serious manner. "So you know what I'm going to say. Lois Scannell said no. But your Helen got a little money for a smaller project. She knows Hebrew and Yiddish as well as Russian. I am happy for her she has some work. I can never understand Americans; never, never will I understand them. A promise to them is nothing, nothing at all."

David was annoyed by this criticism of Americans. "Don't people break promises in Europe, in Russia, and in Germany and in England?"

"Of course, but not when they make a definite promise." He looked around. "I must go. Someone is asking me to come over. So very nice to meet you, Mr. Podolsky."

David wandered about, listening to this little group or that. They were all talking theatre in mixtures of English, Russian and Polish. What annoyed him especially was that when they burst out laughing it was at something said in a language other than English. At one such group a tall woman with a florid face, thick neck, huge bosom, and small eyes turned to him. "Are you David Polonsky?"

He said yes. Whereupon she almost pulled him aside, threw her arms around him and kissed him first on one cheek, then on his mouth. She smelled of rancid liquor and cigarette smoke. "I so wanted to meet you. Is your name David?"

"Yes."

She straightened out his tie, unnecessarily, then said, still looking at his tie, "Of course." Then she looked him straight in the eye, "You are shy, like Helen says." She patted his cheeks with her big hand. "You are sweet. You must come to have dinner with us, any night after the first. My husband and I have to go to Chicago. He is now in Detroit. He is a furrier. He is not an intellectual, the way we are, but you will like him, everybody does. My name is Anna Kurlandofsky. Take it down please, the name and the address. Mrs. Sergei Kurlandofsky, that is my husband's name, and the address is 229 Seventy-ninth Street."

"East or West?"

She laughed. "I always forget. My husband says sometimes I will forget my own name. Oh, it's East, I think, yes, East. And I will get your address from Goldie. I love Helen."

"She's a lovely woman," said David, feeling a little foolish.

"My best friend, that's what she is. I tell that to my husband, and he says I am foolish that I tell that to all my friends. That is not true. My husband doesn't know me. Helen is my best friend. I say this from my heart." She raised her hand to the sky. "Now you believe me?"

"Of course."

A short woman came over and said to Mrs. Kurlandofsky, "Are you talking to Helen's friend?"

"Yes, to Mr. David Polonsky. I must go now. Remember now what I said."

"Thank you," said David.

"My name is Olga Titiev," said the short woman. "I've heard about you from Helen. I said to myself that anybody about whom Helen talks the way she talks about you, that man must be wonderful."

"You embarrass me, Mrs. Titiev," said David.

"*Miss* Titiev," she corrected.

"Sorry. Miss Titiev."

She smiled. "I'm one of the few remaining Russian-Jewish feminists. I am married to an engineer, Peter Goldfarb, who couldn't come tonight, he had to be in Seattle on some business. I think you would like him. I know he likes you."

"I didn't know he knew me," said David.

"He does. He has read some of your short stories and your articles and reviews. And we have, really, heard about you from the Tobiases."

"Oh, the Tobiases! They are just marvelous, simply marvelous people!"

"We were supposed to come over several times when you were there, but Peter was away or I was away on a production. These things happen. I just want to tell you how glad I am to see you. My husband ordered me to tell you that we would be delighted to have you come over to our house. For dinner, of course, and to meet some people. We have all kinds come to our house, crazy people, brilliant people, *meshugoim*, you know, and I think you would enjoy being with us. I know we would enjoy having you."

"Thank you."

Miss Titiev looked at him and then smiled. "You just don't know how much Helen loves you. All she talks about is you. I'm not exaggerating. Once she said, 'My greatest tragedy is that I didn't meet him forty years ago.' Isn't that marvelous? To have somebody feel that way about you?"

"I guess Helen is my best publicity agent."

"Couldn't be better. Did you know that you and I and maybe one or two other persons, and Goldie of course, are the only Jews here. Goldie spoke about that to me in passing, of course, and she doesn't like it. It just turned out that way. Many think I'm Russian Orthodox or Greek Orthodox, I don't know why, and it would be too much trouble for me to tell all of them the truth, but I do tell them the truth whenever the opportunity offers, but I don't feel right with so many *goyim* around, and Russian Orthodox *goyim* have a special hatred for Jews. I know many of them claim to be free and liberal and they say they are atheists and agnostics and God knows what else, but I don't trust any of them. A *goy* is a *goy,* and a Russian *goy* is one of the worst, maybe even worse than a Nazi."

"Really?"

"Well, that's a little exaggerated. But I'm so glad to know you. You just spoke to Mrs. Kurlandofsky."

"Yes, why?"

"She's a drunkard, and other things. She said she'll invite you to dinner?"

"Yes."

"Maybe she will and maybe she won't. She's very stupid, so is her husband. Both are drunkards, and both are stupid. And

both are anti-Semites. When they get drunk they talk about
zhiden, and their house is full of ikons and pictures of this saint
and that saint. It makes me sick to look at all this stuff. I went
to their home twice. I had to. Her husband is very wealthy, and
he has given us lots of money, and sometimes they invite us to
a party, on Easter or Christmas, you know, and there are flaming
crosses all over and big thick candles, like piano legs or horses'
hooves, all over, and there are priests, those Russian priests make
me especially sick, with their dirty beards and their long, what
do you call them, *kapotes,* those long coats, black, that go
down to the shoes?"

"Yes, *kapotes.*"

"When she finds out you are Jewish, she may forget her invitation. She drinks so much she hardly remembers anything. I
just think I ought to prepare you. Don't be offended if you don't
hear from her. She's a drunken pig."

"Oh, well, I won't be offended whatever she does. One remark
by Mrs. Eleanor Roosevelt I always remember: you can't be
offended by anybody whom you don't allow to offend you."

"Yes, she was a fine woman, Mrs. Roosevelt, much finer than
her husband, who was a liar and a conniver. All the American
Jews think he was so good to Jews, but while they were thinking
so he was having secret conferences with King Saud of one of
the Arabian countries. A trickster."

"Yes, I've been hearing about his trickery. Frankly I find it
hard to believe, because I almost worshiped him, you know."

"I did, too. So did Peter, my husband. He's been simply heartbroken about this. He said that if you can't trust Roosevelt, whom
can you trust? And he said that he is beginning to think like his
grandfather, who was a *maggid,* you know what that is?"

"A lay preacher."

She smiled and touched his hand. "I apologize. From your
writings I should have known that you know more about Jews
and Judaism than I do, much more. My husband said about
you, as a matter of fact, he said it recently when we met the
Tobiases, I forget just where it was, isn't it terrible how you
forget as you get older; this happened only a few days ago, maybe
two, three weeks. Anyway, he said that you, David Polonsky,
know more about Jewish customs than anybody he has ever met.

Oh, he will be so glad to see you. You write about Boston, don't you?"

"Yes, why?"

"Peter, who reads you, says that your descriptions of Boston are just perfect. He went to MIT, the Massachusetts Institute of Technology, when their buildings used to be in Boston, I don't know the street."

"Boylston Street."

She smiled. "That's it. I always used to call it Bulbe Street, Potato Street, I don't know why."

"Boylston Street is anything but Potato Street. I mean it's very fashionable. Of course, MIT now is in Cambridge, and it has many huge buildings. You've been there, of course?"

"Many times. Peter always drags me to affairs at MIT. I go because I like to go to places. But I know nothing about engineering. The people are nice, though. We met the Comptons, the Nobel Prize physicists—two brothers, aren't they?"

"I guess so. My knowledge of physics is exactly nothing."

"That's more than I know. Peter says not only don't I know anything about any science, but what I think I know is all wrong."

"That applies to me, too."

"Are you married, I mean were you ever married? Never mind, I shouldn't ask you these questions. I'm sorry. Sometimes I'm like other women, even though I am a feminist. Forgive me."

"It's nothing at all."

She smiled. "Women are women. It reminds me what my *bobbe* said. Education, art, nothing changes women very much; women are women. Anyway, the most womanly woman I know is Helen. I just adore her. Peter says there are two words for her: *genuine* and *Jewish*. Believe me, David," she touched his hand, "believe me, I mean every word of what I say. If anything happened to Helen, God forbid, Peter and I would go crazy. That's how much we love her. She really is one in a million. Even her mistakes, that's what Peter says, even her mistakes are genuine. Will you do me a favor?"

"Of course."

"I don't know if I should say it."

"I have to leave it you. I don't know what you wish to say."

"I will, then," said Olga. "But remember it comes from the heart. Be good to Helen."

"Of course."

"Please."

David didn't know what else to say. He was dismayed, and he was pleased, and he was dismayed. "I like her very much."

Olga looked at him. "Is that all?"

David was stumped. "What do you mean?"

"You men are all alike. You just don't understand that women like to hear certain words, certain very simple words. My husband is the same. Other husbands are the same. All men are the same."

"I love Helen," said David.

"That's better. Helen will be glad to hear this."

David smiled. "She has heard it."

"I am glad."

"She has heard it from me. Didn't you know it?"

"Forgive me, David. I'm so worried about Helen. If anything happened to Helen, like I said, Peter and I would go crazy. You don't know Helen, you just don't know her, David."

Now David was worried. "What do you mean?"

Olga looked aside, then looked at David, "She has suffered so much, so very much. Never mind. Just be good to her."

Olga was right. Mrs. Kurlandofsky did not call David. Goldie, however, called him the very next day, apologizing profusely. "David, please, please, David, forgive me, I'm ashamed to write to Helen about what happened."

David was startled. "What did happen? I had a good time. I'm grateful you invited me. Everything was just fine."

"Oh, David, you don't have to say that, you really don't have to. It was a terrible party. First of all, I hardly talked to you, but there were so many people, and they all kept on coming to talk to me, and everything, you know. I kept on looking for you, and when I saw that terrible woman, Mrs. Kurlandofsky, talk to you, I thought I would die. She's so coarse. She is simply impossible. That's when I sent over Olga to save you. Isn't she a darling?"

"I like her very much."

"And she likes you. Her husband, Peter, is a diamond. He adores every word you write. But I am so sorry about the party. There were so many terrible people there. I had invited many others, but they couldn't come, for this or that reason. And there was so much drinking. These terrible Russian people drink like sailors, they drink and drink and get so coarse and cheap, you know. I just don't know what I will tell Helen when I write to her about this party. She'll kill me. I can almost hear her say, 'Goldie, what did you do to my David?' "

"Oh, Goldie, don't say that. I had a marvelous party."

"I knew you would say that. But please forgive me for that terrible Mrs. Kurlandofsky. Actually, you are lucky. Her husband is even worse. What he has tried to do with me and with Olga and with Helen. He's so terribly cheap, it's impossible to tell you. Sometimes I think it's hard to blame him, when I look at her. How can any man kiss her and make love to her? But forgive me, please."

"Forget it, Goldie. I had a fine time. Really."

Olga and Peter invited David to their home several times. Their home was a most pleasant gathering place for the kind of people he wanted to meet. Other than the Tobiases', theirs was most congenial. At times he met people there whose opinions dismayed him and disturbed him, but in the main he was at peace at their home. The Goldfarbs were without guile; they had no ulterior motives; they were honest; they faced facts; they were Zionists, and they listened to people as well as talked to them. The more he learned about Olga and Peter the more he liked them. Olga was an actress who, at present, obtained few parts, because she was along in years and also because of her accent, which actually wasn't too pronounced, yet wasn't "pure American." Olga came from an Orthodox family in Russia, but her mother was pretty much like David's mother, Nechame. Her mother was "worldly," read novels and poems by non-Jewish writers as well as by Jewish writers. She was a Zionist, a devout Jew, a good mother, and a loving wife. Olga "revolted" in her youth, she was anti-Judaism, she was anti-Zionism, and "pro-Russian." She became an actress, and for a while preferred to play in "purely Russian" plays. This pained her parents, but they could do nothing about it beyond suggesting that she rethink her position, which, of course, she didn't. She was first married to a non-Jew, an actor. Her parents were heartsick about this. After two years of marriage to the non-Jew, she divorced him because he used to call her, at various times, "a damn Jew, a marvelous mistress, a beautiful vagina, and an untrustworthy female Jew." As their brief marriage continued he drank more and more. One night he struck her on the face and on the stomach when she refused to have intercourse with him. She decided then and there to divorce him. It was then that both her parents died, within three months of each other, and all her life she couldn't get rid of the feeling that she was the cause—that is, that her marriage to the non-Jew was the cause of their deaths. She then suffered a nervous collapse. Not long afterward she met Helen, who comforted her and introduced her to Peter Goldfarb, who at once fell in love with her. Olga could never forget his first serious talk with her. It was brief but it changed her whole life: "Olga, I love you. I love every little hair on you. I love your eyes and all the tears in them. The past doesn't interest me. Your marriage was not a marriage. It was a misstep. You are more of a Jew than you know. I am completely a Jew. I want you to help me be a better Jew. You need me to be a better Jew yourself. Olga, we must be with each other. We need each other equally. You are the Jewish woman I have wanted all my life. I am a scientist. You are an actress. It's a marvelous combination. Let's get married."

David had the feeling that Peter, despite his eminence as an engineer, was at heart an artist—a painter, sculptor or musician—yes, a sculptor. How Peter had got into engineering mystified David. David liked Peter's deep Jewishness. Peter once said to him, "If I had been born in no religion, and I had been told about several religions, I am absolutely sure I would have picked Judaism. It is the only rational, mystical, truly complete religion I know of. I feel sorry for Jews who get converted to any other religion. Judaism is a philosophical religion, it's a scientific religion, it's a smiling religion, it's an ethical religion, it's a historical religion. All my hopes and dreams and desires are encompassed in it. Judaism answers no questions. That's one of the beautiful things about it. It makes no promises, the way Catholicism does, or some of the Protestant denominations. It evades nothing. Sometimes I think the Jewish God could be a professor at MIT, the Massachusetts Institute of Technology. It's an open society, Judaism is. It has no top guys, no popes, and stuff like that. I mean every Jew can talk to God any time he wants to, and he needs no introduction from a rabbi, not even a chief rabbi. As you know, I'm only an amateur musician, I'm not a musician at all, I just peck away at the piano. Olga is the piano player in the family. But Judaism has a melody that suits me just fine. I like the violin tone, the oboe tone, the combination of the two, in Judaism. This is strange talk from a hard-headed engineer, but this is the chief truth that gives meaning to my life."

David liked this man, and he wrote to Helen telling her how much he liked him: "This is a man after my own heart. He is a male Helen." To this line she replied by special delivery: "Darling, darling David. With this line alone you have made me happy for the rest of my life. Darling, I kiss your picture every night. I know this is being sentimental, girlish. But that is how I feel about you. I feel girlish about you, deeply, forever." Later David wrote to her: "I am profoundly impressed with his devotion to Jewishness. He is all of Jewish history brought down to date. I hope you don't mind my saying that I feel closer to him than I feel to Olga. I like her, I like her very much, but there is something belligerent about her that troubles me. You, darling, are not belligerent. A woman mustn't be belligerent. A woman is the one qualification to the belligerence of life. That is what a woman is. She is soft, she is doubting, she is loving, she says no to the harshness of life. That is why, Helen, I am so devoted to you. Olga is a feminist. And a feminist is not a woman; she is a woman trying to be a man. I hope I have not offended you. I know how much you like Olga." To this she replied: "Darling, you are, of course, right. Olga is Olga. Frankly, I don't think she's a feminist now. Feminism is only a habit to her. She really doesn't believe in it. If she did she wouldn't be so in love with Peter. She will do anything he wants her to do. He smiles at her feminism. Be charitable to her. And keep on loving me. This is all that matters, that you

263

love me, as much as I love you. You will never know how much I have missed you on this trip. But I had to make it. I need the money, darling, it's as simple as that. I didn't tell you, but my Azriel needed some serious medical attention a little while ago. I'll tell you about it sometime. It has to do with his sex organs, and I was worried. It was very expensive. I had to borrow money. I tell you all this for you to know why I went on this trip. I had to go. I miss you so very much."

At the Goldfarbs' one night, David met three persons different from any he had ever known. These were Dr. Abraham Kasin, a psychoanalyst and psychiatrist; his wife, Thelma, who taught vocational guidance and typewriting in the New York public schools; and Karen Schmidt, a niece of Thelma's. Before David had been in their company ten minutes, Dr. Kasin said, "Call me Abe, and call my wife Toby. Her name is Thelma, but I call her Toby in bed, and that is how I would like others to call her."

David was shocked at this display of bad taste, and could merely reply, "As you say, Abe and Toby." Whereupon Abe added, "And call Toby's niece Kushy. Her husband is always kissing her, and kissing, as you know, in Yiddish, is *kushing*. So Karen is Kushy. Don't you think this is sweet?"

David wanted to say he thought this was all horrid, but he said, "It's interesting. So it's Abe, Toby, and Kushy."

"Right," said Abe.

Olga interrupted, "David, you call them anything you please. Abe is rather domineering, which is strange for a psychiatrist. He is henpecked, that's why he's so combative. Is that the right word, Abe?"

"Absolutely. The male must always be combative. Women like that." He turned to David and said, "Don't be alarmed. This is all a show. Olga and Peter like to have me act this way when I meet new people, I mean when they introduce me to new people. We are really very simple and complicated. I am simple and complicated. We all are. I really don't know what I mean. Anyway, I'm glad to meet you." He shook hands with David a second time. "You've met Toby and Kushy?" David shook hands with them also a second time.

Olga came over to them and offered drinks. She looked at

Abe first, apparently expecting something special to come from his mouth. He did not disappoint her. "Well, my love," he said. "Make mine an absinthe straight."

Olga looked around: "Do you want it in a glass or without a glass? Or will a cup do?"

"Without a glass," he said.

"Would you like it without something else, perhaps, if I may ask?"

"Yes, without everything, but put anything in," he said.

"Very good," said Olga. "The usual. Straight vodka with a little French vermouth."

"You are a darling," he said. "Come right over here and I'll kiss you, first chastely, then honestly."

She did as she was told, and he did as he promised. She took the drink orders from the others. David asked for a mixture of port and sherry, half and half. "Did you ever try it, Abraham?" he asked.

"Abe is the name," said the psychiatrist. "Now, as they say in movie courtroom scenes, repeat the question, please."

"Did you ever drink a half-and-half mixture of port and sherry?"

"I heard you the first time," said Abe, and burst out laughing. "I just wanted to be a professional lawyer. Yes, I've had the mixture, and frankly I like it better than the vodka concoction."

"So why don't you change your order? Olga will be glad to do it."

"No. If I change my order, Olga will be disappointed."

"Disappointed? What do you mean?"

"I know it's *meshugge,* but that's how we all are. It's the only thing I have learned in my business of analysis and psychiatry and all that. We're all *meshugge.* Oh, we know a little bit, and we do help people. I'm not a complete fraud, and psychiatry is not a complete fraud, but there's so much we don't know and there's so little we can do." He became serious, and David liked him better this way than when he was carrying on with his jokes. "I get case after case, people who look perfectly normal, married, in business, in professions, men and women, and yet they're all tied up in knots with all sorts of problems. There's a story that will interest you. It's about a man who saw giraffes. Have you heard it?"

"No."

"It's a real good one, David. You'll like it. I can tell by just looking at you that you'll like it. This man was having trouble. He couldn't sleep. Every time he went to sleep he heard giraffes and elephants and buffaloes running under his bed, making all sorts of noises. This went on all night, he said. Naturally, he couldn't sleep, and he was in a bad way. He went to a psychiatrist, and he had him for six months. You know, he asked him if he ever hated a girl who looked like a giraffe or if his mother looked like a buffalo, and he hated her, and he asked him similar questions about his father and brothers, whether they looked like lions and tigers, you know. Oh, yes, all kinds of animals ran under the bed. Well, the psychiatrist couldn't help him. So he went to another psychiatrist, and he put him through the same analysis, and he couldn't help him either. Then he went to some super-super analyst. People said that if this one couldn't help him, then there was no help for him. Of course, this super analyst couldn't help either, and the poor man was left to shift for himself. Six months passed, and this super analyst was walking down Fifth Avenue, and there he sees the man, all smiles, without a worry on his face. He stops him and he says, 'You look fine. Who was the analyst who helped you?' The man answered, 'An analyst? I didn't go to another analyst.' 'Then who helped you?' The man answered, 'My brother-in-law. He's a carpenter. I told him my troubles, and he said that he could fix it. All he did was cut the legs off the bed, and now I don't hear any more lions and buffaloes and giraffes running under the bed.' So that's how valuable analysis is sometimes, and how common sense sometimes solves all sorts of problems. Isn't that some story? Every analyst I tell it to just roars with laughter."

"That is funny," said David, who was really touched by the story, but he didn't quite know how to express his pleasure.

Toby Kasin merely wandered about the room. Now and then she stopped at this or that group, listened, smiled, and went on. David couldn't quite make up his mind about her. Somehow she offended him physically. When she smiled, which she did most of the evening, her poor teeth showed. Long before, David had developed a deep revulsion for poor teeth or false teeth, especially in women. He knew that this was unreasonable, but he couldn't help himself. She came to where Abe, her husband,

and David were talking. "Abe has wanted to meet you for some time," she said. "He used to be, maybe he still is, a great admirer of the *World*."

"Oh, yes," Abe said. "That used to be a wonderful magazine, still is, in a small way, and I heard you were the man behind all the hard work."

"Well, I wouldn't say that," said David.

"We'd like to have you over our house sometime soon," Toby said. "Kushy would also like to meet you. You met my niece."

"Yes. I was hoping to talk to her sometime during the evening."

"Not here," said Toby. "This place is like Times Square. Over at our house, you'll have a real chance. What about two weeks from tonight, for dinner?"

"I guess that's all right. But I'm a little confused. If you don't hear from me in two days, it's a date. I hate to be so difficult, but I have a vague recollection I have something to do then. Is that all right?"

"Perfectly," said Toby. "You just have no idea how deeply Abe is attached to the *World*. For a psychiatrist he really has an obsession."

"A little knowledge is a dangerous thing," said Abe.

"He says that to me all the time," said Toby.

David had learned a great deal about the Kasins from Helen, and from others. Abe Kasin had been a high school teacher in Brooklyn for almost fifteen years. He taught general science and social sciences. He had a Ph.D. from New York University in psychology, or, to be more specific, educational psychology. His wife taught typewriting and vocational guidance in the New York City junior high schools. At present she was at one school, the Fiorello La Guardia Junior High School, where she did both: she taught typewriting and she practiced vocational guidance. How she had got into vocational guidance she didn't know. Apparently, as she admitted to her teacher friends, "The real reason, I guess, is that Abe, my husband, is a psychologist, so I suppose they figured that a little of his psychology had rubbed off on me. I know nothing about guidance, if there's anything to know. I confess it frightens me a little, no, not a little, but a lot. Think of it, telling somebody not to study engineering but to go into social work. It's terrible. There are late developers, there are all sorts of other considerations. In junior high, what does anyone really know what he wants to do? I didn't know. In a sense I still don't know. The only thing I know, I admit, is type-writing. So I'm frightened."

She came from a radical non-religious Jewish family. Her father, a physician, belonged to the Sholom Aleichem organization, the non-religious but deeply Jewish group. These Sholom Aleichem people were for Jewish culture, and against "organized" Jewish religion. He had received his M.D. in a Russian university— his father had been wealthy, and he was able to get his son into a Russian medical school . . . few Jews were admitted, and her father was one of them. Soon after he came to America and had passed his State Boards in medicine in New York State, he became ill. Just before that he had been accepted by an insurance com-pany, which had a wonderful proviso for people, especially doctors, who became disabled in the practice of their profession. Not long afterward his heart became affected, and he had to retire from medical practice. At the moment he was on a very generous in-surance allowance and had no financial problems. But he had other problems. He was idle, and lying in bed was a dreadful bore to him. Also, he could not go out at night, which meant he could not attend meetings of his Sholom Aleichem society, and he could not participate in any "social movements," such as sup-porting the Paterson, New Jersey, textile strikers, or the Gastonia, North Carolina, strikers, and he could not go to their protest meetings. But he made up for his delinquency, as he called it, by reading their literature and writing letters to their publications, and also, of course, talking to various officials on the telephone. Toby told David once, "I wish he had never taken out that policy. It's wonderful, and it's terrible. I believe he could practice medi-cine now, and he'd be a happy man. But the policy says he must be totally disabled, and so he rots away. But I can't say it to him."

Toby's father had been a militant socialist in Russia. He had been arrested several times for participating in anti-government activities, and through a fluke had never been sent to Siberia, as had some of his colleagues. "Why they let me go," he said to whoever would listen, "I don't know. There was some legal technicality. I don't know exactly what it was. It embarrasses me. But that's how it was."

The reason might have been that he was a physician, that he was admitted to a medical school even though he was a Jew, and the authorities apparently didn't want to take a chance with a man who had such "privileges." In the United States, before he became ill, he joined various organizations that aimed to "democratize" the American economic system. He was a vigorous Yiddishist, arguing that Hebrew was the language of "a fanatical minority, and that also reflected the views of the capitalist class in America." His daughter, Toby, who was not too well informed about the situation in the United States, and who really knew almost nothing about the relative merits of Yiddish and Hebrew as the dominant language of the Jews, accepted whatever her father said, and became a Yiddishist-Socialist, with vague ties to Zionism, so vague, in fact as to be non-Zionist. Abe's parents were pretty much of the same political-economic persuasion, insofar as world affairs were concerned, though in the realm of Zionism they were somewhat inclined to Dr. Herzl's views. Abe's father used to say, "They don't like us, the *goyim,* not a single one of them. There is no exception, none at all. I used to think some of the *goy* intellectuals were different, but I have discovered so many of these same intellectuals who are also anti-Semites, polite ones, of course, that I have given up hope. I don't think Israel will solve all the problems of the Jews. The *goyim* still won't like us, but at least we'll have a state that will be able to answer them in the name of all the Jews. It's the best we can hope for in the *goy* world."

It was, indeed, at a radical-liberal-progressive meeting of Jews in Brooklyn, to which both Toby's and Abe's parents went, that Abe and Toby met. They had both come along with their parents, and they took to each other at once. Toby was a bit taller than Abe, but she was so warmly chubby, and there was such an endearing smile on her face all the time, and she seemed so agreeable that he could hardly keep his eyes off her. They were married less than two months later. Both were "advanced," and hence were married secretly in the City Clerk's office. Much to their surprise the two sets of parents insisted that they go through a religious ceremony as well, and that they also have a "regular wedding"—with relatives, a supper, dancing. Toby and Abe wondered why. The answer was simple, "What we believe and what we feel are two different things. Anyway, a *chasineh* is a *chasineh*—a wedding is a wedding."

After the wedding Toby went back to her typewriting teaching and Abe went back to his high-school teaching. His Ph.D. naturally gave him status and also a larger salary than many of the other teachers got. But he was vaguely unhappy. First and most important there was his marriage, which was far from what he had hoped it would be. Toby turned out to be a *shlump* as a housekeeper. She also was dull in bed, and she read the New York *Post* at night, which was a slightly superior New York *Daily News*, a shabby tabloid. She clearly enjoyed the *Post* much more than *The New York Times*. Still, she had her uses, as he shamelessly said to himself—shamelessly, because he was so disappointed in her. She did make breakfast during the week, also supper, and on Sunday she made lunch. She attended to the bills. When they had married he had tentatively suggested that she take care of the rent, telephone, gas and electric, and other bills, because it bothered him to do so. She agreed, and he thought that she did this because of her love for him. She did do it for love, but she also did it, it was clear, because she liked detail. He had read, in his psychological studies, that women love detail and find great joy in it, but he had hoped that his wife would be different. Alas, she was not different. She was just another sloppy, faithful, dull Jewish girl-woman, who spouted whatever ideas her father or husband expressed, but really had no convictions of her own. She was reasonably clean and neat, but sometimes he wished that she had fixed herself up more, with more delicious perfume, more fetching clothes; in short, that she was more alluringly feminine. She did nothing of the sort, and he found that, when making love to her, he had to imagine that the one he was making love to was Claudette Colbert or Greta Garbo or Kathryn Grayson, a second-class actress, the very sight of whom excited him sexually.

There were other matters that troubled him. Though a Socialist, he wanted to be well-fixed financially. But he didn't know how to accomplish it. There was the moral-spiritual problem, which, while it didn't trouble him as much as it would have a half dozen years ago, it nevertheless still did so. He had obtained his A.B. at Syracuse University, where he had been a firebrand, according to the local press, in the various protest meetings of the student "liberals" and "radicals." In fact, the university president had told him, "Because of you, we have lost more than two million dollars in gifts. Donors demanded that I dismiss you, because of your un-American speeches and activities. Of course, I refused. A university is a place of free speech, for both faculty and students. Still, I must admit that I didn't like to lose two million dollars. A university can always use money. Syracuse University especially can use money, since we have so many projects in mind." Abe was flattered by this confession from the president of his university. Abe was an important man. The Socialist and Communist publications in New York praised him for "the vital spark of academic progress that Abe Kasin had instilled into the staid halls of Syracuse University." *The Nation* and the *New Republic* praised him, and this worried him, in the deepest recesses of his mind . . . he wasn't altogether sure that what he was doing was the right thing at the university. He had said several things he wasn't sure of, for example that "the university is a cesspool of reactionary colonialism, and the university is an arm of capitalist exploitation . . . the arm of Wall Street is long and has reached to Syracuse University." He spouted all this stuff because it sounded very "realistic" and "intelligent" and "advanced," but deep down in his own mind and heart he wasn't at all ready to defend the logical aspects of his statements. He was exhilarated by his statements, but not at all certain of his facts or his arguments. What especially troubled him was that he was really repeating things that he had been fed by "outsiders"—he didn't quite know who they were. They came, they went . . . sometimes they spoke to those he knew at the university . . . these people were also vehicles. He felt vaguely unhappy, but there was something very heady about being quoted in the local newspapers and in *The Nation* and the *New Republic* and in *The New York Times*. He was surprised that these publications he had trusted so much had fallen for his "line." He was not going to take them too seriously hereafter. He was sorry . . . it wasn't pleasant to stop believing in periodicals that you had believed in completely for so long. . . .

But despite these reservations Abe was still a Socialist . . . the capitalist world was not "just and fair to the workers and toilers, and a radical change is needed in society." He looked upon Wall

Street as "the enemy of the people, a cesspool of gamblers, blood-suckers." He wrote for the *Socialist Call* and for *The Nation* and for the *Globe,* and also for the *Journal of the National Educational Association* and some of the more learned psychological periodicals.

Abe had a brother, a dentist, who taught a branch of dentistry at Temple University. This brother, Phil, had for long tried to interest Abe in investing in stocks and real estate. At first Abe had refused summarily: "I will have nothing to do with the most contemptible aspects of capitalism." But slowly he had reconsidered. He thought thus: "I object to the Stock Exchange business. It's a form of gambling. That is true. At the same time, I have life insurance policies, and they buy stock in companies on the New York Stock Exchange, so why shouldn't I do the same?" He did, at first on a very small scale. He bought only blue chips—American Telephone and Telegraph, General Motors, Eastman Kodak, International Business Machines, Alcoa, but he soon learned that Blue Chip stocks were not always the best stocks from the the point of view of growth and profits. So he also bought some "speculative" stocks, such as Xerox and Polaroid. He discovered that while his dividends were small, sometimes as low as three-quarters of one percent, his growth profits were enormous. Abe was learning rapidly the strange and mysterious ways of the stock market. Still more important, he was learning that it was possible to become "independent financially" by playing the stock market, if one really knew the market. He learned the hard way. He made money, he lost money. He learned about the differences between income stocks and growth stocks, and about the differences between the various mutual funds, which no-load funds were really good, which were worthless, and the like.

There was another lesson that Abe learned from his brothers: the marvelous income that there was in real estate, because of various legal technicalities. His brother told Abe to buy into certain hotels and business buildings in Detroit, since they "guaranteed a 14 percent income annually, with so many tax loopholes." Abe bought some stocks in these real estate items, and he was enormously pleased by the yield. He told Toby about his transactions, and she merely smiled and said, "That's good." It troubled him that she wasn't apprehensive about these dealings, violating his resolve never to trade in the stock market, "that cesspool of gamblers." This only added to his annoyance. He said nothing. He only worried about the ways of the world. Before he married her, he would have sworn that Toby was absolutely civilized, didn't care a whit about money, and lived by "ideas and ideals," as the phrase went then, but now he learned that his beloved Toby was the same vulgar, insensitive, money-loving woman that he had decided, years before, he would never marry. How on earth had he ever made this mistake? Were women really, after all, the gateway to hell that the old theologians had been saying all along? It seemed so, but he wished to God that he didn't have to agree with these theologians. What a life, what a life. . . . He became more and more cynical. He plunged more deeply into the stock market, and he discovered that he had an instinct for stocks that would go up and split. Before a year was over he had earned about twenty-five percent over his investment, which was truly remarkable, when one recalled that savings banks were paying only four percent interest and government bonds were paying only three percent. Abe was pleased and shocked. As he said to himself, "The people are being swindled. They are told to invest in safe savings banks and government bonds, but they are really losing money when they do this. The reason is very simple: the interest rate of savings banks and government bonds only accounts for the rise in the cost of living. The people are being horribly swindled. This is terrible. They should invest in common stocks, which are paying much more." He himself had earned in one year twenty-five percent above his investment. And his real estate, protected by various state laws, was giving him fourteen percent. The whole thing was ludicrous and tragic, and American society was sick, very sick.

This, however, didn't deter Abe from buying two slum dwellings in lower Manhattan. He paid little for them, he skirted most of the housing regulations (perfectly legal, of course), and he was earning a net of almost twenty percent on his investment. Some of his tenants demanded new toilets and the painting of halls and lobbies ("They haven't been painted for twenty years"), but he managed to avoid doing what these tenants demanded, with the aid of a clever real estate lawyer. He was more secure now, financially, but he was also vaguely troubled. This was all fine, and it was all not so fine. To his consternation, Toby was more

273

disturbed than he was. "You really should get them new toilets and paint the halls. What they say is true. I don't care what your lawyer says. He's a shyster. These people are right." Abe argued with her, but he knew she was right, and he also knew that the desire for money was powerful in him. He knew he was unfaithful to his old principles, but he was filled with satisfaction whenever he went over his bank accounts. He was in very good shape, indeed, financially. Why should he give up his status? He didn't say this to Toby. He was ashamed. This woman was embarrassing him. She wasn't much in bed, but she was very embarrassing in these financial matters. This pleased him, but it displeased him even more. Slowly he was becoming more and more accustomed to being a stock exchange trader, and his new affluence gave him pleasure. Tenants in his slum dwellings continued to make their demands, but he wasn't as much troubled by them, emotionally, as he used to be. He called them unreasonable, and on several occasions he told them, "If you are unhappy here, get out. I'm not keeping you." He reported this to Toby. He could tell by her silence that she didn't like what he did. This disturbed him. He would say to himself that a woman who was so unsatisfactory in bed was really not worth listening to, but emotionally he didn't really believe this: alas, there was some substance to what she was saying. She objected less and less to his ways of making money. He was glad, and he was unhappy. He wished he knew what she was thinking. He didn't dare to ask her, for fear she would tell him.

Teaching social science in high school now made little sense to him. He didn't need his salary. Besides, there was the matter of prestige. He wanted to be a university professor. He wrote a few articles on "social dynamics" and "the psychological principles of racial integration" for psychological magazines. He got favorable letters; so did the magazines. He used these letters to get a post as assistant professor of educational psychology at Fordham University. He was unhappy there. As he told Toby, "I'm not much of a Jew, but seeing nuns and priests all day long is no pleasure." So he got another job, this time as associate professor of educational psychology at the City College, and now he was content. He had money—from his stock market operations—he had academic prestige. Good. But he didn't have love.

274

He took care of this quickly. At City College there was a young married Ph.D. in history who took a shine to him. At lunch one day she touched his thigh, and in two days they were in bed. She complained about her husband, an accountant: "All he thinks about is money and debits and credits. He has no real values." This relationship was fine for a few weeks, but then she began to demand that they do something "sensible." When he asked what she meant, she said, "Divorce your wife; I'll divorce my husband, and we'll get married." This blunt way of stating the situation offended him. There was also the matter of his dissatisfaction with her lovemaking. She had a strange habit of rushing to the bathroom right after an act of intercourse, and he told her several times, "Do you have to do this? It takes away from the romance." To this she answered that it also takes away from the risk of her becoming pregnant. Again he was offended by her crudeness. Then there was a night when she said to him, "I love you. You are such a wonderful lover. My husband does his thing so quickly. Before I know it, he's finished. You're more refined." When he heard this he decided to get rid of her. This proved more difficult than he had imagined, but he did get rid of her.

He suspected that his Toby knew about his liaison, and this also troubled him. When he finally did get rid of his paramour he decided if he was to have more extramarital intercourse, it would be on a term basis: a few days or weeks and no more—"and no strings." He now found his Toby a bit more satisfying. He decided that in marriage no man can ever be wholly satisfied. All a married can do is have an affair now and then, but to be sure not to let the affair become too serious. "Love 'em and leave 'em," he said to himself. He and Toby settled down to a marriage of mutual tolerance. Then Toby became ill. She needed a hysterectomy. This disturbed him more than he had realized. At the beginning of their marriage they didn't want any children, and Toby took the necessary precautions. Then both wanted children, but none came. Now the hysterectomy made it totally impossible. He felt cheated. She felt cheated. Both were depressed. And both knew that from now on they would be together till the end, that they would not really be happy . . . and that life had played a cruel trick on them. Abe tried to make it up to Toby, and she tried to do the same, as if she

275

were to blame for their childlessness, but both knew that it was no use; this was how it would have to be for the rest of their lives. He had an affair now and then, lasting two, three days. He found little relief in it, but it was "a change of vagina," as he said to himself, and there was something in that, though he didn't really know what the change was. He was sure that Toby had no lovers, never had any.

After a time he started practicing psychoanalysis. He got more patients than he really wanted. They paid well: thirty-five dollars a fifty-minute hour. He met many people this way: doctors, lawyers, department store buyers, bankers, rabbis, priests. He was shocked by the troubles all these people had, and he was comforted by the knowledge that their troubles were pretty much like his own: dull wives, dull husbands, a yearning to sleep with pretty young girls, a yearning to run away from spouses, despair over a job, thoughts of suicide (Abe had had such yearnings himself of late), a desire to kill for no reason. He listened to all these miserable people, he took their money, but he was sure he was of little help to them. Some called him late at night, pleading with him to dissuade them from jumping off the George Washington Bridge or taking poison. He succeeded in the case of all such pleas except one. She was a schoolteacher, married to a lawyer, who found herself pregnant after a week of pleasure with the neighborhood newsdealer, a married man with three children: "Believe me, I don't know why I did it. I guess it was because he smelled like bananas. Isn't that crazy? But I can't lie to my husband, I just can't." Abe thought he had dissuaded her, but two days later she jumped from the Brooklyn Bridge. He couldn't sleep for a whole week afterward. He was all the more troubled because he himself had made a pass at her the very time she was sleeping with the newsdealer. He couldn't tell Toby about this, naturally. She tried to comfort him. "After all, dear, these things happen." He had no answer.

Abe was not at peace with himself for many reasons. There was, first of all, Toby, who was a constant reminder of the failure of his sex life and of his whole married life. After her hysterectomy she became even more offensive than before. She developed an odor pretty much like that of Muenster cheese, which he could barely tolerate. Nearly every night he would douse himself with a lotion. At first Toby remarked about this. "You smell like a woman in a harem, about to give herself to her lord and master," she said.

He couldn't help laughing at this—and at the oblique irony of it. There was no giving in this bed, he said to himself, no giving either way. It was a bed of failure and regret and boredom and sheer dullness and disappointment. But he had to answer her now. He suddenly realized that he had been silent for a full minute. He was being impolite to this creature beside him who had helped him to make a shambles of a great part of his life. He smiled a mechanical smile. "Oh, I read in the *Reader's Digest* the other day, or maybe it's some other magazine, that a man, like a woman, needs a lift at night before retiring, and some cologne helps, a man's cologne."

"Since when have you begun reading the *Reader's Digest*? I thought you said it was cheap and all that."

"So it wasn't the *Reader's Digest*. It was some other magazine. What difference does it make, after all."

"My God, why do you make a federal case out of it?" said Toby.

Abe didn't answer. Thereafter he sometimes used cologne, sometimes he didn't. At first she said nothing. Then she brought it up again. "You're all set for the harem again?"

He turned at her. "Shut up! I don't want to hear any more about my use of cologne. I'll use it when I want. It's none of your damn business. If you knew the truth behind this cologne you'd die of apoplexy."

"What does that mean?"

He didn't answer.

"I think I have a right to know, Abe. That's a mean remark you made. What truth do you mean?"

Still he didn't answer."

"Abe, I repeat, I have a right to know. You are hiding some truth about me, or what you think is the truth. I want to know. Tell me."

"Oh, forget it. It was nothing. Nothing at all."

"I don't believe it, Abe. Something is eating you. Tell me."

"It's nothing, nothing, nothing at all."

"Abe, I'm going to insist. I want to know the truth, I mean the truth you were talking about. I'll keep on all night till you tell me."

But how could he tell her he couldn't tolerate her smell since she had her hysterectomy—she didn't have it all the time but a good deal of the time. Didn't she realize it? Why didn't she use some perfume at night when they were in bed together. But how could he say all this to her?

"Oh, Toby, I made it all up. I was angry with you for bothering me about the cologne. Forget it. I just have nothing more to say about this."

This satisfied her, yet not completely. He had just humiliated himself before her by confessing childish anger. Still, she couldn't get rid of the feeling that there was something to what he had said. But she was getting tired, she wanted sleep, and she decided to drop the matter. He was filled with remorse. He knew he had hurt her, and he decided to make love to her. At first she repulsed him, but not too vigorously. The second time she submitted. He had to make an effort of will to achieve potency. The lovemaking wasn't too satisfactory to either of them, but he knew that it did mollify her a bit, and it also relieved him from making further love to her for three or maybe even four weeks. They had tacitly worked out this arrangement of making love about once a month. Sometimes he thought she looked forward to it, for she would cuddle up to him on the night when she thought there would be lovemaking. He never looked forward to it. The very thought annoyed him. Marriage to Toby was thus a problem that would last all his life.

Then there was his trading in the market. He was now making a great deal of money, not only in the market, but also in his slum real estate. Toby didn't chide him for his slum real estate and his neglect of the tenants, as she had at first, but he knew that she was unhappy about it. Worse, he was unhappy himself, deep down within himself. He had wanted to achieve financial independence. Now he had this financial independence and he also suffered shame because of it. He felt trapped by his success. He still read some of the Socialist journals. He reacted to them in a strange way. He followed them closely, agreeing with their logic that capitalism was the enemy of the people, but at the same time he was offended by the shabbiness of the periodicals, and by the obvious poverty of the men and women whose photographs sometimes appeared in these journals. At the same time he defended the Republican party, among those at the brokerage office where he traded, but he did not vote Republican. Toby called him "hypocrite!" He was shocked. She sensed it at once, and immediately apologized. He said nothing. But now he had another reason for disliking her. He knew that she had told the truth, but a wife mustn't do that to a husband. Well, she must, of course . . . a wife must be a man's best and most severe critic. Abe taught this in his classes . . . but he didn't like it when Toby told him the truth. Life was getting very trying to him, but he saw no way out. Worse, he didn't seek for a way out. He knew he would go on the way he had been. Perhaps he would have an affair now and then, just for a few weeks . . . a man needed some womanly softness in his life. Some of the younger female instructors at City College, recent additions to the faculty, had smiled at him. As a matter of fact, he had inquired about them. They were all married. That was fine. He didn't want to get involved with virgins or unmarried women. Virgins would insist he get divorced and marry them, and unmarried women would hold on to him, act the part of martyrs, and in a moment of anger might even tell Toby. Married women would be best. Mutual guilt coupled with mutual need plus the pleasure of secret sin plus a total lack of obligation, save an occasional expensive dinner or lunch. There was no problem of presents. A lover seldom gives presents to a married mistress.

He didn't quite know how it happened, but his first affair with one of these married women was with a Negress. A new faculty member, she had invited several colleagues to her apartment. All had a really good time, Abe liked her smile. She had a lovely beige skin. Her mother was Portuguese; her father was part Indian and part Negro, who traveled for a surgical instrument company and was away much of the time. She found reasons for seeing Abe often. She taught sociology, and he taught educational psychology, so there was reason for her to seek information and advice from him. He then noticed that she managed to rub her body close to his now and then, and he was smitten with her scent. Once he told her so, and she opened her lovely, white-toothed mouth and said, "You do? I'm so glad."

"What is the name of the scent?"

"You would never guess. Go ahead and guess."

"I have no idea about such things."

"European," she said; "4711."

"I've never heard of it. It's marvelous."

"I'm glad you like it." She patted his cheek. "You're the first man who's told me he liked my scent. Even my husband hasn't mentioned it."

She found a reason for asking him up to her apartment, not far from City College. She took him into the bed-room, and told him to throw his jacket on the bed. "Might as well be comfortable." She helped him with the jacket, folding it neatly as she put it on the bed. She turned to him, came close, and smiled at him. She put both her hands to his face, and they were in each other's arms.

"Your husband . . ." he said.

"He's in Minneapolis or Chicago, some place way out West. He won't be back for ten days. You have nothing to worry about." They made love passionately. No woman had ever embraced him with such ferocity before, and her demand upon his sex was at first gratifying and then enervating.

"You sure want it," he said.

" I wants it when I wants it," she said, lapsing into Negro speech. "And you are marvelous yourself. Jewish, eh?"

"Yes."

She fondled his sex, and said endearingly, "Nice little Jewish boy."

This was too much for him. It was just too vulgar for his sensibilities. He was surprised at himself for being offended.

Then she added, "I've had some Jewish men before, but you're the best. And I know you Jewish men like us black girls too. We give them more than their white girls. Well, King Solomon liked the black girls, too. All them Ethiopian girls were his meat."

Abe laughed, but he was revolted . . . this was not the kind of softness he wanted; this was cheap and vulgar . . . what he wanted was what he thought Toby would give, gentleness with sex, tenderness with delicate frankness, not this sweaty, snickering leering. No, not this . . . and he wondered how many of his friends had looked for what he sought and been equally disappointed. Another thought came to him: perhaps Jewish young men were less inclined to this sort of adultery than *goyim*. He was ashamed for thinking such thoughts. And then he was surprised about something else: he wasn't too troubled about adultery, on his part, and his part alone, of course, that was all right . . .

at no time in his married life, now that he thought of it, did adultery on his own part trouble him. But he wanted the partner in adultery to be someone of taste and loyalty, and he wanted the adulterous situation to last a long time, to be a sort of concurrent marriage. Ah, perhaps man really was a polygamous animal, he did need more than one woman. But then, again, maybe this wasn't so. At the time he married Toby he thought that she would be everything to him, the legendary combination of wife, mother, and mistress. It didn't turn out that way. He began to think, on the basis of his talks with other men, it never turned out that way with anybody. Women lost their charm quickly. They also seemed to lose their minds, it seemed. Some women seemed so intelligent before marriage, then they turned out to be simple-minded. Was it because they never expressed their honest opinions, mouthing only what they thought their men wanted them to say? Was it because they have a knack of picking up phrases instead of ideas, and passing the phrases off as ideas? Abe knew of so many men who were so bored with their wives, the same wives who, as unmarried girls, seemed to be so well-read and so brilliant. Was this part of the great conspiracy of womankind against men?

Sex, delicacy, tenderness, modesty. . . . Abe remembered reading somewhere that real courtesans never use dirty words, in bed or out of bed: they sigh and they touch you tenderly and they kiss you all over passionately, but they never use the words of the street, and they don't appear before their lovers naked, for they know instinctively that the female body, most of the time, is rather lumpy and hairy and even smelly, especially in the areas around the vagina and the rectum. A man wants to make love to what he doesn't see, not to what he has just seen and found not so pretty. Then there was the matter of a married woman's regard for her husband's self-respect. Cheating on him is one thing (and Abe saw little wrong in that so long, of course, as it wasn't his wife), but it offended him to hear a married woman in bed disparaging her husband's prowess as a lover.

The black woman interrupted his thinking: "You sure are doing a lot of thinking right after our little party! You white men give me the laugh. Always worried about a thing like this. My black man just gives it to me, good and hard, and that suits

281

me fine, just fine, I just can't stand his being away so often and for so long. And I do need a change of semen now and then, white boy." She burst out laughing. "You sure is scandalized, white boy! You got semen, haven't you, I just felt it flow right through me, white boy. So why that look?"

Abe had nothing to say. He wished he could run out and hide—but where? He couldn't hide in his own home. He would like to talk to his wife and tell her about what had happened to him, but she would be horrified. Actually, he was the one who was horrified. Toby should also be horrified: her dullness and her coldness and her sheer stupidity had driven him to do this, and what had caused him so much inner anguish. But, again, what could he do? Toby just wouldn't understand. She's that thick-skulled. To her physiological purity was all that mattered. If he told her everything she would run home to mother. It might be a good idea for her to run home to mother, but that would solve nothing. Her mother would call him, and her father, perhaps, would call him, and they would talk to him, and nothing would be said that would in any way implicate Toby, and they would hint that he was foolish, that such incidents of intercourse had little value, "they only hurt those you love most, and look where it's got you, it's all so silly, after all, you're a grown man." What can you say to people who talk this way? They lie and they know they lie, but they get a sick satisfaction in talking the way they do. It makes them feel virtuous or superior to the person they are condemning. On his part, he could not tell them the truth: that he was bored and disappointed with Toby, that she was dull, that she was a slob, that she was disappointing in bed, that he wished to God he could get rid of her without hurting her too much. But he would have to add that he was not sure he wanted to get rid of her. That was the strange aspect of the whole situation. He wanted to get rid of Toby and he didn't want to get rid of her. She added no joy and no comfort to his life and she was a bore, but he wanted her around the house, not just to be his maid, but also because at times her talk and her presence, foolish as both were, put him at ease. How could he tell all this to her parents or to anybody else? The world conspired against all truth-tellers. And he thought, how far apart intellectual interests were from emotional obsessions. Well, obsessions was not quite the right word, it implied something not quite right, but actually being encompassed by a girl's or woman's legs, in an act of love, made so much sense in itself that one didn't have to argue about it. At the same time, such legs about one did not always bring contentment. That was the real tragedy of life for a man. Abe didn't know exactly what women yearned for in their relationship with men, but he had a hunch that they hoped for far less than did men; they were less romantic, or was it more truthful to say that they expected less out of life than men did? He was bewildered. Meanwhile, there was Toby, with her obnoxious smell, who was home waiting for him, and that was not a pleasant prospect. And here in front of him was this black woman who was vulgar and cheap and utterly disappointing. He couldn't say who was more disappointing, this black woman or his wife. All the talk he had heard about black women being more sexy was just not true. They were more demanding, they sighed and grumbled more, but they also uttered more obscenities, and this offended Abe. These black women were really not very much. Abe thought, I am a white man, and I must have satisfaction from white women. All other intercourse really made little sense. Intercourse in itself was of little consequence. It was a form of hydraulic engineering. What mattered was the meaningful silence before and after. Uniting sexually was a spiritual act, hardly a physical act.

Abe, however, did not learn his lesson from his session with this black woman. Not long afterward he had an affair with a Jewish married woman, a "liberal, free-thinking, emancipated woman," the wife of a professor of philosophy at Wagner College, Staten Island, New York. The professor was a Lutheran—Wagner College was founded by Lutherans, though in theory it was non-denominational. The woman's husband was an ordained Lutheran minister, born a Jew but converted. He had never explained his conversion satisfactorily to her. The Jewish woman was an educational statistician at Wagner College. At first she was a mere secretary, but in three years she obtained an M.A. in educational statistics, and this gave her the right to her title. Deep down, she was very dubious about her competence, but "a job is a job." In that capacity she met the professor of philosophy, who was attracted to her. He was over forty, unmarried, and apparently making a last search for a wife, and for reasons best known to himself he chose this Jewish woman to be his wife. She wasn't especially drawn to him. As she told her friends, "He's greasy, and so obvious, I mean he touches me all over, even in public, and I don't like it." She was thirty-nine, though she admitted to only thirty-four, and her "remaining time" was limited. Her final comment to her friends was, "Well, it's either now or never. I can't say I'm in love, but I do want to be married. So that's the way it is."

Her marriage took place in City Hall. He pleaded with her to be married in a chapel of Wagner College, "just for the sake of nostalgia. After all, you're taking my name. Why not at least make a token acceptance of my religion?" To this she answered briefly and emphatically, "No. To this I will never agree. Either City Hall or nothing." They were at his apartment in Staten Island when she said this. He came to her and played with her breasts, and then put his hand under her skirt, and she knew that he knew what this did to her. She was very sensual, and she almost fainted when he fondled her vagina, but, as she thought to herself, only a miracle saved her, she absoultely refused to be married in a Lutheran chapel. "Darling, darling, I am just helpless when you do this to me, but in a Lutheran chapel, never, absolutely never. I just don't believe in all that Virgin Mary rubbish. You will have me as I am or not at all, and I am honest with you when I say I wish you would have me as I am. I want you, darling." He was deeply moved, and they were married in the City Hall chapel. She was disappointed by the prosaic quality of the marriage. It took less than ten minutes, and she was profoundly depressed. She thought of her father and of her mother, and of her whole upbringing. To her great surprise, she so much wanted an old-fashioned wedding, the rabbi, the blessing, the breaking of the glass by the groom, the *kazatzke* dancing, the weeping parents, the overeating. Her husband asked, "Why are you so sad, darling? We're married."

"Oh, nothing. After all, it's more important to a woman than to a man. You know what I mean, darling."

He didn't know what she meant, and she knew he didn't know. This only deepened her sense of loneliness. There was nobody there from her family or his family. It was all so open, and so secretive. It was all so wrong. She sensed what a failure her emotional life was. She did what she did because she was afraid that if she didn't do it, she would be even more miserable. But she was miserable indeed, now. She looked at her husband, this Lutheran, and she said to herself, "He's only a *goy,* he has no idea what is going through my mind, what is cutting into my heart."

They made a life for themselves in an apartment not far from the college. They had three rooms, and she wished they had twenty rooms. She wanted to be alone many hours during the day, and, later, at night, too. Sometimes she had the feeling that it was so unreal, that they were playing a game, that they really were not married. He took her to his parents' home, and she took him to her parents' home, but neither of their parents really accepted them, and when they went back to their own home, to their cold, tight, confined little apartment, they were like strangers. They were together, but somehow the world did not confirm their togetherness. What offended her especially was that her husband did not appear to be disturbed—a professor of philosophy, yet insensitive to her need. Well, she said to herself, that's how God wished it, and that's how it will be. She could do no better, she thought. She just couldn't afford waiting any longer. What hurt her was that the passionate lovemaking, though satisfactory at first, somehow did not compensate for her loneliness. There were times when she looked and looked at her husband and was astonished that he had no notion of what she was thinking about.

Abe met her at a psychological meeting, a meeting of the Middle Atlantic States Psychological Association. Her husband was reading a paper there. She came along with him. Abe liked her on sight, and he arranged that they meet together alone. He was so smitten with her that he decided to be utterly honest. They went to a coffee shop on Eighth Avenue, not far from where the meetings were being held. As they finished their coffee, he put his hand on hers and said, "I like you very much. I like you very, very much. I just want you to know it." She had not been too deeply attracted to him, but this outburst moved her, and she at once saw virtues in him that she had not seen before. "I like you, too," she said softly, squeezing his hand.

"That's all I want to hear," he said, in a matter-of-fact manner, and again he patted her hand. She sensed a wonderful warm feeling going through her, and she wanted suddenly to suck his lips. Apparently she blushed. He said, "You seem embarrassed about something."

"I do?"

"Yes. Is it good or not good?" He smiled apologetically.

"My, you're inquisitive. It's good."

"That's good." He held her hand as often as he could, without being too demonstrative. At one point, when he was squeezing her hand, she smiled and said, "Do you mind if I tell you something?"

"No, tell me."

She blushed and said, "Oh, maybe I shouldn't say it."

"Tell me. Please."

"I like to have you squeeze my hand. God, I shouldn't have said it. Me, a married woman."

"Me, a married man," he said.

He told her about his life with Toby and she told him about her life with the Lutheran professor of philosophy. After they had finished confessing to each other, so to speak, she felt very calm, and he felt content, and they both smiled, and again he said, "I like you very much. I want to call you darling."

"Thank you. I'll call you darling, too. It's all so strange."

He kissed her hand, and she kissed his hand.

"Life is so strange," she said.

"Yes," he said. "You are wonderful."

"You are, too."

They made love within a week, at a hotel in midtown New York. It was glorious for both of them. So intimate and trusting had the relationship become that they wrote to each other, at their respective schools, most endearing notes, without fear that the notes would come into the hands of their spouses. As Abe said to her, "I feel, darling, I am yours and you are mine. I sometimes wonder what would happen if anything happened between us, and I get frightened." She said, "I do, too." Abe became a new man. His wife, Toby, noticed it, and one evening after supper she said, "You have grown so much younger and peppier. Have you come into a secret inheritance you're not telling me about?"

He looked at her, a little sorry for her prosaic character, and seeing in his mind's eye the face of his genuine love, and he said slowly, "Well, I might as well confess to you. Three days ago I got a postcard, marked personal, telling me a favorite uncle of mine, in Bialistock, Russia, had willed me six million rubles, a villa of 50,000 acres, and six yachts. I have rechristened one *Toby*."

"So you became converted to Russian Orthodoxy at the same time."

"What do you mean?"

"You said you rechristened the boat *Toby*."

"Oh, I meant re-Mogen Dovided, is that better?" As he was talking he invented a project that he had had in mind for some time and that would satisfy Toby's curiosity about his new attitude to life. "The real news is that I'm going to write a book. I have the general outline in my mind, and now you know why I have been absentminded these past weeks and taking long walks."

"A book about what?"

"William James."

"The psychologist?"

"Right. And the angle is this: I have been studying his life. There are a great many papers on him at Columbia, at NYU, and at the Forty-second Street Library. He is a perfect example of psychosomatic medicine. He suffered from a nervous heart all his life, because of his hesitations and lack of security, as to his competence, first as a physician, then as a psychologist, and then as a philosopher. He had many doubts about pragmatism, his philosophy. Here there was a special problem. Actually, he did borrow a good deal of his idea from Charles S. Peirce, and Peirce's disciples pointed this out. We have evidence that whenever he read such an article, hinting at a vague form of plagiarism, he would develop violent, sick headaches. Well, anyway, this is what I have in mind. Even more, I have an actual outline. And I plan to get the essence of it down on paper and show it to a publisher."

Toby's face glowed, and at this moment he felt for her the same passionate love he had felt when he was courting her. He wanted to kiss her, but decided not to, for that would be unfaithful to his "true love." He couldn't help smiling at this thought. He slept with Toby, while he had been sleeping with the other woman, yet somehow this didn't seem to him to be infidelity, but kissing her, out of bed, did seem unfaithful. He suddenly recalled that he hadn't kissed Toby in months, not even when making love to her. Not kissing your wife. especially when making love, was the first and most revealing sign of what has taken place between a married couple. There's more love in kissing than in intercourse. Kissing often is a desire for another's total being; intercourse often is a mere impulse for a specific evanescent act. Abe was astonished that he hadn't realized this, despite all his learning in psychology.

He worked on the book intensively for a while. The Wagner professor's wife, whom he called Lekach, because the space between her breasts smelled like honeycake, helped him with the research and the typing . . . there was a good collection of James material at the Wagner College Library. They had worked out an arrangement that seemed proof against detection. He had rented a cottage on South Beach, in the distant part of Staten Island, telling the owner that he was working on a book and needed absolute privacy, and that sometimes he might stay overnight, and he might also have some secretarial help: "I tell you all this so that you'll know everything, and I don't want to waste any energy explaining things later. If you have any objection say so now." The owner said, "Dr. Kaltenborn (Abe had changed his name), you do anything you want. It's none of my business. Pay the rent regular, and keep the place in decent shape, and that's all that matters to me. I may be away a good deal of the time myself, and when I make a trip for several weeks I would appreciate the rent in advance. I hope that's not asking too much." The deal was made, and Abe and Lekach had no trouble—and they were in sheer delight. Abe told Toby nothing about this place, of course, but to protect himself, he said he might now and then take a trip to Cambridge, Massachusetts, or Washington, to look at some documents. To make this lie look absolutely honest he did go to Washington once, and took Toby along, adding, however, "I can't promise to take you along all the time. It's expensive, fare and hotel, and I may have to stay for two, three days sometimes, especially during the school holidays." She kissed him and added, "I understand perfectly. I think your idea for the book is just marvelous."

But then something happened that shook both Abe and Lekach,

One evening, at home, Toby suddenly said, "I heard something today that worried me. It's about the book on William James you're doing, dear. Someone told me that he heard the wife of a professor of philosophy at Wagner College, of all places, is doing a book on exactly the same subject. I couldn't believe it. Do you know anything about this?"

Abe could hardly keep from bursting out, "It's a lie," but he realized that this would make things worse. Instead he answered quietly, "It could be. Such things happen. After all, Wallace and Darwin propounded the theory of evolution about the same time, and Newton and Leibnitz, or maybe it was somebody else, my knowledge of the history of mathematics is not too good, but two people came out with the theory of calculus about the same time."

"Yes, I sort of heard of this, but this is different."

Abe looked at her suspiciously. Did she know more than she revealed. "Why is it different, Toby?"

She seemed troubled. "I don't know. It's all so funny."

"But how? Why?"

"I told you I don't know. Have you ever heard of this woman?"

"What's her name? How can I answer you if I don't know her name? I don't even know her husband's name."

"Do you know anybody in Wagner College? You know, sometimes you talk, perfectly innocently, about what you're doing; somebody listens in, you know. Oh, didn't you tell me that you found the library at Wagner College very helpful?"

Abe felt a tightness in his throat. "Yes, that is true, but I also have used the library at Columbia, at NYU, and this I don't think I told you, I have also used the library at Yeshiva University."

"But Wagner is different," said Toby. "Some girl, a clerk or somebody, probably got wind of what you're doing, and she was looking for a subject for a thesis, or something, who knows what could happen. I only hope whoever she is isn't stealing your stuff, I mean your leads."

"Oh, forget it," said Abe. "After all, I have no monopoly of the material. Let's be reasonable. The material is public property, any scholar can use it. I can't lock it up. Besides, hunting up material and drawing conclusions from it are two different things. This woman will draw her conclusions, and I'll draw mine."

"I know, I know, but that's what worries me. This person who told me in the first place said that this woman is studying the psychology of William James himself, I mean his personal psychology, his reactions, you know. I guess I should have asked more questions, but you know how these things come up, you talk and that's it. Do you think I should try to find out some more from this woman?"

"No, forget it, Toby. I'll just keep on working on my book. Naturally, I'm worried a little, but not much."

Abe wasn't going to see Lekach for almost a week, and calling her on the telephone was out of the question. He now began to suspect that his calls were being monitored. And the thought rushed through his mind, Was the love of Lekach worth all this mounting tension in his own home? And he began to wonder whether Lekach really hadn't spoken to somebody. True, she had promised to say nothing to anybody about his project, and of course she promised to tell nobody about their hideout. Still, who can tell about women? Now he feared to bring the whole matter up when they met again. She might get so offended at his suspicions that she really would spill everything. Of course, she would have to do some calculating, for she was involved in adultery, and that was more difficult to bear for a woman than for a man . . . in this case it would be particularly difficult for Lekach: her husband was a convert to Lutheranism, a teacher of philosophy at a rather religious college; his job would be jeopardized, and what would happen to her, an adulteress? These were not the days of Hester Prynne, true, still, adultery was adultery, and Wagner College was Wagner College.

Of course, Toby did talk to the woman again, the one who gave her the information in the first place. The woman didn't know very much more. Toby, without telling Abe, went to Wagner and ferreted out the whereabouts of "the wife of the professor of philosophy" who was involved in the writing of a book on some aspects of William James. She found the woman— her name was Mrs. Daniel (Irene) Beresford. As soon as Toby spoke to her she knew that there was much more to what she had heard than a mere coincidence of research. She dragged out enough from her to be sure that Abe and Irene were seeing each other. Irene was not very clever. In answer to Toby's

290

question, "Do you know a Dr. Abe Kasin?" she answered, "Well, yes. He uses the name Kaltenborn as a pen-name or something. He has a little cottage not far from here, but he wishes to keep it private. He does his research there." This was all news to Toby. Irene freely admitted that she saw him at this cottage, "helping him out in his research, typing, and so on. I hope you see nothing wrong in that? We're mature people."

"Does your husband know about your seeing my husband and helping him in his research?"

"Oh, in a vague sort of way. I don't have to tell him everything."

"I leave that to you, Mrs. Beresford, but do you know that by babbling about the book that you're helping my husband on, as you put it, you have hurt him, by making his idea public?"

"I didn't babble, Mrs. Kasin. I only said, maybe to one or two people, just in passing, about the idea, but that was all. I don't see how I've hurt him."

Toby tried to get the address of the cottage from Irene, but Irene refused.

"Why won't you tell me?"

"It's private. He wants it as his hideaway."

"He's also kept it a secret from me," said Toby. "Is that part of his wanting to be private?"

"That's his business. I'm only his assistant."

Toby looked at her, and began to smile. "You're stupid as well as a bitch." With this she left her.

Toby told Abe everything. He told her everything. "So that's what's been going on behind my back?"

"Yes, I hadn't planned to tell you, to be frank, but now that you present it to me, I admit it. You're disappointed in me, but I was disappointed in you long ago."

"Then do you want a divorce?" Toby asked. "Maybe I'll take that question back."

"What do you mean?"

"You figure it out."

They continued living together for months, being polite to each other, but no more. They even entertained. No one knew anything about their situation. In point of truth, they didn't either. Toby knew that he had stopped seeing Irene. Abe knew that Toby wanted to continue their marriage, but she didn't know how to suggest it without injuring her pride.

One Sunday morning, as they were sitting at the breakfast table, each reading a different section of the Sunday *Times,* he looked at her from the corner of his eye, and was attracted by the softness and warmth that seemed to come from her neck, and he liked the bulge of her breasts as they pressed against her bathrobe. Her hair was neatly done, and a fine scent came from her. He put his paper down, and said, "You look beautiful this morning."

She looked at him, then went back to her paper.

"You really do. I hope you don't mind my saying it."

She hesitated, then said, almost in a whisper, "I don't mind."

There were a few moments of silence. Then he said, "Toby, I was foolish. I'm sorry. Let's try again."

She didn't even raise her head. Suddenly she got up and walked to the living room. In a few moments, he went in too, and saw her staring into space. He sat down beside her on the couch, and caressed her hair. She didn't move away. Then she turned to him, and said, "Abe, you hurt me so much, so very much," and she hid her face on his shoulder. "Abe, please, please . . ."

"What, Toby?"

"I love you so much, and yet . . ."

"Let's forget it, Toby. Let's start again."

They were in each other's arms, and that night in bed they pledged eternal trust in each other. But both knew that their home would from now on often be a place of tolerance for each other. For the first time he really was ashamed of himself. He had engaged in petty cheating and hiding and lying. He really was immature emotionally, he said to himself. He was immature on so many levels: as a husband, as an author (he was unhappy with some parts of his manuscript, the writing seemed so childish, he had never realized he wrote so poorly), and he was immature as a Jew.

Lately he had been thinking more and more of his stand toward Judaism. Somehow he was being drawn to it, to its history, to its philosophy (insofar as he knew it, and this wasn't much), even to its rituals, which had a warm nostalgia. He had also been immature insofar as his attitude toward the workers was concerned; indeed, he was all mixed up on this point. He used to agree with the writers of the left, during the strange era of proletarian literature, that the workers were, in effect, the salt of the earth, and that all owners of almost anything were devils and bastards. This was all so silly. But so also was his later involvement in the stock market. So now he had money, he said to himself, so what? He never would have starved if he had a great deal less. Now he was spending time every morning going over the small numbers on the stock pages of *The New York Times*. He simply could not get rid of a feeling of shame when he did this. Now, in addition to the shame, there was a sense of futility. Why, why?

Finally, he finished the James book. He was not too happy with it. He had the feeling that he could have said it all in a longish article, but the publisher thought otherwise. Cautiously he asked Toby if she minded if he dedicated the book to her. When she heard this she stopped, looked at him, and burst into tears. "Oh, darling, darling, darling, thank you, thank you," and she kissed him all over his face. Then she said, through her tears, "Don't ever leave me, Abe, please don't. I was so hurt, darling, terribly hurt. I'm sorry to bring it up again. I never will bring it up again. But now I must. Darling, I can't help it. I just can't stop loving you. I have been horrid about several things, darling, especially once when I burst out, 'Hypocrite!' I shouldn't have done it. I cried over that for nights and nights, but I just didn't have the courage to say I was sorry. I don't know what's wrong with me. I know only one thing, that I love you, I love you. And for what you asked, I want to kiss you again."

Abe was deeply shaken. His Toby was simple, tabloid-mindish in speech and in many of her ideas, but there was something genuine and truly precious in her, and her devotion to him was almost monumental.

He took her face in his hands, and as he watched the tears coursing down her cheeks, he himself began to feel tears come to his eyes. To hide them, he quickly whispered, "I love you forever, darling," and he kissed her long and deeply. They spent all that night in each other's arms, kissing each other softly, gently . . . he felt her tears, and he was glad that it was nighttime, because tears were in his eyes too. He felt lost, he felt grateful, he felt bewildered, he felt old, he felt young . . . above all, he was happy that he was in the arms of this true woman who was holding on to him, her face buried in his chest.

293

thirteen

The Kasins invited David for dinner, and he found there also Toby's niece, Karen Schmidt, or Kushy, as Abe called her. Though there were only two in the Kasins' family, they had an eight-room apartment. David wondered why, especially when Toby pointed to only one room as "the guest room." Abe was in high spirits that first time, and he said, "You see, David, we are like English royalty. Queen Elizabeth has three hundred rooms in Buckingham Palace, maybe even more, and all that she and her family can use, at the most, is say twenty. What they do with the rest I don't know. I wish they would let Toby and me stay over when we are next in London. In the summer it's so hard to get a place, reasonable, that is, to stay in. I mean reasonable and decent. Those places around Russell Square are cheap, but dirty."

"I've been hearing about the wasted rooms in Buckingham Palace for years now," said Toby. "My dear husband wants the British to make some money on the extra rooms."

"It's not such a bad idea," said Kushy. "I don't see why the English people should keep all those parasites anyway."

Toby touched her on the sleeve. "Not now, dear," she said,

smiling. "Not till after we eat." She turned to David, "Kushy doesn't like British royalty."

"I hate them," said Kushy.

They entered a large room, a combination library-sitting room. There were several paintings in it, one Picasso, two Modiglianis, four Van Goghs, and several Ben Shahns. "I spend a lot of time here," said Abe. "I get a lot of comfort out of looking at these pictures. So much agony, so much joy. Oh, I also have some Chagalls, in a folder. We'll frame them and hang them up. Two are wonderful things, one the famous one of the bearded Jew with the *tefilim* (phylacteries) and *talis* (prayer shawl), and another of a group of *Chassidim* dancing."

"They are good," said Toby. "Chagall has so much in common with Modigliani, I think."

"More chauvinism," said Kushy.

"Not till after we eat," said Toby gently. "We eat first and argue later."

Abe smiled and came over to David, and also brought Kushy over. "This girl, this woman, really," he said, "she has three children. She's a wonderful writer of children's stories, and she also is a fine dancer, and she can play the guitar really well. She's got all sorts of prizes. She comes from Orthodox Jewish people, she had a fine Hebrew school education, listen to this, she was president of Junior Hadassah, and she used to orate from the soapbox for this or that Zionist cause, and there's more . . ."

Kushy began wandering off, but Abe stopped her, but not before she said, "My God, my horrible past, he always brings it up."

Toby touched Kushy's arm. "Not such a horrible past. All nice Jewish girls should have such a past."

"Oh, well, get it over with," said Kushy.

"There isn't any more," said Abe. "I just wanted to give David a thumbnail sketch of your life. Oh, I forgot the now, the present, contemporary now. Now, she's all for the party; well, I don't think she's a member actually."

"Oh, yes, I am. I became one three months ago. I told you," said Kushy.

"That is right," said Abe. "You see, Kushy does everything wrong side out, or however you say. When people were joining the party, she stayed out. Now that people are leaving, because of the party's anti-Israel attitude, Kushy joins. It's not just anti-Israel, the party is, it's also anti-Semitic. That's what I think."

"Oh, there you go again," said Kushy. "It's not that simple. History is a very complicated thing."

"What's complicated about anti-Semitism?" asked Abe.

"It is complicated. Remember the Soviet Constitution. It guarantees freedom of religion to everybody. It's right there in black and white," said Kushy.

"You can't be that naïve, dear," said Toby. "The Constitution also guarantees free, democratic elections, open discussion, everything, and you know what the real truth is."

Kushy clenched her teeth, and began pulling her hair. "Please, please, let's eat. I'm starving."

Toby embraced her. "We love you just the same. Now we'll eat."

As they sat down Toby said, "Your attention, please. My dearly beloved husband will now make his usual speech about liquor and digestion, and liquor and the heart."

Abe stood up, smiled, and sat down. "I always repeat what Bertrand Russell said. He said: 'I never drank before I was forty, and I have taken several drinks every day since I left forty. I do believe that it's the English gin that has kept me hale and hearty these past forty-five years.' "

David interrupted, "And Sir William Osler, the celebrated Canadian physician, or maybe it was somebody else, is reported to have said, 'Anybody who drinks before he is forty is a fool, anybody who doesn't drink after he is forty is a goddamn fool.' "

"With that wonderful line, I think we better stop," said Abe. "I can't beat that. So let's drink whatever we wish. Only Kushy mustn't drink. She's under forty."

Kushy said, "That's one area where I don't go along with my radical friends. It's true that they drink a lot, but that's not because they're radical, it's just fashionable, I guess. And I don't drink only because I don't like it. I mean I don't drink gin or whiskey or any such stuff. I do like the old-fashioned Manischewitz wine we used to drink at home during Passover. That I like."

"I do, too," said Abe. "But I've gotten to like gin, too, and whiskey, and one of the things I'm afraid of is to get to like this hard stuff too much. It makes me feel good, so I'm afraid of it."

"He's a Puritan, my husband is," said Toby. "What he enjoys he is determined to be against."

"But seriously," continued Abe, "I've been reading about Jewish holidays, and Passover in particular. It's a wonderful thing the Jews celebrate them. They celebrate freedom, they fled from the Egyptians, they became a nation, they had a great leader, and that is wonderful."

"That's all superstition," said Kushy. "The whole Exodus story has been shown to be fiction."

"Where did you read that?" asked Abe.

"I don't remember, but I read it," she said.

"In one of your party papers, I suppose."

"It could be, and if it appeared there it's so. Much more reliable than *The New York Times,* which is the mouthpiece of big business."

Toby turned to David. "There we go again. Goodness, Kushy, can't you discriminate? Of course, *The Times* is big business; of course, it prints advertising from big business, that's what makes it possible for it to have correspondents all over the world. That takes money. But it's also true that the paper has a code of ethics."

"Don't make me laugh," said Kushy. *"The Times* prints what is good for big business."

"Kushy," said Abe, "for a girl with as much ability as you have, who has sensitivity, a mother of children and all that, you are strangely naïve. I readily admit that things used to be different in the newspaper business, much different, but they have improved greatly. By and large, over a period of time, you will find accurate news in *The Times,* and there are other papers that also print the news, by and large. Sure, newspapers are subject to bribery, so are doctors, so are lawyers, so are judges, so are plain men and women, but they all have codes. Besides, *The Times* is not controlled by the government, not a single branch of it, federal, state, or municipal. *The Times* attacks the President, the governor, the mayor, anyone it pleases, and nothing happens. This is a lot different than it is in Russia."

"How?" asked Kushy.

Abe looked at her, "You don't mean that, do you? How?

You know damn well how. In all the years that the Communists have been in power not a single newspaper has dared to attack the people in power. Even if there was a hint of criticism, that editor didn't last out the week, sometimes he didn't last out the day. Even the novel writers are controlled by the government, even poets, even religious leaders. You know that. Don't be so naïve."

"I don't believe it," said Kushy. "There is no criticism in the newspapers because there is no reason for criticism."

David couldn't help laughing out loud, something he seldom did. "Nothing to criticize! The people can't travel where they want to, without permission; they can't change jobs without permission; they can't leave the country without permission; they can't travel, not just abroad but within their own country; they are spied upon all the time, especially when they talk to foreigners, and especially Americans; and they can't go to their own churches. No, this last I have to change. Some can go to Christian churches, the Russian Orthodox Church, maybe the Catholic churches and the Baptist churches and Moslem churches, or mosques, but no synagogues. No, I have to change this last, too. In all Moscow there is one synagogue, a city with a half million or so Jews, one synagogue!"

"The Jews don't even want to come to that one," said Kushy.

"My God, like Abe says, you are naïve," said David. "I'm sorry to get so excited. The Jews don't come because it's worth their whole careers to be seen in a Jewish house of worship. Even the older people are worried. Because they're spied upon. Let a single one of them complain about the government's stand on Zionism, about its anti-Semitism, and see what happens to him or to his family. Why is it that only Jews have to have on their identification cards their religion, Jew. Not a single other religion is mentioned on any identification card. Yiddish newspapers are virtually barred, religious seminaries are barred. Talmud Torahs are practically nonexistent. Take even *matzohs*. It's very difficult for Jews to get *matzohs* in Russia, you know that. Worse than that, it's almost impossible to import *matzohs* from the United States or England into Russia. And you say they, the Russians, and especially the Jews have nothing to criticize?"

"I think the Russian people have always been anti-Semitic," said Abe.

"That's a strange thing for a psychologist, an educator, to say. You can't describe them all in one phrase," said Kushy.

"Maybe so," said Abe. "Maybe so, though I'm not as sure on this, as I used to be. But you can report a fact of history. Isn't it a fact that there have been more pogroms in Russia than in any other country in the world, except maybe Poland?"

"I suppose so," said Kushy. "But that was not the fault of the people. It was the fault of the Czar's government."

"And also the Communist government, you should add, Kushy," said Abe. "It has been almost as bad under the Communists as under the Czars. As a matter of fact, from one point of view, it was better under the Czars. Under the Czars Jews could be Zionists, hold meetings, talk Hebrew, read Hebrew and Yiddish newspapers, books, and magazines. But they can't do it under the Communists."

"The Zionists are anti-Russia," said Kushy.

"Do you believe that?" asked Toby. "The Zionists are no more anti-Russia than they are anti-United States or anti-France, or any other country. They are against the Communists because the Communists are instigating the Arabs to make war against the Jews, supplying them with ammunition and technical help. Why don't they let Russian Jews leave Russia for Israel? Why not?"

"I don't know, but there must be a good reason," said Kushy.

"You're in the party now," said Abe. "Why don't you ask one of your party functionaries."

"Maybe I will. You know all this talk about Jews and Zionists and the Passover makes me mad. It's time we stopped all this nationalism and parochialism and religious superstition. I don't want to be known as a Jew. I want to be known as a human being. We've had enough trouble from all the old stuff, nationalism and religion."

"All right," said David. "Then why don't the Russians give up their military hold on Poland and Bulgaria and Czechoslovakia, if they're so uninterested in nationalism? This is all rubbish, what you're saying, Kushy. Nobody stops anybody in this country from being a Jew. You can be a Jew and an American at the same time, and you can also be deeply interested in Israel in this country, and nobody says a word. In Russia, no. I say Russia is the most nationalistic, the most chauvinistic, the most superstitious of all countries. Communism is their religion, and Stalin is their Jesus or God. I confess it makes me sick to see Jewish men and women side with Arabs in their attacks on Israel. Here is intellectual and emotional slavery of the worst sort."

"The slavery we have here, in the United States is much worse," said Kushy. "Here everything is poisoned by big business and by the government. Have you forgotten the Teapot Dome scandals, have you forgotten Senator Joe McCarthy and his scandalous attacks on innocent people?"

"No, we haven't forgotten them," said Abe. "They were terrible. But the press and individuals and organizations protested against them, denouncing senators and governors and even the President of the United States, and in the end they won out. We have the right of protest. There is nothing sanctified about the government in this country. In Russia the Communist party is God, Stalin is God, all the politicians in the Kremlin are little gods, they tell people what to think, what to eat, what to say, what not to say, what to write, where to go, where not to go to, my God, only slavery exists in Russia. You know something, Kushy?"

"What?"

"I just have too much respect for you to believe that you believe what you're saying," said Abe. "You're an intelligent girl, you understand things, you know in your heart that there is no freedom in Russia, you know in your heart that not the slightest bit of criticism of any branch of the government is allowed, not even in poetry or in fiction, or in the drama, or in music or in painting—frankly I don't see how music or painting or dancing can be capitalistic or anti-Communistic, art is art, but the despotic Soviet politicians, they have the nerve to tell poets what kind of poetry to write, what kind of music the musicians should write, what kind of dancing the dancers should dance. This is absurd. Even the Czar never did this. He never told Tchaikovsky what kind of music to write, what kind of symphonies, he never told Chekhov what kind of plays to write. As a matter of fact, under the Czars Russia produced a great literature and a great music and a great dancing. What have the Russians produced? Nothing, just nothing, except terrible music by Shoshtakovitch, and terrible novels and essays by Karl Radek and Sholokov."

300

"That's not true," said Kushy, and stopped.

"What's not true?" asked Abe.

"Everything," said Kushy. "You can write everything you want to in Russia so long as it's the truth. Would you want the government to sanction the publication of lies?"

"The truth, the truth," said David, as calmly as he could. "Whose truth? The truth as the government sees it, or as impartial reporters see it? Why doesn't the Soviet government permit outside reporters to travel all over the country and talk to all kinds of people and then send in reports to their papers? Why do Soviet censors censor everything that comes out of Russia? There is no censorship in England or in France, and surely there is no censorship in the United States."

"There's plenty of censorship in the United States," said Kushy. "The censorship of omission."

"That's not true," said Abe. "If *The Times,* the paper you hate so much, but it's really pretty good, if *The Times* fails to print something important, you can be sure *The Nation* will print it or the *New Republic* will print it, or the St Louis *Post-Dispatch* will print it. Somebody will print it, and nothing will happen to them. This country respects the right of dissent. By the way, are there any strikes in Russia? I never heard of any."

"No. There are no strikes," said Kushy. "The workers know the government is looking out for their welfare."

"I get so mad," said Toby, "when I hear an intelligent girl like you talk this way. Workers always have complaints, but not in Russia, you believe that?"

"I do. If they had anything to complain about they would strike."

"And how long would the strike last? And what would happen to the strike leaders?"

"What do you mean?" said Kushy. "Nothing would happen."

"Do you really believe that?" asked David. "I didn't believe there were actual people around, intelligent people, too, who talked this way, it's hard to believe."

"I'll tell you what would happen to the strikers," said Abe. "They'd be arrested at once as counterrevolutionaries, in the pay of capitalistic-imperialists and the rest of this hogwash, they would be sent away to Siberia for years and years, if they were lucky, some would probably be shot or they would develop serious illnesses and die, and, worse, their families, wives and children and cousins and sisters and brothers, all relatives, would suddenly discover that they were being shunned, that they were getting poor service in grocery stores, and some of them might even also be sent to Siberia. People disappear in Russia for the slightest reason, because of the slightest suspicion of their displeasure with this or that act of government. Nobody ever hears from them again. By the way, do you know where Karl Radek is? He was a great Communist pamphleteer in the early days of the Revolution, a friend of all the big shots. He didn't agree with Stalin about something. He disappeared. No one has ever heard of him again."

"He was a counterrevolutionary, probably. I don't know his case," said Kushy.

"My God, Kushy," said Abe, "how can you say that? How can you say anything? Nobody ever heard Radek's side, nobody even knows on what grounds he was censured or exiled or anything. What's going on in Russia now is what went on in Nazi Germany. There, too, there was censorship, there was oppression, no freedom of any kind, and there, too, as in Russia now and always, there was, of course, anti-Semitism. I see no difference, really, of any consequence, between Brown fascism and Red fascism and any other kind of fascism."

"Yes," said Toby, "one of the reasons Radek was banished, maybe killed, was that he was Jewish. Stalin and his whole gang, all of Russia, hate Jews, always have hated Jews."

"I told you, I'm sick of this Jewish business. Jews are only people."

"No," said Abe. "That's what I used to think, when I was a radical or a socialist, or whatever you want to call me then. Jews are more than people. That's how the *goyim* treat them, as more or less people. They refuse to treat them as they do other Christians. They look upon them, the most liberal of the *goyim,* as Christ-killers, as inferior socially. I say to hell with all the *goyim,* you know what I mean. We must look out when we're with them. Oh, there may be some decent ones, but they get fewer and fewer in my experience anyway. That's why I'm for Israel. That's why, only one of the many reasons, why I'm against Russia, because Russia is against Israel, against all Jews. Yes, that's my criterion. I've learned, Kushy. And, frankly, I hope you learn, too. You're just too smart, too intelligent to be taken in by all this stuff. I know, it takes a lot of courage to admit you've made a mistake. It took me a long time to admit it. Learn from me. Now, let's have another drink or a coffee, or anything. We still love you," and he kissed her. Toby went over and also kissed her. Toby, smiling, turned to David and said, "You might as well get in on the act." David also kissed Kushy. She joined in the spirit of this gesture and said, "I guess this makes the argument worthwhile."

As he went home David tried to get into the mental and emotional operations of Kushy. He had thought that this kind of thinking had mostly vanished from the intellectual world of New York, but clearly it had not. He began to think that there always would be such dupes . . . well, not all of them would be dupes, any more than not all devout Catholics who followed every behest of the Pope were dupes. Some doctrines, however absurd and even vicious to others, held a deep attraction or offered much comfort to some people, among them learned and kindly men and women.

fourteen

David didn't fly. He was afraid. He liked riding in trains, even on the short trip from Boston to New York. There was something about trains that gave him a feeling of romance . . . people and places looked better as he passed them by on a train, all America looked better, all life seemed more interesting and mysterious. Riding on a train was always a holiday to David. He recalled having said to Helen as they were sitting by themselves in Central Park, near midnight: "Being with you now, Helen, somehow makes me feel as good as when I am traveling on a train. You are as glorious as the passing scene, as the men and women who come into view and then disappear. Especially at night. You are traveling on a train at night."

"Darling, you say everything so just right, and you make me happy. I want to be like a train to you, like a ride on a train. Only one thing, though."

"What?"

"I want to be with you on a train, especially in the evening and at night, when you hear the whistles of trains. Darling, what is more sad, the whistle of a train late at night, or the whistle of a boat?"

"I never thought of that, Helen. The whistles are different. I feel that, on a train, a whistle late at night is sad, but on a boat it is sorrowful, and the sorrow lasts longer when you're on a boat."

"That is true, David. And I want to be with you on a boat, too, across the Atlantic, a slow boat."

"I want that, too."

"David, you and I will never travel together on a plane. We will travel only on trains and boats."

"What about buses?"

Helen kissed his hand, then his cheeks, then his mouth. "Do you like buses, darling?"

He hesitated. "A little. For short trips. They're too crowded, I mean, too confining."

"That's how I feel, darling. I like to travel, when you can walk a little, like on a train and on a boat. On a boat you can walk a lot. That's what makes a boat so wonderful."

"And the water of the ocean, Helen?"

"Ocean water, darling, is heaven. The sound of the ocean water is the sound you hear in heaven."

"You know that for a fact, Helen?"

"Why, of course, my David, of course. You know it, too, don't you?"

"I know it, because you told me."

"And I know it because you agreed with me, darling. Now, darling, let me put my arms around you and let's just look at the sky. Put your darling head on my breasts, and I'll count the stars, and I will tell you how many there are."

David remembered this conversation as his train rumbled on to southern Missouri, where he was to teach writing for two weeks. The director of the conference, Neil Sutton, had given him very general instructions: "Do anything you want. You'll have four actual classroom sessions each of the two weeks, you'll read articles and some stories. You will see them, the students, whenever you want. Be practical, but also be impractical. It's more important to fill them with ideals of writing than with pointers on how to make money. Do whatever you wish in any way you wish. The students are here not just to learn, but also to be, well, I'll use a cliché, to be inspired by you."

These instructions were fine, but they also were worrisome, because David had never done any teaching before. If only Helen would be with him now, holding his hand, actually and figuratively. His worries mounted as the train rumbled on. He recalled reading about Professor Alfred North Whitehead, the eminent mathematician-philosopher, who, though nearly eighty, always felt very nervous in a classroom. There was also William James, who dreaded entering a classroom, and who on his last day, just before retiring, said, "This is my happiest day, because I will now not have to go into another classroom the rest of my life." Then there were the actresses Helen Hayes and Katharine Cornell, both of whom trembled whenever they were about to go on the stage. After they were on, they were in complete control, but beforehand, for hours, they could barely sit still. He remembered what Helen had told him, "Darling, you don't have a worry. To be a good teacher all you need is to be sure of your subject, and to be enthusiastic about it. You know your subject, and you are enthusiastic." So, he said to himself, he won't think about the matter anymore. What will be, will be. Meanwhile he would make notes about the essentials of article writing and short-story writing. The first could be taught, the second he wasn't so sure about. One could be taught to be a good article writer, but one could not be taught to be a good short-story writer. One could be taught to make less obvious mistakes in the writing of fiction, one could be taught where to look for material, one could be told what stories one could learn from most, but fiction was a highly personalized thing. One could be told that the world is not interested in carbon copies of Faulkner or Hemingway or Dreiser or Sherwood Anderson or Chekhov; the world is interested only in originals. But one also had to be told how difficult it was to be himself, since all of us are subject to the pressures of fashions in fiction and in the criticism of fiction. David had already made several notes about these matters in New York, and he had lists of stories to recommend to his students, and he had decided to draw upon his own experiences as an editor and also as a writer, to make his points in both classes, in nonfiction writing and in fiction writing. Now he would add to these notes . . . and then he would go into the diner. He had heard that the Santa Fe Railroad, on which he was traveling, served fine dinners in very pleasant cars.

The stories about the Santa Fe diners were true. There were soft, lovely parlor cars, with small tables and tasteful tablecloths, and there were lamps on the side . . . and there were pleasant designs on the walls of the cars. He picked a table near a window. He was to have dinner. It was evening, entering into night, a time that David loved especially. "Twilight and sunrise," he had said to Helen, "are the most mysterious and most appealing parts of the day. That's when men and women understand each other best. That's when God and nature and the angels rest and contemplate and dream."

As he sat down, there was no one else at his table, but a man soon appeared and sat down opposite him. They began to talk. The man said, "I am going on a foolish expedition."

"You are?" said David.

"I didn't even tell my wife about it," the man said. "I told her I was going to a convention of teachers of economics. There is a regional convention in Kansas City, Kansas."

"That's strange; I'm going to Kansas City, Missouri," said David.

"That's a much finer city. I'm going to this convention, but I'm actually going for another reason, really. In a suburb of Kansas City, Kansas, there is a small village where a woman lives. She's a widow with two children. Her husband died two months ago. I dreamt that he had died, and that she was asking for me, you know, in the way people talk in a dream. I had never seen this man. I had not seen his wife, this woman—Marilyn is her name, for twenty years, since we were in college together. I hadn't even heard from her. I did ask people about her, you know, when old classmates got together. Some knew about her, some didn't. Those who knew said she was doing all right, that her husband was an accountant. That was about all. And I kept on asking, you know."

"I guess you were interested," said David.

"Oh, yes, I was interested. We were supposed to get married."

"Married?"

"Yes, We didn't tell our parents. We were so in love. You can get some idea of how much I loved her, when I tell you I used to love the little stray hair on her neck, the way she would run her hand across her skirt when she sat down. She liked me, too. I knew it. You know such things, isn't that right?"

"Definitely."

"But we didn't get married. We had a fight instead. About the strangest thing."

"Oh."

"We're both Presbyterians. Not exactly, but for all practical purposes. Actually, I'm a Huguenot, that is a kind of French Presbyterianism but I don't take it too seriously. Oh, I believe and all that, but that's all. She's a special kind of Presbyterian too. Her sect actually believes in the old doctrine of infant damnation and election and things of that sort. All it means, in a rough sort of way, is that if you're born to be in hell, there's nothing you can do about it, and if you are born to go to heaven, that's it, you're lucky. One day she asked me which group I belonged to. I laughed. I said this was all nonsense. I said I didn't believe that God was that cruel. Besides, how could anybody know anyway? She got all worried about that. You see I knew nothing about her sect. She would ask her minister. Was I lucky or was I the other kind? She told me that she had talked to her minister, who told her to ask me what I thought about things like the Second Coming, the redemption of sins, the Virgin Birth, and all that. I said, Hell, I don't know, it all means damn little to me. I guess I said I didn't believe in the Second Coming. I don't remember really what I said, and I said the Virgin Birth was a fable. She seemed upset. And then she told me that she couldn't see me again because she figured that I wasn't among the elect, that I would go to hell. I'll say this for her, she didn't say the minister had told her to tell me this; she said that she figured it out herself, and that her father, who was a sort of lay minister, had told her that I was not for her. She actually said she would have nothing more to do with me. I said I couldn't believe it. I told her how much she loved me, and how much I loved her. She admitted that she loved me, but now she was ashamed of it, because she was in love with a doomed man.

"One late afternoon, as she and I were walking in a park, I could see the struggle she was going through. She loved me, I was sure of that, and I was passionate about her, you know how a young man can fall for a young woman, the mere swish of her skirt, a bit of a beginning smile on her face, can just set you off into heaven. That's how much I loved her. Well, I threw my arms about her, and I almost suffocated her with kisses, and I felt her breasts and I felt her all over, and I kissed her eyes, and I told her we belonged to each other, that this was all that mattered, and then she gave me one big kiss, and bit my lips, and then she took my face in both her hands and almost pulled my lips off, and she ran off, but not before she said, 'You are a messenger of Lucifer. May God forgive me. And I'll always pray that God be merciful to you. This I will do all my days.' And I never saw her again after that. She actually left school, went to another school, so as to be away from me, I guess. At the beginning I was told that she always asked about me . . . then I heard she had married somebody . . . and then this dream."

"I've never heard the likes of what you tell me," said David. "This is a love story that is a love story."

"I've told other people about this, and they tell me it's an obsession. What do you think?"

"I don't know about such things. But I guess you could call it an obsession. It's clear, I should say, you've been in love with this woman, in a way, you understand, all these years, and I imagine you felt that she was really in love with you."

"I have no doubt of that. Not a bit. Mind you, I'm a married man, with kids, and she was a married woman with kids. I begin to think there are all kinds of love, and I suppose they can be at the same time, I mean a man can have two, maybe three or more women at the same time for different reasons. Maybe, in the future, plural marriages or some kind of attachments will be permitted. It's not so impossible, really. I've been thinking about this, since the dream, you know. The Mohammedans have it, you can marry four wives, I think, with them, and the Mormons, I understand the women don't mind at all, they rather like it. That's what I'm told. It's hard to say about such things. What people say and what they really think are two different things. This business of man and woman is so complicated. Love, no love, children, no children, wife, other women, it's all so complicated. I guess you could say I love my wife, in a way. Come to think of it, though, I don't know why I married her and not some other woman. It just happened one night. We were together at her home, after dinner and a show, and I didn't like the idea of going home alone again, and I guess I sort of felt sorry for myself, so I asked her to marry me, and, boy, did she say yes! The way she said it kind of worried me. I don't know why.

"I began to wonder whether I'd made a mistake. Well, I said it, she said it, and it was done. I can't say I was so excited, really. There were times before the marriage when I wished I hadn't got into this, but then she would come close to me, with her perfume that I liked, and I guess she knew it, and she would nestle up to me, her breasts pushing against me—she does have nice breasts, I'll say that for her, and good, firm hips—and she would look at me, and kiss me on the lips and then put her head on my shoulders. I was only human. Like the feller says, I hope you don't mind my saying it, you can't argue with a stiff prick. But, and this is where the catch comes in, on the night of the wedding, I felt a little guilty, on account of Marilyn, the girl with the screwball ideas about my going to hell, the widow I'm going to see now. Why in hell I felt this way I just don't know, I just simply don't know."

"Did your wife know about it, I mean suspect, if you don't mind my asking?" asked David.

"What's that?"

David had the feeling that the man resented his interruption. The man apparently was not looking for advice, he merely needed a listener, and possibly he wasn't even too eager to have the man listen, he just wanted to see a pair of ears in front of him. David repeated his question.

"No, my wife didn't know, and I am sure she had no inkling. I love her and all that and she's the mother of my children, but she's not too bright. Marilyn was really sharp and quick, very alert. Anyway, as I say, I had this strange sense of guilt, but that didn't keep us from having kids, and one has to do something else beside feeling guilty to have kids, wouldn't you say?"

"Of course."

"My wife is all right, but about what I said before, men having only one wife but more than one woman, I get bothered about that. I suppose out of fairness I ought to add that women should also have more than one man, maybe only one husband, but other men as well. I couldn't take that, fair or not. I just couldn't. I guess we men are built that way. The cock of the roost wants it all his way. Oh, I don't mind my telling you I've slept with some other women, not many, maybe a half dozen. It was all right. But even then, listen to this, I felt guilty about being unfaithful to Marilyn, isn't that the damndest thing?"

"It gets more complicated every minute," said David, beginning to wonder about several things: How much of the truth was the man telling him? What was the man really expecting from David? How much longer would he continue his monologue, and how could David leave him without offending him?

"Yes, it's plenty complicated. I suppose I've reached the age— I'm fifty-four, when a man looks for more variety in his sex life before the fires begin to go down, you know what I mean. You married?"

"No."

"Well, I don't know whether I should say you're lucky or otherwise. Living with the same woman year in and year out, sleeping in the same bed year after year, is pretty dull, I mean it gets dull, so damn dull I sometimes have a hard time getting an erection. I suppose women don't mind being with the same man so much. I mean good women, you know. The other kind, they're different. Boy, are they different! There's a young woman assistant professor of statistics, at my college, been married only two, three years, to a friend of mine who teaches business administration at another college. I never would have thought she was that kind, you know. One night, I take her home from a faculty meeting, and she invites me up for a nightcap—no harm in that, I figure. We had a couple of drinks, then she says that Jay, that's her husband, is out of town, and perhaps I wouldn't mind a quick party. So help me, I was so dumb I didn't know what she meant, then she comes over to me, gives me a soft feel between the legs, and then we were in bed. I saw her the next day in school, we passed each other, said hello, like always, as if it never happened. How do you figure that? A man can never tell."

"No, a man can never tell," said David, again wondering how much longer he would go on.

"You, a bachelor, you know more about such things than I do. The married women love to give themselves to bachelors. They're pushovers for bachelors. But about Marilyn, I guess I can't get her out of my system. It's hard to tell. I really don't know whether I should see her or not. She may be quite a dis-

311

appointment. But, then, if I don't see for myself, how will I know?"

"That's right."

"But she seemed eager on the telephone. Through all kinds of maneuverings I got her address and telephone number, and I called her, and she seemed really happy to hear me. And I said, might I see her; she said of course. I said I was sorry about her husband dying, and all she said was 'These things happen,' and she asked about my wife, she knew her name—how she found out, that I will never know, I guess, though I may ask her. So that's how it happened. You know something?"

"What?"

"I wonder if she still believes that about me going to hell? Isn't that a horrible way of looking at things, at life!"

"It's not a kindly way."

The man smiled. "Not kindly is right. I remember asking my minister about that, and he said it's the Old Testament influence. The God of the Old Testament is an angry man, full of hell, fire, brimstone, and all that, and some Christians incline more towards the Old Testament than toward the New Testament, which they really should, they being Christians, and the New Testament really being a religion of love and charity. That's what I go for."

"There's plenty of love in the Old Testament," said David. "Isaiah and Micah and in Deuteronomy and Leviticus there's plenty of preaching of love, loving your neighbor as yourself."

"I thought that was only Christian," said the man.

"Not at all," said David. "It was in the Old Testament long before the New Testament."

"That may be so," said the man, who began to look at David in an inquisitive manner, "but the Jews don't really mean it. I mean they don't emphasize it. Wouldn't you say that?"

"Well, I don't know. Frankly, I don't think so. But this is all such a tender, touchy, complicated question," said David.

"It definitely is."

Both wiped their mouths with their napkins, and both went their own ways. David returned to his roomette. It was after nine. He had picked up a copy of the Chicago *Tribune* in the lounge car. He began to read it, and was depressed by its small-town character, its super-super-Americanism, and he was especially depressed by the innumerable pages of sports news and business news. Then he noticed, near the bottom of a page, a small item from Amsterdam announcing that the Dutch government planned to do some more repairing in the general area where the Great Synagogue stood, and also that it planned to extend the hours that the Anne Frank House would be open to the public. The very last line read: "The Anne Frank House is probably the place in all Amsterdam that every tourist visits. No matter how many people come at one time, it is always virtually silent there, as the people come and stand and look and no doubt pray to God to forgive those who did this to Anne Frank and to the 6,000,000 Jews who were destroyed along with her."

A lump came to David's throat. He felt his eyes filling. But a sense and conviction of pride also began to fill his heart.

fifteen

David had never been to Missouri or, indeed, anywhere in the
Midwest. As the train rumbled toward the Union Station in
Kansas City, David compared its approach to that of the Boston
South Station. The approach to the South Station was among
densely crowded freight cars, surrounded by dilapidated dwellings, which, in turn, were surrounded by garbage cans and rubbish.
The approach to the Union Station in Kansas City appeared
to be neater, even among the freight cars. There seemed to be
more sky in the outskirts of Kansas City than in Boston, and
also a more leisurely pace to the traffic that could be seen on the
highways. In Boston the traffic near the railroad station was
swifter, almost hysterical. But David was disappointed that he
did not see any corn fields or haystacks . . . no doubt they were
to be seen not far away, but he wished he could see them now.
That would put the stamp of reality upon the Midwest. Now
he took it for granted . . . he wanted proof.

The train came to a stop in the station, and David's meander-
ing dreaming also came to a stop. It was early in the morning,
not yet eight, and he would have to be in this station for more

314

than two hours before taking another train to Intercity Community University. The lobby of the station, where the gates to the trains were, was enormous, and so was the waiting room. He bought a copy of the Kansas City *Star* and sat down to read. There, in the center of the front page, was a picture of a cat, followed by three of her kittens, with the caption, "Queen of the Walk and Her Entourage." Next to it was a short article about troubles in the School of Journalism in the University of Missouri. It wasn't quite clear from the article what the trouble was about. Apparently the dean had given one of the professors a terminal contract, and the students claimed that the professor was being dismissed for his "liberal views on public issues." The piece did not say what the public issues were, or precisely what the professor's views were.

The foreign news was mostly on the inside pages, and was rather skimpy. The editorials were so dull that David couldn't finish a single one of them. There was a poem entitled "Yesterday," which said that the past is sad. There were pages of local news, financial news, sports news, and society news. Kansas City was a large community, one of the largest in the United States, yet its only newspaper read like a small-town weekly. David put the paper aside and went to the station restaurant for breakfast. The food was good enough—orange juice, hard-boiled eggs, rolls, butter and coffee. But something was missing, and David didn't know just what it was. He watched the people come and go. The waitresses were polite and neat. One of them, not the one who waited on him, offered him a second cup of coffee, though he had not asked for it. "Our cups of coffee have no bottoms," she said, smiling. He thanked her and said, "This is my first time in Kansas City."

She smiled again. "I knew it from the lost look in your eyes."

"I show it?"

"You all do. And you come from New York, too?"

"Yes. My God!"

"We have a game, we waitresses, guessing where people come from. All kinds come through this station. I think I can tell people who come from New York, those who come from Chicago, and those who come from Los Angeles."

"How did you know I came from New York?"

"Oh, I just knew." She smiled and was off to attend to a new customer.

David checked his suitcase and walked about the station. He still felt something was missing. He walked on and on. He looked at the faces of the people. They were good faces and strange faces and dubious faces and bland faces, and yet there was something about them that troubled him . . . he wasn't sure whether it was something on the faces or something that was not on them. Then he began to think of the faces he encountered in Grand Central Station in New York or in the South Station in Boston. Suddenly, he realized what he had been missing: Jewishness . . . a *Yiddisher ponim* . . . a Jewish face. The realization of what he had been missing somehow gave him a good feeling, he didn't know exactly why. For a few seconds he was a little embarrassed: Couldn't he be "worldly" and "cosmopolitan" and "civilized," as some of the non-Jewish Jewish writers insisted Jews should be? "Get out of your ghetto mentality. Stop thinking of yourselves merely as Jews. You are also people, members of the human race, and you should extend your horizon," and so on. But soon he realized that it was these non-Jewish Jews who were lacking in "civilization," who were parochial, unaware of "the realities of the world." It was the "civilized" world that had forced upon the Jews their so-called parochialism. The history of the persecutions by the Christians, before and after the Inquisition, had made the unconscious in every Jew a little suspicious of every non-Jew, at least, a bit cautious . . . and that had made every Jew feel more comfortable in the presence of a Jewish face. David recalled what he had long ago heard someone say, "Whenever a Jew comes to a strange town, the first thing he does is look for another Jew." What a sad commentary! Not upon the Jews, but upon the whole non-Jewish community! What was there about the Jewish face that made other Jews feel safe and comfortable? There was a feeling of compassion for the plight of fellow Jews who suffered the irrational hatred of non-Jews, there was a strange and warm feeling of resignation to the injustice of the world, there was a good humor in the face of all this misery of life and of Jewish life in particular. Jews understood each other on sight. Jews understood each other at all times and all places. Jews were Jews,

316

no matter what their intellectual pretensions and emotional se-
crecies. Jews were Jews to all non-Jews, and this gave the Jews
everywhere a sense of being strangers in the world. And it is
this strangeness that Israel would at least in part combat, and
make it easier for Jews to be themselves even thousands of miles
away from Israel. Israel was a portable homeland for every Jew
throughout the world and down all time. A Jew was always at
peace among other Jews. A Jew always was not quite at peace
among non-Jews. For even the most liberal of non-Jews, now and
then, revealed an anti-Jewishness that was least expected. Weren't
there Christians who were without any unconscious anti-Jewishness?
Possibly; but every Jew who ever thought so has found, to his
horror, that the number of such non-Jews in his life was mini-
mal.

David walked on and on, and around and around the lobby
and the waiting room. And he saw in the waiting room a plaque
that announced to all who read the places of worship of the
various denominations in Kansas City. He looked down the list,
and to his pleasure he saw two entries under "Jewish." He wished
he had more time to spend in Kansas City, so that he could
visit these two synagogues. But what he had read gave him a
good feeling. There were not only Jews in Kansas City, these
Jews also were sufficiently eager to perpetuate their Jewishness
as to organize synagogues. And probably there were more synagogues than the two whose addresses he had just seen. After all,
the plaque couldn't hold all the Jewish places of worship, any
more than the plaque could announce all the Catholic or Protestant churches. He wished he could discuss this matter with some
other Jew, but he saw no Jewish face as he continued his walk.

The President of Intercity Community University gave a reception to the faculty of the Writers' Conference at his home.
Dr. Morton Jarvis and his wife, Olive, were childless, and David
wondered what they possibly could do in so huge a home—
about twenty rooms, three bathrooms, two kitchens, and a large
garden. The Jarvises took the faculty around the house ("This is
the full three-dollar tour," said Dr. Jarvis, and somehow this
remark didn't sit well with David . . . perhaps it was because
he had expected something more brilliant from the president
of a university . . . perhaps he also didn't like his pinched face,

his thin nose). Mrs. Jarvis merely smiled and made light talk. She looked ten years older than her husband. She was, as a matter of fact, a little dowdy and even frumpy, but a good warmth came from her . . . she was motherly without being matronly. Suddenly she stopped and turned to the group of faculty and said, "I hope you don't get the idea that we occupy all these rooms. This house has just been bought by the university for the use of the president, from a wealthy family, millionaires, people who haven't lived here for years. They got tired of paying taxes, I guess, so they willed it to the university— goodness, I don't mean willed, they're still very much alive— they're lovely people, and that's how we got this house. We just occupy a few rooms. Morton thinks we ought to rent out some rooms, but I told him I am not yet ready to run a rooming house." They returned to the garden where there were cocktails, with substantial sandwiches and cakes and shrimps and hamburgers. David helped himself to everything, he talked to various people. As usual he found it difficult to start a conversation himself, but he was glad when somebody else started a conversation with him. A reporter from the Kansas City *Star* said he would like to interview him during his stay at Intercity Community University. As he walked around he missed the same thing that he had missed in the Union Station in Kansas City. He wouldn't say it to anybody but members of his immediate family and to Helen, of course, but they "looked like *goyim,*" very courteous but cold, devoid of the Jewish twinkle, or whatever you wish to call it, that nearly always identifies one Jew to another. Well, he thought, it will be only two weeks, and he'll make the best of it.

He felt a touch on his shoulder. He turned to see a pleasant woman of about forty-five, well-proportioned but not fat. He smiled at her, hardly knowing what to say.

"You're David Polonsky?"

"Yes."

"I hope you're not busy Friday night. We'd like to have you over for a Friday night supper, real Jewish, with candles, *challeh,* and everything."

David was overwhelmed. "How did you know, I mean . . . how did you know?"

"Well, in the first place," said the woman, "let me introduce

318

myself. My name is Mrs. Manny Schwimmer; call me Fanny. I saw the name David Polonsky and knew right away that any man with such a name can't be an Egyptian. And I know how lost Jews can feel in a little town where there are hardly any Jews. *Goyim* are nice, I mean nice *goyim* are nice, but Jews are, well, you know. *Haimish.*"

David's face lit up. "I can't tell how glad I am that you invited me. Now I feel better."

Fanny whispered in his ear, "Don't tell anybody else. I want a nice Friday-night evening, just for us Jews." She pinched his arm. "My husband will be thrilled. He knows about you. He likes your things. So do I." She looked around, then continued, "You'll have a good time here. The Jarvises are very fine people, Olive especially, she could almost be a Jew. He's a little pompous but he's nice, real nice. Manny and I will show you around. Only be sure to tell us when you feel we're not giving you any privacy. It's not often we get a real New York writer and editor, and one who is a Jew at the same time."

"I don't know how to thank you, Fanny."

"Forget it. I have to run along. See you Friday. Manny will call you and pick you up. Friday."

David was so happy about the invitation and so glad to know someone like Fanny that he got himself another drink and moved around a little more freely. He was now in a group where Dr. Jarvis was holding forth. As soon as Dr. Jarvis saw David he stopped and said, "I'm very glad you finally decided to come over here. You and Fanny seemed to hit it off on sight. She's a marvelous woman, so is her husband. They have three wonderful boys, and they call their home Boys' Hill. Isn't that nice? Listen, David, this will interest you. People nowadays are saying all kinds of things about Sinclair Lewis, that he's only a journalist, that he's no artist. Well, they'll all eat their words. Not everything he wrote was first-rate, but he's written some tremendous things. Anyway, what I was saying is this. Lewis was just great when it came to the Jewish issue. Just great. This I can tell you from my own personal experience. I was there. I heard it. This happened in Topeka, Kansas. Dr. Logan Clendening was at this party that somebody at the University of Kansas Medical School was giving. I was invited. Other college presidents were invited.

There was drinking, of course. Logan is no Prohibitionist, and neither was Lewis. I don't have to tell you that, David. Lewis was a heavy drinker, but this is the strange thing, I don't think he was an alcoholic. I really don't. He had all sorts of problems. He had troubles with his women, not just his wives but his mistresses. I guess it's true what some have said, that Red never enjoyed requited love from a woman.

"That's true. He looked fine to me, hell, a man doesn't think of other men as beautiful or not, he thinks of them only as interesting or not interesting. But with women it's different. You all know that he had a terrible skin condition. He had cancer of the skin, and he had to take X-ray treatments fairly regularly, and these treatments ate into his skin and worsened his condition. I didn't mind his pock marks. But women did, and he had a hard time with them, even the last one he was living with. Maybe I better not mention her name, though some people have. I hesitate. Then, you all know, his son by his first wife, Wells Lewis— Red adored H. G. Wells—well, this son died in the Second World War, and Red was really shattered. So he had troubles, lots of troubles. But listen, all of you, at this party there were speeches, and Logan Clendening, professor of internal medicine, or something of the sort, he gets up and says something about medicine, and about what the 'kike doctors' have done for medicine. He admitted that Jewish doctors had done a great deal, but he did call them *kikes,* and this is what riled Red.

"I was there and I saw his face get red, and I noticed he sort of stopped drinking. I knew that something was troubling him. As a matter of fact, it was troubling several of us, because some of the members of the medical faculty of the Medical School of Kansas are Jewish, and I think one or two of them have been nominated for the Nobel Prize. Anyway, after Logan finished his speech, Lewis gets up and says, 'I have just heard a talk by an erstwhile friend of mine, Dr. Logan Clendening. He's no friend of mine anymore. I don't like his reference to *kikes.* That's a horrible word to use for decent men and women who have done so much for the human race. I don't mind telling you-all I resent it. I came here to have a good time. But I am having a horrible time. I don't want to be in the same room with an anti-Semite. Good night, gentlemen.' It was one of the most moving speeches, no, I will say, it was one of the most moving expressions of decency in the history of the United States. I hope a future biographer will record this, but he probably won't. The really important things in a man's life sometimes escape his biographers. But I thought you people would like to hear this. Isn't that wonderful, David?"

"I am deeply moved. I have met Lewis, but this story I have never heard. I'll spread it around, if you don't mind."

"Not at all," said Morton. "History should know it."

David went to another group where two men were talking about President Harry Truman. Both expressed admiration for him, and this surprised David, who had the general impression that Missouri was not too friendly to Truman, because of Truman's early association with the less reputable politicians in the state, particularly one Prendergast. Said the first man: "I didn't like Truman at first, when he was road commissioner. He seemed cocky, very sure of himself. But then I got to like him more and more. He has no college education, but he's a reader, and he does know American history. I guess the one thing I still don't like about him is his awe in front of generals. I don't know where he got this. A man with as much common sense as he has should know how dumb most generals are. I think it was Clemenceau who said that war is too important to leave to generals. That's why he's so devoted to General Marshall, a dull, thick-headed general who thought the Chinese Communists were only agrarians. Truman should have known better just from his own experience. Farmers can never be Communists by themselves. But outside of this Marshall nonsense, Truman has common sense and courage. He's worth a thousand Eisenhowers, and I am basically a Republican."

"You know me," said the second man, "I've always been a Truman man. I don't even mind his association with Prendergast. I don't mean I like it, but it's not so terrible. Lincoln himself was mixed up with lowdown politicians. So was Al Smith. So was Grover Cleveland. So was Governor Lehman of New York, an honest man if there ever was one. The point is that Truman never himself became corrupt. Even the Republicans have never charged corruption against him. With me, two things stands out, as far as Truman is concerned. He told General MacArthur to go to hell, and that's fine by me. MacArthur looked down upon

321

Truman. I remember a picture, the two were on some island in the Pacific. Truman was man enough to go out there. And MacArthur put his arm around Truman's shoulder, as if he were patting a little boy. Then MacArthur tried to ignore Truman in the running of the war, and Truman did the only thing he could do: he fired him. He did more. He allowed him to talk to the Congress, even though he, MacArthur, had insulted Truman."

"That really was something," said the first man. "Only in a democracy can a thing like that happen. This country must be real strong to take that, and do nothing."

"Then there was Israel," said the second man. "Frankly, I'm not so sure we should have become so friendly with the Jews. I mean, with their new country. My wife, who's been following that Middle Eastern thing closely, she's active in Eastern Star, and they are active in religious things, you know. She says the Jews have been horrid to the Arabs. I'm not so sure of that. The Arabs have been plenty dirty and mean to the Jews, and besides, it's the Jews who built up Israel. Still, I wonder whether we should have come right out in favor of the new country. But what I want to say is that Truman showed real humanity and courage in doing what he did, in recognizing Israel only a few minutes after the UN voted for partition. It showed he has a sense of justice, and I like that. I tell you frankly, I begin to think more and more he was a much bigger man than FDR."

David hadn't meant to say anything, but he interrupted, "I hope you don't mind a New Yorker saying a word. I'm pleased to hear all this good talk about Truman. I confess I thought that in Missouri Truman is not so well thought of."

"Well, actually, he isn't," said the second man, "at least among the people I see. But I think it is true, though, that even these people think more of him now than they used to. The man does grow on people. There's something plain and rugged, and I guess you can say honest, about him."

"I don't mind saying," said David, "that when I'm in Kansas City I plan to drop into the haberdashery place where Truman and Jacobson had their business, and buy a tie, just for sentiment's sake. And I also plan to drop into that hotel, I forget the name, and get a bourbon highball."

"Muhlebach Hotel," said the first man. "And I guess he did like his bourbon. No harm in that."

The Jarvises came over. "I heard you people talking about Truman. There's a big man there, a really big man. One of the things I did at this university I'm especially proud of is to give him an honorary LL.D. the very first year he was President. You know, he went to our pre-law department. He was going to go to a law school in Kansas City or some other place, I forget where, but he couldn't, on account of the Depression or something. I do think he was proud of that degree. He has a high respect for schools and colleges and professors. The funny thing is what we talked about at the time. You people would never guess."

"That really was strange," said Olive.

"Well," said Morton Jarvis, "I was telling the President about a favorite food of mine, raw potatoes, with salt. I love it. I also love raw turnips with a sauce of some kind, and the President said, 'That's one of my favorite foods, raw potato. It tastes much better than baked potato or boiled potato. But I never could get my Cabinet to try it. On the farm lots of people eat raw potato.' I also like raw oatmeal and raw groats, with milk, but mostly by itself. Very good."

"Isn't it strange; raw potato I like, I really do," said Olive, "but raw oatmeal I never could get used to, and groats raw I can't stand at all."

"Actually, all vegetables are best raw. Take cauliflower," said Morton. "It's delicious uncooked; so are parsnips, and artichokes and mushrooms."

"Cauliflower really is good raw," said Olive.

"Goes well with a little whiskey, too," said Morton.

"I like cauliflower with ketchup, of all things," said Olive. "This reminds me, I want to see if there's more coffee. We ran out of it."

"How did this happen?" asked Morton.

"Oh, it happened." Olive rushed off.

"One thing I never could get used to is Irish coffee," said Morton to David. "Oh, let me show you some of the flowers we've planted."

The other two men excused themselves, and Morton and

David walked off to the flower beds. Soon Olive joined them. "I was telling David," said Morton. "that I can't get used to Irish coffee."

"That's because you can't stand your whiskey diluted," said Olive playfully.

"Maybe I shouldn't make a confession right here in the bourbon country," said David, who got to like President Jarvis and his wife, "but my favorite drink is Manischewitz and soda."

Olive became excited. She touched David's sleeve. "Oh, I just love it, I simply love it. We have dinner now and then at the Schwimmers, they're lovely Jewish people. Did Fanny see you, David?"

"Yes, thank you, she did."

"She was looking for you," said Olive. "She wants you over to their house. But whenever we're there, she always serves me Manischewitz with soda. My spouse over here, of course, wouldn't lower himself with that drink, he's a straight whiskey man, but he doesn't know what he's missing, isn't that true, David?"

"I like it," said David.

"I forgot, Olive. I have to call Timothy, you know about what," said Morton, who excused himself to David and walked off.

"We're very glad to have the Writers' Conference here, and you especially. Neil Sutton has told us so much about you."

"I'm glad to be here. You have a lovely home."

"Yes, David, we like it, but it's so big, and we get lonesome here, all these rooms. And I can't do much housework. I have a circulatory condition. But the garden is nice. And in the summer Mort and I like to sit here toward twilight. Oh, look over there! Isn't it horrid? It's a Catholic church, something terrible that a Protestant architect sold to them; it's supposed to be a fish—Peter the fisherman, you know. But Mort says it looks like an abortion. That's a terrible thing to say, but it's true. It's horrid. At first we couldn't stand it, but now we look at it and don't see it. I'm a Presbyterian, the daughter of a Presbyterian minister, and the church my father had was in a little town in Montana, but the church was simply lovely, very bare, all wood, and there was a little hand organ—the kind the Negroes have. My mother used to play it on Sunday. And the outside of the church was plain, red bricks, and that can be very impressive in its simplicity. So you can appreciate how I abhor this thing over there. But the view is really beautiful here, outside of that, isn't it?"

"Very much."

Both remained silent as they looked around. Then Olive said, "One of the things I've missed here in Missouri is spaces, the big, round sky, that we had in Montana where I was born."

"The sense of space is a little new to me," said David. "In my part of the country, all we have is skyscrapers."

"I know, David, I know. Skyscrapers are all right. But they're mechanical, you know what I mean?"

"Yes. I must say, though, that I have come to like spaces, and natural heights, the little time I've been here."

"You put your finger on it, David. Natural heights. You see, there is a difference between the height of a skyscraper and the height of a mountain. The mountain God made, and the skyscraper man made, and that is a difference."

"A very big difference," said David.

"As a matter of fact, Kansas City and all Missouri and this town, they're not Montana. They're flat lands compared to where I was brought up. In Montana I could walk out of the house and see everywhere, you know what I mean?"

"I think so."

"Now, Morton was born in North Dakota, but the part he was born in was lowlands, and that's where we differ. I'm a mountain woman, he's a valley man. So what brings me pleasure doesn't bring him pleasure, and the other way around. I sometimes think, there's mountain living, and there's valley living, and there's plateau living. That makes a difference, wouldn't you say?"

David had never heard this line of thought, and he was a little startled. "I guess you're right, Olive," he said.

"Actually, if I had my way I'd live in the Canadian Rockies. Have you ever been there?"

"No."

"Montana is not far from Canada, as you can see by the map. My father was a great traveler, and in his youth he was a mountain climber. He used to take the whole family nearly every summer to the Canadian Rockies. I've been over Europe, through most of the Alps, including the Austrian Alps, which are the loveliest. But there's nothing, just nothing to compare to the Canadian Rockies. They're simply divine. My father, who was very religious, naturally, being a minister, used to take his family to Canada nearly every summer when we were little, and he would tell us all about the mountains and the glaciers, and why some had snow on them, why others didn't, what happened to the rain on the mountains, how old they were, what was in the mountains—minerals, oil, and so on. I used to be just fascinated. Do you know anything about mountains?"

"Nothing. Less than nothing. Where I come from, the Boston area, there are only hills, and all they have is grass and trees, and naturally they're not very high at all. I've been on top of the Blue Hills myself, and I have flat feet."

"I have flat feet, too. What do you do about your flat feet?"

"Nothing. I used to do a lot, buying all kinds of arches. One pair of arches cost me almost fifty dollars. They were no better than the ready-made arches you buy in shoe stores. So I decided to do nothing. I have pain nearly all the time, sometimes worse, sometimes not so bad, but I had that before."

"David, you are giving me the history of my own feet."

"I consider myself lucky, though, in a way. When I was very young, my father took me to an infirmary or a clinic connected with the Massachusetts General Hospital. One of the doctors wanted to operate on me. He wanted a fee, I think it was twenty-five dollars, and my father didn't have the money. That saved my feet. I learned later on that the operation this doctor had in mind was very dangerous and proved to be of little use. So for once poverty was a wonderful thing."

"Let me tell you a little more about those Canadian mountains, David. There's one place, in Banff, or not far from there, that is simply out of this world. It is called Lake Louise, a beautiful green-blue lake, but that's not describing it. I don't know of anybody who's seen it who didn't gasp with wonder and delight. There's no other lake like it in the whole world. And all around are mountains, one especially, Victoria, that is truly majestic. I do really think that God lives there, I really think that. My father used to say that, but he asked us kids not to repeat it, because some of his parishioners, Presbyterians, can be very rigid on such things, might not like what he said—disrespectful to God, and so on. He was really liberal. Father always admired the Jewish attitude toward God. As a matter of fact he adored the Old Testament. Those are real people, he used to say of Abraham and Jacob and Leah and Ruth and King David and the prophets. I have never met you before, David, but I have a feeling, a woman's intuition, if you please, that you would have liked my father. Isn't it terrible that a minister cannot express his poetical attitude toward mountains without offending people?"

"It is pretty bad," said David, who now liked Olive very much, far more than he did her husband, who had told the story about Logan Clendening and Sinclair Lewis.

"Well, this religion business gets me all riled up," Olive said. "I sometimes think if I had married a Jewish man, I would have become a Jew; if I had married a Buddhist, I would have become a Buddhist. After all, if you take a man's name, you might as well take his religion, because I think a man's name, all your life, is more important than your own religion. I wish people would intermarry more, and mix up all the religions. There's too much hatred among religions, and that's silly. Religion is supposed to mean love, so why hate one another?"

"I guess you're right about religion and hatred," said David, who was a bit disturbed now.

"But I do like Mrs. Schwimmer," added Olive. "Fine Jewish people they are, very fine people. Morton doesn't like them as much as I do. He says they're a little too loud. I don't see it at all. I feel very much at home with them, with both of them and their boys. There's something so warm about them. You'll like them, too, I'm sure of that."

"I liked her on sight," said David, for want of anything else to say.

"You know, David, in Montana there are very few Jews. My father used to go out of his way to socialize with them. We often had them over for dinner or some reception. He especially liked a Dr. Garfunkle, who taught sociology at Missoula. They were lovely people, he and his wife. You know, David, as Father said, he was heartbroken how virtually ostracized Jews were in Montana. I mean that people would do business with them, but after five o'clock all this would end. The Jews had to socialize among themselves. That's terrible. It's just as bad here, right here. I'll tell you more about that as the Conference goes on. I simply can't understand it. Jesus was Jewish, and yet the people who say they believe in him don't want to give any credit to his fellow Jews, they shun them. Isn't that simply terrible?"

"I don't have to tell you how I feel," said David.

"I'll say this about Mort, while he doesn't feel as I do on this issue of the Jews, he is trying to get more Jews on the faculty, but he hasn't had any luck lately. It's simply terrible how unconsciously anti-Semitic professors can be, with Ph.D.'s and all that. They don't say it outright, of course, but, as Mort tells me, whenever a Jewish young man with a doctorate and publications comes up for consideration to be appointed, the others find all sorts of reasons to keep him out. This is just terrible. It makes me sick, it makes me real sick."

"I didn't know this, I mean, that it was so bad," said David.

"Goodness, faculty people can be just horrible. They are among the most narrow-minded people in this whole country. And I used to think that they were the one decent element in the community. Isn't that horrible, too?"

"All this is news to me. I thought as you did."

"You will learn, David, you will learn. In the little time you will be here, you will see and hear all sorts of things."

"I confess I'm shocked," said David.

"I know, I surely do know. I used to feel the way you feel now. I know this is your first teaching position, and I don't envy you your disappointments. I sometimes think that education is just nothing. It teaches people nothing. Prejudice against Jews and against decent ideas remains in people, no matter what degrees they have, no matter how many books they have written. There's the president of a little denominational college not far from here—I can't give you the name of the college or the name of the president—but he's a dreadful anti-Semite. He calls Jews kikes, yes, he calls them kikes, and I simply refuse to go to his house or to invite him to our house. Morton sees him in some restaurant, but I told Mort that I will simply not have that horrid man in my house. Think of it, they haven't got a single Jew on their faculty. Think of it! The only Jew in the whole administration is the bursar. And he's married to a Methodist girl. Think of it."

"Well, all this is discouraging," said David.

328

"It is and it isn't. Education is all we have to make people civilized. It's all we have. But it's a terrible struggle, just terrible. I suppose we just got to keep on trying. Maybe we better go in and join the others."

They walked in to where the others were gathered. David had never before met a non-Jewish woman who was so well-informed about the position of Jews in their communities, and who appeared to have the right attitude. He wondered whether she was just as outspoken about the silence of the Christians during the Hitler days. He wondered whether her minister father spoke up. He wondered, in short, how deep her sense of decency and of honor was . . . and he said to himself again and again, the problems of the Jews are everywhere, Jews cannot have peace of mind or of soul anywhere, except in Israel. But, he asked himself, does it always have to be this way?

sixteen

The Friday evening at the Schwimmers' was one of the most
delightful that David had ever had. Fanny was sheer Jewish
womanhood—warm, round, sweet, smiling, eager to please, and
completely involved in the Jewish way of life. Her husband,
Manny, owned a chain of jewelry shops in southern Missouri,
and while he was the complete businessman he was also dedicated to Jewishness, and he was deeply devoted to his wife. Their
three sons, about a year and two months apart, were quiet, gentle,
and well-behaved. They ranged in age from ten to fifteen. There
were also present the rabbi of the temple they went to, Rabbi
Joseph Nadell, and the director of the Hebrew school at the
temple, Frank Liston.

David felt a warm feeling go through his entire being as he
entered the Schwimmer home. It was a home where Friday night
was a holiday. The table in the dining room was holidayish—
beautiful tablecloth, two candlesticks in the middle of the table,
a *challeh* and an elegant carafe near Manny's chair, and green
leaves here and there. The three boys had just put on fresh shirts
and washed their faces. Rabbi Nadell was a young man, hardly

thirty, and the head of the Hebrew school was only a few years older.

Fanny said to David, "I have two bachelors on my hands. I must get them girls. Oh, I'm sorry. The rabbi is bespoken, I guess, I should say."

Rabbi Nadell said, "You're being a little premature, I think. The girl has something to say about it, too."

"If she has any sense, I know what she'll say, and I know she has sense. But about our school principal, I just don't know what to say or do. Such a fine young man without a wife. Terrible, just terrible."

The three boys were truly little gentlemen. Manny was rather heavy-set, with a huge head that was bald to the very top. He had a double chin and smiled all the time, but when he spoke he made sense. He said, "This is what I look forward to every week. When I'm away and can't come I feel terrible."

"He's really very sweet," said Fanny as she kissed him.

"The one thing I like about the girl I'm going with now is that she's like Fanny," said Rabbi Nadell.

They sat down at the table and Fanny blessed the Sabbath candles. She had a kerchief on her head, which David liked because it reminded him of his mother, but he wished she had said the words so that all could hear. When she finished she kissed her husband and her three boys. Then Manny made the *kiddush* in Hebrew, and very good Hebrew it was, too. David was so moved to find all this deep and sincere Jewishness in the middle of the United States that he felt a lump forming in his throat, and he looked down at his piece of *challeh* for fear tears would come to his eyes. The meal was superb, from gefilte fish to tea and *lekach*. The rabbi said grace after the meal. There was almost an hour before the services at the temple, and the time was taken up with talk and drinking of brandy.

"David," said the rabbi, "this is a small community, there is only one synagogue, or temple. I try to satisfy all forms of worship, Orthodox, Conservative, and Reform. I myself am Conservative. Of course, I can't satisfy everybody, but all realize that we can have only one synagogue in this town, and they're cooperative. I try to point out to them that the Torah is the same to all of us, most of the prayers are the same, and, happily,

331

virtually all Jews are for Israel now. Naturally, some of the super-Orthodox, the elderly folk who are now retired, object to this or that, but I must say that they are not too vehement in their objections."

"How do you like it here?" asked David. "I mean, is Jewish-ness . . . ?"

"I know your question," said the rabbi. "I hope you don't mind if I tell you others have asked me the same question. I like it, I don't like, I am fascinated by it. I like it because what I see here confirms what has been said millennia ago, that Jew-ishness is eternal, that Jews come back to their roots, that there is something about Judaism that satisfies Jews. It's really thrilling to see the number of Jews who come to Friday-night services and to Saturday-morning services. You will see later on. There are synagogues and temples in New York where there is hardly a *minyan* on Friday night. I know. I studied at the Jewish Theological Seminary. Here, everybody comes, virtually everybody. You'll see.

"Now, I know all the propulsions. It's not only religion. No, it isn't. It's social, too. The Jews here, there may be about four hundred, counting children, are accepted during the day but not at night. That's putting it bluntly. So what can they do? They socialize with one another. And the center of socializing is the temple, where the gym and the social activities hall and the lecture hall and the dance hall, most of these are all in the gym, are very important. I am especially glad that so many young men and women come here. At first, what draws them, perhaps, is not so much religion, as the social activities. But they do go to services, and they do go to lectures and recitals. Why? Well, at first, because their boy friends or their girl friends come, but then they also come because they like the lectures and the music recitals, and the religious services, too, of course."

"I don't mind telling you, rabbi," said David, "that this is good news to me. Jewishness is alive in the middle states of America."

"What goes on in the Hebrew school is also significant," said Frank Liston. "The childen like to come."

"Frank is a perfect teacher," said the rabbi.

"He really is," said both Fanny and Manny.

"Well, I try to hold their interest," said Liston. "Many years ago, when I went to the University of Chicago, I took a course in creative writing. Our professor told us that it was an unteachable course. One thing I remember that he told us. He said, 'Write anyway you please. Never mind rules. All you have to do is to keep the reader interested. Remember the recipe for making rabbit stew. First, catch the rabbit.' So that's what I try to do. There are certain tricks, of course, and I use as many as I think necessary. But, as I was saying, I do believe that the percentage of children who go to Hebrew school in this small town is far greater than the percentage of Jewish children in big cities like New York and Chicago and Philadelphia, who go to Hebrew school."

"Tell them about the post-*bar mitzvah* classes," said the rabbi. "That's where Frank really shines."

"As you know, David," said Frank, "in the big cities, all over, I guess, one of the problems is to keep the children interested in Judaism after they're *bar mitzvah* and *bas mitzvah*. Most of the time the day they're *bar mitzvah* or *bas mitzvah* on is the last day they're in synagogue. They're finished. But not here. Almost three-quarters of these young men and women continue their studies, for a year, some for two years, and some for three years. And three of our young men have gone on to study for the rabbinate."

"Isn't that marvelous?" said Fanny.

"Just wonderful," said Manny.

"So one doesn't have to worry too much about the state of Judaism in the Middle States," said the rabbi.

"I used to worry," said David. "You know, I am sure, that others have also worried. But now I'm far more optimistic."

The rabbi said, "You might be interested in our intermarriage statistics. In the past five years there have been a hundred and fifty eligible young men and about the same number of eligible young women. Only two of the men married non-Jews, and of these, one of the girls converted. Of the girls, only one married a non-Jew, and they moved out West and I have lost touch with them. Now, I submit that's not a bad record."

"Not at all," said David.

"It's much worse, I suppose, in New York."

"Much worse."

"I want to tell you something else," said the rabbi. "Out here we have long had the label of being isolationist and conservative. Well, there's some truth in that. But if you will study the records of our congressmen and senators, you will be surprised how many of them have been for Israel and critical of the Arabs. You see, the Christians here are Old Testament Christians, the way the Puritans used to be, and they're all for Israel."

"Truman comes from Missouri. That proves what you say," said David. "But it's still a mystery to me why people who love Israel, or at least are for it, people who are Old Testament Christians, as you say, why they should feel as they do about Jews, socially. I mean why is there this five o'clock ghetto, as they say? It's a mystery."

"Of course it's a mystery," said Frank Liston, "it's more than a mystery, I mean it makes no sense. As an educator here, I am invited to various educational meetings, naturally. Every now and then they will postpone a meeting from Friday night or from Saturday, on account of me. This is fine, of course. But if one of them has a *simche,* say, a wedding, or a homecoming of a soldier son, or something else, they will invite every other member of our educational group except me. No, once I was invited, but then no more."

Manny said, "It's the same in business, although there it's not so pronounced. Fanny and I do get invited to social functions now and then, most of the time in out-of-town places, and I take Fanny along with me, but I don't think I'm looking for trouble, and I know Fanny isn't, we don't feel we're wholly accepted. Once in a great while, we do feel comfortable, but most of the time we're not accepted, as I say."

"That is so," said Fanny. "You get this strange feeling. The women are too polite, the men are too polite. I always send thank you notes, naturally, and I never hear from them again. I have invited them over here, of course. Some come, some don't. But hardly any of them return the courtesy. You get the feeling they have the feeling that you are forcing yourself on them."

Frank said, "The strange part, in my case, anyway, is that they're all such nice people otherwise, really intelligent."

"So it's been this way from time immemorial," said the rabbi. "If Freud didn't know the answer, then we don't. It could be, though, as more and more scholars and writers are beginning to say, it may all be due to the New Testament. One scholar has said that the most dangerous thing in the world—and it's being done in virtually every non-Jewish home in the Western world—is to let the New Testament lie around for the youngsters to pick up. That book is a mine of anti-Semitism. It is fortunate, of course, that few young people, on their own, pick up the New Testament, but when they go to Sunday school, they study it, and there they read the anti-Semitism of the saints and the apostles. If they read the writings of such Christian fathers as St. John Chrysostom and St. Augustine and the others, they get still more anti-Semitism. So, the remedy is to have the Christians repudiate all these sections in the New Testament, and you all know when that will happen. When the Messiah will come."

"But as my mother, *olav hasholem*, used to say, and as my father used to say, it's still better here than in any other country, except Israel, of course."

"Of that there is no doubt," all said.

"I come from the East myself," said Frank Liston. "I used to be Hebrew school director in several small towns in New Jersey, in Maryland, and in Delaware. There were more Jews there than here. What is probably more important is that these small communities in the East were closer to big centers of Jewish population, like New York and Philadelphia, and Baltimore, and even Newark and Passaic. We forget that even cities like Newark and Passaic have more Jews than whole states out this way. My point is that Jewishness is more intense here than there, and that pleases me. Here Jews don't take their Jewishness for granted, as they do in the East."

"As someone once said," remarked the rabbi, "it's easier for a Jew to be an atheist in New York than in Walla Walla, Washington."

"And it's easier for a Jew just to pass or get assimilated," said Fanny, "in a big city. Whenever I go to Chicago or New York, I am amazed how many Jewish women don't belong to Hadassah or are active in the synagogue. Here, that would be almost impossible. I honestly think a Jewish woman would just have to belong. She would be ashamed not to. She'd have to explain herself."

"The same applies to the men here," said Manny.

"All this is new to me," said David. "I read about some of

335

the things you say, but I didn't know it from direct experience, so to speak."

"So it's good and it's bad," said the rabbi. "And maybe it's more good than bad. Now I think we better go to temple. I always like to be ahead of time, to make sure everything is the way it should be."

The service was beautiful. The temple was small, seating about two hundred. Rabbi Nadell was both the rabbi and the *chazen*. The choir consisted of three people: two women and a man— a soprano, a contralto, and a tenor. There were about a hundred people present, young and old, men and women. The rabbi read the prayers clearly, the selections he made from the prayer-book for responsive reading were good. He delivered a brief sermon, urging his congregants to go to Israel. "You will learn more about Jewishness and Judaism by going to the land of Israel, walking along the streets of Jerusalem . . . visiting the grave of King David, visiting the graves of the judges of the Sanhedrin, visiting the Knesset, the Israeli Legislative House, where you will see Ben-Gurion conduct the government, where you will see the Speaker of the Knesset speak for the people of Israel. Somehow he always affects me profoundly, the Speaker is the mouthpiece of the people, *Kol Israel,* where you will see Arabs, because they are citizens of the State of Israel, where you will see all phases of Israeli religious life represented, where you will see open and frank debate, where you will see the Jewish soul at work. Fellow Jews, I have had the inestimable privilege of having been in Israel. I want to tell you, from the very bottom of my heart, that you owe it to yourselves as Jews, as human beings, to visit this holy, this marvelous, this miraculous land, if you possibly can. There is no experience like it for a Jew. There just isn't. Unfortunately, you will not be able to go to the Wailing Wall, that immortal symbol of our people. The Arabs have it. The Kingdom of Jordan has it. They got it from us as the result of the War of 1947. But I do have faith that it will be ours again in the not too distant future. It belongs to us by right of history. It belongs to us by right of justice. My friends, being in Israel is something special. It is the most inspiring thing any Jew can do for himself and for his family."

David felt very much at home.

seventeen

The two weeks of the Writers' Conference passed quickly, bewilderingly, and fascinatingly. David had never before encountered such a group of men and women. There were about thirty-five in all, young and old. Some were in their late fifties and middle sixties, while others were not yet thirty, and one girl admitted to being only eighteen. There were a nun and a Catholic priest. The faculty was made up of a play instructor, a juvenile instructor, a poetry instructor, a novel-short fiction instructor, and David, who was concerned chiefly with articles and "other nonfiction," but who also helped out with short-story manuscripts. Neil Sutton, the director, asked him, "if the need arose" that he read "a few poems, if you have time, that is." Neil Sutton himself gave two evening talks on "markets"—how to submit manuscripts, whether to have an agent or not, "how to deal with editors' letters," etc. The conference was run in an informal manner. There were three sessions every day, usually in the morning and early afternoon, each session lasting about an hour and a half. Each instructor had a total of five sessions, three the first week and two the second. Students submitted manuscripts, and in the second week the instructor discussed the scripts with the authors.

The other faculty members, much to David's surprise, were rather cynical. The play instructor, a man who had several one-act plays produced by little theatres, told David at the very beginning, "You'll find nothing here. I've been going to these things for ten years, and I haven't found a single play manuscript worth a damn. Just a bunch of old ladies with silly little plays, poorly put together, and dripping with sentimentality. They've been carting the same plays from conference to conference, hoping someone will tell them they've written masterpieces that they'll be able to sell to the movies and make a million. They all yearn to be produced by the movies. Why do I come to these things? I'll be damned if I know. I get a little vacation, paid for, I make a few dollars, and it's a good reason for staying away from the wife for a couple of weeks. She claims it's a good reason for her to be on her own for two weeks." The novel instructor, who had written six novels, with only one published, said pretty much the same thing. "I wish I had the courage to say no when Neil asks me," he said. "But I hate to drop the thing. I suppose if I sell another novel—my first one really was not much, even though it got a fair review in *The New York Times*—if I ever sell another novel, and make some dough, I might stop this conferencing."

The juvenile instructor, a woman in her late fifties, had published fifteen juvenile books and won the much sought-after Newberry Award three times. Her juveniles were aimed at the six to eight year group, and her books were very short, seldom more than 2,400 words long, and filled with many illustrations. David read a couple of these juveniles and found them dull, though some of the illustrations were interesting. He wondered how many young readers really liked these little stories about rabbits and ostriches and all-wise elephants. David talked to the juvenile instructor, and found her coy and almost totally ignorant of world literature. When she told him that juveniles formed "a major portion" of the current book industry, he was depressed. The poetry instructor was the most interesting of the entire faculty. He was a young man, about thirty-five, "relaxing between wives," as he said, who had had two books published by legitimate houses in New York and Boston, and his poetry clearly had much strength and lyricism. He reminded David that some of his poetry had appeared in the *American World,* many years before. Somehow David had forgotten the man's name.

He told David, "Frankly, I come to these things because it helps me financially. I'm always broke. I've been trying to get a permanent job in some high school or junior college, but no luck. Everything is fine, as far as my credentials go, but I lack education courses. I haven't had any. They want me to go back to school for two years or a year and a half and take courses in teaching elementary long division, secondary school grammar, the principles of motivation, the principles of classroom participation, and all that garbage. Did you ever see the catalogue of a college of education? It's criminal the kind of stuff those educators get away with. Former students tell me that most of the courses duplicate each other, that whatever there is to learn can be taught in a few hours, by an old-time teacher watching you for a few sessions in the classroom. But these educators have turned their nonsense into a huge industry. It's mostly a fake. And the people who teach the stuff would turn your stomach— dowdy ladies who've long passed the menopause, and seedy men who have taught trigonometry for fifty years and are ending their careers as professors of education. I suppose you know that the Ed.D. degree, doctor of education, is looked down upon by all honest people in universities. Read any of the Ed.D. theses, and you'll puke. Here are some subjects, I believe I quote them more or less accurately: 'The Frankfurter as a Democratizing Influence,' 'The Ice Cream Parlor as a Force in Social Cohesion,' 'The Problems of Persistent Bad Toilet Habits in Young Teen-Agers.' You've got to believe me when I tell you this. And the writing of these theses is unbelievably bad. So why should I waste my time with this rubbish? Meanwhile I have to eat. So now you have my whole life story. Neil lets me do everything I want to. There's one other point. At these conferences there's always one or two ladies, without any real talent, who want me to help them doctor up their verses, for a fee, of course. I do it, with a clear conscience. I pick up another hundred dollars this way."

David was sure this poetry instructor was Jewish, but he had

339

a hunch that he didn't want to be reminded. One afternoon the poetry instructor, whose name was Montgomery Sulzer, and who was called Monty, suddenly exclaimed, "Oh, to have a couple of Nathan frankfurters now."

"You come from Coney Island?" asked David.

"Not exactly. I come from Brighton, not far away," said Monty. "Tell me, David, how in hell did the Jews ever learn to make such wonderful franks?"

"They are wonderful, those Nathan franks. How, you ask? I don't know. You're Jewish, maybe you have a theory."

"I was born Jewish," said Monty, with a strange curtness. "But I don't consider myself Jewish. I do not subscribe to any of the silly rituals, prayers, and all that stuff. The sooner we get rid of all that stuff, in all religions, the better for the world."

"Do you ever use Jewish themes in your poetry, I don't mean only religious themes, I mean Jewish historical, legendary themes, Israel, King David, you know?"

"Hell no. I find them stifling. I prefer to affiliate myself with a larger group, the world, than with a small minority, a parochial-minded, chauvinistic minority at that. I'm not a Communist, but I think the Russians have the right idea on this. Let all religion die on the vine. You seem skeptical."

"Frankly, Monty, I am skeptical. As a matter of fact, I'm more than skeptical. I believe that every writer can find his most enriching material in his own background, and both of us, if you let me include you with a man who enjoys being a Jew, both of us can find a great deal in Jewish history and religion, too, for that matter, that we could turn into art. Zangwill did it, Bialik did it, Isaac Babel did it. But I'm not trying to argue. It came up, and well, you had your say and I had mine."

Monty appeared to be taken aback by David's statement. He looked at David, then said, shrugging his shoulders, "So that's the way you feel." David thought Monty avoided him as much as possible the remainder of the conference.

David read only two short stories. They were so bad that all he could do is tell the author of both, a woman of about forty-five, that "perhaps you ought to try to let the experience it is based on to distill more in your mind. It seems to have caused you much pain, and the pain, or perhaps I should say

340

the ill-feeling, comes through, and I am sure that you do not wish to hurt anybody. After all, it happened long ago."

"Well, Mr. Polonsky, it's only partly based on personal experience, you realize that, I am sure."

David said he realized it, but he was sure that the stories— the ancient ones about the husband who had an affair with his wife's oldest woman friend, who had been to the house "so often, and we were so devoted to each other"—David was sure that the stories were almost entirely autobiographical, and that the author was still seething with hatred against both the husband and the friend. The twenty articles or so that David read were humdrum, a little childish, and clearly aimed at big-money markets. Two were about "My Most Unforgettable Character," a department by that title that the *Reader's Digest* has run for years; two more were about "the oldest human being in my country," one a woman of eighty-five and the other a woman of ninety-two. Both women apparently were enjoying good health, which they attributed to "looking at the bright side of things." There was an article about "the old, great railroad days," by a man in his seventies, who had worked for the Great Northern Railroad when "it was a grand old railroad, with spitting engines and grinding wheels, and when there were real telegraphers. Those were the days. And the Pullmans of those days, they were palaces, believe me, real palaces." The trouble was that this man had no notion of sentence or paragraph structure, and his spelling was haphazard.

There was a long, thirty-five-page article by a retired Salvation Army officer, who obviously was deeply disappointed because he did not go up "in the ranks." He spilled much gossip about the operations of the Army, as he called it, and David had to assume it was substantially true—it was certainly depressing. He said, "My wife and I wouldn't kowtow to the district commissioners or the lieutenants, so we were never promoted. You know, in the Army, noncommissioned officers cannot fraternize with the Big Brass, and ordinary street workers, you know, tambourine girls and people like that, are like dirt. Yes, there is a caste system in the Army. I can't believe that General Booth had this kind of thing in mind, but then, who knows? I hear that in the Volunteers of America it's much more democratic.

341

But don't get me wrong, my wife and I are happy we gave our lives, so to speak, to the Army. We felt we were doing some good. We worked in the slums of Kansas City and Chicago and Buffalo. In some ways the slums of Buffalo are the worst of all." This man obviously had good material, but he had no sense of organization, and he had no idea when to drop an incident and start on another. He asked David whether he would be willing to take him on as a correspondence student. "I'll pay whatever you think right"—but David had to decline. David, however, did recommend Montgomery Sulzer. The Salvation Army man smiled and said, "No, thank you. I don't think he and I would hit it off. I attended one of his talks." He did not elaborate.

There were two Jewish students—one a man of about seventy, the other a woman of perhaps sixty. The man wrote about hobbies. He argued eloquently that "hobbies are important to health, especially to retired people." He himself had two hobbies, traveling and swimming. His two articles were very short, each less than three pages. David hardly knew what to say to him. The man didn't mind. All he seemed to want was to have somebody to talk to about hobbies—and other matters, including his late wife and his one daughter, who was married to an accountant, "who is doing very well, thank God." David asked him what affiliation he had with Jewish life. He said, "Oh, I go to a synagogue on the high holy days. I used to belong to the B'nai B'rith long ago. My late wife belonged to Hadassah, though she wasn't active. After she died, I sort of lost touch."

"Do you belong to anything else?"

"Yes," said the man. "I am active in Rotary and in Kiwanis, and I may join the Odd Fellows again. I belonged there off and on, and I rather liked it."

The Jewish woman wrote a sketch about a Negro mammy she had as a child in Georgia. It was pretty bad. David asked her why she didn't try to write something about her Jewish grandmother ("They're interesting, too"), or some Jewish aunt or uncle ("Some of them are quite colorful"), but her response was, "Oh, it hardly ever occurred to me. But I was very close to my colored mammy." She belonged to no Jewish organization either. She lived with an unmarried daughter, who had no association with Jewish life of any sort. The daughter was mostly

342

interested in a book-reviewing circle in the town library in a suburb of Atlanta.

David had never before met such Jews. They were so different from the Schwimmers. Apparently there was a large group of Jews in the South and in the Midwest who lived in a sort of limbo, between Judaism and Christianity and "plain, nonreligious Americanism," as this woman had said. David asked both the Jewish man and the Jewish woman how they felt about Israel. Neither seemed to have a definite attitude. They were not against Israel, nor were they strongly for it. "I suppose it's a good thing," both said, "to have a country where Jews from other countries can go, I mean when there's trouble for the Jews. Oh, I've given some money for their drives, appeals and things of that sort. Yes, I suppose it's a good thing." On inquiry David learned that the grandparents of these people had come from Austria and settled in the South, "when there were hardly any Jews here." The woman said, "As a matter of fact, my great-grandmother—my mother told me this—used to go to the same school with Judge Louis Brandeis's mother, in Kentucky; Lexington, I believe."

All in all David enjoyed the experience at the conference very much. He had met the Schwimmers. He had met interesting human beings as students. The Jews on the faculty and in the student body interested him especially. He was glad that, at the dinner on the last night of the conference, he was voted "the most popular and most helpful" among the instructors. He had proved something to himself, namely, that he was a good teacher. He had proved something else to himself; he liked teaching.

eighteen

When David returned to New York he found a letter from his sister Adele. It was brief and foreboding: "This letter is no way to greet you on your return from the Midwest. But I have to tell you about father. He is very sick. He is now in Beth Israel Hospital. About a week ago he had a fall, and he's been bleeding ever since, and he is getting weaker. We are all beside ourselves with worry. Two doctors have seen him and taken all kinds of pictures. They can see two definite breaks in the hip bone, but they don't understand why all the persistent bleeding. Please come."

As soon as David came to Boston he got in touch with a friend, a professor at the Harvard Medical School. He was a hematologist, but he got David in touch with an orthopedist and with an internist. These two men examined Moshe thoroughly, and their findings were most discouraging. The internist said: "The breaks in the hip are pretty bad, and it may take a year or two to heal, maybe longer. He will need a cast, and probably also some nails, which work very well with young bones and not so well with older people. But this is minor. I really don't know for sure, but apparently the shock of the fall set a whole

chain reaction in motion, reviving a deep-seated intestinal condition. I don't believe it's malignant. It's probably a long-standing
ulcer that has proliferated, and the body somehow accommodated
itself to this proliferation. How, it's difficult to say. But now this
whole system that the body built up by itself is shot. Arteries,
veins, and God knows what else are just not functioning, and
he is losing blood at a rapid pace, increasingly so. We can stop
it for a while with certain injections and perhaps some trans-
fusions, but it's a losing battle. We thought of opening him up
for an exploratory. Perhaps we can sew something up inside. At
least we can take a look. But there is the additional problem of
the quality of the blood that is leaving the body and that is
remaining. It looks poor to all of us. I don't think there is leukemia,
but there is definitely pernicious anemia. So we first have to build
up your father. I propose we feed him heavy doses of liver, liver
extract, meat. I'm not sure he can tolerate these heavy doses. I
don't know how much will remain within him. But there's no
harm in trying."

At first this treatment seemed to work. Moshe's eyes brightened,
color came back to his face, his voice became firmer. He sat up
in bed more often and for longer periods. He read more of the
Yiddish newspapers, but before a week was over, he began to
weaken once more. His one complaint was, "I feel so tired. I
have no *koach* (energy). Sometimes I think my life is slowly
going out of me." He had less appetite, and then he complained
that he had lost most of his ability to taste things. "Everything
tastes like wet wood to me, if I make any sense, but that's how
it tastes." Then he stopped eating solids altogether. He took only
liquids. David's friend at the Harvard Medical School talked
to the two doctors who were treating Moshe. One afternoon after
both of them had visited Moshe, the friend said, "Look, I must
tell you—your father has maybe two weeks, more probably a
week. They're planning to give him a new ray treatment, it's
brand-new, it will probably perk up your father for a few hours.
I have to tell you the truth. They plan to do it tomorrow. You
will want to talk to him, to hear him, you know. This is a terrible
thing to tell you, and your brothers and sisters. We really don't
understand your father's case. I've examined his blood. It's not
too good, but it's not really bad. There's something else wrong.

345

But we don't know what it is. There are more things that medicine doesn't know than it knows."

David didn't tell his brothers and sisters everything that he was told, but he did suggest that they see Father as often as possible. The sisters especially were alarmed. "What's wrong, what's wrong? Tell us."

"It's about the same," said David. "Only when I see him the way he is now, I get worried. He seems so weak."

"But the orthopedist said they will give him some kind of ray treatment, something absolutely new, that will perk him up."

"I know, I know," said David. "Let us hope."

The treatment worked almost instantaneously. David recalled what this doctor friend had said, but he just couldn't believe that his father, who looked so vital and vigorous now, would not survive much longer. Adele saw what happened, and said, "A miracle, a miracle if there ever was one." The others said the same. This was about noontime. The others decided to go home: "We'll visit him later tonight or tomorrow. Why don't you come, too, David? You've spent so much time here, you've had so little sleep."

David said, "No. I feel fine. I'll stay a little longer."

Moshe himself said, "Let him stay. After all, I've seen so little of him the past few years. I'm sorry it had to be on an occasion like this that we can spend some more time with each other. I would like to hear about the university where you taught, what kind of people there were, what sort of place it is, about the Jewish life there. So let him stay another hour or so. I feel fine, thank God."

David was left with his father alone. David told him a little about the Writers' Conference, about the campus, the faculty, the students, especially the Jewish instructor, the two elderly Jewish students, the nun, the priest. "Nu," said Moshe, "about this Sulzer Jew, him we Jews have always known. All Germany was full of his kind. Sulzer sounds like a German Jewish name. I should think the German Jews have learned by now. So, some haven't. We must be sorry for him. The old Jewish man and the old Jewish woman, what can I say? If they belonged to synagogues, if they had affiliations, they'd be happier. One thing I never could understand, no Jew can understand is how anybody can live without holidays, holidays make life so beautiful. I may have told you this before, others may have told you, but it's true. I know, there are Fourth of July, Thanksgiving, holidays like that. But a holiday to be a holiday must have religion in it. A feeling that comes from another world, from the Almighty. That's what makes a holiday beautiful, warm, nice, makes you feel good for being a human being. Everybody needs holidays. Jews need them more. These two Jewish people, for them, too, I am sorry. Not going to a *shul!* How can a Jew live that way? It's like a day without any sun, a whole week without any sun." He sighed, and David noted his face was getting white. "Anything wrong, Father? Pain?"

"No, just a little twinge. I've had this before. It will pass. So you had a good time at the university."

"I did. I think, Father, I like teaching. I like teaching very much."

"Good, good. What could be finer? By us a rabbi, as you know, is first of all a teacher. Torah, that's the important thing. Teaching Torah is the greatest thing a Jew can do. I tell you, my son"— he began to breathe deeply and heavily—"I tell you, the rabbis were very wise. There's a place in the Talmud where a rabbi tells a student, who told him he has a headache. The rabbi said to him, 'Immerse your head in Torah. Your headache will pass.' And it did pass. I'm glad you'll teach." He raised his head, wiped his face with his hands, and David's heart sank as he noticed how thin his wrists were, how bony his arms were, how thin the skin on his forehead.

Moshe turned to David. "Don't tell any of your brothers and sisters, but I know I am dying."

"You shouldn't think such thoughts, Father. You saw how much good the rays did you, and the injections, how much better you feel now."

Moshe looked at his son, a sad smile flitted across his face, and he said, "David, you don't have to say this. It's natural for a person to die. Our great Leader and Teacher Moshe died, and so did the Rambam, so why shouldn't Moshe Polonsky? A great *tzadik* (holy man) I haven't been. I have worked on the Sabbath. Of course, I had to, children and so on, but when

347

a Jew works on the Sabbath he is ashamed the rest of his life."

"Others have been forced to do it," said David. "God will forgive. After all . . ."

"Yes, I know, God will forgive. God always forgives. But how can I forgive myself?"

David saw a tightness come to his father's lips.

"Nu," continued the father, "there are other things I want to say to you. You are my *b'chor* (the eldest son). Your father was not very wise. Your mother was wiser, much wiser. She saw in Zionism what I didn't see. A man must have a head to understand things. Tradition says the Messiah will come on a white donkey, you know that."

"Yes, that is so, Father."

"Good, but why can't one interpret an airplane to be a modern donkey?"

"Yes, why not?" said David, astonished at the intellectual courage of this man.

"And how do I know that Ben-Gurion is not a messenger of the Messiah? It could be, couldn't it?"

"It could, Father."

"Of course. It's all very simple. But it took your foolish father more than seventy years to see all this. No fool like an old fool. I wish I could take back all the words I said in criticism of Zionism. So many of them don't go to *shul*. But they work for the good of the Jewish people. Many of them have died for the Jewish people, such fine young men and women have died. For this I do wish God will forgive me."

"Israel again belongs to the Jews, Father. That's all that matters." Again David was astonished at the courage it took this man, his father, to admit the mistake of a lifetime. He looked at the thin, bony, dear face of his father, whose mind seemed far away.

"Never forget your mother, David. Never. She was an angel. She was a queen."

"I know, Father."

A sharp twitch gripped his father's face, then suddenly passed away, but it left him bathed in sweat.

"Do you want me to call a doctor, Father?"

"I don't need doctors. They've done their best. A doctor isn't

God. I have one more thing to say, David." He sighed deeply, and again a sharp twitch passed across his face. David didn't know what to do.

The father now continued, in a much weaker voice. "I know you're not so *frum* (pious), but do something for me. Say *kaddish.*"

"Of course, Father, but don't talk that way."

"I don't know, my son, if it will do me so much good. Saying *kaddish* is not an obligation, but a custom, an old custom, true enough. It will be good for you, too. Read the prayers, mostly Psalms, sayings of the rabbis. All Judaism is in them, after the Bible, of course." Suddenly he stretched out his hand to David, who took it.

There were a few moments of silence. Moshe's throat began to gurgle; he twisted his head, and he slumped on his pillow.

David knew what had happened. He kept on looking at his father, whose eyes were now wide open, and whose mouth had fallen. He kissed his father on the forehead. Then he took his father's hand back in his, looked at it, caressed it, put it to his lips, kissed it slowly, and held it to his cheek. At this moment it seemed to him that the whole world had abandoned him.